DEC 2023

CHAMPIONS OF THE FOX

KEVIN SANDS

VIKING

Also by Kevin Sands

CHILDREN OF THE FOX
SEEKERS OF THE FOX

VIKING

An imprint of Penguin Random House LLC, New York

First published in the United States of America by Viking,
an imprint of Penguin Random House LLC, 2023

Visit us online at PenguinRandomHouse.com.

Library of Congress Cataloging-in-Publication Data is available.

ISBN 9780593620953

1st Printing

Printed in the United States of America

LSCH

Design by Lucia Baez • Text set in Rilke

CHAMPIONS OF THE FOX

CHAPTER 1

Was I dreaming?

I was standing alone in the woods. Trees stretched high above me, their trunks overgrown with moss. The light was dim, the only illumination coming from our twin moons shining through the leaves. A forest, much like any other.

Except I couldn't remember how I'd gotten here.

The last thing I recalled was Gareth. It was bedtime, and with little space at the inn, he, Lachlan, and I had piled into one room while Meriel and Foxtail took the other. As usual, Lachlan had asked Gareth to read him a story from the Fox and Bear book I'd given him. Gareth had obliged, telling the tale of the Fox, the Bear, and the Whistling Wind from his blanket cocoon on the floor as Lachlan nestled into his pillow.

I hadn't really been listening. I'd heard the story a hundred times before, told to me by the Old Man—the gaffer who'd raised me, taught me how to cheat people, then abandoned me after we'd had one too many fights. So as Gareth read, I just closed my eyes, letting his soft, low voice drift me to sleep.

Then my mind filled with strange images.

First I stood between giant creatures, reptilian things, lumbering beneath an orange sky streaked with clouds tinted green. As the beasts walked, they stretched impossibly long necks up to strip the bark from spiny trees, lowing with contentment as they chewed.

Then I was in a cellar, the creaking shelves around me smelling of mildew.

Then I was on a boat, and my hand was on fire.

Then I was . . . I don't know where I was. In pitch black. Someone was laughing in the darkness.

Dreams, surely dreams. Bizarre, half-remembered things, already fading from memory.

But now I was here, among these trees. And this didn't feel like a dream. It was too real, too alive. The rustling of the leaves as the wind blew. The peaty scent of moss. The stink of wet, rotting log. And something else. Something below that, hot and coppery.

Blood.

I could smell it. It was coming from the other side of a crooked old oak. Where the ground was dug up, the earth strewn about.

Cautious—and still confused—I approached the hole. There were tracks pressed into the dirt, three-toed, with claws. Each print was twice the span of my hand.

What kind of creature could make these?

The smell got stronger the closer I got. Not just blood anymore, but the reek of decay. Inside the scar in the ground were the ravaged bodies of the animals that had lived in this den.

They were foxes. Whatever had dug up the earth had torn apart the little ones. On the other side of the hole lay the broken body of their mother, killed defending her young.

I backed away, skin crawling. My heel caught on a root,

sending me sprawling into the dirt—where I found myself face-to-face with a pair of eyes staring from under the brush. Orange, with vertical slits for pupils.

Alarmed, I shouted—and the hidden creature squeaked back in fright. It bolted from its hiding place, little paws scrabbling in the earth as it tried to escape.

It was one of the foxes. The only one that had survived. She was small, not a cub anymore, but clearly still a juvenile, with gangly legs and a narrower-than-adult body. She scrambled halfway around the nearest tree before looking back in fear.

Her eyes met mine. Strangely, she stopped. She stared.

Then she ran toward me with a piteous squeal.

I lay there, stunned, as the young fox sprang into my arms. She leaped away, then back onto my chest, her tiny claws poking through my shirt. She whimpered, licking my face, crying in sorrow at the death of her family—but also, I thought, in relief at seeing me.

Did this fox know me? I would have sworn the look in her eyes was recognition. Except I didn't know any foxes. Other than—

I blinked.

Was this . . . *Shuna*? Back when she was young?

I didn't think so. This fox smelled musky; Shuna had never had any scent I could detect. And though it was hard to make out colors in the moonlight, this fox's fur looked more brown to me than Shuna's vivid red. She didn't have a patch of white fur on her belly, either, like I'd seen on the Spirit.

She licked my face in desperation, ears out, tail swishing. She clawed against me as I stood, trying to stay in my arms. Still confused, I held her close. That seemed to calm her, and she looked up at me with sad but friendly eyes.

Then she froze. Her ears went flat, her tail tucked into me.

And a low growl rumbled through the forest.

I didn't even think about it. I ran. Panic fueled my legs, feet thudding against the ground, stomach churning. The fox clung to me, her head nestled in the crook of my neck, mute with fear.

I sprinted, the trees a blur, until I couldn't run anymore. I stopped, back pressed against a giant trunk, listening for that growl, but my heart pounded so hard it was like a drumbeat drowning out any other sound. The fox looked around, alert, but she didn't seem to hear anything, either. As she relaxed, I did, too. A bit.

"What was that thing?" I whispered when I could breathe again.

The young fox gave a soft squeak and stared at me with those catlike eyes. Feeling safe again, her ears went wide once more, bushy tail brushing against me as she licked the corner of my mouth. She definitely knew me; I was sure of it. And even more strange, I was starting to feel like I knew her, too.

I put her down. She sniffed the air around her, returning to the smells of the forest, unconcerned. Maybe this was a dream after all, then. The fox's change in mood was certainly dreamlike— swinging from sheer terror to total peace without any logic—yet nothing else felt like I was asleep. I tried listening once more for that growl, but it was gone. Though there was something else now beyond the rustle of the fox's nose in the leaves.

thwock-thwock-thwock-whop

I strained to hear it. It sounded like something hitting wood.

A woodsman? With an ax? No, the beat was too fast. "What is that?" I asked the fox.

She looked confused, like she didn't understand what I was on about.

thwock-thwock-thwock-whop

"Can't you hear that?" I said.

The fox cocked her head and chirped at me, puzzled.

Was this sound only for me? Oddly, it did feel as if it was calling to me, like I needed to find out what it was. There was something afterward, too. Mumbling? Someone said something.

I stood there, trying to figure out where the sound was coming from.

thwock-thwock-thwock-whop

"Again."

There. A voice. A man's. I didn't recognize it. But he'd definitely said—

thwock-thwock-thwock-whop

"Again."

Why couldn't I find it? *This is important*, I thought, though I didn't understand why.

thwock-thwock-thwock-whop

"Again."

thwock-thwock-thwock-whop

"Again."

Where on earth is that coming from? I thought.

Then I heard a girl scream.

CHAPTER 2

The dream shattered.

That's Meriel screaming, I thought. And it hadn't come from the dream.

I flung myself out of bed, but my legs got tangled in the sheets. Already half off the mattress, I tumbled headfirst to the floor.

My elbow broke my fall—which nearly broke my elbow. Cracking bone on wood sent a jolt down my arm, turning my hand numb with pain. Gripping my wrist, I stood.

Then someone began to laugh.

Meriel's voice came from the other room. "You rotten little—*come here*!" she shouted.

A crash sounded, a vase breaking. I slumped back on the bed. "Lachlan," I muttered. "Shuna's *snout*."

I heard him now, laughing through the wall, furniture banging as Meriel chased him around her room. Gareth poked his head above the bed, blinking away sleep, not sure what was happening. But I knew. Lachlan had played a prank on Meriel. Again.

It had been a long trip out of Carlow. After stealing the Dragon's Teeth—the twin swords, Belenoth and Camuloth, capable of draining and transmuting magical energy—from the underground vault in the Weaver Enclave, we'd fled the city. The five of us had hurried back to Quarry's Point to collect our things, then caught the first wagon headed for Stonewall, a town on the southern border of Carlow province. There, we'd boarded a stagecoach headed west.

Snaffling the Weavers—High Weaver Darragh VII, in particular, the greatest enchanter in the world—was the most insane thing we'd ever done. And that was saying something. Those first few days afterward, Meriel, Gareth, Lachlan, Foxtail, and I had sat in our coach, on edge, watching for signs of pursuit. When no one came for us, we'd started to relax.

Maybe a little too much. We'd been on the road three weeks now, and there wasn't a lot to do but watch the empire pass by. Lachlan had his Fox and Bear book, and Gareth had his deck of cards, so we spent most of our time huddled over those, playing games and swapping stories, sleeping while the stagecoach trundled on during the night.

But being cooped up in a cabin had gotten pretty dull. Meriel, Foxtail, and Lachlan, especially restless, began to alleviate the boredom by playing pranks on each other. They were mostly harmless. Meriel put a frog in Lachlan's pocket. Lachlan cut the seat out of Meriel's dress. Both of them dipped Foxtail's ponytail in a bowl of soup, so it dripped strings of cooked egg down her back when she awoke. That sort of thing.

It appeared this morning was Meriel's turn to get got. And by her shriek, Lachlan had got her good. Judging by his own howl, he was about to regret that.

With one blistering crash, Meriel caught him. "Help!" he cried. "Cal! Help!"

I buried my head in my hands. "The rest of this inn must love us," I said. Gareth just looked glad he wasn't part of it.

"Caaaaaal! Heeeelllllp!"

I went into the girls' room to survey the damage—which was a good way to put it. The nightstand was on its side, a vase shattered beside it, flowers everywhere. Water ran along the cracks between the floorboards. The dresser had toppled onto one corner of the bed, breaking the bedpost, leaving the mattress tilted at an odd angle.

That was where Meriel sat, in a disheveled nightgown, Lachlan firmly in her grip. She'd pinned his hands behind his back and bent him over her knee. Foxtail laughed silently in the corner as Meriel began giving Lachlan's backside a serious paddling.

WHAP WHAP WHAP WHAP

"Caaaaaal!"

It wasn't until I saw Lachlan's face—and recoiled in horror—that I understood what prank he'd played. His flesh was seeping. There were boils all over his skin, swelled, red, and inflamed. Some had burst, streaks of yellow pus oozing down his cheeks. His eyes had sunken into his head, his lips cracked, his tongue swollen and purple. He looked exactly like he had the weeping sickness, the deadliest plague on Ayreth.

It was just an illusion. We knew this, Meriel most of all, as Lachlan had played this prank on her before. The effect wasn't created through makeup, though. Before we'd fled the Enclave, we'd each stolen a few enchanted artifacts from the Weaver treasure vault.

Lachlan had pocketed a collection of rings. One of them had turned out to be useful: it healed the wearer of minor cuts and scrapes, at the expense of making them ravenously hungry while they wore it. The rest of the rings just created bizarre illusions. One turned your skin blue. One gave you the shadow of a giant bird. And one made you look like you were infected with the weeping sickness. When Lachlan first figured out what that ring did, he'd put it on and waited for us to join him inside the stagecoach—which we all quickly dove out of, screaming.

Successful gaffs are always worth replaying, the Old Man had told me once—a philosophy that Lachlan apparently shared. "Let me guess," I said. "You leaned over Meriel as she slept, so the first thing she saw when she opened her eyes was . . . that."

Lachlan laughed. "Shoulda seen her face—*owwww! Stop it!*"

WHAP WHAP WHAP WHAP

Meriel was really going to town on him. Galawan, Lachlan's enchanted construct of a sparrow, sat on the windowsill tweeting at them, though whether he was asking Meriel to stop or telling the boy this was all his fault, I didn't know.

"What did I tell you about those rings?" I said.

"Don't wear 'em no more," Lachlan said, tears in his eyes.

"And why not?"

"'Cause fiddling with nature is for fools."

Though the Old Man had run off months ago, sometimes I still imagined what he'd say to me. At the moment, I could practically see him smirking in my head.

Now, wherever did you hear that? he said. I ignored him. I hated it when he was right—which was pretty much always.

"But it's so funny, innit—*owowowwwwww!*"

WHAP WHAP WHAP

"Help me, guv! She's going to kill me!"

"How can I kill you," Meriel said sweetly, "if you're already dead?"

WHAPPITY WHAP

"Pleeeeeease!"

I sighed. "All right. Hand the ring over."

"Why?" Lachlan complained. "It's mine."

"You stole it from the Weavers."

"Which makes it mine. Don't it?"

"Put it this way," I said. "You can either give me the ring, or Meriel will make it so you'll never sit down again."

"Aw . . . Shuna's paws," Lachlan grumbled.

Meriel let him go. The instant he took the ring off, he looked normal again: a mop of blond hair, smooth skin without a trace of the plague. I slipped the ring in my pocket as Lachlan stood, rubbing his backside. Foxtail continued to laugh in the corner, face hidden behind the polished steel mask riveted to her skull.

"No more magic," I told him. "We don't know enough about these rings. Using them might alert the Weavers as to where we are. And we're trying not to attract attention, remember?"

"All *right*," Lachlan said. "Artha's blessed bum. That hurts, that does."

Gareth had risen and was watching from the door. How did I ever become in charge of this bunch?

In my mind, the Old Man laughed and laughed.

CHAPTER 3

GARETH FOLLOWED ME downstairs for breakfast. We took a table in the corner of the common room, avoiding the glares of the other travelers who'd been woken up a bit too early. Gareth was less concerned about them and more about what I'd said in our quarters.

"Do you think that's t-true?" Gareth had a bit of a stammer, which got worse when he got nervous. "I mean . . . about the Weavers. That they might use the artifacts we stole to find us?"

"No." I called the serving girl over for two bowls of oatmeal. When she left, I continued quietly, so no one else could hear. "It's been nearly a month with no sign of them. If they could track us, they'd have ambushed us already."

"What about the H-High Weaver? He must want us dead. After . . ."

Gareth trailed off, not willing to say it out loud. I didn't blame him. Our showdown with Darragh had been even worse than battling Mr. Solomon. We'd only managed to get away by accidentally knocking the entire Enclave out cold.

Fortunately, that would work in our favor. When Darragh awoke, he'd either have to explain to the rest of the guild what had happened or try to cover the whole thing up. Since telling the truth would weaken his position—he got beat by a handful of young thieves?—he'd want to keep this as quiet as possible. And that meant letting us go. At least for the moment. "It'll be a long time before he comes after us."

That seemed to reassure him, even though it meant that one day, Darragh *would* hunt us down. Still, as the Old Man always said: one problem at a time.

In truth, I was more worried about possible side effects from the artifacts we were carrying. We'd used the Dragon's Teeth to heal Lachlan from the corruption of the primeval magic that had been inside him. As far as I could tell, there hadn't been any trouble with him since, but that didn't mean much. If the Teeth were as deceptive as the other Dragon artifact, the Eye, then I didn't trust their magic one bit.

Gareth was wondering about that, too. "Has the . . ." He waved at the eyepatch I wore. The Eye was hidden beneath it, stuck to my left eye socket. "Has it s-said anything more?"

"No."

The Eye was the strangest artifact of all. It talked to me inside my mind, except when I wore my patch. The metal cup inside it, provided by Foxtail, appeared to have the same enchantment as her mirrored mask: it prevented magical scrying. This had the effect of not only blocking the Eye's sight but cutting it off from the world entirely.

I was grateful for that. It made me feel like I didn't have a spy in my head all the time. But ever since we'd left Carlow, even when I lifted my patch, the Eye rarely had anything to say. And while I didn't exactly want to have a conversation with the thing, its current silence made me uneasy. Previously, the artifact wouldn't shut up. Now all it said was that it needed me to find one more thing. Then it would let me go.

And being rid of the Eye was what I most desperately wanted. When I'd first found it, it had taken over my mind. I'd fought off its control, but later, while searching for the Teeth, the Eye had overwhelmed me once again. It brought some benefits—it let me see magic—but I'd give that up in a heartbeat if it meant being free of the thing.

I was afraid of it. Afraid of losing control to it again. Afraid of what it wanted me to do. It wouldn't tell me exactly what we were looking for, but I knew it wasn't likely to be good. I'd thought about refusing to continue, just keeping it trapped beneath my patch, but then it would never release me. And the longer it was attached to my head . . . Would the artifact grow stronger? Would it take over my mind again—the next time, maybe for good?

I could only hope that whatever the Eye wanted at the end of this trail, I could live with it. As for now, it couldn't even tell me where the end was. When we'd fled the Weaver Enclave, we'd originally just wanted to get away from Carlow. It wasn't until we'd reached Stonewall that the Eye told me to change direction and go west.

"Why west?" I'd asked it.

because that is what I need, the Eye said. do as you are told, foxchild.

Its refusal to say more had worried me. Gareth had offered up a different theory. "Maybe . . . I mean . . . maybe it doesn't know where to go," he'd said. "Where exactly, I mean. Like with the Teeth."

That was certainly possible. Before we'd stolen it, the Eye had been trapped underground, bound in an enchanted cave for thousands of years by Shuna the Fox herself. When we'd freed it from its chamber, it hadn't known where the Dragon's Teeth were. So maybe that was why the Eye wouldn't tell me: it didn't want to look weak. When I confronted the thing, it admitted Gareth was right.

what I seek has been hidden, it said.

"By whom?" I'd asked.

it does not matter. the lifeblood that powers your world will show me the way.

By "lifeblood," it meant the energy of magic. Not just the primeval that ran below the surface of Ayreth but the energy inside every living thing, the source of all enchantments. The Eye could actually see it. Both life and magic glowed when I looked through the artifact: different colors according to the magic type, brighter or dimmer depending on how much energy was within.

"How will the . . . lifeblood"—I didn't like using the Eye's word for it—"how will it show you the way?"

what I seek sends ripples through the blood, the Eye said. I can feel the disturbances. I could find it even more quickly if you would leave me free.

It meant it didn't want to be stuck beneath the patch. "I can't keep you out all the time," I said. Mostly because I didn't want to—to say nothing of what other people would think if they saw an amber jewel stuck to my head. "I told you, seeing the magical world and the ordinary world at the same time makes me dizzy."

you do not need to be conscious when I search. release me when you sleep.

Fat chance. I didn't trust the thing when I was awake. Shuna only knew what it could do to me when I was asleep. Letting it have any more control over my mind was a risk I would never, ever take again.

then do not complain to me of time, foxchild, the Eye had said, and went silent.

Remembering that conversation made me think of what I'd seen last night. "Have you had any weird dreams lately?" I asked Gareth.

He paused, a spoonful of oatmeal halfway to his mouth. "I don't think so. But I never really remember my dreams."

"Neither do I. But listen." I told him the whole thing: being in the forest, the fox, that strange sound, the man talking.

He frowned. "That's awfully . . . detailed," he said when I finished.

"Exactly. That's what's odd about it. I recall it completely. Every blade of grass, every blow of the wind. It felt like I was there. *Really* there."

Gareth put his spoon down. "Do you think . . . I mean . . . was it the Eye's doing?"

"How could it be?"

"I don't . . . well . . . your patch. Did it come off in the night?"

"No." I'd gotten into the habit of checking it every morning. It was automatic now. "But I don't think that dream had anything to do with the Eye. I can't explain it, but it doesn't feel like an Eye thing. Not that that makes any sense, I guess."

"You would know better than any of us," Gareth said. "But it doesn't... I mean... it doesn't mean the Eye isn't keeping secrets."

That, above all, was the one thing we could be sure of. Speaking of which...

I stood. "Time to talk to the enemy."

CHAPTER 4

I NEEDED A private place.

I'd gotten pretty good at uncovering the Eye while other people were around. I'd push the patch up a little and rub my socket, as if the stitching was making me itch. Meanwhile, I peeked through my fingers to use the artifact's magical sight.

To know if we were still going in the right direction, however, I'd need to do more than that. I popped back up to our rooms. This morning's prank was forgiven, apparently, as Meriel, Foxtail, and Lachlan were laughing about something. Though I noticed Lachlan still wouldn't sit down.

"We leaving, guv?" he said.

"Coach heads out in half an hour," I said. "You should grab some food before we go."

The three of them went down to join Gareth, Foxtail only tagging along for the company, since the magic in her mask somehow kept her alive without her needing to eat. I grabbed a lead box from among my things and took the back door outside.

The inn we'd stopped at was along the Emperor's Highway, surrounded by a small section of farmland among the rolling hills of Tullagh province. A creek ran nearby, which gave me a place to duck into where the ground sloped to meet the water. A curious cow, drinking from the stream, raised her head and watched as I removed my patch and looked around.

The world came alive with light. The cow glowed a healthy red, a tinge of brown to its color. On the other side, a bean field shone green behind a fence. Though the water itself had no energy, I could see tiny streaks of light blue flitting about within. Little fish swimming beneath the rippling surface.

Alone now—except for the cow, I guess—I could speak. "Have you been poking around my head?" I said.

greetings to you as well, foxchild, the Eye said, sounding amused. are you troubled?

"You didn't answer my question."

because I do as I please, not as you wish. nonetheless, I will answer by saying I do not know of what you speak.

Was it lying? I decided to test it. "I had a strange dream."

Before we'd found the Dragon's Teeth, the Eye had been temporarily silenced by some magic of Mr. Solomon's, the rogue Weaver who'd hired us to steal the artifact. Though the Eye hadn't been able to talk, I'd still felt its emotions inside my head. Now that it could speak again, I didn't feel them quite as strongly. But I did get a sense of derision from within.

why would I care about your dreams? your mind is already filled with unimportant things. do you believe I wish to experience ones even less meaningful?

Contemptuous and indifferent: that sounded like the Eye telling the truth. "Feel free to let go of me anytime you like."

you are ungrateful, foxchild.

Was that a joke? "You think *I* should be grateful to *you*?"

did I not save your life inside the fire mountain, when the lifeblood threatened to tear you apart? did I not save your companion, when he was dying before your eyes? did I not save your entire world, when one of your kind cracked it and the lifeblood spilled forth to split your planet? you should be on your knees, praising me. instead, you bore me with inane questions.

"You lied to me, Eye. You said you'd attach yourself to my head just so you could protect me when I needed to use my hands."

and so I did. you should have accepted my gift after I was free. if you had not rebelled against me, our task might already be completed. instead you chose to take me to the traitorous one and have me silenced. and what did that accomplish? it was not I who injured you. it was not I who injured your companion. do not blame me, foxchild. the fault is all yours.

I didn't say anything. Mostly because the rotten thing was right. Both the loss of my eye and Lachlan's death were Mr. Solomon's doing. If I hadn't gone back to give him the Eye, I might very well be done with it already.

The Eye took my silence for embarrassment. no more complaints? then follow my instructions. I will free you when our task is done, and not one moment before.

I wasn't sure I believed that. But what did it matter? It was either do as the Eye said or live with this cursed jewel in my head forever. And the thought of that made me shudder. At this point, short of murdering someone, I'd do pretty much anything to get it out. "What now, then?"

what you came here for, the Eye said. it is time to find our new path.

CHAPTER 5

I UNLATCHED THE lead box I'd brought into the gully.

Deciding what to take from the Weaver vault hadn't been easy. The chamber had been filled with enchanted treasures, most without any description as to what they did. So everyone had taken whatever had caught their fancy.

Besides the collection of rings he'd been using to prank the girls, Lachlan had also stolen a small mechanical construct in the shape of a robin. He'd hoped the bird would be a friend for Galawan. At first, it hadn't moved at all. Lachlan had complained he got ripped off, even though I assured him the robin glowed brightly through the Eye. But when he'd placed the two birds together, the robin came alive—and promptly began attacking the poor sparrow, who tried to flap away, tweeting in alarm. Foxtail managed to catch the robin before it did Galawan harm, and when she threw it to the ground, Meriel stomped it into pieces. "He won't do that again, I guess," Lachlan said, a little dismayed.

Meriel had chosen her items strictly for their value: a pair of Fox and Bear figurines, each six inches high and solid gold. That theft had been our most practical. We traded those statues in Stonewall for five thousand crowns, so our wallets were stuffed again.

Gareth had given his choices much more thought. After

some deliberation, he took a pouch with three marble-sized orbs inside and a cloth mask. Of the orbs, one glowed softly like a light globe—but it also lit up the invisible runes that powered enchantments. When he tested it on Galawan, we could see just how complex the runes Mr. Solomon engraved him with were, glimmering in stark white. The other two orbs were protection stones: holding the opal made you immune to fire; the pearl let you breathe underwater. I wished we'd had them earlier. We sure could have used them.

But the mask was the most curious item of all. I didn't quite believe it when Gareth told me what the note he'd found under it said. "It does *what*?"

"It c-copies faces," he said.

The note claimed that if one person put the mask on, the next person to wear it would take on the face of the previous bearer. I thought it was a joke until we tried it.

Lachlan wanted to be the first to put it on, so we let him. "Well?"

"Looks like a cloth mask to me," I said.

Meriel, even more skeptical now, had donned it next. And to our shock, it suddenly looked as if Lachlan's face had been transferred to Meriel's body. "Artha's pounding paws!" Lachlan breathed. "It's me!"

Meriel had stared at herself in the mirror, poking her cheeks in stunned horror. "It feels like linen," she said. "But it moves . . . and . . ." Eventually she just pulled the thing off, shoving it into my hands with a shudder.

But Gareth hadn't taken the cloth for them. Foxtail's mirrored mask meant the only way she could walk in public was with a veil. If this magic worked . . .

I handed it to her to try. She hesitated—I wasn't sure why—but she did slip it on. And as Meriel was the last person to wear the mask, it suddenly looked as if Meriel's face was on Foxtail's body.

Sort of. There was one big problem: The enchantment in Foxtail's own mask seemed to prevent the cloth from fully working, because the copied face didn't move at all. It made Foxtail look like a wax replica of Meriel, entirely lifeless. Close up, it would be obvious something was wrong.

Gareth was disappointed. I assured him that it was an amazing find anyway. As long as no one got too close, it could still prove useful.

As for Foxtail, she'd studied the artifacts in the vault but hadn't taken any. When Lachlan asked her why, she'd shrugged. *Don't need anything.*

I hadn't planned to take anything, either. With the Eye stuck in my head, I'd had more than my fill of bindings. But the Eye itself had its own plans.

walk, it had told me, while the others searched the vault. And as I let the Eye gaze upon the artifacts' glow, it chose what it wanted. take that. and that.

"What for?" I said, suspicious.

I felt a flash of annoyance from the Eye. these will make finding what I need easier.

So I'd taken what it asked for. The first was the lead box, ten inches wide with a hooked latch to keep it closed. There were crystals inside, which the Eye told me to dump; it only wanted the box.

The second was a mannequin, one foot tall, constructed out of wire and smooth stones. The figure was squat and bulky, put together without any particular skill, as if by the hand of an apprentice toy maker just starting to learn his craft. The Eye ordered me to put the mannequin in the box. I had to fold it at the waist to fit it inside.

Our run from the Enclave didn't leave us a lot of time to do anything, so it wasn't until we reached Stonewall that I took the mannequin out. "What do I do with it?" I'd asked.

The Eye told me to find a patch of untampered ground—grass, dirt, stone, whatever, as long as it was unaltered by humans. Then I should place the mannequin on it, and its enchantment would do the work.

The first time, I had no idea what would happen, and I didn't trust the Eye when it said it wouldn't hurt anyone. So I went into the woods outside Stonewall to try it. When I put the mannequin on the ground, the figure stood there for a moment. Then, slowly, it bent over and slammed its stone fist against the dirt.

Nothing seemed to happen. It hammered the ground again.

"What's it doing?" I said.

sending a wave through the lifeblood, the Eye said.

"What does that mean?"

look. look carefully.

I focused on a patch of nearby grass glowing faint green in the

Eye's sight. The next time the mannequin hammered the ground, I saw a ripple through the glow, as if someone had dropped a stone into a pond. The grass's color brightened with the wave, then returned to the same shine as before.

The mannequin continued to slam its fist into the dirt. Each time, the ripple traveled outward. Then, suddenly, the Eye spoke, excited.

that way, foxchild. go that way.

An arrow formed in front of me, glowing in midair. It pointed west.

"What's that way?" I said, uneasy.

what I seek, the Eye said. And it wouldn't say any more than that.

∩∪

So we'd gone west. We hired a stagecoach and followed the Emperor's Highway, changing drivers and horses at the regular stops the coach company had built along the way. Most days, the stagecoach traveled straight through the night. It made the line nearly the fastest way to travel, covering a hundred and fifty miles a day, second only to an airship.

That meant we slept in the cabin most of the time, only stopping at an inn twice a week. When we did, I took the mannequin to a secluded spot to make sure we were still traveling in the right direction. Each time, the figure punched the earth, sending ripples through the life energy that surrounded us. I got the sense the Eye could see even deeper, all the way down to the primeval below the surface, watching the waves drift outward.

The second time I'd used it, a terrible thought had occurred to me. "Is it possible the Weavers could detect what we're doing?" I'd asked, worried.

they could, the Eye sneered, if they understood the nature of this world. instead, they have turned away from the truth. do not worry, foxchild. they are nearly as ignorant as you are.

"Thanks, I guess."

The Eye continued to send us west. We crossed the vast plains of Varlagh, with its endless yellow fields of wheat. We rode through the Rathcarran Gap, its chalk-white, mile-high cliffs rising high on both sides. Then we passed the mountains of Aeric's Spine, traveling through Kildunvan and Lakeland, before entering the rolling, wooded hills of Tullagh province. By now, we'd traveled nearly three thousand miles from Carlow—a full quarter of the entire continent—and each time I took the mannequin out, the result was the same.

So I was surprised when this morning, suddenly, it changed.

there, the Eye said, excited.

"What?" I said.

in that direction. it is there.

That floating, glowing arrow the Eye had shown me before returned. It pointed southwest.

"What's there?" I said.

a collection of your kind.

"You mean a city?"

yes, foxchild. a city. what I seek is there.

Gareth had bought a map of Ayreth at one of the stagecoach

offices. I located our inn and traced my finger along it, heading southwest.

"Is this the one you mean?" I said. "Tullagh's capital? Sligach?"

names are irrelevant, the Eye said, impatient. what I seek is there. go there.

"All right. But what are we looking for?"

I will tell you when we arrive. go.

I packed the mannequin into its box and hurried back.

CHAPTER 6

ODD DREAMS CAME again that night.

I was the last to fall asleep in the stagecoach. Meriel was leaning against me, dozing with her head on my shoulder. I closed my eyes. There was a strange flitting of images.

And then I was back in the forest where I'd found that fox. Though this time, I was alone. There was no dug-up hole, no dead creatures, no smell of blood. Remembering what Gareth had said about my eyepatch coming off, I reached up to check—

It wasn't there.

I wasn't wearing the patch. *The Eye's in my mind*, I thought, panic rising, until I realized that while my patch was gone, the Eye was gone, too. All I felt was an empty socket below a hollow eyelid. In this dream, I was as injured as ever, but no Eye. Strange.

Though again, that word—*dream*—didn't sit right. My mind was awake, alert. My senses were just as alive: the scent of the forest, the sound of the breeze. It was all too real.

So what was this?

And why had I come back here? I'd never been to this forest before—not in real life, anyway, only in my previous "dream." The smell was unfamiliar, as if I'd somehow traveled to a different part of Ayreth entirely. I wondered if that little fox was hiding somewhere nearby. It hadn't felt like a coincidence that I'd run into it the last time.

Maybe it would remember me, remember that I'd helped it. "Hello?"

The only answer came from the leaves rustling in the wind. It occurred to me—a little late, perhaps—that if the fox was around, then maybe so was the monster that killed its family. And yet for some reason, I didn't feel any sense of danger.

I tried again—though I didn't call quite so loudly this time. "Fox? Are you there?"

caw

I looked up. Above me, perched on a swaying branch, was a crow.

"Oh. Hello," I said.

The crow watched me.

"I don't suppose you've seen a fox around here," I said.

The crow cocked its head, as if wondering what I was talking about.

"For that matter, I don't suppose you know where I am?"

The crow blinked.

"I'm talking to a bird," I said to no one in particular. "Maybe I have lost my mind."

The crow continued to watch me curiously as I looked around. I couldn't see a trail anywhere, or anything that indicated some sort of civilization nearby. Though the last time I was here, I'd heard that strange sound, like something hitting wood. And a voice.

I tried listening. Nothing.

The crow had lost interest in me and was preening a wing. I supposed I might as well look around. I chose a direction at random, then headed out.

bonk

An acorn bounced off my head.

"What the . . . ?" I rubbed my hair and looked up. The crow had followed me, hopping to the closest branch above.

caw caw caw caw caw

It sounded like it was laughing. "Very funny," I said.

caw

"Right. Caw."

I continued on, wondering why my head was always everyone's favorite target. This crow, Foxtail and Meriel, Grey, the Old Man . . . I was surprised I didn't have a dent in my skull by now.

The crow fluttered down from the branches. I covered my head, expecting another acorn—or something a little more unpleasant—but the crow just landed in front of me, standing in my way.

caw

"What is it?" I said.

The crow looked at me.

"Are you hoping for food?" I said. "I don't have any."

At least, I didn't think I did. I checked my pockets; they were empty.

"See?" I turned them out. "Nothing."

The crow cocked its head, then flew up into the tree behind me.

caw

I was starting to think it was trying to tell me something. "I don't know what you want."

It flew back down to land at my feet. Then it took off again, returning to the tree. I stepped toward it. "What—"

It flapped over to the next tree, a little farther away.

caw

"Hold on . . . Do you want me to follow you?" I said.

It didn't answer. But when I took another step toward it, it flapped away again.

I couldn't think of any reason not to keep going. "All right, I guess. Lead the way."

It flew off, with me trailing. Occasionally, I'd lose sight of it among the leaves, only for it to reappear overhead, moving in a slightly different direction. Each time, I shifted to match it, and it flew on.

It did occur to me as I walked that maybe it was leading me into some sort of trap. For a moment, I hesitated. Then I shrugged. What could I do about it, regardless? I didn't even know where I was.

I walked a while more before I realized I hadn't seen the crow for several minutes. It had disappeared behind the canopy, and hadn't returned.

"Hello?" I called. "Crow? Are you still there?"

Apparently, it had gone for good. I stood there, hands on my hips, stumped. I'd say the thing had gotten me lost, but then, I'd been lost from the start. I wondered if that fox—

Wait.

I heard something.

thwock-thwock-thwock-whop

There. The same sound I'd heard the last time. Where was it coming from?

To the left? I went that way.

thwock-thwock-thwock-whop

Louder now. I went on. Then the voice joined it, like before.

thwock-thwock-thwock-whop

"Again."

I moved faster, following. Jogging now, I broke into a clearing.

And suddenly there was a door in front of me.

It looked like an ordinary door. Except it was standing by itself in the middle of the clearing. No walls, no roof. Just a door with a big brass handle.

thwock-thwock-thwock-whop

"Again."

The sounds were coming from behind it.

Cautiously, I approached. And then—

caw

The crow flapped down from the trees to land on top of the doorframe.

I stopped. "So you *were* leading me here."

The crow looked at me. It was waiting for me to open the door, I was sure of it.

Again I hesitated. But like before, what else was I going to do? I reached for the handle and the dream shattered.

I was back in the stagecoach, Foxtail shaking me awake. I squinted into the morning sun. "What . . . ?"

"We're here, guv," Lachlan said, rubbing his eyes.

We'd arrived at Sligach.

CHAPTER 7

I'D HEARD SLIGACH called the City of Progress before. I'd read newspapers that described it as a place of technological wonders. But I had no idea it would look like . . . this.

The road into Sligach was lined with contraptions, even before we reached the city gates. On our left, three huge cogwheels clunked as they spun, driving equally giant pistons deep into the ground—though for what purpose, I couldn't tell. On our right was a line of mechanical men dressed in top hats and coattails. They greeted us as we passed, doffing their hats, tapping brass canes against the tiles, their steam whistles playing a chorus in harmony.

It was even more mind-boggling inside. A massive clock, a near-perfect match to the grandfather clock that Grey kept at the front of his shop, its face showing Shuna and Artha chasing each other under sun and moons, stood in the center of a circular plaza—except this clock was fifty yards tall. All around, a menagerie of constructs of different animals from across Ayreth chirped, chittered, and growled from within painted cages, all almost as finely crafted as Galawan. A fountain of eight jets sprayed water into the air; a pinwheel at the top showered down sparks as it spun. The whole place smelled like smoke and oil.

"Shuna's sneezing snout," Lachlan said. He gaped in awe,

pointing out everything to Galawan, who was perched on his finger. Gareth was more reserved, looking with interest but surprisingly not much more than that. Meriel stared about, just as amazed as I was. Only Foxtail wasn't impressed. She covered her ears with her hands and shook her head. *Why does it have to be so noisy?*

She had a point. All the pumping pistons, clanging bells, and whirring gears made it awfully hard to hear. A gaggle of teenage girls in orange dresses with red pinstripes wandered among the travelers, welcoming us. One of them spoke to me; I had to lean in to make her out.

"New to Sligach?" she said, practically shouting. I noticed she had cotton balls stuck in her ears.

I nodded. "First time."

"Then welcome!" She handed each of us a pinwheel on a stick, a miniature version of the giant sparker above the fountain. "Is there something in particular you've come to see?"

"Actually, we were hoping to get settled in first," I shouted. "Is there a decent hotel for working folk?"

She gave me a few names. "You'll want to take the rails to get there. Don't worry, your first ride is free."

She fished a handful of brass tokens from a pouch at her belt and dropped one into each of our palms. The tokens were stamped with a cogwheel; CITY OF SLIGACH, CITY OF PROGRESS on one side, VALID FOR ALL ROUTES on the other. She gave us a map, too, printed on cheap, flimsy paper, pointing out what she called the proper "exchanges."

I had no idea what she was talking about. Even the map was

gibberish to me, with colored lines inked everywhere over a heavily labeled street plan. I turned to Gareth, bewildered.

"I know what to do," he said. With his low voice, I could barely hear a word coming out of him.

"You do?" I said.

"I p-passed through here once. I mean . . . on my way to Carlow."

Right. Even though Gareth had an obvious Westport accent—all stretched-out vowels and clipped consonants—I always forgot he was from the far edge of the empire. The girl pointed us past the clock to a metal staircase leading upward. At the top was a platform on a tower, forty feet above the ground. From there, steel rails stretched off into the distance, disappearing behind the buildings.

"Artha's blessed bum," Lachlan said. "What is all this?"

"Sligach's h-huge," Gareth said. "It's half the population of Carlow but five times the size. I mean . . . spread out. They use a rail system to get around."

When we reached the top, a sign over the entryway told us this was Wellcome Station. There were two platforms up here, divided by several rails, side-by-side. On the opposite platform, a train waited: an engine with three separate cabins behind it, which Gareth called "cars." Most of the people piled into the car closest to the engine. A good number took the middle car, while only a few very well-dressed gentlemen and ladies stepped into the last car. First, second, and third class, I guessed. Rather like an airship.

A man in a bright blue uniform with gold tassels on his shoulders blew a whistle, which was apparently the signal to hurry and get on, as the stragglers rushed to squeeze in. Then he gave two short whistles and one long one, and the doors on the cars closed. The engine in front began to chuff, great puffs of coal smoke blowing out its stack.

The train pulled away, steel wheels screeching against the rails. We watched it go, impressed—again, except for Foxtail, who still had her hands clasped over her ears.

"Did we miss the train?" Meriel asked.

"No," Gareth said. "I mean . . . yes. But there's another coming in a few minutes."

True to his word, we only had to wait a short time before the next train arrived, turning around on an extended rail loop to stop on the tracks on our side. People stepped aside politely as the car doors opened, allowing passengers to disembark, and then it was our turn.

I'd assumed the free tokens the pinstriped girls were handing out would get us into the cheapest section, third class. Instead, Gareth led us right to second class. The conductor smiled and nodded at us as we dropped our tokens into the box. "Welcome to Sligach."

Lachlan chose five seats in the corner so we could sit together. Meriel, who'd taken the rail map, was turning it this way and that, trying to make sense of it.

"What are all these colors?" she said.

"The routes," Gareth said. "Each one is a different rail line."

"What's the point of that?"

"Well ... the city's so big. You need different lines to get where you want to go. The colors make it easier to understand." Gareth explained that part of why it was so complicated was that different routes were owned by different rail companies.

"It's not just one?" Lachlan said.

Gareth shook his head. "There are a dozen. Companies, I mean. It's worth a lot to own a line. The business is very c-cutthroat."

That I could understand. I'd seen plenty of septs drop into those fare boxes when we got on—and crowns to ride first class. I couldn't even begin to estimate how much money the trains might make in a day.

"They're very proud of their rails in Sligach," Gareth said quietly. "Robbing the strongboxes gets you death by hanging."

We all glanced at Meriel. "Why is everyone looking at me?" she protested.

When the conductor blew his whistle, the train pulled away with a jolt. Our car rocked gently with the sway, wheels rumbling underneath.

Lachlan bounced on his cushion in excitement. "This is something else, this is," he said. "Why don't we have no trains in Carlow?"

"They're banned," Gareth said.

"They are?" Meriel said. "Why?"

He pointed out the window. "Th-that."

Up here, we should have had a great view. But the smoke that belched from the train's engine—and from the smokestacks all over Sligach—covered the city in a gray haze. All cities had some smog, especially in the winter when everyone burned coal to keep warm, but I'd never seen it anywhere near this thick.

"The emperor visited Sligach years ago," Gareth said, "after he took the Ruby Throne. He h-hated it here. How dirty and noisy the city was, I mean. So he banned the rails everywhere else. Along with any mechanical device that would take the job of a man."

"That's just good sense," Meriel said.

Gareth shrugged. I could tell he didn't agree, but he wasn't the type to argue. "The Weavers are the other reason rails are banned."

That got my attention. "What do you mean?"

"It's . . . a power struggle. The Weavers against the rail companies. Rails between cities would make it quick and easy to move people and goods. The Weavers have their airships, but they can't carry as much, and they can't travel through bad weather. Trains can. If Ayreth built rails, the Weavers would lose a lot of status."

"And since the High Weaver is the emperor's main advisor . . ."

Gareth nodded. "His Imperial Majesty couldn't ban trains in Sligach. The city was too invested; there would have been a revolt. But Darragh convinced him to stop the spread and b-ban them outside Tullagh province. Weavers aren't much welcome here anymore."

That was good news, as far as I was concerned. I'd had enough of Weavers to last a lifetime.

Foxtail was gesturing to Meriel. Meriel suddenly looked surprised and bit her lip. "I hadn't thought of that," she said.

"What's the problem?"

Foxtail gestured toward the rooftops. She pointed at us, then made a running motion with her fingers. *We can't use the Thieves' Highway. We'll be seen.*

The Thieves' Highway was what we called the rooftops: where thieves like us could move without being spotted by the Stickmen, the city guard. Here, with all the rooftop rails, we'd be spotted instantly.

"In Sligach, the Thieves' Highway is underground," Gareth said. "I mean . . . the Breakers use the sewers to get around."

Meriel's face fell. "I *hate* sewers."

Gareth shrugged. "They're big. And they go everywhere."

Then we'd have to familiarize ourselves with them. We watched the city for the rest of the ride, Lachlan pointing out the sights to Galawan—at least the ones he could see through the smog. We passed through several stations before Gareth told us our stop was coming up. From there, we went down another stair tower to the streets. For a busy city, the roads weren't nearly as bustling as Carlow. Whatever smog troubles the rails brought to Sligach, they certainly cut down on traffic. Though the whole city still smelled like smoke and oil.

Gareth led us to our hotel, using the map and the directions that the pinstriped girl had given him. I was glad we'd arrived. After weeks of waiting, I was keen to finally get to work.

CHAPTER 8

THE HOTEL GARETH chose was called the Stokefield Hub. It was a good location: central, with a window in our suite to a back alley so we might climb in and out unseen. There was also a pumping station and manhole cover nearby, both of which could give quick access to the sewers.

"What now, guv?" Lachlan said.

"We should prepare," I said.

Foxtail gestured. *For what?*

"Anything and everything. There's no telling what the Eye will ask me to do, so let's start by getting tools and making connections. Lachlan, I know you only ever lived in Carlow, but is there any chance you can find us a fence?"

Lachlan scratched his head. "Shouldn't be too hard. Just need to head out to the plainer places, ask about. Breakers are same-like the world over, eh?"

"We should map out our escape routes first," Meriel said.

"Those'll be through the sewers," I pointed out.

Foxtail tapped her chest. *I'll do it.*

Meriel looked relieved. We'd need more than Foxtail on it, though. "Is there some way we could get a map of the underground?" I asked Gareth.

Gareth nodded. "Yes. I mean . . . there should be. In the city records office. Someone will have the plans."

That would be his job, then. Lachlan and Foxtail followed him out. "What about us?" Meriel said.

"Do you still have that beige dress?"

"Yes. Why?"

"Put it on. I'll be back," I said, and I left before she could ask me anything further.

At the front desk, I asked for directions to some nearby shops. From those, I bought a selection of cheeses, roasted meat, a loaf of bread, a bottle of wine, and a basket. By the time I returned to our rooms, Meriel had changed. The room smelled faintly of jasmine; she'd dabbed some perfume on her neck, too.

She watched, puzzled, as I collected a couple more things. "Grab your parasol," I said, "and let's go."

"Go where?" she said.

I lifted the basket. "We're going to have a picnic."

Slightly wary, Meriel followed me downstairs. She hesitated when I offered her my arm.

"What are you up to?" she said.

"Don't you want to have a picnic with me?"

She opened her mouth, then closed it again without saying anything. Eventually, she just took my arm, her fingers resting lightly inside my elbow.

"Smile," I said, and that made her even more flustered.

We walked down the street together. She kept looking over at me, touching the malachite dragon pendant I'd given her, which she always wore around her neck. As for me, I kept thinking about jasmine. In my head, I could see the Old Man smirk. Though whether it was at her or me, I didn't know.

On the way to the hotel, I'd kept an eye out the window for nearby green spaces. I led her to the largest I'd spotted: a park a half mile from our hotel. There weren't a lot of folks around— Gareth had told us the City of Progress was a city of business, where all but the poorest and wealthiest would be at work—but I still picked the most secluded spot I could find.

"Help me spread out the blanket," I said.

Meriel hesitated, but she did as asked. I began to lay out the food. Meriel just watched.

"You're enjoying this, aren't you?" she said.

"Aren't you?"

She sat with me, trying to hide a smile. Eventually, she said, "Are you going to tell me what you're really doing or not?"

"The Eye said we had to come to Sligach to find what it needed."

"You told us already. So?"

"So . . ." I waved my arms around the park.

She glanced over her shoulder as a young couple strolled by. "You want to use that thing *here*?" she said quietly.

"It has to be on natural ground." Shifting the basket so it was on the grass, I punched a hole in the bottom. Then I opened the lead box, which I'd hidden in the basket, and removed the mannequin. Now I could place it in the hole, and being inside the basket, no one would see the mannequin hammering the ground.

We'd still have to shield the Eye, though. "Block me with your parasol, would you?"

Meriel angled her shade so no one passing could see my face. I pushed up the patch. "We're here," I said.

excellent, foxchild. The Eye said it the way you'd praise a dog for fetching your slippers. **proceed.**

I placed the mannequin on the grass. As before, the clunky little figure bent over and hammered its fist against the ground. The life energy rippled outward, a bright green ring spreading through the grass.

And then, suddenly, I saw the ripples come back. Except now they seemed to reflect from all directions—like a thousand pebbles dropped into a clear, still pond. It was almost disorienting.

what is this? the Eye hissed in my mind.

"What do you mean?"

It sounded angry. **where have you brought me?**

"Sligach," I said, confused. "Where you told me to go." When the Eye didn't respond, I said, "What are all these waves?"

something is interfering with my sight.

"What would do that?"

SILENCE

the Eye roared in my mind. It left me reeling.

Meriel steadied me, concerned. "What's going on?"

I held up a hand. I was afraid if I said anything, the Eye would thunder at me again. The mannequin continued to hammer on the grass, and each time a thousand echoes came back. With each thump, I could feel the Eye seething inside.

someone is playing a trick on me, foxchild. I will play back. and they will not like the way I play.

"I don't understand," I said. "Who's playing the trick? What is all this?"

the path to what I seek. it has been obscured more skillfully than I anticipated.

I was beginning to get it. "These . . . reflections. They're what you've been looking for? The directions they come from show you the way?"

yes, foxchild. but there should be only one. someone has used their powers to shield the location of what I need.

"Who?"

an old enemy. it does not matter. we will defeat them together.

I didn't like the sound of that. "How?"

I have a new task for you, the Eye said. you must find the hollow man.

CHAPTER 9

I PAUSED. "THE what?"

were you not listening? the Eye said. *must I say everything twice now? find the hollow man. your path is through the hollow man. is that clear enough for your feeble mind to comprehend?*

"What's it saying?" Meriel asked.

"It wants me to find the 'Hollow Man,'" I said.

She frowned. "Who's that? Or is it a place?"

"Place?"

"Like the name of a tavern or something."

Good question. I asked the Eye. It didn't answer. "Eye? Are you there?"

of course I am here, fool. where else would I have to go?

"I asked—"

I am tired of your questions. pester me no further. I have given you your task. complete it.

Confused, I put the patch back down. The Eye always hated when I covered it, but this time, I got the sense it welcomed the solitude, if for no other reason than that I couldn't bother it anymore.

"That was the strangest conversation I've had with that thing yet," I said to Meriel. "And that's saying something."

"What going on?"

"The Eye's really angry." I explained what had happened—at least as much as I could figure. "Someone—or something—has blocked it from finding what it wants."

"What does that mean for us?" she said.

I sighed. "It means if I want to get rid of this thing, our job just got a lot harder."

Gareth was the first to return. He'd found us a map of the sewers. We cleared off the dining table so he could unroll it. It was incredibly detailed, finely printed on thick paper.

"This looks official," I said.

"It's . . . I mean . . . it's their main blueprint."

"They let you borrow this?" Meriel said, surprised.

"Well . . . no." In other words, he stole it. He was a little sheepish. "I'll return it."

I told him what Meriel and I had learned in the park. "Have you ever heard of a Hollow Man?"

Gareth shook his head, frowning. "The Eye wouldn't tell you what it was?"

"Not even if it was a person or a place."

He sat, thinking. "Maybe it's neither."

"What do you mean?" Meriel said.

"It could be an object. I mean . . . an artifact. Like that mannequin. Or the Teeth." Gareth didn't seem too surprised at the Eye's reticence. He was more interested in the fact that the path had been hidden at all.

"Do you think a Weaver did that?" I asked him. "Like Mr. Solomon did to silence the Eye?"

"It's possible," he said. "Or . . ."

He looked at me meaningfully. An old High Weaver, Veran IX, had hidden the trail to the Dragon's Teeth. But a Spirit—a *dead* Spirit, Kira the Sheep, whom none of us had ever heard of before—had been part of that artifact hunt, too. "You think it's a Spirit that's playing tricks?" I said.

"The Eye said it was 'an old enemy.' Could be Shuna. Or maybe . . . someone . . . something else."

I knew what he was thinking of. Back in Westport, Gareth had met a librarian. The man had been a friend to him, showing him how to do research, teaching him ancient languages like the Old Tongue. Then, after three years, the librarian had vanished without a trace. And no one else even remembered he'd ever existed.

Gareth believed that vanished librarian was a Spirit. And thinking about it reminded him of something. "Do you recall what Professor Whelan said? Back in Redfairne?" Professor Whelan was the scholar who'd told us about the Pact the Spirits had made with each other, forbidding them from using their powers to affect humans. "There's a man who believes there are more than two Spirits. Professor—"

"Keane," I said, remembering. "Whelan said we should talk to Professor Keane, in Sligach." I stared at Gareth. "I told Whelan that Sligach was three thousand miles away. We'd never get to meet him. And yet . . ."

Gareth's eyes went wide. "Now we're here," he said.

Meriel was confused. "What are you two talking about?"

"Remember back in the vault?" I said. "After Artha disappeared, I pointed out to Shuna just how many things had to go our way for us to defeat the Bear. First the idol to summon Artha had to be placed in the vault and made unmovable. Then, a thousand years later, Veran had to hide the Teeth behind the idol. Then, two thousand years after that, the Old Man had to steal that crystal ring from that Weaver, then give it to Grey, who gave it to me, so I'd have exactly what I needed when we robbed the Enclave."

I held up my right hand. When the crystal ring shattered, it had left a burn mark on my finger. The mark was the same seven-banded pattern as the ring.

"Now we find ourselves needing to know more about the Spirits," I said. "And here we are in Sligach, three thousand miles from where we started—where the only other man who can tell us about them just happens to live."

Meriel looked from Gareth to me. "What does it mean?"

"It means none of this is a coincidence," I said. "And Gareth and I better find out why."

CHAPTER 10

VISITING PROFESSOR WHELAN back in Redfairne was the first time I'd ever been to a university. It had been peaceful and pretty, and like the Old Man always said, *First impressions count more than anything else. Show a man you're lazy for a month, then work hard the rest of the year. At the end, he'll still think you're a bum.* So peaceful and pretty was what I expected from the University of Sligach. What we saw was anything but.

Contraptions littered the university grounds. Some were functioning: an eight-armed cylinder, twenty feet long, marching awkwardly, steadied by a team of students; a coal-powered catapult; a spinning dumbbell that rode back and forth on a rail, flicking a line of switches, to what purpose, I didn't know. Others were works in progress—the steel framework of a nine-foot box; a half-built engine—but several of them had failed outright. Machines lay scattered across the lawns, their bodies rusting, their guts blown out by steam explosions, or burned by runaway coal fires. Most of the grass had been worn down, trampled by boots and wheels. And the *noise.* Cranks, bells, gears, whistles; I had to cover my ears. Poor Foxtail would have hated it here.

I didn't much like it myself. "Easy enough to see why the emperor banned this sort of thing," I shouted to Gareth over the din.

He shrugged. "For now."

"You think he'll change his mind? Who would want *this*?"

"These are the experiments," Gareth said. "The f-failures. But things like the rails, they work. And if someone can exploit that . . . it's why business rules this city, and Weavers aren't welcome. Tullagh's the w-wealthiest province in the empire. They mine half the gold and three-quarters of the steel. And all of that runs through Sligach. Eventually other provinces will learn they can make money like Sligach, too. And then . . ." He waved a hand around us. "Either this or spilled blood."

Gareth likes these machines, the Old Man said, *so he can't see what's coming. But you do, don't you, boy?*

I looked over the field of broken steel. *This is a threat to the Weavers' power*, I said. *And if there's one thing I've learned about the Weavers, it's that they're not going to go quietly. It'll be blood. I'd bet everything on it.*

The Old Man nodded. *Good bet.*

The noise wasn't the only difference between the campuses. In Redfairne, everyone had been helpful. Here, not so much. We asked a passing student if he could direct us to Professor Keane's office. He snorted and kept on walking. A second student smirked and said "'Professor.' Ha!" before moving on.

Gareth, clutching his satchel, was confused by the hostility. But I understood. Professor Whelan had said this Keane fellow was a bit of a crackpot. The campus was embarrassed to be associated with him. We eventually asked an older woman, who sighed and directed us to a low building made of old stone—a stark contrast to the rest of the university's more modern architecture of steel and glass. A directory was posted to a board in the entryway. We found Keane's office number—206—and went upstairs.

Keane's door was closed, but we could hear someone shuffling papers on the other side. I knocked. When no one answered, I knocked again.

A muffled voice came through the door. "Go away."

I looked at Gareth, surprised. He'd told me back in Redfairne how scholars loved to talk about their work, and Professor Whelan had proven that true. I hadn't even needed a gaff to get us in Whelan's door. This time, I hadn't bothered to prepare one.

"Professor Keane?" I called.

A chair scraped on the floor. Then the door opened. A squat man in a loose-fitting suit with hair on the back of his hands looked from Gareth to me. "Am I speaking out loud?" he said. "Can you hear me?"

"Um ... yes?"

"But can you understand me? Do my words make sense to you?"

"Yes?"

"Then what," he said, "did you find confusing about 'go away'?"

He slammed the door in my face.

We stood there a moment. "You know, Gareth," I said, "I don't think I like Sligach all that much." Gareth turned to go, but I stopped him. "We're getting some answers."

Gareth shied away; he didn't like conflict. But I was certain our being here wasn't a coincidence, and it wouldn't be smart to miss whatever this man had to say. I knocked again.

"Professor Keane? We need to talk to you. We need to ask you about the Spirits."

No answer.

I tried again. "Professor? How did Kira die?"

There was a pause. Then the door flung open. I half expected a fist aimed at my face. Instead, Keane stood there a moment, a little wild-eyed.

"Don't know where you came from," he said, "but I think you'd better come inside."

CHAPTER 11

WE PILED INTO Keane's office. It was a tidier place than Professor Whelan's, but more cluttered, knickknacks and artifacts everywhere. Much of it was pottery and ceramic fragments: chipped bowls, broken plates, sections of crumbling clay tablets in a box. There were a number of weathered scrolls, too, yellowing with age. The room smelled dusty, like the basement of an old museum.

Gareth, mesmerized by the history scattered around him, jumped when Keane shut the door behind us. The professor looked us up and down. I wasn't sure what he was looking for—or whether he found it.

"How do you know about Kira?" he asked.

I didn't really have a good answer to give him. I obviously couldn't tell him the truth, and not just because Shuna had warned us we couldn't tell anyone else we'd interacted with the Spirits. I decided to try the most likely approach.

"A professor in Redfairne showed us one of your papers," I said.

"Really?" Keane said. "Which one?"

The man looked like a brute. Short, squat, square jaw unshaven, muscles obvious even through his ill-fitting garb. His brow was thick and bony, giving the added impression of dullness. Yet his eyes seemed to pierce into my soul. I didn't give myself good odds on bluffing through this.

"I can't remember the title," I said.

"Do you know why?"

There was only one reason he'd ask that. "Because you never wrote a paper about Kira."

He smiled. "You're not stupid. That's good. It will make this quicker."

His hand shot out with alarming speed. Grip like a vise, he grabbed my collar and slammed me backward. The corkboard on the wall rattled, toppling free of its nail. It hit my shoulder coming down—*ow*—and would have hit Keane on the head if the man didn't swat it away.

The board tumbled into Gareth's thigh. He cried out and limped off to cower in the corner, satchel clutched to his chest. Keane held me against the wall, hand tightening. I struggled; it was getting hard to breathe.

Keane pointed a finger in my face. Swatting the corkboard had bloodied his knuckles. "A lot of students think it's funny to make fun of me," he said. "The first time, anyway. Never had one do it twice."

"I'm not making fun of you," I croaked.

"Then answer my question. How do you know about Kira?"

His grip was making me reconsider telling him the truth. But I had the sense that that would make things even worse. So I told him a different lie. "I saw her in a dream."

"A *dream*?"

He curled his bloody knuckles into a fist. Maybe the truth

would have been better after all. Instinctively, my hands rose to protect my face.

And suddenly, he stopped.

He stared at my right hand, mouth open. "Where did you get that?"

I couldn't catch enough breath to answer. Not that it would have mattered; I didn't have the faintest idea what he was talking about.

He released my collar. I slumped against the wall, gasping for air, as he grabbed my hand, splaying the fingers.

"This tattoo," he said. "Where did it come from?"

Now I understood. My crystal ring. The burn it had left looked like a tattoo.

This was another thing I couldn't tell the truth about. But finding a reasonable lie was easy. "My mother was superstitious," I said, rubbing my neck where he'd grabbed me. "She paid a wise man to mark me with it when I was little. It's supposed to offer good luck."

Keane couldn't stop staring. "Luck it brings, boy," he said. "Though I don't know about good."

"What do you mean?"

"These dreams of Spirits. How long have you been having them?"

My first instinct was to say, *All my life.* But then I'd have to make up a lot of dreams. I decided to play it safe. "Just recently."

"Anything important happen to prompt them?"

"Like what?"

"Did you have them before Bolcanoig erupted? Or only after?"

The volcano? What a strange question. *But it's not strange to Keane*, I thought, so I ran with it. "After. Right after."

He nodded, letting my hand go. "Luck, indeed." He regarded me with new scrutiny. "How many Spirits have you seen in your dreams?"

I decided to give him the right number, though for the wrong reason. Fox, Bear, Sheep, Deer, Leopard. "Five."

"And how many Spirits do you think there are?"

"I don't know."

"Yes, you do."

"I do?"

"Everyone does," Keane said. "They just don't see it. The number is right there in front of them. Always has been. But they never, ever recognize what it means."

I frowned. *The number's always been in front of us?* "That doesn't make sense," I said. "We've seen all kinds of numbers all our lives. How many Spirits? It's a riddle without an answer."

But Gareth gasped.

He'd been huddled in the corner since Keane had attacked me. Now his eyes widened, and in his revelation, his fear melted away. "No," he said. "There is an answer. It's *seven*."

CHAPTER 12

I STARED BACK at Gareth. "How do you know that?"

"The number," Gareth said. "I mean . . . seven. It's everywhere."

"It is?"

He explained, so excited he barely stammered at all. "Think of how many times seven shows up in anything that stretches back to the old days. The Weavers, with their seven-pointed stars. Their Hall of Elements: seven times seven times seven feet a side. Or our money. Crowns—and *septs*."

"What's that got to do with seven?" I said, puzzled.

"What do you think 'sept' means?" Keane asked.

I didn't know it meant anything. "I thought it was a reference to the emperor's articles of office. Crown and scepter."

"No," Gareth said. "'Sept' is an old word meaning 'seven.' But there are sixty septs to a crown. There's no reason to name it that."

"Because it's nothing to do with counting," Keane said. He pulled a handkerchief from his pocket and used it to wipe the blood from his knuckles. "It's an homage to our bond. Crown and sept. Man and Spirit."

"And the volcanoes." Gareth spoke so quickly he was tumbling over his words. "The Seven Sisters volcanoes." He looked at me meaningfully. "*Sisters.*"

My breath caught in my throat. The Spirits we'd met . . . they were sisters.

"All right," I said slowly. "I get that our ancestors would have named things after the Spirits. And that they might have known about Spirits we've forgotten. But the Weavers . . . the seven-pointed star is a reference to magic, isn't it? The number of different kinds of enchantments or something?"

"The Weavers believe that," Keane said, "because they've forgotten their own history. No, that's not true. They didn't forget it. They *rewrote* it."

"What's the Weavers' history?"

"They're an offshoot of the old dragon cult."

I looked at Gareth in surprise. "We've heard of the dragon cult," I said, "but we've never been able to find any information about it."

"Because it's outlawed." Keane tossed his handkerchief on his desk. "Has been for so long, almost no one even remembers it existed."

"How is the dragon cult . . . I mean . . . how is it related to the Weavers?" Gareth asked.

"You ever heard of primeval magic?"

I almost laughed. We just nodded.

"The dragon cultists were the ones who learned to trap it," Keane said. "They created the first enchantments."

I recalled what Bragan had told us about Mr. Solomon's dragon staff. *It was made four thousand years ago by the Dragon's Light himself.* "The Dragon's Light," I said.

"You've heard of him?" Keane said. "That's what they called their high priest. The cult was brutal, and the Dragon's Light was the worst of the lot. With the primeval so hard to control, once he realized he could steal the life from other living things instead, he turned the cult to human sacrifice to power their bindings."

Dragon cult, Dragon's Light, Dragon's Teeth, Dragon's Eye. "Why is everything named after dragons?" I said. "Dragons don't exist."

"But they used to," Keane said. "At least one did, anyway. The cult worshipped it. Then it died—or maybe it was already dead; the old texts aren't clear."

"Did it have a name?" Gareth asked.

"The dragon? No. It was just called the Adversary. Or sometimes the Devourer. Possibly because the cult was linked to the human sacrifices. No way to know anymore. If the cult still exists, they've gone deep underground."

They definitely existed. We'd met at least one cultist: Bragan. I was starting to wonder about Mr. Solomon, too. "You said they were related to the Weavers?"

Keane nodded. "The Weavers began as a splinter from the cult. Weavers wanted to enchant things, but they didn't want to hurt anyone to do it. They realized they could just draw the life energy from other sources: plants and animals. Their items wouldn't be as powerful, but their consciences would be clear.

"As you might guess, the cultists didn't approve. They tried to stamp out the heretics. Almost succeeded, too. The few Weavers who survived the purge fled and hid away in the forest, where Carlow is now."

"Then they allied with Aeric," I said, remembering Fergal's tale of the Dragon's Teeth in that sailors' tavern. "Our first emperor."

"That's the story. Once the Weavers had the emperor's ear, the tables turned. Now they could stamp out the dragon cult instead. It's been outlawed ever since. In the counterpurge, the Weavers deliberately erased any link between them and the cult. Most enchanters don't even know their own history—and that's the way the guild likes it."

Hearing the way Keane talked about this, something suddenly occurred to me. "You used to be a Weaver, didn't you?" I said.

He looked at me shrewdly. "You really aren't so stupid." He shrugged. "Started in the guild. Made it all the way to Associate before I crossed the wrong Grandmaster." He shrugged again. "Never was one for following rules."

"H-how do you know about the Spirits, then?" Gareth asked. "I mean . . . the other Spirits."

"Old writings. Illustrations. Artifacts. The truth is there, if you look hard enough."

Keane grabbed a scroll from a pile on his desk and tossed it to Gareth. Gareth, startled, unrolled the parchment with care.

The writing inside looked similar to what we'd seen in Veran's journal, the book that had told us where to find the Dragon's Teeth. The Old Tongue. Gareth read it silently. I couldn't make out a word of it, but there was also an illustration on the page, illuminated with faded colors and gold highlights. A fox standing with a deer. Or rather, *the* Fox, Shuna, standing with her sister, Fiona.

"If you have these," Gareth said, looking longingly at the rest of the scrolls, "why does nobody believe you? I mean . . . about more than two Spirits?"

"Most scholars think they're just illustrations of old Fox and Bear stories," Keane said. "That, or outright forgeries. Many of them probably are. But not all. Especially this. Look."

He pulled a long box from the bottom drawer of his desk. What was inside appeared more ancient than anything we'd seen yet.

It was a tablet—a part of one, anyway, broken from some bigger work thousands of years ago. A mosaic was set in the clay, semiprecious gemstones turned cloudy with age. Along the crumbled border was a fragment of what looked like a gilded, intertwining pattern, most of it lost when the tablet was removed. But the images in the center were intact. Seven animals.

"The Seven Sisters," Keane said. "Fox. Bear. Sheep. Deer. Leopard. Wolf. And Rabbit."

I couldn't believe it. I felt like we'd uncovered some long-lost secret. And yet, like Gareth had said, the truth had been staring us in the face all along.

That gameboard in the Weaver vault, I thought. *The one that was supposed to transport us out of the Enclave. There had been seven pieces, seven animals—seven sisters. Fox, bear, sheep, deer, leopard, wolf, and rabbit.*

Here they were. The Spirits.

"Wolf," Gareth said, breathless. "And Rabbit. Do you know their names?"

If Keane wondered why Gareth didn't ask about the others, he didn't say so. "The Wolf is Nuala. The Rabbit is Lila."

"What could make the Spirits be forgotten?"

Keane studied the tablet thoughtfully. "According to what I've read, the Spirits made a pact, long ago, not to interfere with us. I would think that was easier if we just forgot they existed. It's possible the Spirits themselves *made* us forget."

"But we know of Fox and Bear," I said.

"Because they're still alive. I believe the other five are dead."

That was the first thing he'd said that I knew he'd got wrong. Fiona the Deer and Cailín the Leopard were definitely alive. I wondered about Wolf and Rabbit. Had they died, like Kira? Was that why they hadn't appeared with the others in the vault?

"What could kill a Spirit?" I asked.

"No way to know, exactly. It's never mentioned in the stories. But we know the Spirits created Ayreth, and we know that at some point, they faced the Adversary—that dragon the cult worshipped. It stands to reason that anything that could fight the Spirits could also kill them."

"But what were they fighting over?" Gareth said.

Keane shrugged. "Again, no way to know. But in the oldest stories, it says the Spirits used the Eye of Creation to form the world."

A chill ran down my spine. "The Dragon's Eye."

Keane nodded. "That's what the cult called the stone; the Weavers kept the name. I think that's what the battle was fought over. Who controls the Eye. If the Spirits could use it to create the world, I imagine the Adversary could use the Eye to destroy it."

The power to create or destroy the world . . . stuck to my head under my eyepatch. I was too stunned to say anything.

But Gareth pushed on, clearly wondering about his vanished

librarian. "Are there . . . I mean . . . is it possible . . . there are more than seven Spirits?"

"Not as far as I know. Why?"

"What about B-Bran? Bran the Crow?"

We'd seen a Bran the Crow mentioned in the old Fox and Bear story that Shuna had led us to in Carlow. Though no crow had appeared with the other Spirits in the vault.

Keane looked pensive. "I don't know what the Crow is. He may exist, but if he does, I'm not sure he's a Spirit. At least, not like the others. There's something . . . different about him."

Now I was wondering, too. I'd just seen a crow in last night's dream. In fact, come to think of it, I'd seen one before, in a different dream. Back when I first lost my eye. A crow had saved me from Artha.

That couldn't be a coincidence. Could it?

"How is the Crow different?" I said.

"Well, the obvious is that he's male. But he's also different in other ways. It's always the Seven Sisters, never eight. He's never referred to as a brother or something similar. He's not on this mosaic with the others.

"In fact," Keane continued, "when he shows up in the stories, he always has his own agenda. Sometimes he's helping the Spirits. But sometimes he's against them—or one of them, at least. One time he sides with Shuna, another time with Artha. I mentioned the Adversary earlier. It's possible that Bran *is* the Adversary."

"But you said the Adversary was a dragon," Gareth said.

"He might be. Except no dragon ever appears in the stories. Just the Crow. And they do have one similarity: they're both flying creatures—and none of the Seven Sisters can fly. Maybe as the years passed, 'the dragon' changed into 'the Crow.'" Keane nodded toward me. "Shame we can't ask your old wise man."

For a moment, I was confused, thinking he was talking about the Old Man. Then I remembered I'd lied about how I'd got my burn mark. "Why would the wise man know?"

"He knew enough to give you that tattoo."

I looked over at Gareth, but he didn't understand what Keane was getting at, either. "What's so special about my tattoo?"

Keane was amused. "You didn't see it? Look at the mosaic again."

Puzzled, I looked at the Spirits on the tablet he'd shown us. There were Fox and Bear. Pretty good likenesses, actually, capturing Shuna's cheerfulness and Artha's haughtiness. I studied the others, but I couldn't see what the man was talking about.

"The border," he said. "Look at the border."

There wasn't much of the border left. It had been made with hammered gold, very fine. At first, I thought it was just a decoration, gold leaf intertwined. Now I saw it was actually made of tiny letters weaving in and out of each other, almost too small to make out. "What does it say?"

Gareth had missed the letters, too. Now he read them, growing excited again. "It's the names of the Spirits," he said, "in the Old Tongue." He read them out, tracing the lines with his finger. "Shuna . . . Artha . . . Kira . . . Fiona . . . Cailín . . . Nuala . . . Lila."

But there was something even more special about them than that. As I followed Gareth's finger, I saw that each name was written on a separate band. Seven names . . . seven bands.

The mark.

The burn mark from my crystal ring. Seven bands intertwined. "The pattern's the *same*," I said, breathless.

Keane nodded. "It's the Mark of the Seven Sisters. Whoever put that on you gave you a connection to the Spirits. That's what's allowing you to dream about them. Except they're not actually dreams at all."

I stared at him. "What do you mean, not dreams?"

"A dream is just in your head," Keane said. "I don't think that's where you were when you saw the Spirits. I think you were *there*, with them. I think you were in Shadow."

CHAPTER 13

S HADOW.

The realm of secrets, Bragan had called it. *Where extraordinary, magical creatures may speak with us and endow us with blessed wisdom.* Veran had said almost the same thing in his journal. *I taught Galdron the nature of Shadow, and how it may be used to communicate with greater beings like the Spirits.*

When I fell asleep, had I somehow entered that place? That... realm?

"What exactly is Shadow?" I said.

"Exactly?" Keane said. "I'm not sure. Back when I was with the Weavers, I found an old work in the Enclave library written by one of the early Grandmasters. He claimed that there are different realms, different realities. Where entire universes follow different rules. Worlds where magic doesn't exist, for example, that sort of thing.

"Shadow is supposed to be the place *between* these realities. 'The realm between realms,' I heard it once called. I don't know if that's true. What I do know is that the Spirits have the power to move through Shadow—and thereby move between realms."

"What would be the purpose of that?" Gareth asked.

He shrugged. "No idea. Tell your friend to ask the Spirits the next time he dreams about them."

"But h-how would he know he's there? In Shadow? That he's not just having a dream?"

"He'll know," Keane said, "because he'll *know* it's a dream."

"What do you mean?" I said.

"Most of the time, when you dream, you don't realize you're dreaming. Things are bizarre. You're in one place, then suddenly you're in another. Or you're talking to people you don't know or who are long dead, yet somehow it's all normal. It doesn't even register how strange it is. Right?"

Gareth and I nodded.

"But sometimes," Keane said, "you *do* know you're dreaming. Your mind is conscious, even though you're asleep. And you look around and say, *This is a dream.* Right?"

"Sure," I said.

"That's the irony. Because at that point, when you know you're in a dream, *you're not in a dream anymore.* You've moved into Shadow. You've slipped into the realm between realms. Or at least your mind has. Or maybe your soul. I don't really understand how it works. I don't think anyone does, except the Spirits."

A dream where you know you're dreaming. I'd had *two* of them recently. The one where I met that fox. And then last night, where the crow led me to that door.

I was in Shadow. The thought chilled me to my bones.

"Entering Shadow," I said. "Could it be controlled? Could you make yourself do it?" *Or not do it?* I wondered.

Keane looked pensive. "There are Weavers who've attempted it. Tried to travel into Shadow by forcing their mind to realize they're asleep. Lucid dreaming, they call it. Some have even succeeded. Though whether they brought back truths or lies, who knows?"

"Lies?"

"Of course. Shadow is sometimes called the realm of secrets. But the secrets that the beings who live there whisper . . . well, every living thing has its own agenda. Are they trying to help you? Or hurt you? The things they tell you: Are they true? Or are they false? How would you tell the difference?"

Keane nodded toward the mark on my hand. "I've known Weavers who would kill—literally—for what you've been given. But ask yourself: the wise man who gave you that tattoo . . . what did *he* want? Your mother wanted the Spirits' protection. What did the wise man want for you?"

"What's the danger?" Gareth asked. "I mean . . . besides being l-lied to. What could it do to him?"

"Shadow exposes you to magical, alien forces. Not just the mind, but the soul. The things that live there can tear both of those apart."

I stared at him. "You mean it could kill me?"

"Oh, much worse." Keane looked grim. "When I was still with the guild, I had a friend—Aerlan was his name—who experimented with entering Shadow. When I first met him, he was a middling enchanter, nothing more. But once he started visiting the realm of secrets, his skill began to grow at an alarming rate. Barely a few months after he first made it into Shadow, he crafted a Grade V enchantment, when the best he could have done beforehand wouldn't even have reached Grade III. You're not Weavers, so you don't understand what that means. It's like a five-year-old suddenly telling you the secrets of the universe."

"What happened to him?" Gareth said.

"He went to sleep one night and never woke up."

"He d-died?"

"Not at first," Keane said. "It was like he was in a coma, from which nothing could wake him. We tried for weeks, keeping him alive by forcing food and water down his throat. Eventually, one of the Grandmasters discovered a binding that would let him peek into a sleeping person's mind. He used it . . ."

Keane trailed off.

"And?" I said. "What did he see?"

"He didn't see anything. It's what he heard." Keane shivered. "Screaming. Endless, terrified screaming."

CHAPTER 14

WE EXITED KEANE'S office in silence.

What he told us had left me completely rattled. A million fears slammed around inside my head, each one crazier than the last. I'd been all but certain getting that crystal ring wasn't a coincidence. Now there was no doubt. Someone—something—had been manipulating us. Me most of all.

I rubbed the mark on my finger. Though it felt like normal skin, Keane believed the magic within was pulling me into Shadow. If that was true, then the question was: For what purpose? To help me? Or hurt me? Keane had had no answers. Neither did I.

Gareth wasn't any help, either. As we rode the train back to our hotel, he sat by the window, that thoughtful look on his face, the slight frown and pursed lips he had whenever he was mulling over something serious.

"Wondering if I'm going to end my days in a coma?" I said. "Screaming into the void?"

He looked startled—and somewhat stricken. "I . . ."

I held up a hand. "Sorry. Bad joke." I sighed. "I just don't know what to make of anything anymore."

We hadn't even gotten an answer from Keane to the most pressing question we had. Who—or what—was the Hollow Man?

We'd asked him just before we left. Keane had shaken his head. "Never heard that term before. Don't think it's anything to do with the Spirits. At least nothing I've ever seen."

Now, on the train with Gareth, I had an idea. "Maybe it's to do with this Adversary—Devourer. Dragon, or Crow, or whatever."

Gareth agreed that was possible. But without more information, we were right back where we started.

Both Foxtail and Lachlan returned to the hotel a few minutes before us. I was still so caught up in my own thoughts, I barely noticed they were there.

"Everything all right, guv?" Lachlan said.

"Huh?" I looked over to see everyone watching me. "Oh. Yeah. Um...any luck?"

Foxtail nodded. She gestured, jabbing a finger at the map of Sligach and the sewers until we understood her. *There are four ways in near our hotel: a pumping station behind the grocer, two manholes in the streets, and a drainage grate for runoff in the alley. The pumping station's the most secluded, but it's locked, so we'll have to either find a key or break in if you want to use it.*

We could work with that. "Did you check out the sewers themselves?"

She nodded, gesturing again. *Big. And they go everywhere. Lots of nooks and crannies to hide, if it comes to that. Lots of tracks inside, too. Looks like the Breakers use the tunnels a lot.*

That was promising. It meant the Breakers had keys to the pumping stations. It might be worth contacting them, seeing if we could buy a copy.

Lachlan said we were already halfway there. "Found us a fence." He scratched his head. "Least I think I did."

"You didn't go in?" I said.

"Weren't nearby. Things is proper strange round here, guv. Should have been quick-like snooping what I need, but I couldn't get no one to yap for the longest time. Don't make no sense, it don't."

"Why not?" Meriel said.

"Can always find someone wanting an extra coin in their pocket, eh? Makes getting the scoop as easy as feeding bread to a duck; just start slipping septs into palms. And I got crowns to donate." Lachlan waved his wallet at us. "But no one would talk. The shops, too. Can always tell a Breakers' friend; they got a key in the window, like. But none of the blokes behind the counter seemed to know my signal."

I remembered the one Lachlan had used on the hotel clerk in Carlow: three fingers on the left, two on the right. "Maybe it's a different sign here in Sligach."

"Nah, guv. Every club's got their own flash, true enough, for the times you got to show you're in the immediate family, right? A town changes them up on the monthly so's the Stickmen don't crack yer walnut. But this one's good for Breakers everywhere, always the same." He repeated the sign he'd given that clerk. "Ask Gar."

Gareth nodded.

"So what does this mean?" I said.

"Things're tighter than a mouse's pucker in a cat's claw," Lachlan said. "Something must have rattled the Breakers sometime recent. Anyhow, I finally found a tavern with loose lips. Geezer said a bloke named Collins is the man to see. Runs a pawnshop called the Lemon Tree over in the Sun district. Though only Shuna knows where that is, eh?"

The Sun district was labeled on our map. No Lemon Tree, though. "We'll have to go there and find it," I said.

"Do you need me and Foxtail to go with you?" Meriel asked.

"I suppose the three of us can manage by ourselves. Why?"

"I want to run our escape routes, make sure they're open," she said. "Especially if Lachlan's right, and something's made the Breakers cautious. Foxtail can show me which ways to go."

That was probably a good idea. "All right. Don't go lifting a key to the pumping station if you find one, though. We'll ask the fence about it first."

She made a face. "You're no fun anymore."

CHAPTER 15

EVEN THOUGH GARETH had warned us, I hadn't truly comprehended just how sprawling Sligach was. The city had been founded at the confluence of five different rivers, all feeding into the massive Cardogh River to the north. Over time, settlers had spread out across the banks, originally as different villages, eventually joining over the centuries to form one huge metropolis.

The Sun district was in the far southwest of the city, nestled between the Blackwater and Kilcrow streams. It was a more upscale part of town, lacking the industrial centers that belched coal smoke over most of Sligach, so there was barely any smog out this way. Between pockets of shops and residences, wide orchards stretched from river to river in bandlike rows. They grew citrus trees here, giving the whole area a faint lemony smell.

Since we didn't know exactly where the pawnshop was, Gareth, Lachlan, and I hopped off at the first stop and asked one of the uniformed attendants. He directed us six stops down, using a different rail company—costing us several more septs each. *A nice gig these rail barons have going here*, I thought. They must be swimming in coins.

The Lemon Tree was a surprise, too. Unlike the pawnshops

I was used to—narrow spaces jam-packed with goods, tags with hastily scrawled prices hanging down—the Lemon Tree was bright and airy. It almost could have passed for a museum: well-lit merchandise, with plenty of room to study the pieces. What was on display was mostly furniture, with figurines, curios, silverware, and the like neatly arranged on the shelves.

"Are you sure this is the place?" I asked Lachlan.

"What I was told." He motioned to the window, where a sign announced LOST KEYS RECUT HERE. "We need the owner."

The owner, Collins, didn't seem particularly enthused to see us—and strangely, even less so after Lachlan flashed him the sign of the Breakers. He regarded us coolly, looking down his long nose at us from behind the counter. "Yes," he said eventually. "I believe I have what you need in the back."

He left the clerks in charge and escorted us through hanging curtains into a small warehouse. At the far end was a separate room filled with chests of drawers. He locked that door behind us and regarded us once more.

"You're from Carlow?" He'd recognized Lachlan's accent, broad and drawling, from the poorer part of that city. "I thought the Stickmen took the Carlow Breakers out."

"Couldn't catch us lot," Lachlan said cheerfully. "Slippery like foxes, we are."

"Hm. So what is it you're looking for?"

The fact that Collins was wary made me a little wary, too. Best to start off with simple business. "Whatever you have," I said. "We're out of tools and looking for new kit."

If his attitude wasn't welcoming, his stock more than made up for it. He opened the drawers to show us the largest assortment of thieves' tools I'd ever seen. Chain cutters, purse snippers, disguise kits, grapples, blackjacks; you name it, he had it. And all top quality. I plucked out a set of steel snips and tested its edge against my fingernail. It sheared off a sliver with ease.

Lachlan was impressed. "Shuna's snout. I'm in the emperor's vault, I am."

Collins smiled indulgently. "Take your time," he said, not sounding like he meant it.

We piled up a solid collection of gear. What I was most interested in, though, was what Breakers called "one-shots." These were small vials of liquids or powders, one use only. We'd made good work of two of them back in the Enchanters' Enclave, and I had a feeling that whatever was coming, they'd be just as handy here.

Collins's one-shots were as impressive as his gadgets. Puffs (smoke bombs), dead juice (stink bombs), matchsticks (flame bursts), bugs' legs (itching powder), boo-hoo (tear gas), snooze goo (sleeping draughts), achoo (sneezing powder) . . . It was like a candy shop.

"Artha's pounding paws," Lachlan said, and he plucked out a small vial filled with what looked like flakes of metal, incredibly shiny.

Collins put a hand out. "Don't open that."

Gareth leaned in, peering at the silvery flakes as they flashed in the lamplight. "W-what is it?"

"Sunshine," the fence said. "The metal ignites in air. Look right at it, the light'll blind you for a week."

That almost made me nervous to cart it around. But I pulled a couple and added them to the pile with the others.

"Quite a purchase," Collins said, tallying it in his ledger.

I shrugged. "Never hurts to be ready. That reminds me, if you have a key to the pumping stations, we'll take that, too."

"Hm. I presume you've already checked in?"

"To a hotel?" I said, confused.

Collins paused and looked up at me. "No," he said slowly. "With Mr. Fox."

Ah.

Mr. Fox, I remembered the Old Man once telling me, was the title they gave to the head of a city's guild of Breakers—named, obviously, after Shuna the Fox, patron Spirit of thieves. When pulling a job in a Breaker city, it was customary for freelancers like us to get the thumbs-up from the locals first. Like any other guild, the Breakers didn't want outsiders playing on their turf.

Most of the time, accommodations could be made—as long as the Breakers got their cut. Standard rate was a full third of your take. A hefty sum, which was why most freelancers only operated in towns too small to have a guild chapter.

Sometimes, however, the Breakers would refuse to let free-lancers work. This was usually a peaceful process: they wave you off, you move on, no harm done. If you stayed to break the rules, then you got broken yourself. Your arms, your legs . . . and if you really made them mad, your neck.

We hadn't worried about that on the last two jobs. With the

Carlow Breakers gone, there was no need to ask permission. As for Sligach, we still didn't know what we were doing here. Would we need to stick around or just find the Hollow Man and move on?

I decided to play it safe. "We just got in," I said. "Of course we'll talk to Mr. Fox. I only wanted to get our tools before we started wandering about. Like I said, never hurts to be ready."

"Naturally." Collins finished his tally. "Nine hundred and sixty-three crowns and twenty-seven septs."

At first, I thought I'd heard him wrong. It was an eye-watering sum, twenty times higher than what we'd have paid in Carlow. Lachlan was outraged. "You having us on, mate?"

Collins shrugged. We'd already seen everything was more expensive in Sligach, but this was more than an outrageous price. It was a message. *You're not welcome here, outsider.*

It left me in a tricky spot. I didn't want to burn any bridges—a great fence was a precious thing—so I couldn't haggle him down too hard. On the other hand, if we accepted a gouging this bad, he wouldn't respect us. In the end, I talked him down to three hundred and fifty crowns flat. Still way too much, but there really wasn't anything else we could do. Other than robbing him, of course, which would not have been a good idea.

As Collins began to put his collection away, it was time to ask what I'd put off. "One more thing," I said casually. "We're looking for the Hollow Man."

He paused, ever so slightly. Then he continued shutting the drawers. "Never heard of him."

Well. I'd learned two things from that. One, from the way he'd paused, he was lying. He knew very well who the Hollow Man was. And two, that it was, in fact, a "him." Maybe someone in the guild?

"You sure?" I said. "We just need to talk. There's a hundred-crown finder's fee."

Collins shrugged. "I can't sell what I don't have. Anything else?"

Clearly, he wouldn't be budged, so we left. On our way back to the rail station, Lachlan looked troubled. At first, I thought it was just that he was offended the fence had ripped us off. "I guess everything really is more expensive in Sligach," I said.

"Huh?" Lachlan said. "No, that ain't it."

"Then what's wrong?"

"Dunno, guv. Can't put my finger on it. But something's all off about this town."

"What do you mean?"

"Shouldn't've been so hard to find a fence," he complained. "Shouldn't've been so much to spend. Just . . . everything's on edge. Like the whole city's locked down when there ain't no lock-down. I dunno, maybe that don't make no sense."

No one would ever accuse Lachlan of being the brightest. But he had genuine street smarts, and he knew the ins and outs of Breaker ways cold, even if he'd learned them halfway around the world. What he'd felt, I'd felt, too, just from Collins alone. Something was off. I suspected finding this Hollow Man was going to be more trouble than I'd hoped.

In the morning, I'd learn just how much.

CHAPTER 16

THAT NIGHT, I returned to the forest. And there wasn't any doubt. Not anymore.

This wasn't a dream.

I said it out loud. "This is Shadow."

It was strange. The forest didn't look any different. It didn't sound or smell any different. And yet saying those words did change something: me.

I felt different. It wasn't anything I could put a finger on. But it was as if something went *click* inside. Like a switch had flipped, and something new had opened in my mind.

The realm between realms, I thought. *The realm of secrets.*

I looked down at the seven-banded mark on my finger. According to Keane, this was what kept bringing me here.

"What do you want?" I said. "What secrets am I supposed to find?"

As if the forest could hear the question, I suddenly heard a sound. The same as I'd heard before.

thwock-thwock-thwock-whop

And as I heard it, I realized this was where I'd been the last time. Not just the forest, but *here*, this very spot. I'd passed through it while following that crow. And . . . yes, there. One of my own footprints in the dirt, where I'd stepped around a bush to avoid its thorns.

I knew the way to go. And like before, as I walked the path, a man added his voice to the sound.

thwock-thwock-thwock-whop

"Again."

I pushed past the leaves of a low-branched tree. And there was the door.

No crow this time. But the door was the same. I stood in front of it, listening.

thwock-thwock-thwock-whop

"Again."

The realm of secrets. That crow, I wondered . . . Was it Bran the Crow? Or just a Shadow-bird?

And why had it brought me here?

Every living thing has its own agenda, Keane had told us. *But are they trying to help you? Or hurt you? The things they tell you. Are they true? Or are they false?*

How would you tell the difference?

I wasn't sure. But I'd been taught by the Old Man. "And if anyone knew how to crack a lie," I said to him, "it was you."

Steeling myself, I opened the door

and found myself somewhere entirely new. I was in a gallery, a stone wall on one side, pillars on the other. The stone was smooth and plain, no carvings or artistic flourishes. But it was crafted with precision and care, the work of a master mason.

The gallery overlooked a training arena fifteen feet below. Wooden posts, straw targets, and dummies sat like fat scarecrows around the square. The ground was white sand, churned by untold numbers of feet stomping through it. Here and there, dark splotches marred the grains. Blood, soaked into the ground.

There were two people in that arena. One was a man, dressed in a plain beige shirt and brown pants. His long gray hair was tied in a ponytail, and he held a wooden staff. His back was to me, so I couldn't see his face. Just dry, wrinkled skin over strong hands.

Before him, perched barefoot on a sawed-off tree stump, stood a girl, about eight years old. She was lightly dressed in a short, loose skirt and a sleeveless top that wrapped around the upper part of her torso, leaving her midriff exposed. Her body was covered in sweat. She'd been training.

The girl had raven-black hair, tied in a ponytail of her own. Her dark eyes—

Wait.

"Meriel?" I whispered.

That girl . . . it was Meriel. The shape of the eyes. The high cheekbones. The intense, brooding look as she focused. This was Meriel, sometime around six years ago. It could be no one else.

I stared, barely able to believe

(the realm of secrets)

what I was seeing. Beside the tree stump she stood on was a bucket. She reached down, sweat dripping from her chin, and drew four throwing knives from it. If there had been any doubt before that this was Meriel, there was none now. I'd recognize those knives anywhere.

She tucked two of them into the top of her skirt. The other

two she held, one in each hand. She stood there, watching the man in front of her. Waiting.

The man nodded.

Suddenly, Meriel spun around. Twirling, she flung the knives she was holding, aiming at two wooden circles on the far side of the arena. As the blades sailed through the air, Meriel drew the other knives from her waistband. Still turning, she threw one of them, aiming at a different target. All three hit their mark.

thwock-thwock-thwock

As she completed her spin, the man swung his staff at her hip.

Meriel twisted, eyes tracking the incoming staff. Holding tight onto her last knife, she brought the blade down to block the attack. She caught it with the tip.

whop

The man nodded. "Again," he said.

Meriel let out a breath, blowing drops of sweat from her lips. She reached down and pulled more knives. Once more the man nodded, and once more she spun, hurling the blades. This time, when she spun around, the man struck at her head. She blocked the attack.

thwock-thwock-thwock-whop

"Again," he said.

Meriel slumped a little. But she pulled new knives once more. She spun. He aimed the staff at her legs. This time, she was too slow.

thwock-thwock-thwock

CRACK

Meriel cried out as the staff walloped her on the thigh. She toppled from the stump, crumpling sideways into the sand. She lay there, gripping her leg, sobbing in pain.

The man said nothing.

"I can't," Meriel said. "I can't do it anymore. I'm too tired."

"Then we're finished for the day." The man picked up the bucket of throwing knives. "Remember that phrase, Meriel. For when your uncle Dathal finally comes to take what is your father's—what is *yours*—you'll need it. 'Go ahead,' you can tell him. 'I can't fight today. I'm too tired.'"

He turned to leave.

"Wait."

Meriel pushed herself up. The sand stuck to her skin, a tear dragging a jagged thunderbolt through the grains on her cheek. Limping, she stepped back up on the stump.

"Again," she said.

Silently, the man placed the bucket beside her. She drew the knives and spun.

thwock-thwock-thwock-whop

"Again," she said.

thwock-thwock-thwock-CRACK

The staff hit Meriel in the ribs this time. But she didn't fall. She drew a shuddering breath, eyes closed, and wiped the tears from her cheeks.

"Again," she said.

thwock-thwock-thwock-whop

"Again."

I awoke.

CHAPTER 17

BREAKFAST THAT MORNING was oatmeal and bacon, the plates brought to our room. Meriel was stuffing her face. Gareth picked at his food, eating small bites as usual. Foxtail joined us at the table, but just for company. Lachlan was sleeping in.

I ate alongside the others, but I barely tasted my meal. My eyes kept wandering to Meriel and thinking of that eight-year-old girl.

The realm of secrets. Well, I'd certainly learned one. There was no doubt in my mind that what I'd seen wasn't just a vision, but a memory. Something that had actually happened in Meriel's past.

It explained a lot. Why Meriel was so good with those knives, for one. She must have been training since she could walk. And though her master had been brutal, it was obvious she'd looked up to him. Despite his stern manner, it was easy to see he'd cared about her, too.

I'd also learned something special about her family. Her father—and an uncle who would come to take "what was hers." So her father was . . . someone important? A landowner? Or something more?

The realm of secrets. Yes, I'd learned a few.

But why?

That crow, Bran or not, had led me there. For what purpose? What was it trying to show me?

The Old Man answered in my head. *I doubt that particular scene is finished, boy. There's something more there to discover.*

I had the sense he was right. I felt like I'd walked into a theater in the middle of a play. I could tell by what happened on the stage what had come before. But the ending had yet to be revealed.

Tonight, maybe, I began to answer the Old Man, when Meriel nearly choked.

She'd had the misfortune to be guzzling from her glass when she spied what walked out of Lachlan's room. It made her spit milk all over the table.

I whirled in my chair, heart skipping a beat, to see Lachlan's corpse lumbering toward us. His eyes were sunken, his flesh covered in weeping boils and open sores. He had his hands out, like the dead returned to life, come to drag us down to the under-world.

"Gaaaah," he said.

"You *weasel*," Meriel hissed.

Lachlan laughed, a wild peal of delight. That *stupid* weeping sickness ring.

Meriel plunged her hand into the pot of oatmeal and threw a fistful at Lachlan. A good glob of it smacked him on the chin, splashing his shirt. He dodged, still laughing, as she flung strips of bacon at him, spattering him—and the rest of the room—in grease.

Foxtail laughed along silently. Gareth just looked bemused. And though I was peeved at being startled by Lachlan's prank, I had to admit I was impressed, too: he'd discovered something that scared Meriel, and she didn't scare easily.

"You're lucky I don't let her strangle you," I said to him as he ducked behind Foxtail, dodging the flying breakfast.

"Shuna's ears," Lachlan said. "What's put the bee in your underpants, eh?"

"Look at this mess." I'd already taken that ring from him once. "How did you even get that?"

"Lifted it from your pocket," he said, as if that should have been obvious. "You know, you wouldn't think so, but for a gaffer, you're right easy to snaffle."

For Shuna's sake. There was food everywhere now. "Give me the ring."

"Why? It's mine."

"Meriel?" I said. "Kill him."

He ran to the far side of the table, ducking behind an alarmed Gareth as Meriel stormed over, a fistful of oatmeal oozing through her fingers. Foxtail just laughed harder. "Nooo!" Lachlan cried. "Guv, please! Don't let her hurt me!"

"Let her?" I said. "I'm going to sell tickets to the show."

"Nooooooo! Oh . . . all *right*." He pulled the enchanted ring from his finger, and his flesh returned to normal.

I took the ring. "You snaffle me again, I'm going to dip your head in the river."

"Artha's paws," he grumbled. "You'd think you'd never seen bacon in the carpet before."

Our bundle of stolen enchantments was hidden in Foxtail's room. She brought it out so I could put the ring with the others. Part of me thought I should palm it and slip it under my belt instead, so Lachlan wouldn't know where to look in case he went for it again.

Meriel was doing her best to warn him off either way. "I'm going to ram oatmeal in places you never even heard of," she said.

He laughed, even as he used Gareth as a shield again—who looked worried that Meriel was going to return to throwing breakfast. I gave the possibility even odds.

Shaking my head, I unrolled the bundle and tossed the ring in with the other artifacts. Suddenly, Foxtail perked up, alert.

"What is it?" I said.

She held up a hand. *Shh.*

Meriel thought we were still talking about pranks. "What's Lachlan done now—"

Foxtail waved her off, too. She cocked her head, listening.

Then she grabbed the bundle of enchantments—Dragon's Teeth, plague ring, and all—and jumped straight out the window.

We stood there, stunned. Meriel had opened the window this morning to air our rooms out, but I was pretty sure Foxtail would have leapt through even if it had been closed. Which could only mean—

The door to our rooms smashed open.

A horde of brutes swarmed in. Lachlan, closest to the entryway, was the first to go down. One of the thugs barreled into him, knocking him to the ground. Another grabbed Gareth by the neck and flung him into the corner. Five more ran around the table, coming for Meriel and me.

I was still on my knees. As I stood, I tried to pedal away from the onrushing brutes and tripped over my own feet. I sprawled onto the rug. Meriel snatched a knife from the table, even as one of the intruders grabbed the far corner and flipped it over. It slammed into her, knocking her off balance and ruining her aim. Her knife clattered harmlessly against the wall.

The table came down hard, pinning me to the rug. Bruised and in pain, I tried to wriggle out, but one brute grabbed me before I could move. Meriel quickly regained her balance and tumbled out of sight, into her room. Two of the thugs chased her, only to fall back as a pair of knives sailed through the doorway, thunking into the wood panels.

One of the men—though he had the most brutish face of them all, there was cunning in his eyes—kept Gareth pinned to the ground with a foot on the back of the boy's neck. He hardly needed to bother; Gareth wasn't going to put up a fight. At this point, neither was I.

"Go get her," the man said calmly to the others.

Run, Meriel, I thought. *Climb out the window and follow Foxtail.*

But Meriel would never leave us behind. Two more knives sailed from the door as the brutes stepped forward, then ducked back again. One of them cursed and pressed a hand against his shoulder, blood staining his shirt.

The head brute just looked sort of bored. One of his ears was half-gone, scarred over from an injury long ago. He tugged casually at what was left of the lobe. "Come on out, girl," he said.

"Why don't you come on in instead?" she called back.

He chuckled. "A pretty offer. But I like my blood on the inside. Your friends, though . . ."

"Leave them alone!" she shouted.

"Come out, then. Hands empty. Pockets, too."

"It's all right, Meriel," I said, still pinned to the rug. "He won't kill us."

The head thug regarded me with interest. He nodded, as if to confirm what I said was true. And I did believe it. If they'd really wanted to kill us—at least, kill us *here*—then Gareth, Lachlan, and I would already be gutted on the floor. They were, however, clearly more than willing to hurt us along the way. I hoped Meriel would understand that and surrender.

There was no answer from her room for long enough to make me nervous. When she finally stepped out, hands up and empty, I was relieved.

The man with the scarred ear nodded his men forward. "Pat her down."

She stood silently, mouth clamped shut, as they searched her for knives—and not gently. She glared at the man in command, but she didn't fight back as the brutes shoved her around. Her dress had already been torn at the collar before she left her room, but it got ripped in a few more places as they kept discovering more blades and dumping them on the overturned table. Their final tally was eight.

Their leader looked amused at the size of the pile. "The rest now," he said to her.

She gave him an innocent look.

"Give 'em over," he said reasonably. "Or I'll strip you down and carry you off full starkers."

She glowered at him. But silently, she removed two more

knives from hidden folds. He seemed to accept that that was all of them, because he stepped off Gareth's neck, letting one of his mates haul the boy up.

"Where are you taking us?" I asked as my own brute dragged me to my feet.

"Boss wants to see you," the leader said. "Hush-hush till then, lad. Or I'll cut out your tongue."

He stood aside as his men marched us out.

CHAPTER 18

NO ONE WATCHED us leave.

Whether the hotel's other guests had seen these thugs coming, or whether they'd heard the fight after it started, every door remained shut as the toughs prodded us down the stairs and out the back. The leader walked ahead, whistling, as our captors led us through the alleys to what I recognized from our map as the nearest pumping station.

It was near deafening inside. A narrow walkway, a suspended metal grate surrounded by thick steel pipes, led from the door to the back, where a piston-driven pump and a boiler bled off steam with an ear-piercing whistle. The thugs seemed used to it; they just pushed us around the pump to a ladder going down.

Foxtail had told us the sewers were big, but I hadn't really understood how big she'd meant. We found ourselves in a tunnel twenty feet wide, a broad channel of water flowing between two side walkways of stone. A sign riveted into the wall marked this ladder as leading to Pumping Station J-C-16A. The smell was foul, though not nearly as bad as I'd thought it would be. The water pumped in from the rivers that divided Sligach kept the waste from stagnating. I'd certainly been in worse.

Another member of the gang was waiting for us down there. He was carrying a bunch of hoods, which he placed over our heads. I thought Meriel might refuse, start another fight. Instead, she just stared into the distance, jaw clamped shut, before he covered her up.

Blinded, we were pushed forward, guided so we didn't fall into the water. I had no idea how far they walked us. It felt like at least a few miles, but they kept making us turn at the junctions, so I ended up totally lost. If Foxtail was with us, she could probably have figured it out, but I was glad she wasn't. At least one of us had escaped.

Eventually, they made us climb a ladder into another pumping station. Still wearing the hoods, we were led into what sounded like the back of a tavern, laughter and music echoing through the walls. And though I didn't like not seeing where I was going, in my head, the Old Man reminded me this was a good thing.

If they're keeping you blind, he said, *then they don't want you to see the route, have too much information. Which means they're still considering letting you out of this alive.* I clung to that thought as we were pushed through a corridor into a small room. There, they finally pulled off our hoods.

They'd brought us into a back office, definitely part of a tavern. With the sackcloth off our heads, I could smell the faint whiff of ale permeating the air. We'd been positioned in front of a desk, which was kept tidy. A ledger near the corner had THE FOX DEN imprinted in silver lettering on the leather. The tavern's name, I guessed.

Meriel, Gareth, Lachlan, and I weren't the only ones in the room. The eight toughs who'd kidnapped us stood behind us. Another dozen or so people were piled around the office, watching. Some looked the same as the toughs, but not all of them. There was a white-haired man with spectacles and a young, haggard-looking girl. She was smaller than Lachlan, though I got the sense she was a year or two older than him. Her chin was dotted with pimples, angry red, and one of her cheeks bore the scars of an old pox.

Still, it was clear who the true leader of this group was. He sat behind the desk, leaning back in his chair. He was thin and decently tall, with friendly-looking eyes and carefully coiffed hair. His clothing was impeccable: a high, crisp collar and fashionable vest of embroidered jade. Most of the gang surrounding him had tried to copy his style, with varying levels of success.

But what really caught my eye was that he was a gaffer.

I saw it instantly in the way he sized us up. His gaze moved over each of us with the practiced eye of a man who knew how to read someone. Their clothes, their gait, their comportment, and all the little subtle things the Old Man had taught me to watch for.

I was sure he could see what I would. How Meriel's stance— one foot slightly forward, the other angled outward—left her ready to spring to the attack. He glanced at Lachlan, saw the boy's casual air, and dismissed him immediately as no threat. Gareth, too, was dismissed, though when the gaffer saw him, he frowned. Gareth, frightened, kept his head bowed, not willing to look any of them in the eye, so the man couldn't get a good look at his face. But he'd seen something there. Something he recognized? Curious.

Eventually, the man focused on me. I met his gaze pleasantly, as if this was nothing more than two strangers meeting in the street. When I did that, he tilted his head back with a half smile. Like me, he'd recognized one of his own kind.

A boy and a girl of around sixteen squeezed into the office after us. The girl carried a pair of satchels—mine, which was empty except for our maps; and Gareth's, filled with his books— plus the few coins, wallets, and trinkets they'd pulled from our pockets before they'd marched us here. The boy had the bundle of thieves' tools we'd bought at the Lemon Tree.

The boy also carried Galawan, which he held with some care. When he and the girl placed our things on the desk in front of the man, the little sparrow flapped into Lachlan's hands, tweeting with worry. The gaffer watched with amusement as Lachlan clutched the bird protectively to his chest. Then the man spoke, his voice smooth and friendly.

"Is this all of them, Byrne?" he said. "I thought there were five."

Byrne, the lead thug with the scarred ear, shrugged. "Only four in the room when we picked them up, boss."

The gaffer stood and began sifting through our things. He paused on a few of them, studying them curiously—Meriel's collection of throwing knives; the journal of High Weaver Veran IX we'd found under Lake Galway—before opening the pouch of enchanted orbs Gareth had taken from the vault.

He pulled one out. It shone faintly in his palm. "A light globe?"

I knew Gareth wasn't going to answer, so I did. "Sort of," I said. "It detects enchantments."

"Really?"

I nodded my head toward Galawan. "Look at the bird."

In the dim light the orb cast, Galawan blazed bright white, the Weaver runes glowing on his metal feathers. His shine disappeared when the gaffer closed his fingers and covered the orb.

"Interesting." The man tucked it back with the others and dropped the pouch on the table. "So. Welcome to Sligach. Why are you here?"

"We're on a job," I said.

"Do you know who I am?"

There was only one person he could be: the head of the Sligach chapter of Breakers. "You're Mr. Fox."

He nodded and smiled. "Sheridan's the name. Voral Sheridan. And if you know I'm Mr. Fox, then you also know you should have come to see me."

"It's not that kind of job."

"Are you getting paid?"

We weren't. But since I'd have to explain why not, and there was no way I was going to tell him about the Eye, I gave him the easy lie. "Of course."

"Then," Sheridan said, "it *is* that kind of job."

In other words, anytime money changed hands in Sligach, Sheridan expected to dip his beak. "Fair enough," I said. "But we're not here to snaffle anything."

Sheridan raised an eyebrow. "This"—he waved his hand at our thieves' tools—"says otherwise."

"Like I told your man Collins at the Lemon Tree, it never hurts to be prepared. Honestly, we were just hired to find someone."

"Who's that?"

There was no point in lying, since he already knew the answer to that question. It was why he'd brought us here, and why he'd done it in this way. "We're looking for the Hollow Man," I said.

The haggard-looking girl to our left stiffened at the name. Interesting. That meant Sheridan knew why we were here, but he hadn't told his crew. And the name meant something to this girl in particular.

"The Hollow Man," Sheridan repeated, as if the name was a surprise. "I see. And what will you do once you find him?"

I shrugged. "At the moment, that's the extent of our orders. Once we know where he is, we're supposed to ask our client what's next."

"Who's your client?"

"A man in Carlow."

Sheridan regarded me carefully. Then he nodded toward Lachlan. "I wonder," he said to me, "how your story will change when I start pulling off that boy's fingers."

"Wait—" I began.

But I didn't speak fast enough, even as I knew what was coming.

CHAPTER 19

SO FAR, MERIEL had been quiet. Too quiet. It was so out of character for her that I knew she was just laying low. That she'd somehow kept a knife or something hidden up her sleeve, waiting for the right time to use it—and the threat to Lachlan was it. She'd never stand around and watch him get tortured to death.

Meriel suddenly spat out a piece of metal I'd never seen before. It was a small disk, an inch in diameter, razor-edged all around, with a weighted center, designed for throwing. She caught it in the air, gripped the edge, and reared back, ready to hurl it at Sheridan.

All around the room, metal slid on leather as the Breakers drew their pistols and aimed them at her. Gareth cowered, hands covering his head. Lachlan cringed, body arched to protect Galawan as much as himself. I just stayed absolutely still.

Sheridan turned his gaze to her with that same pleasant half smile. Meriel smiled back, lips flecked with blood. The disk she'd concealed in her mouth all the way from our hotel had cut her.

"So," she said. "How do things change now?"

His smile remained, but when he spoke, a tinge of contempt edged his voice. I could read it in his expression, too. It was less her violence that failed to impress him than the fact that it wouldn't get her what she wanted. He thought she was a fool.

"Never seen that trick before," Sheridan said. "Surely you know it's suicide."

Meriel remained perfectly still, arm cocked back. "Yes. But in the time it takes for your men to gun me down, I'll throw this disk into your eyes. So while I'll die, you won't be around to see it."

Sheridan regarded her for a moment. Then he said, "It appears we are at an impasse. At least tell me: Which of my lieutenants sent you to kill me?"

I kept my own hands where everyone could see they were empty. "We're not here to kill you," I said. "We're not here to make trouble at all. We just need to find the Hollow Man and report back. That's it."

Sheridan was a gaffer. He had to be good at spotting truth from lies. And by the change in his expression, I think he was starting to believe me. "You really *don't* know what you're doing, do you?" he said, surprised. He waved his men off. "Everyone out."

Byrne had his pistol pointed at Meriel's back. "You sure, boss?"

Sheridan nodded, unconcerned. "There's no danger here." He looked squarely at me. "Is there?"

"None at all," I said. I looked at Meriel, holding my hand out. *Trust me.*

She hesitated, but she placed the disk in my palm. I could feel how sharp it was just from its touch against my skin.

With Meriel disarmed, the Breakers lowered their pistols. "Well?" Byrne barked. "You heard Mr. Fox. Get your sorry backsides gone."

The thieves piled out of the office. The haggard-looking girl gave us a brief, intense glance before scurrying away with the others. Byrne was the last to leave; he shut the door behind him.

I held the disk out to Sheridan. He laughed. "No, thanks. I know where that's been."

He turned his back on us and began rooting in the cupboard behind him. I recognized the action for the power play it was. *I'm not afraid of you at all*, it said. Fine by me. I wasn't here to challenge his Breaker empire.

He pulled a bottle of wine and a pair of glasses from the cupboard. He poured one for himself and the other just for me. Another gaffer's gesture. *I know you're the one in charge.*

I accepted it and took a drink. It was unbelievably good; smooth, without a hint of the typical sourness. Sheridan saw my expression and nodded. "Comes from Garman," he said. "They make the best wine in Ayreth. Only Torgal makes better, and, well, who wants to trade with them?"

I was careful not to look at Meriel. She was from Torgal, and I had no idea how she'd take the insult to her homeland. But she stayed silent as Sheridan held his glass up to the light, admiring the ruby liquid.

"They say it's the volcanic ash that makes the soil so good for Garman's grapes." He laughed again. "So I suppose we'll be getting some amazing wine for the next few years."

He lowered himself to his seat. Another power play. *I sit, you stand.*

"So," he said, "you've been sent to Sligach to find the Hollow Man. But your client didn't tell you anything about him."

"That's right," I said.

"That doesn't strike you as odd?"

"I make it a habit not to ask questions that are none of my business."

"Normally, I'd say that's sensible. But one also needs to know when the questions *are* one's business." He poured himself more wine. "After you found the Hollow Man, how were you supposed to contact your client? It's three weeks to Carlow by stagecoach; surely you're not going all the way back. Or are you planning on an airship?"

"Neither." I motioned to Galawan, still cupped protectively in Lachlan's hands. "The bird's enchanted to deliver messages; he'll carry it."

Sheridan leaned forward, suddenly intent. "So your client's a Weaver?"

A solid deduction. Only a Weaver could make something as fine as Galawan. Of course, the truth was much stranger—but I decided to run with it, pretending like he'd caught me out. "I . . . yes. The plan was to do whatever Mr. . . . our client wanted, then head on to Westport."

Sheridan frowned. "Westport? Why go all the way to—" Suddenly, he pointed at Gareth. "That's where you're from!"

Gareth had tried to make himself small enough not to be noticed during this whole encounter. I'd taken it for his usual nervousness around strangers. But from Sheridan's reaction— and the flush in Gareth's face—it was much more than that.

"You know each other?" I said, startled.

"It's you, isn't it?" Sheridan said, laughing. "The Freak."

Gareth cringed at the cruel nickname the Westport Breakers had given him. I didn't get the chance to defend him; Lachlan was already there. "Don't call Gar that," he said, angry. "He's cleverer'n you."

I put a hand on Lachlan's shoulder—and Meriel's arm. She hadn't much cared to hear Gareth insulted, either. "No one calls him that anymore," I said.

Sheridan seemed amused by Lachlan's outburst. He put his hands up in surrender. "No offense meant. Gareth, wasn't it?"

Gareth nodded.

"How *do* you know each other?" I said.

"We worked together briefly a few years back," Sheridan said. "A museum job."

Suddenly, I knew what he was talking about. Gareth had mentioned him when he told the story of his vanished librarian. The Westport Breakers had brought in a gaffer from another chapter. "That was you?" I said. "I thought you came from Slipsey."

Sheridan looked surprised but also pleased. "He told you about me? Why, Gareth, I'm touched." He turned back to me. "I was working out of Slipsey at the time. My predecessor, the previous Mr. Fox, had had me transferred there. He had the strangest notion I was after his job." He smirked. "As it turns out, he was right. But really, Gareth, I thought you were smarter than this. Coming for the Hollow Man, without even knowing who he is. It's madness."

"I don't understand the problem," I said.

"That *is* the problem. You're a child playing a man's game. All of you are."

"So tell us. Who is the Hollow Man? Is he a Breaker? A friend of yours?"

"No friend of mine, I assure you." Sheridan leaned back in his chair, thinking. Whatever he was weighing in his mind, it landed on telling me the truth.

"I don't know who the Hollow Man is," he said finally. "I'm not sure anyone in Sligach does. But I know where he is. It would be hard not to; he's lived in the same place for nearly a century."

"A *century*?" I said. "How old is he?"

"No idea. Word is, though, that he was already older than that when he came here."

Impossible. Unless . . . could the Hollow Man's life have been extended by magic? Even then, two hundred years old—or more—it sounded almost too mad to believe.

Meriel certainly wasn't buying it. "So where is he?"

Sheridan gave her a thinly veiled look of contempt. Her stunt really hadn't impressed him. "Telling you won't do any good."

"Why not?" I said.

"Because you'll never get in to see him. He's in his own private suite at the Rose Garden."

I stared at him.

What Sheridan had just said was a joke—a thieves' joke. "Private suite" meant a prison cell. And the Rose Garden—that was slang for the prison of Castle Cardogh. Where the emperor himself sent traitors to wither and die, their names erased from history.

If Sheridan was telling the truth, then we really would never see the Hollow Man. Because he was being held in the most secure, most brutal prison in all of Ayreth. And he'd been locked up there for nearly a hundred years.

CHAPTER 20

A TWO-HUNDRED-YEAR-OLD MAN, the Old Man said curiously, *in the emperor's own prison. Quite a task the Eye has set you.*

Task. What a laugh. Even if all this was true, how could we possibly do what the Eye wanted? Though it occurred to me the Eye had never actually told us what it needed from the Hollow Man. It had just said we should find him. Which we had. Sort of.

I needed to probe at Sheridan to learn what I could. I knew it would cost me more of his respect, but he already didn't think much of us regardless. "Is there any way you could get us in to see him?"

"You have a strange sense of humor," he said.

I threw my hands up, as if embarrassed I was even asking. "The job's the job. There's a lot in it for you if you help us."

Sheridan studied me. If he was a good enough gaffer that he'd risen to the top of the Sligach Breakers—even after being exiled by his predecessor—then he'd be an expert at hiding his true feelings. In this case, he didn't. He wanted me to know he was disappointed in me. That I'd fallen in his estimation, just like Meriel.

"A child playing a man's game," he said again. "Very well. To answer your previous question: Yes. I could get you in to see him. To answer your next question: No. I won't help you."

"Why not?"

He leaned back in his chair, arms behind his head. "Have you had the chance to see Sligach since you arrived?"

"We didn't come to go sightseeing."

"But you've seen enough, yes? To know this city is different from the others."

"Sure," I said. "The rails, the contraptions, they're banned in other provinces."

"Doesn't that prompt a question in your mind?" Sheridan said. "If the emperor doesn't like trains and steam whistles, why not ban them outright? Why not ban them even here?"

"Gareth said there's a power struggle. Between the corporations and the Weavers."

"Gareth is correct. There's trouble brewing between the emperor, the Weavers, and us. But we mine the gold that fills the emperor's coffers, and we mine the iron that gets forged into his gun barrels. So this is a fight the emperor does not want. Because even with the Weavers on his side, there's a chance that he will *lose*. And no emperor worth his salt will risk a third civil war that would tear Ayreth apart for good."

And even if the emperor did win, the Old Man said, *it would only give the Weavers more power. He'd be beholden to them more than any ruler in history.*

I repeated what the Old Man said in my head to Sheridan. He nodded, as if I'd finally started speaking sense.

"So you do see," Sheridan said. "For the moment, the emperor pretends to look elsewhere. And that's just how I want it. Because if he were to turn his gaze back this way—which he certainly will, if you go snooping after the Hollow Man—that would be bad for business. What's bad for business is bad for Sligach. And what's bad for Sligach"—Sheridan spread his hands—"is bad for me."

"I understand," I said, trying to sound desperate. "But we have a debt. Doing this job is the only chance we have to repay it. I promise, we won't cause any trouble—"

"You are *still* not listening."

I went silent. An edge had crept into his voice.

"Your debt is not my problem," he said. "Your *problem* is not my problem. Things are carefully balanced here. And that is how they will remain."

Sheridan recorked his wine bottle, then sat there, as if thinking. Finally, he said, "This is what I'll do for you. Just for old times' sake, for my young friend Gareth. You've seen the city—at least enough of it to know it practically bleeds gold. There are plenty of opportunities here for a band of thieves.

"So: if you want to stay in Sligach, pull a couple jobs, you have my permission. I won't waive my cut; it's a third, same as always. But otherwise, you can play any gaff you wish, except one. Don't. Poke. The emperor. Stay away from Castle Cardogh. Do you understand?"

I nodded.

"Good." His smile returned. "Because if I find you nosing around there, I'll ask Mr. Byrne to visit you once more. And this time, he'll send your corpses floating down the river."

CHAPTER 21

THEY LET US leave through the front door of the tavern. Sheridan even allowed us to take back our things. That was a good sign; it meant he really wasn't going to kill us. At least not today.

Meriel pocketed her knives before leaving. She handled the weighted disk gingerly, careful not to cut herself on its edge. "Never seen that one before," Lachlan said curiously. "Where you been keeping it?"

"My collar," she said, and she touched her dress where she'd torn the seam. "Ardal—uh, my old . . ." She cut herself off, then changed what she was going to say. "You keep it near the collar because it's small enough to be hidden there, and it's a place no one ever searches. It means you always have a weapon, even if you're captured."

"Don't it hurt, though? Keeping it in your mouth like that?"

She sighed. "Yes."

Her lips were still red with blood. I offered her my handkerchief. She took it with a quiet nod of thanks, dabbing her mouth.

At least we'd made it out alive. Though I had no idea where we were. I'd lost all sense of direction in the sewers.

"I know the way home, guv," Lachlan said. "I been here before."

"You have?" I said.

"Sure." He led us through the streets. "This's one of the first places I checked for the Breakers. I mean, Fox Den, eh? Come on." He seemed annoyed that they hadn't revealed themselves to him at the tavern. "They ain't too friendly here, is they?"

No, they weren't. And now I knew why. Sheridan had all but told us that he'd done away with the previous Mr. Fox and taken control of the guild in Sligach. He'd even asked us which of his lieutenants sent us to kill him. Clearly, he was still consolidating his power. That meant he'd keep things close to his vest. In the end, he'd dismissed us instead of killing us, at least in part because he thought we were too bad at our jobs to be any threat. We certainly hadn't made a good impression, stumbling about looking for the Hollow Man without even knowing where he was.

"What do we do now?" Meriel said.

"I don't know," I said. "Let's just head back to the hotel."

What really bothered me was that Sheridan hadn't been wrong. We *had* looked like fools, bumbling about. What's more, how were we supposed to get to the Hollow Man now? And who was he? The fact that he was supposedly two hundred years old was only half the story. If Sheridan was right, the emperor—five emperors back, actually—had sent the Hollow Man to the Rose Garden a century ago. What crime had the man committed to be locked away for a *hundred years*?

Gareth might have some thoughts, but he hadn't said a word since we'd left the Fox Den. He looked ashamed, as if he'd somehow let us down.

"So that was unexpected," I said to him.

He wouldn't even meet my eyes. "I'm s-sorry . . . I mean . . . I should have . . . I d-didn't know Sheridan had become Mr. F-Fox."

I didn't blame him. There was no reason he would have. Gareth had been a Breaker in Westport, a thousand miles away. But he had worked with Sheridan before. "What was he like?" I asked. "When you did the museum job."

"Friendly," Gareth said. "I mean . . . he seemed to be. He was always nice to me, even when the other Breakers w-weren't. But you could tell. I mean . . . that deep down, he didn't care about you. That you were just a tool to him. That he'd do whatever he could to get ahead."

Gareth struggled so much around people that I sometimes forgot how perceptive he could be. He'd certainly pegged Sheridan right. Superficial charm, soulless underneath. Like just about every gaffer out there.

It's good that our Mr. Fox is a gaffer, the Old Man said. *You can exploit that.*

How? I said. *He's going to be watching everything I do.*

Of course. But he doesn't think much of you, does he? That's your way in, boy.

The Old Man sounded awfully sure of himself, and he was usually right. This time, I didn't see how. Even now, Sheridan had sent people to follow us. As we headed home, I spotted a pair of men trailing us some thirty yards back. They acted like they were just strolling, browsing the shops through the windows. But I'd seen them in the common room of the Fox Den when we left, and they were matching every turn we made.

As it happened, they weren't the only ones following us. As we passed an alleyway, Foxtail suddenly appeared. She stepped from between the buildings, striding next to me as if she'd been with us all along, slipping her hand into mine as we walked.

"Welcome back," I said.

She put a hand to her chest, then held it out. *I'm sorry.* What she really meant was *I'm sorry I abandoned you when the Breakers came. I should have heard them earlier. I'd have warned you if we had the time.*

I shook my head. "You did exactly the right thing. We can't risk losing the Dragon's Teeth." I wondered what Sheridan would have done if he'd seen them. Would he have recognized them for what they were?

Speaking of which . . . "Where are our enchantments now?"

She made a subtle digging motion. *I buried them. They won't be found.*

That was good. In fact, it was probably best to leave them in the ground for now. We'd retrieve them when there wasn't so much heat on us anymore.

Still holding my hand with her left, Foxtail walked the fingers of her right up my forearm, then dragged her fingernails across it. I think I understood what she was trying to tell me. *You're being followed.*

"I know," I said. "The two men standing in front of that bakery."

She shook her head and held up three fingers. *There's another.*

"Where?"

Keeping her hand concealed by her body, she jerked her

thumb backward, then put her palm low, then grabbed her skirt and shook it. *A young girl, farther back.* She wobbled her hand again. *I'm not sure the men know she's there.*

A second, secret tail? Did Sheridan not trust the other men he'd sent?

I wasn't sure what to make of that. I walked on, lost in thought.

Our rooms were a disaster.

Everything had been tossed. Our valises had been dumped, our clothes all over the floor. Sheridan's thieves had tipped over our mattresses, flipped the cushions on the sofa, and even taken down the paintings, in case we'd hidden something behind them. It was as thorough a job as they could have done without actually shredding the furniture.

At least Sheridan hadn't robbed us. Mostly. Our things were here, but Lachlan noticed, with a string of curses, that our wallets had ended up about a thousand crowns light. "Artha's paws. Where's the professional courtesy, eh? Can't trust no one these days."

He was right about that. "I suppose we shouldn't wait for housekeeping." I was just bending over to pick up a cushion when Foxtail put a hand on my arm. *Wait.*

Head cocked, she listened. Then she pointed to the hall. *Someone's coming.*

Meriel pulled her knives, pressing her back to the wall beside the door. Foxtail took the other side, still listening. She opened and closed her hand at Lachlan, Gareth, and me. *Keep talking.*

"So is anybody hurt?" I said.

"Only my faith," Lachlan said, still miffed. "Shuna's sneezing snout, a thousand crowns. Coulda bought..." He tried to do the arithmetic on his fingers. "Ten thousand syrup fizzes with that. No, a hundred... no, wait. Um..."

Foxtail motioned to Meriel. She held three fingers up, then silently counted them down. *Three... two... one.*

Then Foxtail yanked open the door.

CHAPTER 22

M ERIEL POUNCED.

She jumped on the figure eavesdropping outside our room—a young girl—and dragged her in. The girl squealed in alarm as Meriel pivoted, bending the girl's body over her hip, flipping her to land hard on the rug.

Meriel jammed a knee into the girl's spine, then yanked her head backward by her hair, a blade to her throat.

"Wait," I said. I recognized her. This was the haggard-looking girl who'd been with the Breakers in the back office of the Fox Den.

She looked terrified. Her eyes were wide, her hands trembling on the rug. "Don't!" she said.

"We're not going to hurt you," I said, calming. "Meriel's going to let you up now. But no tricks, all right?"

The girl nodded. Truth be told, I'd said that more to cool Meriel off than anything. Sheridan wouldn't have let us leave the Fox Den just to attack us at our hotel. He certainly wouldn't have sent this girl to do it.

Meriel hauled her up roughly. "Why were you following us?" she demanded.

"Did Mr. Fox send you?" I said.

"No." The girl was still trembling. "He don't know I'm here."

If she was telling the truth—and my instincts said that she was—then we didn't want him to find out. "Foxtail, keep watch. Make sure no one else is listening in on our room."

Foxtail nodded and headed into the hall, closing the door behind her as I looked the girl over. She was a scraggly thing, small even for her age, which was probably eleven or twelve, and rail thin, almost underfed. I'd noticed back in the Fox Den that her clothes weren't particularly well kept, despite the fact that the boss liked to dress nicely—and to get ahead in the Breakers, most thieves would imitate the boss. *Something of an outcast, then,* I thought.

Interesting, the Old Man said. *And potentially useful.*

Meriel let her go. "What's your name?" I said.

"Diana," she said, still trembling.

"I'm Callan. Come sit."

I motioned for Lachlan to get us some water. The pipes in the lavatory burbled as he filled a glass and handed it to her. "Here you go, luv."

She took it but didn't drink, just cupped the glass in her hands.

"Is there something we can do for you?" I said.

"You really going to peep the Hollow Man?" she blurted.

I glanced over at Gareth. "Mr. Fox told us we couldn't."

"But if you could. Would you?"

Meriel shook her head, warning me off. This girl may not have come to attack us, but she could have been sent as a trap, to try to weasel out our intentions. I didn't think so, but it usually paid to be cautious.

"Even if we would," I said carefully, "what's it to you?"

"I can get you in."

Meriel scoffed. "The emperor's own prison? Sure you can."

"I can," the girl said indignantly. "Anytime I want. Mr. Fox already has his hooks in. He just don't do nothing grand, 'cause he don't want to peeve the emperor, like."

"How do you mean?" I said.

"The Rose Garden's on Cardogh Island, in the middle of the river. The way in's by rail. There's a train that goes there every week."

"Why would a train go to the prison?" Meriel said. "Visitors aren't allowed there."

"Train ain't for visitors," Diana said. "It's for supplies and the like. Changin' of the guard. Ain't no other way for 'em to get there."

"What about a boat?" I said.

She shook her head. "Warden don't allow it. Ain't as controlled, like. He don't let nothing near. Guards on the wall shoot you up good if you try. It's the rails or nothing."

"So how does that help us?"

"Work crew goes in with the supplies. Stockers, cleaners, and whatnot. I can get you on it."

Meriel frowned. "How?"

"I told you, Mr. Fox got his hooks in. The foreman, Sullivan. He's our man."

"A Breaker?" I said.

"Yeah. Use him for smuggling and the like. Guards stuck out there cold and lonely, yeah? Sneak 'em a bottle or two, some cake. They pays so much."

I doubted Sheridan kept an inside man on the work crew just to make a few crowns off smuggled cake. He had to have his own, more lucrative reasons for wanting the connection.

Even more likely he's keeping his options open, the Old Man said. *In case he ever ends up there. Might offer him a way out.*

That was more a gaffer's style: work any angle to sweeten your odds. Either way, this sounded like a real possibility. A work crew would have serious access.

Still . . . "Why would Sullivan let us on? No way Sheridan agrees to that."

"Sully don't talk to Mr. Fox," Diana said. "Not direct, anyway. Sends runners like me to do the words. I tell him lies, you get on."

Lachlan, who'd been a runner himself with the Carlow Breakers, nodded. "Snoops in risky places don't talk face-to-face with the big boss," he confirmed. "Keeps 'em insulated, like."

Well, then. This was a real possibility. "Say we're interested," I said. "What do you want out of the deal?"

She bit her lip. "You ever heard of Oran? Oran of Sligach?"

We looked at each other in surprise. "Sure. He stole the emperor's scepter. Why?"

"He disappeared after, right? Ain't no one know where he got to."

That wasn't true. *We* knew. Mr. Solomon had offered for Oran to join us on the job to steal the Eye. He'd refused, saying it was too dangerous. He'd been right. But in crossing Mr. Solomon, Oran had ended up dead, killed by the Weaver's elemental, the Lady in Red.

I had a hard time deciding what to tell Diana. When she'd

mentioned Oran, there'd been more than pride in her voice. There'd been familiarity. She'd known him, and liked him. Maybe it wasn't a kindness to tell her the truth, but in the end, she had the right to know.

"Diana . . . Oran died," I said. "He was murdered by a Weaver in Carlow."

Diana's face fell. "Oh. I didn't . . . oh."

I wondered if Sheridan knew. He must have; Oran's death had been in the Carlow papers. To a gaffer, there's nothing more valuable than information. There was no way news that big would get past his network.

But he didn't tell his underlings, the Old Man said. *Keeps what he knows close to his vest, our Mr. Fox.*

I knew what the Old Man was getting at. If Sheridan had a habit of keeping his people in the dark, this could be good for us. It meant his Breakers wouldn't necessarily know what any of the others were doing.

"Why did you ask about Oran?" I said.

"My brother Cormac. He was on Oran's crew," she said. "When they stole the scepter, like. But when Oran got away, the rest of 'em . . ."

"They got caught."

Diana nodded. "Emperor's guard rookered 'em all. Tortured 'em to get his scepter back. But they wouldn't turn nose, not one of 'em," she said proudly.

Probably couldn't even if they wanted to, I thought. When Oran disappeared with the scepter, none of the others would have known where to find him. Still, no point in spoiling her pride.

"The others died," Diana continued. "'Cept for Cormac. But his crime was against the emperor straight-like. So he put him—"

Meriel finished, surprised. "In the Rose Garden."

"So you want to help us get in there," I said, "to pass him a message?"

"No," Diana said. "I want you to break him out."

I scoffed. "Come on."

"You don't know what it's like inside," she said desperately. "You ain't heard the stories. Ain't no one to talk to. Ain't nowhere to go. Ain't never let out. You got to help him."

"You have a way in. Why haven't you?"

She looked down, ashamed. "I can't. I don't have . . . Ain't no one going to go with me. Ain't no one going to cross Mr. Fox."

What she knew, but couldn't bring herself to say out loud, was that she wasn't respected enough by the other Breakers to have anyone on her side. More than that, she didn't have the courage to try. But courage wasn't really the problem. Even the thought of breaking someone out of Cardogh was ridiculous.

So I was shocked beyond belief that Meriel even considered it. "How could we get him out?" she said.

I stared at her, stunned. She ignored me as Diana spoke, hopeful. "Like I said, I can get you on the work crew. You go in, pull him out."

"That's not a plan," I said, irritated now. "What's the layout of the prison? How many guards? Which cell is Cormac in? Where are the keys?"

"I don't know none of that."

"You've never gone in with the crew? Not to break your brother out, just to see him?"

"I can't," she said, wringing her hands. "I can rooker Sully once to get someone on the train that ain't supposed to be. But Sully's suspicious-like. When it's done, he'll check that things is righteous."

"Wait—you mean we can only go in *once*?"

"'Less you want Mr. Fox to know you done it."

This was even more ridiculous than I thought. And yet, bizarrely, Meriel turned to me and said, "We can at least look into it. Right?"

"No," I said. "Shuna's teeth, *no*. We can't break someone out of prison without scouting it first and knowing exactly what we're going to face. You're talking suicide."

"Don't we have to go in anyway?"

I was so confused by her pressing me on this that it took me a second to understand what she meant. She nodded toward my patch.

Right. The Eye. "Wait here," I said, fuming.

I went into my room and shut the door. Alone, I pulled off the patch.

I don't know if the Eye could sense my temper, but it spoke first. do you need something, foxchild? it said, sounding amused.

"Have you been toying with me this whole time?" I said.

what do you mean?

"What do you want with the Hollow Man?"

have you found him? The Eye sounded excited. where is he?

"So you really don't know where he is."

I have told you I do not.

"Then answer my question. What do you want with the Hollow Man?"

I have told you I require him. that is enough for now.

"No, it isn't. *What* do you require? Do you need to speak to him? Do we need some information from him? Or do we need to take him somewhere?"

The Eye didn't answer right away. It could clearly hear my anger—which gave me the sense that it was trying to decide how much to let me know.

he must accompany you, it said finally.

"So we do need him with us."

that is what "accompany" means, foxchild. why do you waste my time with these questions?

"Because the Hollow Man is in prison."

and?

"It's the most secure prison in the *whole world*."

Suddenly, my head was filled with derision. The Eye was laughing at me.

no, foxchild, it said. I was in the most secure prison on your world. I was bound inside it for countless ages, held there by the treachery of the fox. do you think I should be impressed by your pathetic walls of stone and steel?

"But—"

if you freed me, the Eye said, then freeing one of your own should be trivial. bother me no more with such petty troubles.

Conversation over.

Still fuming, I put the patch back. But angry or not, what difference did it make? If I wanted this thing out of my head, I didn't have a choice.

I went back into our common room, a bitter taste in my mouth. "Tell me everything I need to know."

CHAPTER 23

THERE WASN'T MUCH more Diana could give us. She did assure us that it wouldn't be any problem to get us on the work crew any week the train was running.

But since we could only go that way once, we'd have to do our own scouting. And I didn't want Diana knowing anything about that. When she left, Lachlan went to collect Foxtail, who'd apparently been spying on the street.

The two men who followed you are waiting outside the hotel, she gestured.

"Sure there aren't any more watching?"

She put her hands on her hips and tapped her foot impatiently.

I threw my hands up. "Fine." I might have been on the edge of losing my temper, but nobody was better at spotting tails than her. And Sheridan only sending two men to spy fit with the terrible impression we'd made. In his mind, we weren't much to worry about; he knew he could control us. Given how things had gone so far, I wasn't so sure he was wrong.

"Diana said the weekly train is the only way into the prison," I said. "Let's see if that's actually true. Gareth, would there be records of the rail routes? Official documents or something?"

He nodded. "They'll be at the city offices."

"Go look at those, then. Foxtail, you check out this Cardogh Island. Get Gareth to show you on the map."

Foxtail nodded, then pointed out the window, holding two fingers up. *What about the men outside?*

Another thing we had to worry about. The Breakers were certain to trail us whenever we left the hotel. If they saw Foxtail going anywhere near Castle Cardogh, Sheridan would hear of it.

We'd have to play this safe. "Lachlan, go with Gareth. Make yourselves obvious; look like you're up to no good. You need to draw off the spies so Foxtail won't be followed."

Lachlan gave me a thumbs-up. "Too easy, guv. Can we get lunch on the way, Gar? Nothing like getting roughed up to make you peckish."

Gareth gave him a bemused look as they left. Foxtail waited a few minutes until they drew off the tails, then climbed out the window.

"So what do we do?" Meriel said once she was gone.

"You tell me," I said.

"What does that mean?"

"You were awfully keen to side with Diana. Why are you so helpful all of a sudden?"

She pressed her hand to her chest in mock hurt. "Am I such a monster?"

She was trying to dismiss me by being cute. It made me angrier. "Have you been to Sligach before?" I said.

"I'd have told you if I had."

"And you never met Diana? Or her brother, or Oran, before Mr. Solomon?"

"You know I didn't. I've never been to Sligach, and I'd never been to Carlow before we rode on the *Malley*."

"So what gives?"

She chewed a fingernail, clearly struggling with something. Something she wanted to tell me—but also didn't want to tell me. "I just . . . It's her brother. Family's important, isn't it?"

"How would I know?"

She flushed at that. "I didn't mean . . ."

I put my hands up. "You know what? I don't care."

"Cal—"

"Forget it. I need to think, anyway. Someone has to, after all."

I threw on my jacket and left.

∩∪

I took a train—first class, expense be hanged.

I sat in my seat, fuming as the car rumbled on the rails. Meriel had touched a nerve. She hadn't meant to, and I knew that, but it still stung.

That's not why you're angry, the Old Man said.

Oh, good, I said sarcastically. *I was hoping you'd show up.*

The truth was, he was right—which only made me angrier. What I really was was *tired*. Tired of being manipulated. Tired of being a pawn in some grand game. Tired of this stupid artifact in my head, with its snide remarks and secrets.

But most of all, I was tired of being asked to do the impossible. Tired of putting my life on the line—and the lives of everyone I cared about. It was too much weight. Too much. So I'd had enough. Enough people. Enough gaffs. Enough everything.

You're being childish, the Old Man said.

"I don't care," I muttered, getting a few odd looks from the other passengers. "You left, remember? So leave me *alone*."

Temper, temper, he said, but he went silent after that.

Good. I wanted silence, and everywhere in Sligach was full of noise. I wanted clear air to breathe, and everywhere in Sligach was full of smog. Except for the Sun district, with its citrus fields and wooded groves. So I took the train there. I rode it to its terminal station, then walked into the green until I couldn't see anyone around. I snuck through someone's orchard and stole an orange. But just when I thought I was finally alone—

snap

I turned at the sound of a twig breaking. And I saw, marching through the trees, a fox.

I'd have known that fox anywhere. She had fluffy red fur and a soft white underbelly. Even if my finger with the seven-banded mark hadn't already begun to heat up, the twinkle in her eye would have given her away.

My jaw grew tighter as she approached. "You cannot be serious," I said.

"I can't?" Shuna looked puzzled. "I haven't even said anything yet."

"What do you want?"

"My goodness. That was rude, even for you." The Fox sat in front of me. "I ran into Foxtail by the river. She told me you're sad. I thought I'd stop by and cheer you up."

"I'm not sad. I'm angry." Though as I said it, I realized that was only half true. I was both.

"You have every right to be angry," Shuna said. "But you don't have to take it out on Meriel. It's not her fault. She has wounds of her own inside, just like you."

"How would you even know about— Was Foxtail snooping outside our window?"

"Of course," Shuna said. "Snooping is what she does. So don't go yelling at her, either. She cares about you. They all do."

"Like you do, I suppose? And that's why you keep playing me for a fool?"

"Exactly." She swished her tail. "So tell me: How can I help you right now?"

"You can take this stupid Eye out of my head!"

"I wish I could, Cal. I really do."

I sat on the grass and buried my face in my hands. "This is never going to end, is it?"

Shuna came over and sat next to me. "Sure it will. Everything you do brings the end closer."

"And what does that look like?" I said. "What happens to us? To me? I don't even know what the Eye wants. But you do, don't you?"

"Yes."

"And you're not going to tell me."

"Nope."

I laughed bitterly. "You're just using me. You're all just using me."

"I'm not *just* using you," Shuna said. "I genuinely am trying to help."

"Oh? Then tell me this, at least: Who's the Adversary? The Devourer?"

She looked at me curiously. "Huh. You really have learned some things."

"Who is it?" I demanded.

"I can't tell you that."

"Is it that trickster you mentioned back in the vault? Or is it Bran the Crow?"

Here she paused. But she said, "I can't answer that, either."

"Because of the Pact? I don't believe you."

She seemed surprised at that. "You know better than anyone that the Pact is real."

"Sure. I saw what you and your sisters did to Artha. But I also saw they knew you'd been talking to me when you weren't supposed to. And they didn't make *you* disappear."

"Because I didn't break the Pact. I may have bent it a little, but I never actually broke it."

"Except that's what you're hiding behind, isn't it?" I said. "No doubt there are some things you can't tell me. But I'd bet everything I've ever stolen that you could say more than you have. You're hiding behind the Pact so I won't realize which is which."

Her ears went out, amused. "You always were a clever one."

I glared at her. "If you weren't a Spirit, I'd kick you."

"You'd kick a harmless fox?"

Of course I wouldn't—and the fact that she knew I wouldn't

really got my goat. I loosed a stream of curses at her.

Her eyebrows shot up. "I see those sailors on Lake Galway taught you some new words."

I saw what she was doing. She was letting me vent at her instead of my friends, because no matter how many curses I flung her way, her feelings wouldn't be hurt. Deep down, there was a part of me that was grateful for it—even as I remained irked that she was manipulating me once more. "I knew you were lying to me."

"No, Cal. I've never lied to you. Not once."

"You've been gaffing me this whole time!" I shouted.

"But I *told* you I was. I told you that right from the start. There's something else you're missing, too."

"Oh, what a surprise. What's that?"

"Not everything is about you."

That made me pause. My mind churned, trying to understand what she was hinting at. I'd have asked, but I knew she wouldn't tell me. Though maybe I could get something else out of her instead.

"I've been visiting Shadow in my dreams," I said.

"Really?"

"You didn't know?"

"Why would I?"

"Because the first time I went, you took me there."

"Well, I'm not doing it now."

I stared down at my finger. It hadn't got as hot as the crystal ring had outside Carlow, but it was still uncomfortably warm this close to a Spirit. There was no question now that its magic—or at least part of it—had made its way into me. "So it *is* this mark that's sending me."

"I warned you about wearing that ring," Shuna chided. "What are you seeing when you go?"

"Different things. I rescued a fox."

Her tail thumped the ground. "See? That's why I like you."

"I also saw Meriel. When she was younger. I feel like someone's trying to show me her secrets. But I don't know why."

"Well, Shadow's a big place, and there are a lot of things in it—none of which I'm going to talk about, so don't ask. All I'll say is watch yourself. Shadow can be dangerous. If you get into trouble, I won't be around to help."

It did sound like she was genuinely concerned. Though, as she pointed out, that wouldn't save me if things went south. "I still don't think I should believe you."

"Why not?"

"Gaffers can't be trusted," I said. "And you might be a Spirit, but you're definitely a gaffer."

"So are you," she pointed out.

"So?"

"So should your friends trust you?"

"That's . . . I'm not trying to cheat them!"

"But you would have," she said. "If you'd met them a few years ago, you'd have seen them as nothing but marks. You would have worked them for what you could get, then left them with nothing. Even though it made you feel guilty. Even though you knew it was wrong. Right?"

I didn't know how to answer that. *Sure you do*, the Old Man said. *You just don't like what you'd say.*

Shuna looked at me seriously. "People can change, Cal. If they're good inside, then you have to believe in them. You have to give them the chance."

"You're saying I should trust you, then?"

Her nose twitched. "Of course."

She almost made me smile. "Every gaffer would say the same," I said dismissively.

She stood and shook out her fur. "Then I suppose it's up to you to tell the difference."

"Wait," I said. "Can't you . . . can't you just tell me something? I don't know what I'm supposed to do."

"You mean about the Hollow Man? You don't need my help for that."

"He's in *Castle Cardogh*."

"And you're the five thieves who robbed the Weaver Enclave. I keep telling you, Cal, it's not just other people you should believe in. Try aiming some of that back at yourself."

She trotted off into the trees.

CHAPTER 24

No one was at the hotel when I returned.

The place was still a disaster from this morning: tables over-turned, food everywhere. Meriel's room was empty. I'd sort of hoped she'd be here. Though I hadn't really got much informa-tion out of Shuna, I wasn't so angry anymore. For some reason, talking to the Fox always made me feel better.

The Old Man nodded. *That's an old gaffers' trick. She's quite clever, that one.*

I couldn't tell if he was trying to show me I'd been played or just saying I should learn how to do that myself. Regardless, now that I wasn't so cross, I felt bad about snapping at Meriel.

Push her a bit first before you apologize, boy, the Old Man suggested. *You saw; she has something she wants to tell you. Never pass up the chance to uncover a secret. You never know what you might learn.*

"I've had enough secrets to last a while," I said to the empty room.

Too bad, the Old Man answered. *Because I suspect you're about to learn many more.*

As usual, he was right.

I'd planned to clean up the place before the others returned. No, honest. But I was tired, and I just figured I'd lie down for a few minutes and rest. The next thing I knew

I was standing in a garden.

I blinked, confused. "How did I . . . ?"

I must have fallen asleep, I thought. Which meant—

I was in Shadow again?

I looked around. I certainly didn't remember coming here. I didn't even know where "here" was. But it was definitely a garden, around the back of what looked like a palace. Behind me was a high wall of smooth stone, the same sandy beige as the training arena where I'd seen eight-year-old Meriel. I couldn't see much else from where I stood. Tall, neatly trimmed hedges blocked my view. Intertwined with the hedges were vines blooming with bright multicolored flowers. They smelled sweet and rich, like ripe tropical fruit.

It was beautiful here. I'd have almost said paradise.

But someone was screaming.

Somewhere toward the center of the garden, a man was ranting. Cautiously, I pushed through the hedges to see.

On the other side were two figures. One was Meriel, older than the last time I'd seen her in Shadow, maybe eleven or so now. She was pleading with the ranting man. And there was no question of who he was.

This was her father. The resemblance was unmistakable: same raven-black hair, same cheekbones, same shape ears. Meriel's love for him, too, was unmistakable, the wounded desperation in her eyes.

"You have to take your medicine, Papa," she said, pleading. "Come inside."

The man stomped around the garden. The ground here was laid with a circle of patterned stone, a fountain in the center, water burbling from some underground spring. Around the stone circle were animal statues shaped from the same rock as the wall and pillars. He waved at the statues, ranting.

"No, no, no, no, *no*. Why does no one *see*? The bird fights. The beast fights. But the bird cannot fight the beast. The bird *cannot* fight the *beast*."

"Papa—"

"The bird doesn't kill the beast. The beast doesn't kill the bird! The bird kills the bird. The beast kills the beast!"

"Papa, please." Meriel's voice trembled. "Uncle Dathal is coming. If he sees you like this, he'll lock you away. He'll take everything. *Please*."

"Bird kills BIRD. Beast kills BEAST. Only like kills LIKE. Do you see?"

"Yes, I see," Meriel said, trying to mollify him. "But—"

"Do you *see*?"

I froze.

Meriel's father was staring at me.

"Can . . . can you see me?" I said, startled.

Young Meriel couldn't. "Papa, there's no one here except us."

But her father, wild-eyed, stormed around the fountain straight toward me. "*Do you see?*" he was practically screaming now. "DO YOU SEE?"

I stepped back, nearly stumbling into the bushes. And though I had no idea what he was talking about, like Meriel, I tried to calm him.

"Bird kills bird," I said, as if it were the most obvious thing in the world. "Beast kills beast. Only like kills like. Of course I see."

Meriel's father closed his eyes in relief. He slumped, half-bent over, hands on his knees, and laughed softly. "Yes," he said. "You *do* see. You do."

One of the doors to the palace swung open. An older woman hurried toward us, carrying a potion. Meriel put an arm around her father. "It's time for your medicine, Papa."

"What? Oh. Yes, darling." He ran gentle fingers through Meriel's hair and kissed the top of her head. "All's well now."

When she gave him the potion, he drank it without protest. "Take him to my rooms," she said to the woman. "Don't let *anyone* know he's there." The woman nodded, escorting Meriel's father out as quickly as the weary man would allow.

The moment Meriel was alone, she sobbed. But when she heard more people coming from the building beyond, she wiped her eyes with her palms and put on a careful appearance of casualness.

There were three who entered the garden. Two of them were clearly related, father and son, the boy around twelve or thirteen, a year or two older than this Shadow Meriel. While they were also clearly part of Meriel's family—they, too, had similar features—the man had a hardness to his character that seemed to show just from his stride: purposeful and commanding. The boy tried to match his father's presence, but he couldn't carry it off. The child's swagger was just an act—and not a very good one.

The other man with them I recognized. He was the master who'd been training Meriel in the arena. And now that I could see his face—sharp features, narrow eyes—I was sure I'd seen him somewhere else, too. I tried to remember where.

"Uncle Dathal," Meriel said. "How kind of you to visit me all the way from Prinn. And Ellmere, what a delight to see you, cousin. If I'd have known you were coming, I'd have arranged a puppy for you to kick."

The boy sneered at her. His father didn't rise to the bait. "Where's my brother, Meriel?"

"Didn't Ardal tell you?" She motioned to her training master. "My father isn't in Caerlagh. He's gone hunting in the Boneyard. He won't be back for days."

"You're a lying cow," Ellmere said.

Meriel's expression didn't change. But with one quick motion, almost dismissively, she pulled a throwing knife from her dress and flung it. The boy squealed, flinching too late as it sliced a thin red line across his cheek.

"Oops," Meriel said.

Ellmere pressed his hand to his face, lower lip trembling. "She cut me!" he whined.

Though the knife had passed between Dathal and his son, the man hadn't reacted at all. Now, however, as Ellmere looked to his father to defend him, Dathal's lip curled slightly. Contempt.

"Ready the horses," he said to the boy.

"But aren't you going to—"

"Is someone speaking?" Dathal said to the air.

Ellmere cringed in shame. He left—but not before sending a vicious look at Meriel. There was a promise in those eyes. *I'm going to enjoy killing you.*

Meriel mostly kept her pleasant expression. I doubt Ellmere noticed the difference. But the slight edge in her glance said, *I hope you try.*

When the boy was gone, Meriel shook her head at her uncle. "That's who you think should be the next Lord of All Names? The Orlagh would steal our lands the week he took the throne."

"It takes time to temper steel," Dathal said. "And I have a great deal of time yet." He didn't say what he really meant: *Until then, I will rule.*

Meriel smiled, a dismissal. "Wonderful to see you as always, Uncle."

"You can't hide your father forever, Meriel," Dathal said. Then he walked away.

The weapons master, Ardal, escorted Dathal out before returning. On his way back, I finally remembered where I'd seen him before: in the vision Shuna showed me of the future. Ardal was the man I'd seen executed in that village, the man whose body Meriel had wept over.

"That was unwise," Ardal said to her.

She spat on the stone. "I'm not afraid of Ellmere."

"It's not Ellmere you should be afraid of. And don't spit, it's graceless."

Meriel looked embarrassed at the rebuke. "At least I got them to leave."

"Because your uncle chose not to press the issue." Ardal shook his head. "You know I only pretend friendship with him. But he's right: your father won't live much longer. Even now, there are rumblings among the earls. People say the Spirits have cursed him."

"He's not cursed!" Meriel said, upset. "He's just sick."

"It doesn't matter what he is. Rumors create a truth of their own. You must leave these lands. *Before* your father passes."

Meriel's eyes hardened. "I'll never leave him. And I'll never abandon his legacy."

"Listen to me, child." Ardal took Meriel by the shoulders, insistent. "You will never be allowed to take his place. You have only two choices: leave or die. You'll have to decide which of those best serves his legacy."

He left her alone in the garden.

CHAPTER 25

WHEN I WOKE up, any remnant of my anger was gone. Now I felt guilt instead. Like I'd been going behind Meriel's back, betraying her trust. And while I knew that wasn't exactly true—it wasn't like I'd asked to be shown any of this—I couldn't shake the feeling I'd done something wrong.

Either way, that visit to Shadow had told me a lot about Meriel, going all the way back to the first day I'd met her. I remembered how upset she'd been when we went to Clarewell Sanatorium and spoke to the mad thief Seamus. Now I knew why. It made her remember the pain of her father, whom she'd loved deeply.

There had been another revelation inside that vision, too. Talk of titles, landholds, living in a palace, if an austere one . . . Clearly, Meriel had come from some sort of Torgal nobility. I wasn't sure of her rank, but she'd had lands and wealth. How in the world had she ended up with the likes of us?

It was just one of a million questions I had buzzing around my head. And one question remained above them all.

Why was I seeing this?

That crow—whether it was Bran, a Spirit, the Adversary, or just a plain Shadow-bird doing someone else's bidding—had led me to those memories. It had wanted me to see Meriel's past. But for what purpose? What was so special about Meriel's former life? Was there something there I was supposed to learn?

I lay on my bed a long time. I couldn't come up with an answer.

When I finally left my room, Meriel had returned. I wasn't sure when she'd got in, but she'd started on cleaning up the mess from this morning. She'd already picked up the bacon and wiped most of the grease off the wallpaper. There wasn't much left to do other than scrub oatmeal out of the rug.

Meriel, shoving the armoire into place, straightened when she saw me. Her eyes flicked down and away.

"Hey," she said.

"Hey."

She began to turn back to the armoire. Then she said, "I'm sorry. I shouldn't have said . . . I'm sorry."

"I'm sorry, too," I said, still feeling guilty.

"You didn't do anything."

"Then save it for later. I'll mess up eventually."

She laughed. "All right. But I really am sorry."

"You were right, though," I said, thinking of her father—by now, surely dead. "Family does matter." I looked at her. "No matter how you come by it."

She nodded, understanding. "No matter how."

"Of course," I said, "if you're still feeling guilty, how about I put the furniture back and you take care of the oatmeal?"

That made her laugh again. "I already spent half an hour plucking out bacon." But two sets of hands made for quicker work, and before long, everything was as it should be.

Gareth and Lachlan were the first to return. And from the books they were carrying, they'd had some luck.

Lachlan dumped his stack on the table, which made Gareth wince. After smoothing out the dents in the covers ("Sorry, Gar," Lachlan said), Gareth flipped to pages marked with scrap paper to show us what he'd found. From what I could tell, it looked like these were some sort of company records. Or government records of the companies. Or something.

Gareth tried to explain it. I decided to save some time and held up a hand. "Let's just assume I don't understand anything you're telling me," I said, "and I'm never going to want to. What did you discover?"

"There are s-several rail companies," Gareth said, "and they all make a fortune." He turned over a few pages to point to a decree from the emperor. "But only one company, J.R. Morrigan and Sons, has the rights to operate the train to Castle Cardogh."

Apparently, they'd got the rights despite some brutal competition. "Bloke where we got the books told us there was a big dustup," Lachlan said. "Burned-up rail cars, conductors cracked on the noggin, and the like. Morrigan geezers took a proper beating, they did." Gareth had told us that business in Sligach was cutthroat. It appeared he wasn't exaggerating.

Meriel frowned. "Why would anyone want the rights to the prison line so badly? Don't the rails make money by charging the riders?"

"The prison line's customer is the emperor himself," Gareth explained. "I mean . . . he pays to keep it running. For the supplies.

For everything. Morrigan can charge whatever they w-want for it. It might be the most lucrative railway in Sligach."

Hmm. That might give us an angle in. "Is Morrigan the biggest of the companies?" I said.

"Actually, they're one of the smallest. They own the Cardogh route and a handful that go to the gold mines. They just lost a big bid to add more."

"Not enough bribes, I'd guess," Lachlan said cheerfully.

"Um . . . yes. Probably."

"If Morrigan's so small," Meriel said, "then how did they win the prison contract?"

"Each company makes their own cars," Gareth said. "Morrigan's are the most secure."

That didn't sound like good news. Morrigan cars being *more* secure was the last thing I wanted to hear. It would make it a lot harder to sneak inside.

So far, then, we had nothing. We'd need to wait for Foxtail and hope she had better luck.

She didn't come back that night.

At first, as it turned dark, I wasn't worried. But after I fell asleep on the couch in the common room—to my surprise, without any trip to Shadow—and woke up with Foxtail's bed still empty, I started to get alarmed. I paced through the early hours, growing more and more concerned, until she finally arrived.

"I was starting to think the Breakers had caught you," I said.

She patted my cheek. Then she began gesturing. Though I'd

got better at working out what she was saying, it still took quite a while to get all the details.

Diana was right, Foxtail said. *There's only one way in: through the rails.*

"No other road? Or bridge?"

Nope.

"Could you sneak onto it?"

She hesitated. *The station that leads to the prison is watched pretty heavily. I'm not sure I'd like to try.*

If Foxtail didn't like her odds, then I didn't, either. "What about the water?"

Diana was right about that, too. You'd never reach the prison without being seen. They use bright lights to scan the water at night.

"What about underwater?" I said. Foxtail's mask let her breathe, even without air. And we had that water-breathing orb Gareth had taken from the vault.

I could get onto the island that way, Foxtail said, *but I wouldn't know how to get inside the prison. I might be able to scale the walls, but then there's a*—it took me a long time to work out her gestures here—*a spiked drum at the top. It makes it nearly impossible to get over. Even if I did, I'd never be able to bring somebody else out.*

That was it, then. The train was our only option. And the only way to get on that train was through J.R. Morrigan and Sons. It seemed hopeless.

The Old Man returned. *Nothing's hopeless, boy,* he said.

I began to dismiss him. And yet, as he spoke, my mind started to churn.

J.R. Morrigan and Sons, the Old Man said. *Small company. Secure rails. Just lost a big bid.*

So? I said.

So maybe they'd be interested in some new business, he answered.

New business?

In my head, I flicked through every gaff I knew. Ones the Old Man and I had played. Ones we'd talked about. Ones that were nothing but dreams of mine.

Possibly ... possibly.

But that still leaves us with a problem, I said. *A very big problem.*

Sheridan, the Old Man said. *You need to get him off your back first.*

How could we get him to not pay close enough attention? He'd never believe we were staying in Sligach and not trying to work a job. Unless ...

The Old Man grinned. *Told you, boy: even a mistake can be useful.*

I went to wake up Gareth—and found he was already awake, lying in bed, reading that pocket dictionary of the Old Tongue I'd bought him in Quarry's Point. He looked up, questioning.

"The rails," I said. "They're hugely profitable, right? From the money made from the ridership?"

"Yes," he said. "I mean ... the ones in the city. Yes."

"Where does that money go?"

"Each rail delivers what they collect to their main hub. There's a big safe there. Then they take it to the bank."

"And what about the mines?" I said. "The gold and silver Sligach's known for. What happens with that?"

"The ore is processed out of t-town. Into ingots. Then sent to the ports."

"Sent to the ports how? On the rails again, right?"

"Yes."

I paced Gareth's room, mind working faster and faster. "Sheridan," I said. "You told me he's ruthless and cunning. Just how cunning?"

"Well . . . enough to play the angles. Like you."

"Every gaffer does that. I'm asking how smart he is."

Gareth thought about it. "Very, I suppose. He's certainly . . . I mean . . . he's incredibly confident. He doesn't think much of other people. Always thinks he's the smartest man in the room."

Lachlan came in, rubbing his eyes, dressed in nothing but his underpants. "What's going on?" he said, not wanting to be left out. "You talking 'bout Mr. Fox?"

"We are," I said. "I think it's high time we showed him exactly what we're made of."

"We going to impress him, then?"

"Exactly the opposite," I said. "We're going to show him we're complete and utter fools."

CHAPTER 26

EVERYONE GOT THEIR own job to pull.

We gathered in the common room as I handed out the assignments. "Gareth," I said, "where's the best place in Sligach to lift wallets?"

He thought about it. "There's a few . . . I mean . . . probably the rail stations? Lots of people. No one staying around too long."

"Great. Choose a station and pick some pockets. But I want you to do a bad job of it."

Gareth blinked. "A bad job?"

"Absolutely. Act like you're afraid to be doing it. A lot of starts and stops, aborted attempts, that sort of thing. Go for only the easiest of marks. And when you dip your fingers in their pockets, come up dry most of the time. Don't bring home more than a crown or two a day. But do *not* get caught. If you see a Stickman eyeing you, head to a new station right away. Got it?"

Gareth looked puzzled, but he said, "All right."

Now it was Foxtail's turn. "I need you to rob some houses," I said. "Start by casing a few choice places. Make it painfully obvious what you're doing. If any of Sheridan's Breakers are following you, I want them to know exactly what homes you're planning to crack. Then choose one and go in, only one a night. But I want you to botch every job."

Foxtail cocked her head. *How?*

"Make noise. Knock over furniture, drop a glass. Alert who-ever's home that there's a burglar inside. When they chase you off, take an embarrassingly bad haul. A single silver spoon, something like that. Same as Gareth, come home with practically nothing—but don't get caught."

Foxtail shrugged. *If you say so.*

"As for you two," I said to Meriel and Lachlan, "you're going to run a gaff. But first, Lachlan, I need to borrow Galawan. And you need to pay a visit to the Lemon Tree."

Meriel and Lachlan's gaff was called the Damsel's Ring. It was a simple one, but it would take both of them to pull it off.

On Gareth's advice, I chose the Dunmore Rail Station as our location: a busy junction which ran a line into the wealthier parts of the city. That was important, as Meriel, who'd be playing a young lady, needed a good reason to be there.

I took a position on one side of the track, but I was only there to observe. Meriel and Lachlan would be doing all the work. After Lachlan returned from the pawnshop, I'd spent the day training them in what to do. Now, fresh in the morning, they were ready.

Meriel was the one to kick it off. I waited until a train was pull-ing into the station, then scratched my chin: the signal for her to start.

From her position against the wall, she joined the crowd of people changing trains. But before she could get on, she stumbled and fell—right in front of one of the station's employees. "Oh!"

The attendant, dressed in a dark blue uniform with bright brass buttons and a billed cap, hurried to help her to her feet. "You all right, miss?"

"Yes," Meriel said, looking flustered. "Just clumsy, I'm afraid—oh no!" She stared at her hand in dismay. "My ring! It's gone!" She grabbed the attendant's arm, looking frantically at the ground. "It's fallen off!"

Meriel went to her knees, searching, oblivious to the commuters streaming around her. The attendant helped her search. When he saw nothing, he called over a coworker from the station office to assist.

The crowd thinned as the train pulled away. Empty-handed, Meriel stood, near tears. "Oh . . . oh no . . ."

The attendant tried to comfort her, but she wouldn't be consoled. "You don't understand," she said, half sobbing. "That was my betrothal ring. My fiancé, Padraig, gave it to me last night. His family doesn't approve . . . they'll be furious."

Her desperation made the attendants look again. "It's here somewhere, miss," the first man said. "Give us time, we'll find it."

"But I can't wait! I'm already late for brunch with Padraig's mother. I'll have to lie, or she'll hate me."

"We have a lost and found, miss. Surely some good soul will spot your ring and return it."

She grabbed the man's arm, hopeful. "Would they? I'd be so grateful. I'll offer a hundred-crown reward to whoever returns it."

Their eyes bulged. A hundred crowns! That was nearly a full year's pay for them. They scanned the ground again, now hoping to find that ring more than Meriel. "We'll find it, miss. Don't you worry."

"Have the finder contact me, Penelope Winthrop, at the Langham. It's a hotel in the Shrewsbury district."

The attendants had already recognized the name. The Langham was the best hotel in Sligach. "You'll hear from us the moment it's in our hands."

Meriel smiled through her tears. "Artha bless you."

We waited fifteen minutes after Meriel was gone. Now it was Lachlan's turn.

He strode past the station office, whistling. With his hand out of view below the window, he dropped something in front of his shoe, so he'd kick it as he walked. There was a little metallic rattle on the tile, then a *ding* as it hit the door.

Lachlan bent down in surprise, laying his accent on thick. "'Ere, then. Wot's this?"

He stood right in front of the office—holding a ring. It was a very pretty ring, pure gold, with seven diamonds set in a flower pattern on the band.

The attendants stared through the glass. Then they scrambled through the door. They got jammed up, the two of them trying to exit at the same time. I had to smother a laugh.

"You found it!" one of the men said.

Lachlan, admiring the ring, acted like he hadn't heard them. "Shuna's snout, lookee 'ere," he said. "Must be me lucky day."

"Hold on there," the second attendant said. "That ring's not yours."

"I found it, didn't I?" He peered at the inside of the band. "Don't see no name on it."

"It belongs to the Lady Penelope Winthrop," the attendant said sternly.

"Does it, now?" Lachlan said, skeptical. "And oo's this Penelope, then? Yer molly, most like."

The first attendant put his hand on his coworker's arm. "She's a proper lady, boy. But you are in luck. Miss Winthrop has offered a reward for finding that."

"That so?" Now Lachlan looked interested. "'Ow much?"

The attendant gave a quick glance at Lachlan's garb: worn cap, dirty clothes, ratty shoes. Plus the poor-boy accent. I could practically see the man doing calculations in his mind. *A stock boy or the like. Makes twelve septs a week, at best.*

"The reward is one whole crown," the attendant said.

Lachlan made a rude noise. "Pull the other one, mate. Lookit them diamonds! This ring's worth way more'n 'at." He turned, ready to slip it in his pocket.

"No, no," the second attendant said. "It was ten crowns for this ring."

Lachlan perked up. "Ten, you say? That's more like it. Where's me money, then?"

"Uh . . ." They didn't have ten crowns on them. "It's . . . in the office."

Whispering among themselves, they dipped into the till and pulled out ten crowns. They gave the money to Lachlan, who stuffed it in his pocket before handing over the ring.

"Tell the Lady Penelope to lose more things," Lachlan said, laughing as he walked away.

The attendants watched him go, flushed with excitement. They had the ring! Now all they'd have to do was go collect the reward, use that to pay back the till, and the two of them would be ninety crowns richer.

Except, of course, they would soon discover there was no Penelope Winthrop, and no reward. And the seemingly valuable gold-and-diamond ring was nothing but plated lead and cut glass—worth a few septs, maybe, from a corner stand hawking cheap gewgaws.

Meanwhile, Lachlan had walked away with ten crowns. "I can't believe that worked," he said later, staring down at the bills in our hotel room. "Guv, it was so *easy*."

A sweet little gaff, the Damsel's Ring. And the reason it worked was because it preyed on the very thing the Old Man always said was most important. *Need, greed, and speed, boy. These are the three pillars of a most effective gaff.*

And we weren't done with it yet.

Over the next few days, while Gareth and Foxtail kept deliberately botching their jobs, Meriel and Lachlan pulled the Damsel's Ring another dozen times at different rail stations across the city, using the fake rings bought from the Lemon Tree—which I'd sent Lachlan to specifically because I knew Collins would get word back to Sheridan about what we were doing. And indeed, after the first day, I spotted a Breaker tail following us to the stations, watching from the far platform as Meriel and Lachlan pulled their gaff.

And it nearly always worked. The amount Lachlan was able to wheedle before handing over the ring changed according to how much the attendants thought they could get away with—five crowns was the lowest, twenty the highest—except for one attendant, who was strikingly honest, simply telling Lachlan there was a hundred-crown reward and he should go to the Langham to collect it himself.

In the meantime, I returned to the stations where we'd pulled the gaff and kept a lookout for visits by the Stickmen. It was the original station we'd hit, Dunmore, where I first saw our crime get reported. A pair of Stickmen questioned the two attendants while their supervisor looked on with folded arms. The men looked in trouble—and scared.

This was what I'd been waiting for. Time to play the gaff once more. It just needed one little change: me.

I took Foxtail and Meriel this time. I made Lachlan stay at the hotel.

"Nooo, guv, don't stick me on the side," he pleaded. "Ain't I been doing a good job?"

"A perfect job," I said. "But we need to change up the players. Trust me, you want to sit this one out." He sulked, but that couldn't be helped. He'd understand why soon enough.

Meriel kicked off the gaff, as usual. She waited until there was a different attendant near the office entrance than the first time she'd pulled it. Then she went down, crying about her lost ring as before.

Even if I hadn't already spied the Stickmen, I'd have known right away our gaff was rumbled. The attendant's eyes were hostile, and his commiseration with Meriel over her lost ring bordered on sarcasm. He clearly didn't buy her story—and of course he didn't, since he knew his coworkers had already been snaffled by it. If I'd been running the gaff for real, I'd have waved her off with a quickness.

I let her play it out instead. Though there was a small chance of violence, I knew she could handle herself if it came to that. Besides, she wouldn't be the one they'd jump. Swindler or not, none of these men would have the heart to punish a pretty girl the way they'd punish a boy. They'd wait for her accomplice to arrive.

I was right. They let her play out her part, then Meriel got on a departing train as usual. I watched carefully to see if—

There.

Two doors down, a man got on the same car Meriel did. He was dressed in plain clothes, but from his closely cropped hair and polished, sensible shoes, that was an undercover Stickman.

I signaled Foxtail, waiting among the crowd, and nodded toward the man. She got on after him, positioning herself between the two as the train pulled away. When the Stickman made his move to nab Meriel, Foxtail would trip him up, giving both of them time to escape.

Now came my part. The attendant was watching for Meriel's

accomplice to arrive—and today, that was me. I passed the office, dropping the ring hidden in my palm and kicking it.

"Goodness, what's this?" I said, picking it up.

The attendant glared at me. "Looks like a valuable ring," he said sarcastically.

"So it does. What do you think it's worth?"

"For you?" The attendant smiled nastily. "About three years in prison, I'd say."

A strong hand grabbed me from behind and slammed me face first into the window. Pain throbbed in my cheek. I was lucky the glass didn't shatter.

The attendants piled out of the office, surrounding me as I was held there. I slipped into an accent like Lachlan's. "'Ere! What you doing? Leggo!"

I already knew who had me. I'd spotted him in the crowd earlier, and watched him come at me from the corner of my eye. It was another Stickman, this one in full uniform.

He pulled me from the window, keeping a tight grip on my collar. "What do we have here?" he said.

"A thief," the attendant said. The whole gaggle that surrounded me looked pretty hostile.

"Liar! I ain't no thief!" I protested.

"No?" the Stickman said. "What's this, then?" He snatched the cheap ring from my fingers.

"What d'you mean? It's a ring, innit? I found it."

"Planted it, more like," the attendant said.

"I did not! You got no right."

The Stickman wasn't interested in a debate. He turned toward the two attendants we'd gaffed a week ago and held me up by the collar. "Is this him?"

They shook their heads, looking worried. "The boy before was shorter, younger. And he didn't have an eyepatch."

"See?" I pried myself from the Stickman's grasp. "I ain't done nothing."

"A likely story," the hostile attendant protested. "He's got to be working with them. Take him in."

But I could already see in the Stickman's eyes that the bust had been, well, busted. I turned as smug as I could. "Take me anywhere you like," I crowed. "You ain't got nothing on me, and you knows it. Put me front of the magistrate. Stick me front of the emperor hisself. I'll be flying birdlike before the sun says nighty-night."

The attendants closed in, ready to throttle me themselves. The Stickman put a hand out. "Here, now. There'll be none of that." When the attendants began to argue, he shut them down. "If he's not the boy, there's nothing to be done. Take it up with the sergeant." He looked down at me. "But you're going to make yourself scarce, you are."

"Don't need nothing here, anyway," I said, and I began to leave.

The Stickman put a hand on my shoulder. "I'll go with you. Just to be sure."

"Ain't no need," I began, but the Stickman kept a firm grip. He pushed me through the circle of attendants into the office. "Where we going?"

"Out the back way," the Stickman said. "Can't scare the passengers with sight of a possible thief, can we?"

"I ain't no thief!"

"Right, right."

The back exit led to stairs down to an alleyway at street level. I knew what was coming. It was why I'd taken Lachlan's place in the gaff. Since the Stickman couldn't arrest me, he'd send me a different, more satisfying message instead.

It happened as soon as we reached the ground. The Stickman whirled round and rammed his nightstick in my gut.

He hit me just below the solar plexus. The pain doubled me over, spreading through my body, making me gasp for air. I felt the panic as my lungs wouldn't cooperate.

He hit me again, a knee in the abdomen this time. Then he jammed the end of his club into my kidney.

The agony was beyond belief. I collapsed, in too much pain to make anything more than a strangled cry.

Then he really began to beat me. I didn't move as he put the boot to my gut, over and over again. I just curled up, protecting my head, my face. I couldn't let him mark up my face.

Fortunately for me—well, sort of fortunately—he didn't want to mess up my face, either. He'd rather keep the bruises where no one could see them. A few more kicks, and he was done.

He leaned over, panting with the effort of the thrashing. "Won't be seeing you round here again. Right?"

I couldn't even answer. He took that as agreement.

"Scuffed my boots, you did," he complained. Then he walked off whistling into the street.

It was Foxtail who found me.

I don't know how long I lay there. For the first little while, I couldn't move. Then I just didn't want to. It hurt too much.

I didn't hear her footsteps coming. *Like a cat, that girl is*, I thought when she appeared. She kneeled next to me with a sigh, though as always, she made no sound.

Cool water touched my lips. Foxtail had a flask; I drank from it greedily. Had she known I'd take a beating? She'd returned to check on me, either way.

I rolled onto my back. It hurt. "Meriel got away?" I croaked.

Foxtail nodded. *Everyone's fine.*

"Me too," I said. That hurt. I laughed. That also hurt.

She helped me up.

Yes. That hurt, too.

The others were horrified when Foxtail brought me home. They fussed over me as she brought me to the couch.

"Cal," Meriel said in dismay.

"All part of the plan," I groaned as I lowered myself into the cushions.

Lachlan was upset. "That why you snaffled me place? Artha's rump, guv. Took plenty of beatings, I have. I coulda taken another."

"You already died for us. Twice, in case you forgot," I said, wincing. "More to the point, if you'd have been there, you'd be in jail right now. Either way, it had to be me."

"Why?" Meriel said.

I was too worn out to explain. But there was someone who already knew the answer.

I could almost see the Old Man standing behind them. He looked over my bruises, then lit his pipe and nodded. *Nicely played, boy*, he said.

I couldn't remember the last time I felt so proud.

CHAPTER 27

I GAVE MYSELF a present: a full day of bed rest before limping back to Sheridan.

In the morning, I sent Lachlan to the Fox Den to see if he could set up a meeting. Word came to our hotel that Mr. Fox would see me that evening.

I took Gareth with me. It was a deliberate choice: Sheridan liked him, and I thought that would give me an advantage. Of course, Sheridan would know that, too, so whether it actually affected the outcome was a toss-up. That was the problem when dealing with gaffers. You never really knew where you stood.

His lieutenant, Byrne, was sitting at the bar when we arrived, one of the barmaids on his lap. He nodded and raised his mug as we passed, waving us through to the back. I decided I liked the man. With Byrne, I *did* know where I stood. He'd be perfectly pleasant, even helpful—right up until the boss told him to put a bullet in our heads.

Sheridan was alone in his office, his glass already filled with Garman's finest. He watched, amused, as I stepped up painfully to his desk and tossed a pouch on it.

"We've been doing some jobs," I said. "That's your cut."

He smirked at the meager pickings inside. His third amounted to forty-one crowns and fourteen septs. "Quite a haul," he said.

He wasn't wrong to mock. It was an embarrassing take, barely a rounding error compared to the amount his Breakers would earn him in a week. I gave it even money he tossed the pouch back out of pity.

He kept it. He did, however, wave for me and Gareth to sit, and poured us both some wine. "You look like you need this," he said.

"I've had worse beatings," I said, trying not to grimace as I drank.

"I bet you have."

That wasn't commiseration; it was an insult. *You're exactly what I thought you were when you first walked in here*, he was saying. *A child playing a man's game. A bumbling fool.*

Perfect.

"I have a problem," I said.

Sheridan raised an eyebrow. "Didn't we talk about this? Your problems aren't mine."

I pushed on. "I sent Galawan—our mechanical bird—back to our client. He won't let us out of our debt."

I had actually faked doing that. When I'd come up with the gaff, I borrowed Galawan from Lachlan and gave him instructions to fly to Redfairne, check that Grey the clockmaker was still recovering from the Weaver healing I'd arranged for him, then come back. He'd tweeted his cheerful agreement and taken off, returning late last night. Grey had sent a message back with the little bird: an extremely vulgar thank-you.

When I'd let Galawan go, I'd made sure to do it in the street, where our Breaker tails would see it. So Sheridan wasn't surprised at what I told him. "Of course your client wouldn't drop the debt," he said, barely able to believe I'd be so stupid. "Why would he?"

I ignored that. "We need a score," I said, sounding desperate. "A *big* score."

He looked skeptical—*you couldn't pull one off if you partnered with the Fox herself*—but he raised an eyebrow, waiting.

"The trains," I said. "The ones to the mines. They ship gold on those, right?"

Sheridan stared at me with outright amusement. "Gold, silver, crowns," he said. "The rails transfer money all the time."

"Have the Breakers ever robbed them?"

"Many times. Though not for a couple of years."

"Why not recently?"

"Because each time it happened, the companies' security got better. Stronger safes. More guards. Changed their routines, their keys. In fact, it was the Breakers' last attempt that took down the old Mr. Fox. Tried to pull off one final job, got himself burned. Why?"

"We want to snaffle a shipment of gold," I said.

Sheridan's smile got wider. "And what do you want from me?"

"Just to make sure we're not stepping on anyone's toes. That you don't already have a gaff in the works."

"I do not."

"And if you had any . . . insiders, say, among the rail companies, if we could get access to them."

Sheridan pretended to consider it. "I don't think so," he said finally. "You can keep buying from Collins at the Lemon Tree. But otherwise, I believe we'll stay out of this one."

I could tell he was sure we'd never pull it off. In fact, he was near certain we'd get ourselves killed. Which was why, when Gareth and I stood to leave, he stopped me.

"We haven't discussed my cut," he said.

I pretended to look confused. "Your cut's a third, like usual."

"Not this time." He poured himself more wine. "For this job, the cut will be half."

"Half?" I said, indignant. "Why?"

"Because if you succeed"—his tone belied his confidence that we wouldn't—"it'll cause a world of trouble. Make things harder for us. We deserve compensation for that. Also . . . because I say so."

I let him see me fume for a moment. "Fine." I turned to go.

"I'm not finished."

I stopped.

"I want one more thing," he said.

"What?" I said.

"Gareth."

I froze. "You . . . what?"

"I want Gareth," Sheridan said. "Succeed or fail, Gareth stays with me."

Gareth stared at me, wide-eyed, almost panicked. This time, Sheridan *had* caught me by surprise.

"I can't," I said. "I need him. To do the job."

"And you can have him. For the job. After that, I keep him."

"But—"

"You have a rare talent in Gareth, Callan," Sheridan said. "He has so many useful skills. Yet you squander him. You had him picking pockets in a railway station, for Shuna's sake. He'll be better off with me. Besides, *you* may be a freelancer, but Gareth is a Breaker. He swore an oath."

Gareth had told me. *Until the earth takes you.* Once a Breaker, always a Breaker. Until the day you die.

"So," Sheridan said, "half your take, and Gareth. Don't like it? Go back to your client and beg for mercy. I'll keep Gareth either way. Are we agreed?"

What could I say? Defeated, I nodded. "Yes."

∩∪

When I told the others back at the hotel what had happened, they were furious.

"How could you?" Lachlan said.

"Over Sheridan's dead body," Meriel said.

Foxtail gestured rudely.

I was a little offended. "You really think I'd deal away Gareth?" I said. Gareth looked relieved, even though I'd already told him that right after we'd left the Fox Den. "Sheridan's not getting him, or you, or any of us. I just need him to think he is so we can play our gaff."

That mollified them. But it also made them realize the stakes had changed. This wasn't just a prison break anymore. When Sheridan didn't get what he wanted, he'd kill us. From here on out, we were playing for our lives.

"Righto, then," Lachlan said. "What happens now?"

"What else?" I said to him. "Put on your good shirt. It's time for you to go get a job."

CHAPTER 28

A LONG GAFF is a delicate chain of events.

The Old Man had taught me that long ago. When he first took me in, he'd started by only running simple pulls. *You distract the fruitmonger*, he'd tell six-year-old me. *I'll slip a few pears under my jacket when he's not looking my way.* Or: *Bump into that woman. Fall down and start crying. When she leans over to help you, I'll snaffle her purse.*

As I got older and more experienced, as I learned to read people, he began to teach me gaffs that relied less on simple distractions and more on how others would behave or react, like the Damsel's Ring or the Pigeon Drop. After I'd mastered those, he finally brought me into his most complex schemes.

But right from the beginning, he'd begun preparing me for the long gaff. *It is the pinnacle of our profession, boy*, he'd said, back when I was still small enough to ride in front of him in the same saddle. *I will show you how to make an entire city bend to your will.*

He'd started that night, by the campfire, when he pulled out a gameboard and some pieces. *This game is called Standing Stones.*

The board was circular, with different-colored squares painted on the wood, seemingly at random. But it was the pieces that had captured my interest. They were odd little things, different sizes, strange shapes. Some looked like men, tall or squat. Some looked like animals. And some had no particular shape at all, just amorphous blobs, with arms sticking out here or there. The only thing they had in common was an unstable base. You could balance them, but they were easy to knock down.

As it turned out, that was the point. The rules of the game involved placing your pieces in turns around the squares, with each piece having its own rules of movement. Slowly, the board would fill up with the shapes. And then, when your plan was complete, you'd strike. You could tip over a single piece of your own—which would hopefully knock over another piece on the board, and then another, and so on. If, when the pieces stopped falling, you had at least one standing while all your opponents' troops had toppled, you won. If your try failed, you lost. One shot, that was all you got.

The key, boy, the Old Man told me, *is to look far into the future. This piece is here now. But where will it be in five turns? This one has arms on either side. You can knock over three pieces with it—if you topple it right. But how will you set it up? How far ahead will you see?*

Originally, the game had fascinated me because it was fun knocking things down. But as I learned the strategy over the years, I started to get really good. On our longer gaffs, I began to use the board with other people to win a treat here and there. If we joined a household, pretending to be a father-and-son servant team, for example, I'd challenge the rest of the staff, playing for candies or septs. And winning.

But I never once beat the Old Man.

It was infuriating. When we played, he'd look like he was barely paying attention, puffing his pipe, placing a piece without a moment of thought. Yet as soon I was one or two moves away from shifting the piece that would win me the game, he'd reach over, lazily flick the giraffe, and I'd watch in dismay as my haphazard army was flattened. One winter, when I was nine, I got so mad I flipped the board, scattering the pieces into the river. He made me wade out there, freezing water and all, to collect them.

I thought of him now as I planned our gaff, studying it move by move, as he'd taught me to do.

We needed to break both Cormac and the Hollow Man out at the same time.

Diana could get us in on the work crew only once.

We needed to find a way inside before that, then, so we could scout the layout of the prison and learn everything we needed to pull off an escape.

The only way to do that was to go in on one of J.R. Morrigan and Sons's trains.

And to do that . . .

I could see the Old Man, sitting on the other side of the board.

A delicate chain of events, he said.

There were so many pieces to place. I could only hope, at the end, mine were the ones left standing.

All of my ideas began and ended in one place. If J.R. Morrigan was the way into the prison, then we needed to get into J.R. Morrigan. And the Morrigan offices were where we would start.

Nothing makes a job easier than an inside man, the Old Man always said. While that was certainly true, in this case, we had a bit of a problem. Meriel, Gareth, and I were all past the age of decision and eligible to apply for a job in the rail office, but an entry-level position would require too many hours and offer too little access. A quicker way to get an inside man would be through bribes, but I wasn't keen to try that right away. If we paid off the wrong person, they'd alert their bosses, and we'd be sunk.

So we got Lachlan a job instead.

Businesses never handled their own mail. They hired the work out to courier companies, who used runners to deliver letters and packages across the city. We found the company who handled Morrigan's mail—Swift, they called themselves—then found the runner who worked that specific route: a nine-year-old girl name Eve. And we bribed *her*.

She eyed me with wary curiosity when I stopped her in the middle of a run. She was a rangy thing, long legs like a young doe, cloppy shoes and stockings spattered with mud.

I told her what we wanted. "Whenever you get a package for Morrigan," I said, "bring it to this apartment"—I gave her the address of a room we'd rented just for this purpose—"and leave it with him." I pointed at Lachlan, who'd accompanied me.

He grinned at her. She ignored his charm. "Why should I?"

"How much do you get paid per run?"

"Quarter-sept a bag."

"I'll double it."

That was just the right size bribe. Enough to make it worth her while, not enough that her newfound wealth would set off any alarms.

She hesitated. "I'll get sacked if you don't deliver it straight. Or'n you mess with the packages."

"Everything will leave his hands the way you put it there," I promised. "Anything goes missing, that's on you."

She shrugged. She knew we were up to no good, but she didn't care. The extra money was too good to pass up. She tossed her bag to Lachlan.

"Quick-quick, now," she said. "You already made that one late."

With his new job, Lachlan became our eyes and ears inside the Morrigan offices. It was the perfect position, as no one paid attention to either his appearance or his presence. With the right letter in hand, he could walk up to just about any desk in the building.

Over the next week and a half, he learned the names of the employees, and where their various offices were. What we needed most, however, was to get our hands on the company's private records. That, Lachlan couldn't spy out—because he couldn't read.

But he could watch and learn. While we distracted the Breakers that Sheridan sent to tail us with irrelevant trips to the docks, the train stations, and other pointless feints, Lachlan discovered where the company's records were stored and where the keys to the cabinets and the front door were kept.

And so it was on to step two.

Only trusted Morrigan employees would ever be allowed in their records room. To get to them, then, we'd have to break in. Normally, that would be Foxtail's job, except she had the same problem as Lachlan. She couldn't read, either.

That meant one of us would have to break in with her. The obvious choice was Gareth. He'd find what we needed the quickest by far. I'd have sent him alone, but for all Gareth's smarts, he was no burglar. So the two of them would do the job together.

All three of us went to case the place during the daytime, when the streets were busy and we weren't likely to be noticed. The Morrigan offices, I saw, were in a three-story brownstone in an awfully public place: on the corner of two major streets. Across one street, high on its platform, was a railway station. Across the other was a canal.

A Stickman walked the beat nearby. There was a path along the canal, pleasant for sightseers and strollers. Which meant that besides the Stickman, there'd be a lot of people here, even at night.

"What do you think?" I said to Foxtail.

She wobbled her hand, then pointed to the top floor. The offices up there had broad panes of glass, with tiny windows at the top, hinged to swing down to open. *It's a little exposed. But I could crawl through there.*

Foxtail might be small enough to squeeze through those windows, but Gareth would never fit. We'd have to get him in a different way. Fortunately, I had a plan for that.

Gareth was nervous. "Will the w-windows be open after h-hours?"

Foxtail shook her head, then punched her fist into her palm. *I'll have to break one.*

That would make noise. But I had a plan for that, too. And for dealing with any Stickmen along the way.

"Then let's get home and get ready," I said. "We go in tomorrow night."

CHAPTER 29

IT WAS A nice, cool evening for a heist.

The canal was pretty at this hour, too. The streetlamps lit the water, orange flames from the gas dancing off ripples in the waves. Meriel and I strolled along the path, arm in arm.

I'd bought a bag of candied corn from one of the street vendors. Meriel kept popping pieces of it in her mouth, restless.

"You're supposed to be enjoying yourself," I muttered under my breath.

"You know I don't like sitting on the sidelines," she mumbled through a mouthful of corn.

Unfortunately for her, that was our job tonight. We were only here as a distraction. If it came to being backup, something had gone very, very wrong.

Lachlan was around, also as a distraction. His job was to make a nuisance of himself—a role which he was awfully good at indeed. He'd come armed with a rubber ball, which he had a knack for bouncing in just the right direction to clip a passing gentleman by the shoulder ("Ah, sorry, mate") or lose itself in the folds of a lady's dress ("Apologies, miss. Shuna's snout, I'm clumsy, eh?") all the while looking like he'd done it by accident. The passersby mostly forgave him, though he got a few cuffs about the head and one shoe square in the backside.

"You could have Lachlan's job instead," I said to Meriel.

She snorted and stole more candied corn.

"Leave me some, at least," I complained.

"I told you to buy two bags," she said.

"Speaking of two bags, did you hear the one about the sailor and the—" I cut the joke short. I'd spotted Foxtail.

Her head peeked over the gable of the Morrigan building. She'd covered her mask with a black veil to prevent any shine from the lamplight.

"We're on," I said under my breath.

Meriel turned toward the water. I leaned against the rail, facing her, as if in conversation. This way, I could watch Foxtail out of the corner of my eye.

She crawled over the gable, her body hugging the roof. She'd dressed in a prowler's outfit: a black, form-fitting, full-body leotard, carrying a small black leather rucksack. In the dark, she was nearly impossible to see.

She inched forward, gripping the roof tiles all the way to the edge, positioning herself above one of the upper-floor windows. Carefully, hanging facedown, she pulled a cloth from her rucksack, unrolled it, and pressed it onto the window, covering the glass.

The cloth had been brushed with the contents of one of our one-shots called the "burglars hug." It was a thin, gummy paste, which meant when Foxtail pressed it there, it stuck. The cloth was meant to muffle the sound: when Foxtail broke the window, the fragments would stick to the cloth, so no one would hear it shatter.

But breaking it would still make a crack. So, Foxtail said, we'd need something to hide the sound. That was Lachlan's job. Meriel and I waited, talking idly, while Lachlan annoyed everyone some distance away.

Then we heard the rumble of an incoming train. As soon as it began, Lachlan hurried over to the snack vendor and tossed him two septs for a bottle of lemon fizz. When the vendor went to pull the cork for him, Lachlan said, "Nah, mate, I'll take it like that," and jogged away.

The train moved into view. Lights burned in the cars as they rumbled over the rooftops.

"Stickman's coming," Meriel muttered.

She'd spotted him farther down the path. It was a different man than this afternoon, walking casually, nightstick swinging from one wrist by a leather strap. He tipped his finger to his cap as he passed a group of young women. "Evening," he said.

The rails rumbled louder now as the train approached the station. People raised their voices to be heard.

Foxtail dug her toes into the roof tiles and hung half her body over the edge, ponytail swinging down. She waited, head level with the window.

Lachlan began to shake his bottle of lemon fizz, keeping his thumb over the cork.

"Excuse me," I called. "Officer?"

The Stickman strolled over to join Meriel and me. "Evening, young sir," he said. "What can I do for you?"

The train began to slow as it pulled toward the station.

Foxtail raised her fist.

Lachlan stepped close to the curb, shaking the fizz as hard as he could.

"Will we be safe walking back to our hotel at this hour?" I asked.

"Certainly, sir," the Stickman began. "Sligach's well patrolled, and—"

The train blew its whistle.

Foxtail smashed the window.

I heard the crack. Barely, just over the sound of the train. But no one else noticed it—because at the exact same time, Lachlan dropped his bottle of fizz.

It shattered on the curb. With the liquid inside shaken, the bottle exploded under the pressure. Glass tinkled everywhere on the cobbled street, sticky lemon drink spattering an older lady's dress nearby.

"You absolute pillock!" the gentleman accompanying her said, and he grabbed Lachlan by the collar.

"Right, that's it," the Stickman said, marching toward the boy. He cuffed Lachlan a few times. Lachlan was lucky there were people around, otherwise he would have gotten the stick.

"Ow!" Lachlan protested. "It were an accident!"

"I've had enough of your 'accidents' tonight. Pick all that glass up before someone steps on it."

"But I'll cut me hands!"

The Stickman cuffed him again. "Then you best be careful about it."

With everyone looking at Lachlan, no one spotted Foxtail. She wriggled through the window, and she was in.

∩∪

Now it was Gareth's turn.

Lachlan picked up the pieces of his broken bottle—ever so slowly—the Stickman tapping his foot behind him. I pulled out my pocket watch and counted the minutes. One. Two.

Three.

Gareth, stuffing his own watch back in his pocket, appeared from down the street. We'd made him look older, dressed in a fine suit, false spectacles, and a beard from our disguise kit, and he was carrying a briefcase. He looked like any other young office employee leaving work—except, of course, this late at night, his office would be long closed.

He looked nervous—at least to me. I'd worked with him all day to try to keep him relaxed. *Just think to yourself: You're not doing anything wrong*, I'd told him. *You're a young man walking home. Remember, the way to not get caught is to act like you belong there.*

It was hard to drive the nervous instinct out of him. Out of most people, really. They tended to cringe, keep their heads down, as if, if they could make themselves smaller, no one would see them. Their eyes darted here and there, to spy if anyone was watching. That was the big one: the eyes doing the "witness check," the telltale sign you were up to no good.

So I'd told him: *Keep your head up, your back straight, and don't look at anyone except me. When it's time, I'll give you the signal.*

Now he watched me as he approached from the other side

of the street. That alone made him look nervous—he was only supposed to glance; why would he be staring so intently at some couple across the way?—but what might really tip someone off was how bad he was sweating. It wasn't warm enough for that.

Don't stick your finger in your collar, I thought as he strode toward us. *You're breathing just fine. Don't stick your finger in your collar—*

He stuck his finger in his collar.

Ah, well. You can't have everything. At least Lachlan was keeping the Stickman distracted. Meanwhile, I glanced toward the window nearest the front door of the Morrigan offices for Foxtail's signal. We'd given her three minutes from entry to come down from the top level, grab the key to the door, and unlock it before Gareth arrived. If she wasn't ready in time, I'd have to wave him off.

Lachlan could only stretch out picking up his broken bottle for so long. As he collected the final shard, he glanced my way. I shook my head.

Lachlan held the dripping glass out to the Stickman. "Here ya go."

"What do you want me to do with it?" the Stickman said. "Put it back together? Throw it out, you clown."

Lachlan shrugged and went over to the rail. He heaved back his arms to toss the shards into the water.

"Not in the canal, you idiot! Throw it in the bin. The *bin*." The Stickman cuffed him on the back of the head again. "I swear, you're doing this deliberately."

He certainly was. And thank Shuna for that, because Lachlan had bought us a few more seconds. I glanced back at the window—to see a handkerchief rumpled in the corner. Foxtail had unlocked the door.

Gareth was almost there. He looked my way, desperate.

I took off my hat.

That was the signal. It was on.

And here, Gareth did it perfectly. Without looking around, without even breaking stride, he opened the door and walked in.

I couldn't have been prouder.

Now we waited. In the dark—we couldn't risk a lamp shining from the supposedly empty offices—Foxtail would lead Gareth up to the records room. Once in there, since that room didn't have any windows, Gareth could use the light orb he'd stolen from the Weaver vault to find and copy the records we needed. On the way out, he was also to steal a rubber stamp the secretaries used to mark their mail. That would come in handy later on.

Lachlan's task done, he let the Stickman run him off. "If I see you again tonight," the man said, "I'll feed you my truncheon."

That left Meriel and me, pretending to enjoy the view. The Stickman returned to his beat, passing the Morrigan building every eight minutes or so. When we saw the handkerchief in the window again, it meant Gareth was done. All I had to do was wait until the Stickman was out of sight, then take off my hat again.

Gareth came out the front door and walked away. Foxtail locked the door behind him, then went back up to the top floor and climbed out the window, disappearing behind the roof.

She still had one more job tonight. While she could close

the drawers and return the keys, leaving no sign anyone had rifled through the office, there was nothing she could do about the broken window. It was sure to be spotted; if not tonight, then certainly in the morning, when the employees of J.R. Morrigan and Sons returned to work. So we had to disguise we were ever inside.

After a few minutes, Foxtail came out of the alley. She'd put on new clothes over her burglar's outfit: a raggedy dress and a cheap veil, still carrying her leather pack. She walked across the street, stood next to the canal, and waited until the Stickman returned on his rounds.

Then she reached into the pack, pulled out some rocks, and began throwing them through the windows of the Morrigan offices.

The Stickman jumped at the sound of shattering glass. "Hey! *Hey!*" He sprinted toward her. "Stop!"

Some citizens began to close on her, too, trying to capture the vandal. Meriel and I were the closest. I moved in to grab Foxtail and let her trip me up, sending me sprawling into the passersby who were coming to help.

The Stickman ran to tackle her. But before he could get there, Foxtail hopped over the rail, straight into the canal.

People milled around in confusion as she sank below the surface. A young gentleman helped me to my feet as the Stickman stared down into the water. She never came up.

"Goodness," the gentleman said. "She's drowned."

The woman with him put her hand to her mouth. "Oh, how horrible!"

"Sorry," I said to the Stickman. "I tried to catch her."

The Stickman removed his cap, confused. "Not your fault, sir. Appreciate you trying to help."

We left him there, scratching his head. "Must be something in the air tonight," he muttered to himself.

Foxtail was still wet when she returned to the hotel.

She was shivering, the cool water and the cold night air having taken their toll. She changed into dry clothes, then curled up in a blanket in front of our stove, which we'd filled with coal to warm her up. We ordered some hot lemon water from the desk downstairs, too. She couldn't drink it, of course, but she could wrap her hands around the steaming mug.

"You all right?" Lachlan asked her.

She gave him a thumbs-up. Jumping in the canal had been her idea. Since her mask let her breathe underwater, it gave her the perfect route for escape. She'd swam off below the surface, no one the wiser.

As for Gareth, he'd come away with a wealth of information from the records room. Armed with what Lachlan had gleaned from his spying, Gareth had combed through the staffing records, looking at job titles, finances, expenditures, anything that might give us a leg up. He'd copied down what he could. Now he was seated at the table, hunched over his papers, drawing what he called an "organization chart" of all Morrigan's bigwigs from his hastily scratched notes.

I leaned over his shoulder, watching as he inked the names

and titles. One in particular caught my interest: *Director of New Business—Aidan Farrell, 19.*

"Nineteen?" I said. "The person responsible for bringing in new business is nineteen years old?"

Gareth nodded. "According to their records."

"How's someone that young a director of anything?"

"He's a M-Morrigan." Gareth pulled out his notes and showed me. "His mother is J.R. Morrigan's daughter. He's the founder's oldest grandson."

Director of New Business, I thought. I scanned through Gareth's notes, reading carefully. According to this, young Mr. Farrell had a new wife, was making payments on a new home, and his position as director in his grandfather's company paid for a membership in the Progress Club, the most exclusive private club in Sligach.

I paced the room, mind racing.

"Do you have something?" Meriel said.

Thank Shuna for nepotism—because indeed I did. "That's him," I said. "Aidan Farrell. He's our mark. That's how we'll get into the prison."

CHAPTER 30

I RETURNED TO Shadow that night.

It had been nearly two weeks since I'd last been pulled there. So I was surprised when I found myself back in the training arena where I'd first seen eight-year-old Meriel. But I wasn't in the gallery this time. I was standing on the sand.

And something was burning.

Meriel was there with her weapons master, Ardal. She was older than the last time I'd seen her in Shadow, though this still had to be a couple years ago; she looked twelve at the most. She had a throwing knife in each hand, but she wasn't here to train.

I could smell smoke in the air, hear shouting from outside. A battle?

No. A raid.

Meriel's home was under attack. I could see it in her face: flushed, angry, and defiant. "I'm not going anywhere," she said.

Ardal stood impassive. "Dathal has taken the palace. The council have thrown their support behind him. It's over, Meriel."

"My father's body is barely in the ground," she said, "and you want me to surrender his home to that traitor? I'll die first. I don't care."

"But I do," Ardal said softly. "You can't fight them. No one defeats an army by herself."

"Then what did you give me these for?" She shook her fists at him, knives between her fingers. "Why did you train me to defend my father if you wanted me to run away?"

"I never trained you to defend him."

That made her pause. "But—"

"Your father knew he was doomed the moment he first grew ill. He knew that as the years passed, he would lose his mind, and that his brother would use this to turn the council against him—and you. You were never going to rule here. Your father knew this the day you were born."

Meriel was stunned by that. "So . . . why—"

"Why did I train you? Because he asked me to. Not to defend him. So when the time came for you to leave, you could defend *yourself.*"

Ardal went down on one knee before her. "You're all that's left of your father's line," he said. "The land doesn't matter. Only you do. You must go. For your father. And for me. Please."

The word startled Meriel, disarmed her. It appeared she'd never heard her master say "please" before. And as she stood there, smelling the smoke, listening to the shouts and the cries, I could see her new reality creep inside. There was nothing left for her here. Her home, and everything that made it her home, was gone.

It might have broken someone weaker than Meriel. But as I saw her realization, I saw also her resolve.

"Come with me, then," she said.

Ardal shook his head. "I, too, made a promise. This night is why I pretended friendship with Dathal all these years. So when he came, I could remain and undermine him for the rest of his days. I assure you, his reign will never solidify. His son will never rule your lands."

Suddenly, Meriel seemed small and vulnerable. "But I don't know anyone outside Torgal. I'll be all alone."

"No," Ardal said. "He'll be with you."

And he turned and pointed—at me.

I stepped back, startled. This was the second time someone in a vision had seen me. But when Meriel turned my way . . . *she* could see me, too.

She looked at me, puzzled, as if she'd met me somewhere before but couldn't quite recognize my face.

I was too stunned to say anything. I didn't understand what was happening at all. This couldn't be a pure vision of the past. I'd never been here.

Yet young Meriel walked up to me, trusting, and said, "You'll go with me?"

"I— Of course," I said.

She took my hand. It felt absolutely real.

"You have to go now," Ardal said. "This way."

He hurried out of the arena. I followed, still confused, Meriel near dragging me. The palace was in the distance, the east wing on fire. I heard shouting and dogs barking—Dathal's men, searching the grounds.

Ardal led us through the stables. The horses, nervous at the smell of smoke, stomped in their stalls, eyes rolling with fear. A groom held one of the horses' bridles, trying to calm it. He nodded to us as we passed. "Spirits ride with you," he whispered to Meriel as we ran out the back way.

Beyond the stable was a short wall. We hopped it and found ourselves by a dirt road. An ox-drawn wagon was there, its cargo space full of barrels, one with its lid ajar.

A man waited on the seat up front, holding the reins. He was wearing a heavy hooded cloak and gloves. I couldn't see his face, but Meriel recognized his silhouette and cart. She flinched, skidding to a stop.

"That's old Brannigan!" she said, alarmed. "He'll turn me in!"

"No," Ardal said. "Like me, he only pretends to support your uncle. He's loyal to you."

The wagon driver, Brannigan, called with a crotchety voice from beneath his hood. "Time's ticking, girl," he said. "Hop in that barrel, now. Boy rides with me up front." How he knew I was there, I had no idea. He hadn't even turned our way.

"But they'll stop him," Meriel said to Ardal. "They'll search his cart."

"No," Ardal said. "Dathal's men think he's one of them. That's why I chose him to take you. It's as your father always said: only like kills like." He turned to me. "Isn't that true?"

Meriel looked up at me, eyes wide. I stared back at Ardal, stunned and confused.

He said it again. "Only like kills like. Isn't that true?"

Meriel waited for my answer.

Only like kills like, I thought. "Yes," I said slowly, finally understanding what that meant. "It *is* true. It's like . . . *nothing makes a job easier than an inside man*."

I'd said that to Meriel—my Meriel, in the real world—a couple times before. And as I said it to this Shadow Meriel, she grew puzzled again, as if trying to recall who I was.

Then, suddenly, she did.

"Cal? What are you . . . How did you get here?" She looked around in confusion. "This is—"

I opened my eyes.

I was lying in bed again, back in my room.

I sat up. My clothes were still on, my lamp lit. Strangely, I thought I could still smell the smoke from Meriel's burning home.

That's just the flame in the lamp, I thought. But I wasn't sure anymore.

I heard soft footsteps outside. Then my door opened.

Meriel stood in the doorway. She was in her nightgown, barefoot, hair loose and tumbling over her shoulders. She stared at me.

"I was just asleep," she said. "And . . . you were in my dream. You were *there*."

I almost lied. I'm not sure why. But I didn't.

"That wasn't a dream," I said. "We were in Shadow." I told her what Keane had told Gareth and me about my crystal ring and the realm of secrets.

Meriel looked at her own hand, uncertain, as if she might suddenly find the same mark. "But why was *I* there?" she said.

"Keane said anyone could drift into Shadow while asleep. But I think this might be because of me. I think I drew you there, somehow entered your dream. Saw the things you know from your past."

I remembered what Artha had said to me back in the Weaver

CHAMPIONS OF THE FOX

vault. *You visited me in Shadow.* I hadn't meant to do that, either. I didn't have any control over this—but it made me wonder once more who did.

I explained how I'd seen her training in the arena, then trying to calm her father in her garden. She was shocked. "That happened," she said. "*All* of that happened."

"The night you escaped, too?"

She nodded. "My father died. Then Dathal came, and Ardal made me run away in the back of Brannigan's cart. Everything was the same . . . except you. Why were you there?"

"I think someone's trying to show me something," I said. "Or tell me something. But I don't know who, or what." I spread my hands. "I *am* sorry. I wasn't trying to go through your memories. I didn't mean to snoop."

"It's all right," she said. "I . . . I should have told you anyway."

"We all have our secrets."

"But I should have told you. I wanted to. I just . . . I don't know why I didn't."

I think I did. "You were ashamed of leaving Ardal behind."

She sighed. "I really miss him, Cal. There were days I hated his guts, wished he'd walk out of that arena and get eaten by an alligator." She smiled sadly. "But I always loved him, too. Almost as much as I loved my father. Now they're both dead, and . . ." She trailed off, upset.

But . . . wait.

Could it be?

"Ardal isn't dead," I said.

Meriel shook her head ruefully. "I'm not a little girl anymore. I know better. Ardal was good, but he wasn't *that* good. He couldn't keep sabotaging Uncle Dathal forever."

But he had. And I knew it.

I remembered what Shuna had said to me in the woods. *Not everything is about you, Cal.*

Was it possible . . . that *this* was why I'd seen Meriel's past in Shadow? Was Shadow's secret not for me, but for her?

"Ardal's not dead," I insisted. "And I can prove it. I've seen him."

She stared at me. "Where?"

"I told you that after I lost my eye, Shuna said I needed to get the Dragon's Eye back from Mr. Solomon. What I didn't tell you is what convinced me to do it. Shuna showed me the future."

"The *future*?"

"Not the whole future. Just you. And the others, I mean. Well, not Foxtail, but . . . it doesn't matter. I saw all of you die."

She looked horrified.

"That's not going to happen anymore," I reassured her. "We changed the future when we stole the Eye back. But in that other future, you went home to Torgal. And you got caught."

"What did they do to me?" she said.

"They . . . well . . . beheaded you. They wrote something on your forehead first, though."

Her jaw dropped. "*Feyc anrygán!*" she said. "That's why you asked me about it in Redfairne! You never saw it on a wall. You saw it in your vision!"

"Um . . . yes. Sorry."

To my surprise, she didn't seem angry, just amazed. "*Feyc anrygán*," she said again.

"What does it mean?" I said.

"It's tradition. Part of the old ways. When a new Lord or Lady of All Names is chosen, they mark your skin with paint. *Feyc anrygán* is from the ancient language of Torgal. It means 'Behold your queen.'"

So Gareth had got it right. I should have trusted his translation. You'd think by now, I'd know better.

"Wait," Meriel said, snapping out of her reverie. "You didn't tell me about Ardal."

"Right. Well, as they were taking you to be executed, I saw they'd already beheaded Ardal on the platform."

Meriel got very still. "So he *is* dead."

"No, don't you see? They'd *just* executed him. But that was in the future where you returned to Torgal. My guess is that you got caught, and when Ardal tried to help you escape again, he got caught, too. But he only died because you returned—and in *this* future, you haven't. So he's still alive. He must be."

Her thoughts churned behind her eyes. And then . . . she stilled. It was like everything in Meriel just relaxed, as if the weight of the world had suddenly lifted from her shoulders. I'd seen her happy, but never like this. It seemed to go straight through to her bones.

"What's going on?" Lachlan said. He squeezed past Meriel into my room, rubbing his eyes. "Are you lot leaving me out of stuff again?"

"No," I said. "We were just—"

I stopped. It wasn't my secret to tell. But Meriel said, "My full name is Meriel Kilgalán. I'm the rightful Lady of All Names of Kilgalán Prefecture in Torgal."

"You're the whatsit?" he said.

"Lady of . . . it's . . . like a duchess."

Lachlan frowned. "You having me on?"

He looked from Meriel to me. I shook my head.

"Artha's fuzzy bum," he said.

Meriel laughed and kissed him on the cheek. Then she gave me a lingering glance and went back to her room.

Lachlan stared at me, mouth open. "Did ya see that? She kissed me!"

I laughed, too. "She sure did."

CHAPTER 31

MERIEL BOUNCED ON her toes with nervous energy.

"Stop that," I muttered out of the side of my mouth. We were standing on the sidewalk and supposed to be in character. And Meriel's character would definitely not bounce.

She stilled her legs and linked her arm in mine, hand resting on my forearm. But I could still feel her impatience through the way her fingers tapped absently on my skin.

Meriel had never liked waiting for the job to start. Usually, her impatience made her a little irritated, prone to snapping over unimportant things. But since our visit to Shadow three nights ago, she'd found a new inner calm.

In that way, she'd been different from the rest of the team. Both Lachlan and Gareth had found genuine peace in our friendships since we'd formed our band. I wasn't entirely sure about Foxtail— that mask of hers made it nearly impossible to know what she was feeling inside—but she'd been cheerful from the start. Of all the others, Meriel had carried the biggest weight inside. Now she was free.

I found it hard to believe giving Meriel peace was why I'd been pulled into Shadow, that that was the secret I'd been meant to find. But maybe it was. Even Shuna had pointed out that not everything was about me. Though the Fox had denied dragging me back into the realm of secrets, I was starting to think she'd been lying—despite her protests to the contrary. It made me almost disappointed I hadn't visited Shadow again. I wondered what else I could learn, what good it might do.

Isn't daydreaming wonderful? the Old Man said. *Much better than focusing on the job.*

Even when he wasn't around, he made me feel guilty. *All right, all right,* I grumbled, but I couldn't really argue. Tonight would make or break our whole gaff.

It was dark, well into the evening. Meriel and I had positioned ourselves so we could see our marks coming. Lachlan and Gareth were waiting at their starting places, too. Foxtail wouldn't be working this gaff directly; we'd used her instead to draw away the Breaker tails, so Sheridan wouldn't know what we up to.

"Are those them?" Meriel said suddenly.

She was antsy enough that I thought she might just be jumping the gun. But no, there they were: a young man of nineteen, sharply dressed in top hat and coattails—Aidan Farrell, Director of New Business at J.R. Morrigan and Sons Railroad Company—walking arm in arm with his new wife, Orla, a slightly homely girl in a moderately stylish blue dress with frills and lace.

Meriel's arm shifted in mine, a subconscious desire to get started.

"Wait for it," I said quietly.

"Right," she said. "Right." She waited. "Oh, come on."

"Timing is everything in a gaff," I muttered, but soon enough we began to move.

Aidan and Orla were walking toward us. In about ten seconds, we'd pass them. But before we could get there, a shabbily dressed boy—Lachlan—darted from a nearby alley and ran up from behind.

Lachlan snatched Orla's purse from her elbow, snapping the leather strap clean off. As he yanked it away, he bowled her over. She fell to the ground, crying out, more in surprise than pain.

Lachlan bolted, purse in hand. Aidan, staring in horror at his wife sprawled on the sidewalk, froze between helping her and chasing after the fleeing cutpurse. "Stop!" he shouted. "Thief! Stop him!"

As we'd planned, Lachlan ran straight toward me. He shifted direction to pass by—

I tackled him. There was a short wall to our left, a patch of grass on the other side. I rammed into him, and we both toppled over the wall, wrestling on the lawn.

Aidan had finally collected himself, helping his flustered wife to her feet. After checking she was all right, he hurried over.

By now I had Lachlan in a grapple. "That's enough," I whispered to him.

He surrendered immediately, as if I'd won the fight. I hauled him up by his ear. "Ow!" he said. "Leggo!"

"Quiet, you," I snapped as a red-faced Aidan hopped onto the lawn. "You're lucky I don't fill your guts with lead." Still twisting Lachlan's ear, I turned to Aidan. "This belongs to your wife, I believe," I said, offering him her purse.

"Thank you," he began, but before he could say any more, a Stickman arrived—or what looked like a Stickman. It was Gareth, dressed in a Stickman's uniform bought from the Lemon Tree, filled with padding so he wouldn't look so skinny. Truth be told, it made him look more fat than muscled. I was counting on Aidan being too flustered to notice.

"What's all this, th-then?" Gareth said, teetering on the edge of being convincing. I'd worked with him a lot, too, the last three days.

"This ruffian stole that lady's purse," I said. I shoved Lachlan into Gareth's waiting hand. "Teach him a lesson, officer."

That was Gareth's cue to hit Lachlan with his nightstick. He didn't do a very good job of it.

"Is that all?" I protested.

With a look of apology, Gareth rammed his club harder into Lachlan's stomach. Lachlan bent over, this time in genuine pain. "Arrggghh!"

"It's the magistrate for you," I called as Gareth hauled Lachlan away. "And that's not half of what you deserve!"

Meriel cooed over Aidan's wife, who still looked rattled. "Goodness, are you all right? Did he hurt you?"

"Just a little shaken," Orla said.

"Naturally. You should sit down."

"Thank you," Aidan said again, shaking my hand. "That thief would have gotten away without you."

"It is one's duty to help decent folk," I said, sounding snooty.

"Quite right, sir. Still, we're incredibly grateful—"

"Alastair!" Meriel said suddenly, pointing at my leg. "You've ruined your trousers."

I'd returned to using Alastair Quinn, the old name I had forged patents of nobility for, in case anyone decided to check on my background. And my pants leg was indeed ripped, just below the knee. I should know: I'd ripped it on purpose myself.

"Oh no, you're bleeding!" Orla said.

The blood was also fake, dabbed on under my trousers from our disguise kit before we'd left the hotel. "Artha's eyes," I cursed. "That scallywag . . ." I stared off after the departed Lachlan.

"Oh dear," Meriel said, swooning. "I feel faint."

Both Aidan and Orla steadied Meriel as she wobbled. "Some refreshment would do you good," Aidan said. "And you, sir, could use a bandage. Please, come inside. The Progress Club is right here." He motioned to the great gray stone building beside us.

"I appreciate the offer," I said, "but I'm not a member."

"Why, Aidan is, sir," Orla said. "We'd be indebted if you'd enter as our guests."

"I wouldn't like to impose . . ." I made a show of thinking about it. "But you're very kind. How can I refuse?"

And we were in.

CHAPTER 32

THE PROGRESS CLUB was everything I thought it would be.

Every inch of it bled wealth. From the soft glow of the mottled walnut-wood paneling to the curved steps with gilded rails to the sparkling crystal glasses behind the bar so polished it gleamed, there was no doubt what kind of place you'd entered. *Welcome,* the club seemed to say to its members. *You deserve this.*

Amusingly, what there wasn't inside was a hint of anything to do with "progress." No clanking gears, no whistling pipes, no belching stacks of smoke. Though they did have some very nice clocks, I supposed.

Orla escorted Meriel to the bar. Aidan directed me to the lavatory, which was so decorated with marble it could have been a quarry. When the attendant inside saw I was "injured," he became annoyingly persistent trying to help. I kept him away for the most part—I couldn't let him see that the blood was fake—but once I'd bandaged my shin, I relented and let him mend the rip in my trousers.

The others had ordered drinks by the time I returned. Meriel had been working the gaff hard, doing her best to charm the considerably plainer Orla. The two were already hunched over, heads together, gossiping. Aidan seemed pleased they were getting along, if a little left out.

My gaffer's eye saw it immediately: Aidan, who hadn't earned his job but had been given it, was a man looking to impress, yet lacking the confidence to take control. I filed that away, as the Old Man had taught me. I'd play that angle hard on this job.

"Ah, sir." Aidan looked relieved I'd returned; now he had someone to talk to. "Your lovely sister Scarlett"—he motioned to Meriel—"told us you like brandy. I've taken the liberty of ordering you one."

"Most kind." I took a sip and made sure he saw me look around the place with admiration. "A fine club this is, sir."

"Please, call me Aidan. Aidan Farrell. And my wife, Orla."

"How rude of me," I said, and I offered him my hand. "I haven't even introduced myself. Alastair Quinn. And my sister Scarlett, as you know."

I made some small talk, steering the conversation away from any topics of significance, until I'd finished my brandy. Then I put my glass down and picked up my hat. "As refreshing as promised, Aidan. I feel fortified to take on the world again."

Meriel spotted her cue. She stood, placing a hand on my arm with an indulgent smile. "Please forgive my brother. We were on our way to dinner when that thief attacked you, and he quite forgets his manners when he's hungry."

Orla had looked disappointed that we were leaving. So she bit the easy hook Meriel dangled. "We ourselves were about to dine. Please stay and join us."

"Indeed," Aidan said. "It would be our great pleasure to host you. The Progress Club has the finest chef in the city. I insist."

I pretended to hesitate. Then I smiled. "As you like."

They settled us into a table for four. As we took our seats, Orla said, "You have the most beautiful accent, Scarlett. I can't quite place it. May I ask where you're from?"

We'd practiced this hard the last three days. Meriel's natural lilting, melodic Torgal accent marked her as being from somewhere unusual. So unusual, in fact, that despite the Old Man's education in accents, I hadn't ever heard hers before. (As it turned out, Gareth had recognized she was from Torgal right away. The Westport Breakers had had occasional dealings with smuggling goods across the border. Meanwhile, I'd spent days wondering about it. "Why didn't you tell me?" I asked him afterward. "I thought you already knew," he said. Fair enough.)

But here, her accent presented two problems. First, as her brother, I'd need to speak the same way. I could copy her well enough, but that led to the second problem: for this gaff to work, we could absolutely not be from Torgal.

So I'd practiced with her to adopt a new accent. I smoothed out her lilt and replaced it with broader, fuller vowels, to the extent that she could do it comfortably. Then I matched it. It made us sound more or less from where I planned to pretend we came— though a lilt did occasionally slip in.

"We're from Garman," Meriel said.

"Really?" Aidan said with interest. We were a long way from home, almost the full breadth of the empire—which was another good reason to choose Garman. It was unlikely we'd meet anyone who would recognize Meriel's accent was off. "Are you on your Grand Tour, then?"

The Grand Tour was a common custom among wealthy families. Soon after reaching the age of decision, the father would send their son or daughter on a yearlong trip away from home to learn more about the world firsthand. "We were," I said, "in Carlow. But our Tour was cut short when Bolcanoig exploded."

Even so far away, the whole world knew about the volcano's eruption. Not only had it devastated Garman, it had colored the morning sky a bright orange for weeks afterward. "We'd planned to return home, of course," I continued, "but as I was already out this way, my father tasked me to visit Sligach to explore new business."

"What business is your father in?" Orla asked politely.

This was where the gaff turned. *If you chase somebody for something*, the Old Man had always said, *it will raise their hackles. Their suspicions will be up. But if they discover what you want on their own—make them chase you—they'll believe you from the very start.*

"He has several interests," I said vaguely.

Meriel laughed. "My brother is being modest," she said. "There's no need to keep it a secret, Alastair. Our father is the earl of Garman Minor."

"Oh!" Orla straightened in her chair, as if she'd just been told I was the son of the emperor himself. Aidan was equally impressed.

"We're here for something to do with trains," Meriel continued. "I don't know what it is; Alastair can tell you."

"Just some exploration," I said, as if Meriel shouldn't have let the cat out of the bag. "Meeting a few companies to discuss opportunities."

"I see," Aidan said. He was definitely paying attention now. "May I ask with whom?"

I pondered it, as if weighing whether it should be kept confidential. Then I shrugged as if there was no harm in telling him. "Sligach Central seems most promising," I said. "But I'll also be meeting with Western Line, Tullagh Mining and Rail . . ." I rattled off a half dozen names.

"Had you not considered J.R. Morrigan and Sons?" Aidan said, disappointed I hadn't mentioned them.

"I would have," I said, "but they are apparently not interested in my father's business. I don't think I would trust them, regardless."

Aidan blinked, confused. "I beg your pardon?"

"I wrote to Morrigan as I did the others, informing them I was coming to Sligach on my father's behalf. They didn't even offer the courtesy of a response. If they weren't interested, I'd accept that. But to not even answer? So disrespectful."

Orla stared at her husband in horror. Aidan had gone beet red. "Sir . . . there must be some mistake."

"How so?"

"Well . . . *I* work for Morrigan."

"I see," I said, somewhat coldly.

"I assure you, I would never—*we* would never . . ." He was so embarrassed, he was stumbling over his words. "I don't know what could have happened. I apologize most sincerely."

"I'm sure no offense was meant," Meriel said, to keep the peace.

"Quite right," I said. "Think nothing of it. The dinner table is no place for business, regardless. My apologies."

Meriel changed the subject. Orla warmed to the conversation again, though she continued to give her husband the occasional worried glance. As for Aidan, he only picked at his food for the rest of the dinner. When we finished, we offered our thanks for their hospitality and made to go.

As I knew he would, Aidan pulled me aside before he left. Make *them* chase *you.*

"Alastair," he said, still flustered, "I feel terrible about what I can only promise you was a grave oversight. I would be most grateful if you'd stop by the office tomorrow and give me the opportunity to mend it. I assure you, we can serve whatever business your father needs."

"I'm afraid I already have appointments tomorrow," I said. I let that hang there a moment, so when I changed my mind, his mood would swing wildly. "But you've been so kind to us. I suppose . . . I'm free the day after. I could come by then."

He nearly fainted with relief.

CHAPTER 33

FLUSH FROM ANOTHER successful gaff—at least the start of one—I wondered if I'd go back to Shadow that night, like the last time. And I did, almost exactly like the last time. Though something about this trip felt strange.

When I opened my eyes, I was sitting on a wagon. *This is Brannigan's wagon*, I realized, the one that had snuck Meriel out of Torgal. Brannigan himself was beside me, dressed in the same hooded cloak and gloves as I'd seen before.

Except it wasn't dark anymore. The sun blazed high in the sky. The heat pouring down made Brannigan's garb seem all the more odd. In the back of my mind, an alarm went off.

Why is he wearing that here?

Come to think of it, I had no idea where "here" was. The wagon was trundling slowly down a bare dirt road, nothing but empty grassland for miles.

"Are we still in Torgal?" I asked Brannigan.

He didn't answer. I looked behind me. The barrels were in the back, covered by a tarp.

"Is it all right if I let Meriel out?" I said.

Still no answer.

I didn't want to spring a gaff too early, but there was no one around. Surely I could let Meriel out safely and seal her in again if we approached a checkpoint. Assuming Brannigan would stop me if I was wrong, I kneeled on my seat to pry the lid off the barrel. It popped away.

But there was no Meriel inside.

"Where'd she go?" I said.

Brannigan didn't answer.

"Did you let her out? Brannigan? Hello?"

He just sat there, not saying a word, as the cart bumped over the road.

My skin started to prickle. "Where are we?" I said.

At that, Brannigan finally moved. He nodded his cowled head forward. I turned to look.

There was a farmstead up ahead. I saw a house with an open barn beside it.

Wait. This wasn't right. That farm hadn't been there before.

And what was that noise?

clang

clang

clang

It sounded like someone hammering on metal. From the barn, I saw smoke rising from a stone chimney. A forge? A blacksmith?

The wagon rolled on, slowly approaching the farm. The sound was definitely coming from the barn. From here, I could see someone inside, though it was hard to make out the figure in the shade of the roof.

clang

clang

clang

We began to pass the farmstead. Suddenly, Brannigan reined his oxen to a halt. He waited, staring forward, as if expecting me to hop off.

"What is this?" I said.

He sat there, not moving, not saying a word.

"I'm not going anywhere," I said, "until you tell me where we are."

He turned toward me.

And I fell backward out of the carriage.

I hit the dirt hard, but I barely felt it. I scrambled away, turning only after I'd crawled a safe distance.

Brannigan's face. It was *gone*.

No. Not gone, exactly. It was ... scratched out. Like I was looking not at a man but at a painting of a man, except someone had taken a knife to the canvas. As if they hated the man so much, they couldn't bear to look at his visage.

"What are you?" I whispered.

Slowly, he pointed a gloved hand at the barn.

Then he turned away, hiding that awful scratched-out face. His cart trundled down the road. I watched it go, staring until I was sure it wouldn't come back.

All the while, the hammering continued behind me. Still shaken, I stood, my clothes dusted with dirt. I looked around at where the wagon driver had left me.

There was something odd about this farmstead, something I couldn't place. The Old Man and I had traveled much of Ayreth. We'd passed through countless hamlets, villages, and towns. Yet I'd never seen anything built like this. The house was circular but unusually squat, barely seven feet high, made of a mixture of dried mud and straw. The roof was a broad, gently sloped cone, fashioned out of what looked like dark green moss. The door—it appeared there was only one—was just simple wooden slats held together with a crossbeam.

The barn was made out of the same wood, slats nailed together loosely; the roof would leak badly in the rain. Cautiously, I walked around to the open side.

It was, indeed, a blacksmith's place, though a crude one. The forge was simple brick, the tools rudimentary, without refinement. A fire blazed in the hearth.

The blacksmith was there, facing away from me. The noise—*clang, clang, clang*—came from him hammering something on the anvil. He was dressed in a long multicolored patchwork tunic and heavy canvas trousers; an odd style of dress I'd never seen before.

The strangest thing, however, was the man himself. He was tall and lanky—too lanky, really, to be a blacksmith. He didn't have the muscles that would come with long hours working the forge. In fact, he looked awfully similar to—

"Gareth?" I said.

I walked around to the front of the anvil. Yes. It was Gareth. He was hammering away at a blade, but it wasn't steel. It looked like enamel, an odd milky-white—

That's one of the Dragon's Teeth, I thought with a shock.

"Gareth? Gareth!"

He looked up, barely a pause, before returning to hammering the ancient blade. "Oh. Hello, Cal."

"What are you doing?" I said.

"I have to make this," he said.

"Why?"

He just kept hammering.

"Gareth!" I said sharply.

He looked up, hammer still striking.

"Why are you doing that?" I said.

His arm faltered. He frowned. "I . . . don't know."

He stopped, looking down at the blade. Then he stepped back, startled, as he realized exactly what he'd been forging. "What am I—"

He looked up at me. "I'm dreaming," he said. Then realization dawned on him. "No . . . I'm not dreaming. Because if I know I'm dreaming . . . then I'm not dreaming anymore. *I'm in Shadow.*"

I half expected the vision to break apart, like it had when Meriel recognized me. This time, nothing changed.

Gareth stared at me in wonder and awe. "Cal? Is that really you?"

"Yes," I said.

"And we're *here*. We're really here. In Shadow."

Interestingly, Gareth's stammer had disappeared completely. Not mostly, like it usually did when he was happy or distracted, working hard on a problem. He still had that hesitant pattern of speech, but otherwise he spoke as if he'd never had any stammer at all.

"Do you know this place?" I said. "Where are we?"

Curiously, he walked around, touching the tools, the wall. He stared at the house beyond, frowning. Then his eyes went wide.

"I don't think that's the right question," he said.

"What is?"

"*When* are we?"

"When?"

"This is . . . Look at this construction," he said. "The house is wattle and daub, with a thatched roof. The tools are simple. And look at this. Look."

He beckoned me to follow him, pointing to a mark on the house. From a distance, I'd thought it was just a random shape in the mud. Now I saw the design was deliberate. A simple curve looped around itself three times in the center to form a three-bladed leaf.

"What is that?" I said.

"A triquetra," Gareth said. "It's an ancient symbol of eternity."

I traced the pattern with my finger. "I've never seen one before."

"Because no one draws it anymore. It's only found on our most ancient artifacts. The house, the tools, the symbol . . . if I had to guess, we're somewhere four thousand years ago."

Four *thousand* years? "Why are we here?"

"I don't know." Gareth wandered around the house, studying it. Then suddenly, he gasped. "Look!"

There were more symbols carved into the daub. But these ones, I recognized. They were animals.

Fox. Bear. Wolf. Rabbit. Sheep. Deer. And Leopard.

"The Spirits," I said. "The Seven Sisters."

If Gareth was right about this being four thousand years ago, then Keane had been right about the Spirits. We apparently did once know all of them. "I think—wait." I cocked my head. "Can you hear something?"

Gareth listened. He frowned. "That sounds like . . ."

"Singing," I said.

There was a hill behind the farmhouse. We headed to the top and suddenly we were looking down at a village. The houses were all the same squat wattle and daub with thatched roof—though a quick glance behind me showed the farmhouse we'd just come from wasn't there anymore. It had disappeared.

There was some sort of festival going on in the village. The singing we'd heard earlier came more clearly now, along with laughter. At the edge of the village, a half dozen girls, about seven or eight years old, danced in opposite directions, weaving in and out among each other in a circle, flowers in their hair. Every so often one would skip into the circle, then hop out as quickly as she could. Some sort of game?

The singing—at least some of it—was coming from them. It sounded like some strange, alien language; I couldn't understand the words. There was a boy watching them, sitting cross-legged on the grass. He clapped his hands in time to the beat—

"Lachlan?" I said.

He turned his head. "Oh, hey, guv. Gar."

We approached him. "Are you here?" I said.

He looked puzzled. "Where else would I be?" Though now he looked around, even more puzzled. "Wait. How'd I get here? Cal? What the . . . ? Is this a dream?"

"It's more than that. We're in Shadow."

"Really?" He stood, excited. "Shuna's sneezing snout. Never thought I'd get to see the place."

"What were you doing?" I said.

"Huh?"

"What were you doing?"

He pried his gaze away from the village. "Dunno, really. Just enjoying the music, I guess. Odd tune, eh? Never heard the like before."

Neither had I. But Gareth's eyes widened as he listened.

"Do you recognize it?" I said.

"Not the song," he said. "But the words . . ."

Suddenly, he paled.

"What's wrong?" I said.

"That's the Old Tongue," he said, breathless.

I suppose that wasn't unexpected. If this was four thousand years ago, then the Old Tongue was what they'd have spoken. So why was he so startled?

Gareth translated the lyrics. And then I understood exactly what had him so rattled.

> *The Hollow Man will meet you*
> *The Hollow Man will greet you*
> *He'll dip his bowl into your soul*
> *Then slurp you up and eat you*

"That . . . don't sound good," Lachlan said.

Suddenly, the girls broke off their dance—and ran to me. Two of them took my hands, pulling me into the village. Two more pushed me forward from behind, another two tugging me by the hem of my shirt. They chattered excitedly.

"Gareth?" I said, alarmed, as they dragged me through the crowd. "What are they saying?"

Gareth and Lachlan followed, wide-eyed with amazement. "'You have to meet him,'" Gareth translated. "'You have to come and meet him.'"

Did they mean . . . the Hollow Man? After that song, I really didn't think I wanted to. I resisted, but these Shadow children were impossibly strong.

"Ask them who they're talking about," I said, starting to panic.

Gareth spoke to them haltingly, the words of the Old Tongue unfamiliar in his mouth. When they answered, his eyes went wider.

"The Dragon's Light," he said. "They want you to meet the Dragon's Light. The Dragon's Light will guide you."

The Dragon's Light? The high priest of the dragon cult? Now I *really* didn't want to meet him. But the decision was already made. As the girls dragged me into the crowd, the crowd began pushing me forward, too, encouraging me on in the Old Tongue. Though I lost Gareth and Lachlan, stuck behind in the crowd, I didn't need Gareth's translations. The words were the same as the girls had said before. *The Dragon's Light will guide you.*

They pushed me toward a platform in the center of the village. There was a large stone statue atop it. A dragon. The statue was a dragon.

A man stood before it, blue-eyed and square-jawed, radiating command. He was bare-chested, his arms, shoulders, and face glowing with runes. His chest was glowing, too, but the figure wasn't a rune. It was an image of a dragon.

Like Bragan's tattoo, I thought, but that wasn't quite right. This man's dragon was much more detailed, much more refined. And it wasn't just an image. Even from here, I could feel the power that lurked within.

The crowd pushed me up the steps. The man—the Dragon's Light—beckoned me forward, a soft smile on his lips. As I approached, the crowd quieted.

The Dragon's Light spoke. *"Tavair damina tavartha."*

I looked into the crowd for Gareth. I couldn't see him.

"Tavair damina tavartha," the Dragon's Light said again.

"I don't understand," I said, scared now. "I don't understand what you're saying."

The Dragon's Light listened to my odd words, head cocked. Then he seemed to go *ah*—and spoke again. But this time, though he said the same thing, I could understand him. It was as if the answer was somehow whispered underneath.

"The gifts," he said. "Give me the gifts."

"What gifts?" I said, puzzled.

He looked down at my hands. So did I.

I was carrying the Dragon's Teeth.

"Where did—"

The Dragon's Light took them from me and lifted them high. *"Isbuídelend,"* he said. "Thank you."

Then he stabbed me in the chest with the blades.

And behind him, the dragon statue came to life.

CHAPTER 34

THE VISION SHATTERED. The pain didn't.

My chest. My chest was *burning*.

I lay there, tangled in my bedsheets, writhing in agony. I think I screamed. I must have, for the others piled into my room, alarmed.

Meriel was in her nightgown, but her knives were already in her hands. She looked around, confused. "What's wrong?"

I could barely answer. "He stabbed me," I gasped. Shuna help me, it hurt so *much*.

Foxtail sprang onto my bed and pulled away the sheets. She lifted my nightshirt, ran her fingers over my skin, searching. Other than the scars I'd had since I was six, there wasn't a mark on me.

It seemed impossible that I could feel this kind of torment without actually being wounded, but I did. There was nothing I could do but wait. Slowly, agonizingly slowly, the pain subsided, until it was a dull, aching throb in my rib cage. Foxtail sat cross-legged on my bed, a soothing hand on my burning skin.

Gareth and Lachlan looked at each other, horrified. Meriel saw that. "What is going on? What happened?"

"We were in Shadow," I said, exhausted. Lachlan spared me the conversation. He told the girls what he'd seen in that ancient village. Gareth filled in the rest.

"Getting stabbed in your dream did *that*?" Meriel said.

But she had it wrong. Even though she'd been there with me, she hadn't really wrapped her mind around it. We called it a dream, but it wasn't a dream. It was Shadow. I remembered what the Fox had said to me the first time we'd met.

Dreams are in your head, Cal. This is real.

Keane, too. *Shadow exposes you to magical, alien forces. Not just the mind, but the soul. The things that live there can tear both of those apart.*

That's what had happened to me, I realized. When the Dragon's Light stabbed me with the Dragon's Teeth, it wasn't my body that got hurt. It was my soul.

I pressed my hand to my chest, wondering if those blades had created their own scars, ones that would mark my soul the way the Stickman's whip had marked my flesh. Would this pain go away? Or would it remain, added to the pain I already felt every day?

The thought made my spirits sink. Regardless, there wasn't anything anyone could do for me. "I'm fine," I lied. "Let's just go back to sleep." Though tonight, I knew I'd be too afraid to even try.

It took some more encouraging, but they finally left. All except Meriel. "I can stay," she said. "If you want. In case something else happens."

I wanted her to. But if I said yes, she'd know I was worried. "It's all right," I said. "Probably be a while before I go back again, anyway."

She hesitated. "So . . . let's just talk. Or play some cards. Or something."

I looked at her. "Sure."

She borrowed Gareth's deck, and we played for a while, sitting on my bed, swapping jokes while she cheated outrageously and I pretended not to notice. I didn't really want it to end. But after a couple of hours, I saw she was getting tired, so I yawned and said, "We should try to get a few winks before sunrise."

I could tell she didn't want this to end, either. But she said, "All right," and collected the cards. At the door, she stopped. She opened her mouth, ready to say something—then at the last minute, changed whatever she was about to tell me. "Shuna watch over you," she said instead, and left.

"Meriel?" I called softly.

She stepped back into my doorway, waiting.

I changed what I was going to say, too. "Um . . . the wagon driver," I said, "who helped you escape. Brannigan. What did he do after you left the palace?"

I think she'd hoped I was going to ask something different, because she looked disappointed at the question. But she thought back, remembering. "He talked his way past Dathal's checkpoints, then smuggled me across the border into Ayreth. I hid in the barrel until we'd entered the empire. There was a city close by where he traded. Dunvegan, I think? I got off there. He gave me a few crowns to make my way; that's the last time I saw him."

"Did you ever see his face?"

She looked at me, puzzled. "Of course. I knew him my whole life. Why?"

"So you never saw it . . . scratched out or anything?"

"Scratched *out*?"

I lay back down. "Never mind."

It took nearly the whole day for the last of the pain to subside. Obviously, I was grateful it was gone. But the way it had lingered, even after I'd woken, made me wonder: If I hadn't fallen out of Shadow in time, would I have died? *The things that live there can tear mind and soul apart*, Keane had said. Which made me pretty sure the answer was yes.

I forced myself to put it out of my head. We had a gaff to continue. Though there wasn't much for me to do at the moment. I'd put off meeting Aidan until tomorrow because there was something Lachlan needed to do today. He took care of it early, heading to the Morrigan offices under his guise as a courier. When he returned, he gave me a thumbs-up. "Too easy, guv."

The stage was set. That made me feel a little better. And even better still when, though I was terrified to go to sleep that night, once I did, I had no dreams at all.

The next day, Aidan wasn't the only one to welcome me to the Morrigan offices. "May I introduce my uncle, J.R. Morrigan Junior," Aidan said.

J.R. Junior was a big man. He carried himself with the supreme confidence of hard-won, and no doubt occasionally brutal, success. He gave me what he probably thought of as a firm handshake. A better word for it was "crushing." It was all I could do not to howl.

"Delighted to meet you, Mr. Morrigan," I said.

"The pleasure is mine, Mr. Quinn," he said. Despite my obvious youth, he was treating me seriously. Aidan had told him I was here representing my father, and adding a noble house of Ayreth to his client list would bring even more prestige to his firm. "Mr. Farrell"—he motioned to Aidan—"informed me of our oversight. I want to assure you that this is *not* the way we do business."

He looked to Aidan, who stepped in, trying to show the same confidence. He couldn't really match it. "I must apologize," he said as he launched into his explanation: How they'd found the letter I wrote to them weeks ago, after all. How it had unfortunately gone overlooked.

I listened, already knowing this—because Lachlan had planted that letter yesterday.

After I told Aidan I'd written to his company and they never responded, I knew the first thing he'd do in the morning was search through his firm's correspondence. Had his clerks missed something? When they looked, they'd find nothing, and that might make him suspicious about what I'd said.

This was where Lachlan came in. That same morning, he'd entered their offices with a satchel of mail. As he delivered it, he slipped a false letter—my letter, asking for a meeting—between Aidan's secretary's desk and the wall. Then, on his way out, he'd pretended to spot it.

"Looks like one's trying to escape on ya, miss," he said cheerfully.

Lachlan had lingered just long enough to see the reaction. When the secretary read the letter, her eyes nearly popped out of their sockets. Here was the message from Alastair Quinn they'd been searching for and it was marked RECEIVED, stamped with that Morrigan stamp Gareth had stolen during his and Foxtail's break-in.

The secretary ran to Aidan, who turned as white as she did. This *was* their fault. And best of all, it confirmed my lie—a perfect setup for our gaff. Once again, I wished the Old Man were here to see what I'd done.

Now Aidan looked genuinely embarrassed. A less-decent man would have blamed his underlings for their mistake. Instead, he took the blame on himself. I liked him for that—which made me glad my gaff would end up helping the both of us.

I turned to his uncle. "Mr. Morrigan," I said. "I confess: When I came here this morning, I had no intention of doing business with you. But if there's one thing my father values, it's honesty. Mr. Farrell could have pretended your firm never received my letter. Instead, he's shown himself to be a man of great integrity. So I do believe I've changed my mind."

J.R. Junior nodded in satisfaction. "He shows great promise, our Mr. Farrell."

I smiled. "He certainly does."

The reputation of his firm protected, Aidan's uncle left us to continue on our own.

I leaned in, speaking quietly, even though, behind the glass walls of his office, no one could hear us. "Let me tell you why my father's sent me here," I said to Aidan. "I must impress upon you: what we discuss must be kept completely secret."

The Old Man had told me something once about big gaffs,

while waiting in a coffeehouse for a mark to pass by. *The best lies,* he'd said, *are built out of truths.*

What does that mean? I'd asked him.

He'd stirred his mug with his spoon. *At its heart, every gaff is a lie,* he'd said. *What you're offering is a lie. What the mark will get out of it is a lie. Often, these lies are nearly impossible to believe. Here's a scheme, you might say, that will make you ten thousand crowns, risk free. On its own, it's ridiculous. The gaff is obvious. No one would ever believe it.*

So you don't approach the mark like that, he continued. *First, you tell them something true. Something they already know, or even better, don't know but can learn for themselves, without you. Then build your lie on that.*

The thing to remember is that the mark wants to believe your lies, because deep down, he wants what you're offering. The more your lie is built on a truth, the more plausible it will be. And your mark will fall for it every time.

In this gaff, it wasn't Aidan's money I wanted. Yet I still needed to build this lie on a truth. "As you know," I said, "Bolcanoig's eruption has brought devastation to Garman. My father sees this as an opportunity. We need to rebuild our cities, our infrastructure. Instead of rebuilding the way it was, my father wants to do it better—with the technology already developed by Sligach. He wants to build a rail line in Garman."

"We'd be delighted to assist," Aidan said hesitantly. "But— forgive me, surely you're aware—the emperor has banned railways outside of Tullagh province."

"Yes," I said, "but Garman is nearly destroyed. My father thinks this might be the tragedy we need to change the emperor's mind.

We want to free ourselves from the Weavers' influence and improve the lives of our people."

Like the Old Man said, a lie based on the truth. Garman was in trouble. It did need to rebuild. Lots of people, especially here in Sligach, were unhappy with the influence the Weavers had. There was no evidence that the emperor would ever change his mind about rails, but given the tragedy, it was plausible. So Aidan would believe it. Because he *wanted* to believe.

I could already see it. He sat up straighter in his chair, getting more and more excited about the possibility. His firm stood to make a lot of money if this came to pass, sure. But it was more than that. He'd be the man who helped change the course of Ayreth's history.

"What is it your father's looking for?" he said, eyes alight.

I told him we wanted an experienced company to do everything: build our rails and the cars to ride over them. Aidan eagerly spent the next few hours showing me Morrigan designs and blueprints, trying to convince me.

Gareth might have understood what Aidan was showing me, but I didn't. It made for a boring afternoon. Eventually, I said, "This all seems very impressive. But as my father says, 'What the contract promises is rarely what the factory delivers.' He'll need proof that your lines are the most secure."

"I can provide it," Aidan said. "We own the contract that services Castle Cardogh."

"The emperor's prison?" I leaned back, acting impressed. "I wasn't aware."

"Indeed. So you see, we already have a good reputation with His Imperial Majesty. He would trust us above all to do the job."

"That does sound promising," I said.

Now he moved in for the kill. "There's no need to take my word for it. I can show you the Cardogh line itself."

"But . . . doesn't that train go *inside* the prison?" I said, sounding worried.

Aidan laughed good-naturedly. "I've been inside many times. It'll be no trouble; we have an excellent relationship with the warden. It's perfectly safe, I promise you."

"Well, then," I said. "I would like that very much. When shall we go?"

"We run the line every week. The next delivery is in three days, if that's convenient."

That was too soon for my gaff to play out. "I'm afraid I'm already engaged that day," I said. "Would next week work instead?"

"Of course," Aidan said. "I'm at your convenience."

I stood and shook his hand.

Back in our hotel, I told the others about our arrangement.

"You did it," Meriel said.

"No need to sound so surprised," I said, somewhat offended. "But I haven't done it. Not yet."

"Ain't you getting in the prison now?" Lachlan said.

"Yes, but we need to do more than get in there. We need to be able to explore the place, see how they operate."

"Can't you do that when you're inside?"

"Not if it's just me and Aidan. I won't have a good reason to look around, and no opportunity to go where I shouldn't. We need to create a distraction. A big one."

Foxtail gestured. *So what now?*

"Now," I said, "we have some fun. We're going to throw a party."

CHAPTER 35

WE RENTED A room at the Langham.

Meriel and I had already rented a pair of suites at that hotel last week under the names Alastair and Scarlett Quinn, in case someone checked up on us to prove we were who we said. Now we needed a private dining space for our party. There would be twelve of us: me and Meriel, Aidan and Orla, plus eight other guests.

In going through Morrigan's papers, Gareth had identified three people Aidan was looking to expand his business with. One, a Mr. Finn Campbell, was said to be a bit of a daredevil, a real risk-taker, so he and his wife became my first invites. The other two, plus their wives, were men who'd welcome the opportunity to hobnob with Aidan and the others. That just left my special guest, the most important guest of all—and the one who made me the most nervous.

I forced myself to stay calm as Meriel and I waited, dressed in our finest evening wear. I'd borrowed Galawan for the night, letting him perch on my shoulder. He was a good affectation for a young noble—half pet, half designed to impress. I'd already arranged for cocktails, so we stood around talking as people arrived, mixed, and mingled.

Meriel and I came as something of a surprise to our guests.

Though our invitations had referred to us as the son and daughter of the Earl Quinn, they hadn't expected us to be so young. It was a little awkward when they saw who their hosts were, but nobility was held in high esteem here, and the way Aidan treated me as a serious business contact went a long way toward smoothing out the age differences.

Finn Campbell, our daredevil, was particularly intrigued to meet us. "From Garman, eh?" he drawled. A bit of a dandy, it looked like he might have already had a cocktail or two before he arrived. "Never been out that way, alas. Always meant to go and scale Bolcanoig. Too late now, I suppose."

His wife, a woman with big hair who'd been cooing at Galawan, tittered. It was a bit vulgar to make a joke about the volcano's explosion, but I needed Finn to like me, so I said, "Go anyway. At least now you won't have to worry about your fear of heights."

He guffawed. "And I thought this party would be boring." With a wink, he and his wife went off to torment one of the other couples.

Aidan, for his part, was happy to sing my praises to the others. He'd been worried that his office botching my letter hadn't just put a bad light on his family's business, but our growing friendship. Orla appeared particularly grateful that hadn't been the case. She seemed to have a hard time fitting in with the other ladies here—they didn't take her seriously because she hadn't come from the same class as them—so she spent most of her time clinging to Meriel, gossiping with heads together like old school friends.

As for me, I waited for my final guest, growing more nervous with each passing minute. I was starting to think he wouldn't come. But then he arrived, his wife on his arm.

The others were surprised to see him. They recognized him, even though he wasn't wearing his uniform—because this was Phelan Riley, Chief Superintendent of the Sligach City Watch.

It was hard not to feel jittery at his arrival. I'd never met the man, but he was the head of the Stickmen in this city. And, aside from the obvious danger that presented, in a very real way, the Stickmen had shaped my entire life. There had been a young girl—I never knew her name; I'd just always called her "Mum," though she was clearly too young for that—who'd taken care of me in my earliest years. But after she disappeared and I got caught for stealing an apple, it was the Stickmen who'd flogged me, marking me with scars that would brand me forever as a thief.

Still, as nervous as Superintendent Riley made me, I was glad he'd come. His wife, Elva, who was known to be a bit of a social climber, was delighted to have the opportunity to rub elbows with some of Sligach's most influential couples. But the super-intendent had a wary look about him, certain I'd invited him to curry some sort of favor. No doubt he was expecting a bribe of some sort. *My family has this small legal problem, Superintendent. If you'd just look the other way, we could make it worth your while . . .*

That's actually what I wanted him to think—at least for now. So I just thanked him politely for coming, then returned to speaking with the other guests. Let the man wonder about it before I sprang my gaff.

After cocktails, we had dinner, during which Meriel worked to charm the other ladies. Once dessert was finished, she entertained them with parlor games and even did some simple card tricks I'd had Gareth show her, which the other women then tried to do themselves, to much giggling. Among the men, Finn dominated the conversation with broad stories and sardonic remarks.

Superintendent Riley remained aloof, and I could tell he was growing impatient. He kept looking at his watch, and when he checked it for the second time in ten minutes, I knew he was ready to leave. Time to move in.

He was studying one of the paintings on the wall without interest, alone. I brought him a fresh drink, which he looked ready to refuse, but ever polite, he accepted it. He only took the barest sip, giving a short glance to Galawan on my shoulder.

"Superintendent," I said quietly, "I'm glad you came. I was hoping to speak to you about something of a delicate matter."

I could see it in his eyes. *Ah. Here it comes.* He already looked prepared to refuse—and possibly cart me away, if what I suggested was outrageous enough. Lachlan had confirmed through Breaker contacts that Riley was that rare bird: an honest Stickman. So he was surprised when I said something entirely different.

"You've heard, no doubt, of our troubles in Garman," I said. "With the eruption, and the subsequent unrest? The rise in banditry?"

He nodded curtly. "Terrible business. My condolences."

"And what of our prisons?"

"Sir?"

I lowered my voice even more. "Our prisons. Have you heard of our . . . troubles?"

He paused. Whatever he was expecting, it wasn't this. "I have not."

"When Bolcanoig erupted," I said, as if passing along a secret, "two of our prisons were destroyed. Many of the inmates were killed, but several escaped. They're on the loose now, doing what criminals do, if you get my meaning."

"The bandits," he said, surprised. "They're not just desperate people. They're the convicts."

I nodded. "Our prince is doing what he can to round them up—quietly, so as to not cause general alarm. But as you might imagine, we have nowhere left to keep them."

He frowned, understanding. "A genuine problem."

"Indeed," I said. "His Highness has tasked my father with rebuilding the prisons. My father sees this as an opportunity to build them better: more humane, as well as more secure. He knows you have an excellent system in Sligach, so he's asked me—would you grant me some time to talk to you about your prisons? Perhaps even see your facilities?"

"Of course," he said, disarmed that I wasn't looking to bribe him after all. "I'll arrange a tour of Sligach Prison at your convenience."

"Very kind of you. And no doubt you have much to say about Castle Cardogh, as well."

"I'm afraid I have no familiarity with it."

I pretended to be surprised. "Really?"

"Cardogh is the emperor's prison. It's run by a regiment of the Riflemen."

"Surely you've visited the grounds, though? To observe?"

"Never."

"Oh!" I said, as if that was a terrible oversight. "Well, then, perhaps we can help each other. Would you like to see Cardogh? Mr. Farrell will be escorting me there on a tour of his rail system. It would surely be no trouble for you to accompany us."

He paused. I'd finally captured his interest. "I would like that, yes."

"Then let's arrange it." I went straight to Aidan, who was in conversation with the rest of the men. Meriel caught my eye on the way. She'd already started drifting the ladies toward them when she saw me go talk to Riley. Now the two groups were right next to each other—more than close enough to hear.

"Mr. Farrell," I said, "would it be any trouble for Superintendent Riley to join us at Castle Cardogh? He's expressed interest in seeing the grounds."

Aidan looked a little surprised but agreed easily enough. "Certainly. We'd be glad to have you."

Finn interjected. "Are you lot going *into* the prison?" he said, intrigued. "That sounds fascinating."

Meriel jumped on that right away. "It does, indeed. Can ladies come, too?" She turned to Orla. "We could have a picnic."

Orla laughed. "Oh, you're wicked."

But Finn's wife, Shuna bless her, thought that was a grand idea. "An expedition to the darkest place in Sligach? That sounds *delicious*, darling. I would very much like to see it."

"What say you, Mr. Farrell?" Finn said. "Is there room in that train for all of us?"

We'd boxed Aidan into a corner. While it was impolite for

Finn to invite himself, it would be even more impolite for Aidan to refuse. Besides, the reputation of his firm was at stake. "We have not only the most luxurious of cars, Mr. Campbell, we have the most spacious. Why, we could fit three times this many and still be comfortable."

"Excellent," Finn drawled. "Then it's a date."

Aidan looked to me, wondering if I'd object. He'd set up the trip for my benefit, after all. I gave him a look of pleasant innocence. *Fine by me.*

The party broke up not long after. Superintendent Riley shook my hand as he left—a touch more warmly than before. "Pleasure to meet you, Mr. Quinn."

"Likewise, Superintendent. We'll see you again soon."

And that was it. The last piece of the gaff we needed.

We were in.

CHAPTER 36

THE NIGHT BEFORE a big gaff was always the roughest.

When you were planning a job, your mind was full of possibilities, hard at work, preparing. And when you were pulling the gaff, there was no time to think at all. You were in the thick of it, in full focus.

But the night before . . . that was when the worries crept into your mind. You'd already done the scouting, the setup, the rehearsal. Now there was nothing to do but wait—and think of all the ways you could fail.

This had always annoyed the Old Man. We'd be sleeping by the fire—or, rather, he'd be sleeping by the fire; I was wide awake—and he'd know me so well that he'd suddenly call across the campsite. *Stop it, boy.*

I didn't say anything, I'd protest.

But you thought it. They can hear you fidgeting all the way in Westport.

So I'd lie there, completely still. As if that would fool him.

Boy . . . he said threateningly.

I can't help it, I said.

Breathe, he said. *Just breathe.*

Usually, that worked. Just breathe. In and out. Relax. Sleep. Dream.

I sat up, no longer in my bed. And I knew right away I was back in Shadow.

I stood, fear gnawing at my guts. The last time I'd been to the realm of secrets, I'd taken two swords in my soul. I wasn't keen on repeating that.

But I wasn't in that old village. I was in the forest again, the first Shadow-place I'd visited. And none of the other things I'd seen there were here this time: no frightened fox, no door to Meriel's past. Just the soft rustle of leaves in the breeze. I wondered if I'd see that crow again, or—

bonk

An acorn bounced off my head.

caw caw caw caw caw

I sighed and looked up. The crow perched on a branch above me.

"You're a real comedian," I said.

It cocked its head, as if trying to understand my strange sounds.

"Seriously," I said, "what are you? Are you Bran? A Spirit? Something else? Or are you just a bird? A curious bird trapped in Shadow. Sort of like me. Hey, do crows dream?"

The crow seemed to have no idea what I was saying. The whole thing was making me feel like a fool. "So did you come here to pelt me with acorns?" I said. "Or did you have something else to show me?"

I didn't know if the bird understood me this time or whether it had already planned to do it, but it flapped away, landing in a tree off to my left.

caw

When I came closer, it flew away again to another tree. And so it led me, once again, to another door standing free in the woods.

This door looked different from the one to Meriel's past. It was made of petrified oak and carved with a dizzying array of symbols. I hesitated, but they didn't look like Weaver runes. They were more intricate, curving and overlapping with each other. And when combined . . . it was odd. As if each symbol was its own but somehow became more than that when bound together.

The crow perched atop the door.

caw

it said. Then it flew away.

If I'd seen a door like this in the real world, there would be no way I'd touch it. Those symbols were enchanted with power—*massive* power. I could feel it, even without being able to see the magic through the Eye. In fact, thinking of the Eye reminded me of another door I'd seen not so long ago: the door to its chamber, in that cavern underground.

The thought made me pause. Things hadn't gone so well the last time I'd walked through a portal like that. And yet . . . I didn't feel this one was a threat. I didn't have any reason for that, but I felt it all the same.

The last place the crow led me was good, I told myself. I'd helped Meriel find peace with her past. Maybe this would help someone else, like Foxtail? She was the only one of my friends I hadn't yet seen in Shadow. On the other hand, that same door had eventually led me to Brannigan, which had led me to the Dragon's Light. Which had led to a pair of swords in the heart.

"This is stupid," I said out loud. I could go in circles like this forever. So I just took a deep breath, pushed the door open, and walked through . . . and found myself still in the forest. Nothing had changed.

No—almost nothing. The forest was the same. But when I turned around, the door I'd just entered was gone.

"Hey!" I called out. But the crow was long gone, too.

Was this another of the bird's pranks? With nothing else to do, I kept walking, in the same direction I'd been facing when I went through the door. After several minutes, the trees began to thin, and I came to a creek.

I decided to follow it because of something the Old Man had told me once. *If you're ever lost and you find running water, let it guide you. If you see any trash, go upstream. If you don't, go downstream. That way, you'll eventually run into people.*

The creek was pristine, so downstream I went. The trees thinned further as the woods came to an end. The water ran through a short grassland, then onto white sand, a beach along a riverbank.

And someone was there.

There was a girl sitting cross-legged on the sand by the river. She looked to be a year or two younger than me, maybe twelve or thirteen. She was dressed similarly to those girls I'd seen in that old village, in a light thigh-length tunic that matched her chestnut-colored hair, braided in a ponytail, with similarly colored strapped sandals. Though feminine, she looked toned, like an athlete.

She was singing softly to herself. The tune was pleasant but also a bit alien. I couldn't make out the words.

"Hello?" I said.

She barely turned her head to glance at me. "Hello," she said dismissively, sounding bored.

Then she did a double take, looking closer.

"Are you real?" she said. She sounded surprised.

"Um . . . yes?" I said. "At least I think I am."

"You're human!"

"Well . . . yes. Aren't you?"

She laughed, a friendly sound. "Of course not, silly."

I didn't know what to make of that. "You look human," I pointed out.

"What's that got to do with anything?"

I would have thought it was everything. But then, what did I know? "Fair enough, I guess."

"What are you doing here?" she said.

Good question. "I'm not really sure," I admitted. "I think I might be looking for a secret."

"Ah." She seemed to think that answer made sense. "Well, there are plenty of secrets around. Though you should be careful, human. You won't like all the secrets you find."

She didn't say it as a threat, more of a warning. Either way, I wouldn't have disagreed. "What are you doing here?" I asked.

She looked out over the water again. "It's pretty here." She sighed. "Besides, I have nothing else to do."

"What do you mean?"

"No one visits me," she said sadly. "They're angry."

"Who's angry? And why?"

She sighed again. "I did something I wasn't supposed to."

She sounded lonely. So maybe it was time to make a friend? She might help me understand what I was doing in this place. "Well, I'm here," I said.

That seemed to brighten her. "You are, aren't you?" She stood. "Do you want to play a game?"

"Um . . . sure."

"Come on."

She took off down the beach. I ran after her, my shoes churning the sand. "Hey!" I said. "Wait up!"

She turned, running backward, laughing. "You've got to move faster, human!" But she slowed down enough for me to keep pace.

I followed her onto the grass, then into the trees. We ran for a while, until I started to puff. I called after her. "Are you going to show me this . . ."

I trailed off.

". . . game?" I finished weakly.

I couldn't believe the view.

We were standing on the peak of a mountain. A stream sprang from the rock below us, the water sparkling in the sun, crystal clear. The air was cold and crisp, but in a refreshing, pleasant way. Down the mountainside, a trail led through the snow, the flakes a perfect white, unmarred.

And I could see for miles. For *hundreds* of miles. Forever, it felt like. There were woods, grasslands, lakes, a desert of burnt-umber sand, and an ocean in the distance. And we were high enough that I could see the brightest stars, even in the day-time. It felt like I was so close, if I reached up, I could touch them.

"Wow," I breathed, because I couldn't think of anything else to say.

The girl nodded, looking wistful. "It really is a beautiful world, isn't it?"

There was that sadness again. Before I could ask her about it, she pushed it away. "So do you want to play?"

"What are the rules?" I said, still gawping at the view.

"Let's have a race," she said. "Fastest one down the mountain wins."

It took a moment for what she'd said to register in my brain. A memory dredged up from long ago.

And my breath suddenly caught in my throat.

A . . . race?

"We can even have a wager, if you like," she continued. "I have some honey. Do you want to bet something? If you have any strawberries, I really like them."

I stared, barely able to hear her over the thumping of my heart. "You're going to jump in the stream," I whispered, "and swim down."

She stomped her foot, pouting. "Who gave it away? Did my sister tell you?"

Her . . . sister?

Oh *no*.

"You're . . ." I didn't finish that sentence. I didn't dare.

"How did you know I'd use the stream?" the girl demanded. "Have we met?"

"No. No," I said. "I just heard of this trick before. In a story." I looked frantically for a way out of here. I saw nothing.

Now the girl was frowning. "Come to think of it, you do look familiar. Where have I seen you before?"

"You haven't. I mean . . . I've never been here."

Out. How did I get *out*?

She studied my face. Then, suddenly, she stilled.

"You," she said.

"If I could just—"

"*You.*" She clenched her fists.

"Wait, now," I said. "Wait—"

"YOU!" she roared.

She came toward me. I stepped backward. I slipped.

I fell from the mountain

and hit the floor with a thud.

I lay in my hotel room, heart pounding so hard I genuinely thought it might stop. I stayed there, I don't know how long. I was scared to move. As if, if I moved, she'd catch me.

Eventually, I forced myself to get up. I went straight to Gareth's room. A light sleeper, he woke the moment I opened the door and turned up the gas on his lamp.

"What's wr-wrong?" he stammered, half cowering under his sheets.

"Oh, nothing," I said. "Except I'm pretty sure I just met Artha."

CHAPTER 37

GARETH STARED AT me, wide-eyed.

"The *B-Bear*?" he said, horrified. "You m-met the *B-Bear*? Where?"

"In Shadow," I said. "Except she wasn't the Bear. I mean, she wasn't *a* bear. She looked like an ordinary girl."

I started from the beginning, telling him everything: the woods, the crow, the door, the river. And the girl. "She led me to the mountaintop. I don't know how we got there, but there we were. And then she says, 'Let's have a race,' and I knew she was going to jump into—"

"The crystal stream," Gareth whispered. He knew the stories better than any of us. "The Fox, the Bear, and the Crystal Stream."

"Exactly. That story. *Exactly* that story. Even the bet was the same: honey for strawberries."

Gareth could barely believe it. "You were in a Fox and Bear story."

"It was more than that," I said. "That door I opened to get there was covered with these strange symbols. And I can't explain it, Gareth, but after seeing Artha . . . I think those symbols were put there by the Spirits. I think that was the door to Artha's prison."

After Shuna had told us they'd trapped her in "a prison for Spirits," I'd wondered what that looked like. I certainly hadn't expected what I saw. It was open and beautiful, and I got the sense that the Bear could go anywhere she wanted—as long as she stayed inside, whatever that meant. But the things she said. *No one visits me. They're angry. I did something I wasn't supposed to.* She had to be talking about her sisters.

I told Gareth all of this. He seemed surprised. "She was sad about it?"

"That was what was so odd," I said. "You saw how Artha was in the vault: raging, mad for power. She wasn't like that in Shadow. It's why, even after she said she wasn't human, it didn't occur to me she could be the Bear."

"So what was she like?" Gareth said, fascinated.

"She was . . . a girl. An ordinary girl. Lonely because she'd lost her family. In fact, you know how Artha is in the stories? The early ones, I mean, when she and Shuna are still friends? She was like that, friendly and playful. She didn't get mad until she realized who I was."

I remembered Shuna's words to her sister in the vault, as she pleaded for her to stop. *Won't you listen to me? Won't you remember who you were?* Long ago, Shuna had known a different Artha. I felt like that was the girl I'd just met.

Gareth looked pensive. "The s-stories were never clear about why Artha turned," he said.

"If you had to guess?"

He didn't have to think about it too long. "The Eye," he said. "Or the power the Eye promised. Or both."

Was he right? Was the Eye's influence what had corrupted Artha? And if it could do that to a Spirit . . . what could it do to me? How long could I keep this jewel in my head without losing myself?

It was terrifying to think about. Though I had an even bigger problem at the moment. "What do I do if I end up in Shadow again?" I asked Gareth.

He didn't really have an answer. "You might . . . I mean . . . you're not always in the same place. In Shadow, I mean. Maybe next time you'll be somewhere different."

That wasn't the most comforting thought. "I don't want to be in Shadow at all."

"But you keep going. Because s-something wants you to learn these secrets." He looked at me. "You said the same crow that led you to Meriel's past led you to Artha's prison."

I knew what he was getting at. "I asked it if it was Bran."

He paused. "What did it say?"

"Nothing. It just acted like a crow. But that doesn't mean anything. It could well be Bran, keeping its mouth shut about it. Or the Adversary itself, like Keane said, trying to fool me. Either way, how do I figure out whether what it wants is good or bad?"

Gareth was surprised to hear that from me. "You're . . . I mean . . . you're the . . ."

"I'm the gaffer. Except the Old Man never taught me to read birds," I said ruefully. "I wonder if the Eye knows."

Gareth's eyes went wide. He didn't even have to say it.

"That's a terrible idea, I know," I said. If there's one thing I couldn't trust, it was the Eye.

Still. *Are you friend, crow? Or enemy?*

I couldn't shake the feeling the bird was gaffing me. In fact, I was sure of it. But how? And why?

I thought about it, and wondered.

CHAPTER 38

With the morning came the day of our prison tour.

The tour group was in excellent spirits. Armed with the chance to show off his family's business, Aidan had ensured a trip fit for the emperor himself.

The typical train to Castle Cardogh, he told me, would just be the engine, a third-class passenger compartment for guards transferring in and out, and a pair of cargo cars, which carried both the supplies and the work crew, crammed in among the goods. For this adventure, however, Aidan had attached his company's most luxurious first-class car, laid out with wide chairs and broad couches upholstered in fine, soft leather. The walls were lined with varnished rosewood, with a gold silk carpet and blue velvet curtains tied back with gold rope to let the sunlight in.

Aidan had provided refreshments as well. For the morning, it was ripe fruits, plump berries, and creamy pastries, with freshly squeezed lemonade, coffee, and, for those who wanted it, sparkling wine. Finn Campbell, our resident daredevil, had brought along his own bottles of brandy, already cracking one open, though to his disappointment, none of the others wanted any at this early hour.

Thinking he might be a real asset today and wanting to stay

on his good side, I accepted a snifter. "That's our man Quinn," he said, clapping me on the shoulder and pouring me a measure that would stun a moose.

"Of course, for a proper journey," Aidan said, "there would be a separate dining car for additional comfort."

"We shall endeavor to survive our present hardship, Mr. Farrell," Finn drawled.

"Er . . . quite."

Meriel was farther back, keeping Superintendent Riley and his wife entertained. As the train pulled away from the city, the smog dissipated. We were now riding a hundred feet above the Cardogh River, its mile-wide expanse rushing below.

Everyone flocked to the windows, astounded. Even Finn, no stranger to wondrous sights, was impressed. "You should sell tickets, old boy," he said to Aidan.

The excitement quieted, however, as we approached the Rose Garden. The name Castle Cardogh conjured up romantic notions of old-time emperors like Aeric, sweeping across Ayreth with his dragon blades. The sight of it brought something else.

There was no doubt we were headed into a prison. Castle Cardogh was on an arrowhead-shaped island surrounded by craggy rocks, foamy white water crashing against it in waves. Walls of stone rose imposingly from the rocks, first a low wall, then a higher interior barrier, the main keep and three other stone buildings within. Riflemen manned both walls, protected behind crenellations.

The walls were twenty feet thick. It would take days of pounding with cannons to break through. And the prison had cannons of its own, mounted around the island on the towers, ready to return fire. If that wasn't enough, I saw the traps Foxtail had told me about. Near the tops of the walls on both sides, long rotating drums had been placed horizontally, spiked with two-foot-long edged blades. Any prisoner trying to scale those walls would have to climb over the drums first, and that would be near impossible. Putting aside the spikes, grabbing the drum would make it roll with their weight, dumping them back down to the ground.

"Fox and Bear," Finn murmured to his wife. "Remind me not to offend the emperor, darling."

As the initial shock of seeing the prison subsided, the buzz of excitement returned. The train began to slow as we approached the island. Morrigan had built a loading station inside the inner wall, and that's where the train chuffed to a stop. The guests stepped out eagerly, keen to actually be inside the prison.

I hung back slightly, watching. The replacement guards, in their crisp red Rifleman uniforms, hopped out of the third-class compartment. One of their own officers—Captain Wilkins, I heard one of the soldiers call him—was waiting. He checked their names against a list, then sent them straight to the barracks to stow their gear. Beyond them, the workers piled out of the cargo cars.

Diana had told us the jobs on the crew were doled out by the Breakers to the poor who needed to earn money through honest work: a community service Sheridan had instituted to keep the Low Quarter, where many of the poor were housed, on his side. To that end, the crew was as varied and raggedy a bunch as I'd ever seen. The youngest looked to be around eight—judging from the soot caked under her fingernails, she was their chimney sweep—with the oldest around seventy, though he was probably younger and just aged by a hard life. I was pleased to see such a motley group. We'd fit in easily when we returned.

The crew captain, Blocker, was a no-nonsense sort of man with a gaunt face and beady eyes. Diana had told us Blocker wasn't a Breaker himself, though he worked for Sully, the foreman, who remained behind at the station. Blocker waved to Captain Wilkins, then shouted at his crew to get moving. They started by unloading the cargo cars, bringing out carts, chests, and barrels, which two of the children began rolling immediately down the ramp.

"What is all that?" I asked Aidan curiously.

"Hmm? Oh—fresh water, mostly," he said. "The river's a little too foul to drink here. But there's beer for the guards as well, and some wine for the officers."

I lingered, studying how the crew worked, until Aidan invited me over to meet the warden.

Colonel Deavers was a fussy fellow. I could already see it in his dress: jacket spotless, boots polished to a mirror shine, hair carefully coiffed, nails filed. Even the way he shook hands, cautious and perfunctory, said he wouldn't have done it at all if politeness didn't demand it.

"Welcome to Castle Cardogh, Mr. Quinn, Miss Quinn," he said to me and Meriel.

"Very kind of you to allow us inside, Colonel," Meriel said.

"Not at all."

"Have you met Superintendent Riley?" I said.

"I don't believe I've had the pleasure."

I caught the condescension in his voice. It was slight, almost undetectable, but to my gaffer's ear, it was there. Colonel Deavers was a Rifleman, the emperor's own. Riley, head of the City Watch or not, was just a common Stickman.

Interestingly, Riley caught it, too. I saw it in the way he held on to the warden's hand, keeping his grip a little too long, just enough to make Deavers uncomfortable. For his part, Riley had the contempt of a working peace officer for the danger-free living of a modern soldier. Deavers would have never seen real combat; the emperor already ruled all but Torgal, and we were currently at peace. I'd seen that thought in Riley's eyes as he'd studied the prison's defenses. He'd been impressed by the walls, but he thought the cannons silly. No one had attacked Castle Cardogh in six hundred years.

If Deavers didn't care much for the superintendent, he cared even less for the other guests—least of all the dandy Finn, who'd disembarked with his glass of brandy still in hand. Finn noticed the look and smirked.

Deavers glanced at his pocket watch, then snapped it shut. "Shall we begin?"

Before we arrived, Meriel and I had gone over the plan. We had five critical goals on this trip. Learn the prison's layout. Discover where the prisoners were kept. Watch how they moved about. Study the patterns of the guards. And most of all, find out where the guards kept the keys. A sixth, secondary goal was to watch the work crew and how they operated. The next time we came here, we'd be with them. And we'd only have one shot at getting Cormac and the Hollow Man out.

The warden led us toward the main keep, waving at the other buildings as we passed them. "That's the barracks," he said. "The mess hall is there, and the castle's physick. The third is the administrative center, which contains our offices."

The grounds were remarkably well kept. I was expecting nothing but dirt; instead, it was mostly grass, with a few well-tended gardens. Here I saw how the prison got its nickname: the beds were blooming with roses. It gave the place a heady, floral scent.

"That's unexpected," Finn said.

"Our groundskeeper manages the gardens," Deavers said. "We send the roses to the emperor. For some reason, they grow better on this island than anywhere else in Ayreth."

Meriel and I exchanged a glance. I'd seen enough enchantments by now to know that didn't sound natural.

Superintendent Riley walked beside me, studying the prison with a practiced eye. Believing I wanted to learn about it, he pointed out various aspects of the security. I filed away what he said about the guard patrols; I already knew the walls offered no way out.

One of the guards stepped out of the door to the central keep just as we arrived. He looked startled to see the group of tourists in front of him—and interestingly, when he saw the warden, for the briefest moment, he looked guilty. He stood aside, stepping somewhat farther back onto the grass than he needed to, saluting as we strode past.

Deavers paid no attention to the man at all. If he had, he might have noticed the flush of the guard's cheeks. Thinking I knew why the man's face was so red, I walked a little off the path, just to get closer to him as I passed, and smelled a faint whiff of beer. I was right; he'd been drinking on duty. That information could be useful. I memorized his face and filed it away.

The warden shuffled us inside. While it was bright and fresh on the grounds, the keep was dank and gloomy. Since the castle had originally been built for defense, virtually no sunlight penetrated these halls, just what little streamed through the old arrow slits. Whale-oil lamps hung instead, giving the whole place a fishy smell. Some of the ladies covered their noses with handkerchiefs.

Deavers was used to it. He took us through what had once been an entrance hall into the narrow corridors of the prison. Some of the cleaning crew were here already, scrubbing at the stone.

At the top of a long staircase down was a guardroom. The guard inside was sitting behind a desk; he stood and saluted as the warden entered. "Sir."

Deavers acknowledged him. "Greeley. I'm going to show our guests one of the cells."

"Of course, sir," Greeley said, and he hurried round the desk to a peg on the wall. A key ring hung from it, four large keys attached. I caught Meriel's eye as the soldier handed the warden the ring. *That's it. That's what we need.* Meriel nodded.

Keys jingling on the ring, Deavers led us down steep, narrow stairs. "There are cells on each floor," he said, "but they're all essentially the same. Most of them are empty, so we keep the prisoners next to each other, down here."

"Empty?" one of the ladies said. "I thought this was the emperor's prison."

"The emperor's *special* prison, my lady. Normally, the men kept here would be hanged for the seriousness of their offenses. On occasion, however, His Imperial Majesty chooses to make an example of certain criminals who have offended him greatly. Those, he sends to us. It happens only rarely."

"Didn't I hear the Kingsthief was here?" Meriel said. "The boy who stole the emperor's scepter?"

"Not exactly, miss," Deaver said. "The Kingsthief, Oran of Sligach"—here he gave a pointed look at Superintendent Riley, as if it was the Stickman's fault he'd allowed such a terrible child to grow up in his city—"escaped after his crime. The boy we have was a conspirator of Oran's who was captured during the theft. His cell is at the end of this hall."

"Really?" Meriel said, as if fascinated. "Could we see him?"

"I'm afraid not. Our prisoners are allowed no contact with anyone, except during their monthly examinations. Even then, they are not permitted to speak unless commanded."

"But . . . what about exercise?" Meriel said, shocked, barely playacting anymore. "When do you bring them out of their cells?"

"Never," Deavers said. "They never leave their cells. They live inside them until the emperor chooses to offer clemency. Or death."

And he used one of the keys on the ring to show us.

CHAPTER 39

THE CELL HE unlocked was next to the stairs. I'd assumed the cells would be barred, easy to see inside. Instead, a thick steel door, secured with a heavy padlock and a bar on the outside, kept each prisoner sealed in their own isolation.

At the base of the door was a swinging slat with its own sliding steel bar to keep it shut when not in use. "The prisoners are fed through that," Deavers explained. "They receive their daily meal in the evening: bread, stew, and water. They pass the bowls back through the slot in the morning, along with their waste bucket."

He swung the door open. There were no jokes now, not even from Finn, as we saw the inside of the cell.

It was the bleakest place I'd ever seen. Just four stone walls with the tiniest arrow slit near the ceiling to provide light. On cloudy days, it would be near dark; at night, pitch black, even with our twin moons. There was no furniture inside: no bed, no chair, nothing. The prisoner housed here would sleep on cold, hard stone.

The walls had been carved with graffiti. Some were drawings: a few skilled, most crude, several vulgar. Some of the prisoners had scratched their names or curses or pleas for freedom. And some were tick marks, counting the days—or maybe the years. It was impossible to tell.

I didn't need to pretend. I shuddered at the horror of it. Even Superintendent Riley looked grim at the way these poor wretches would live. "I can't imagine a man could survive in such conditions," I said.

I was trying to lead the warden to give me information. He took the bait. "On the contrary, sir," he said. "Our prisoners are given sufficient nourishment, and medical care if they become ill. And we keep no implements of torture within these walls. The emperor wishes them to live long lives, so they have time to reflect on how they've wronged him. Why, the oldest prisoner we have has been here ninety-seven years."

"Ninety-seven *years*?" Finn said. "Fox and Bear, what's the man done?"

"Treason," Deavers said simply.

"How in the world could anyone live that long?" Finn's wife said, skeptical.

"Some form of enchantment, no doubt. Our physick has always reported him in perfect health, if frail."

"But who *is* he?" I said.

"I don't know his name."

That was too much for Superintendent Riley. "For mercy's sake, man, how can you not know the fellow's name?"

The warden gave him a cool look. "The prison was not provided one when he arrived. For the man's crime, our previous emperors wished his name to be forgotten. And so it has."

I glanced at Meriel. We knew his name—sort of. The Hollow Man. "He's lived in one of *these* for a century?" Meriel said, horrified.

"At the end of the other hall," Deavers said. "Opposite the Kingsthief's accomplice, in fact."

Horrible or not, now we knew where our targets were. The tour continued, the warden showing us some of the more historic places in the castle, where famous prisoners had been kept, and the like. I was surprised—and more than a little puzzled—to note there were almost no guards inside the keep itself. Just the man in the guardroom and the drunk, who wandered by occasionally on patrol. I commented to Superintendent Riley about it.

"Why would they bother?" the Stickman said, unhappy with what he'd seen. "The cell doors are closed, and the men inside are never let out. There's no reason to stand around watching prisoners you can't even see."

"But there are so many guards on the walls. Dozens of them."

"That's for show. To make His Imperial Majesty's prison look impressive to anyone who approaches it. None of it's needed. These wretches couldn't break out if the Fox herself helped them." He shook his head. "Our trip here was wasted, Mr. Quinn. If your father wishes to build a more humane prison, there is nothing in Castle Cardogh for him to learn."

For my fictional father, no. But I'd learned exactly what I needed.

And now there was only one thing left to get.

I didn't spot anything else of interest during the tour—except in one particular chamber. It was a shrine room, tucked away in a separate space among the cellars under the keep. Inside it were two idols, one of the Fox, the other of the Bear. A Spirit acolyte—someone who dedicated their time to caring for Fox and Bear shrines, collecting donations to keep them in good repair—had come in with the work crew this trip. She'd already polished the shrines and was currently collecting the offerings laid there by the guards. It was interesting to note that all of them—coins, flowers, a ration of bread, a written note—were offered to the Bear, the patron Spirit of soldiers. The Fox got nothing.

The acolyte smiled at us as we came in. I found my gaze drawn automatically to the Bear. I was still rattled by meeting her in Shadow.

None of the other guests were particularly fascinated by the shrines, which made my interest stand out to the acolyte. "You can make an offering, if you like," she said to me.

That pulled me from my thoughts. "Sorry?"

"An offering. I'll collect these later if you have something to give."

The others were watching me. Oops. To cover up, I said, "I was just—these shrines are incredibly detailed. Colonel Deavers said they were ancient?"

The acolyte nodded. "I believe they were part of the original build of the castle. What's interesting is how they're made of different materials. The Bear is the same stone as the castle walls, whereas the Fox is petrified wood."

Both idols were well made, but whoever had shaped Shuna had done an extraordinary job. It wasn't just lifelike. It had actually managed to capture her personality. Shuna gazed out at us, looking friendly and somewhat mischievous. It was almost as if the sculptor had—

Wait.

No.

I didn't believe it.

CHAPTER 40

MY FINGER WAS heating up.

The one with the seven-banded mark of the Spirits. It was growing warm.

I stared at the idol of the Fox. "It can't be," I whispered.

"Is everything all right? Alastair?"

I turned as Aidan touched my arm. The others were watching me curiously. Meriel was chewing her fingernail.

"Sorry," I said, trying to cover up my alarm. "The shrine just reminded me of . . . There was one in Garman. My favorite. My father told me it was destroyed in the eruption."

"Of course," Aidan said. "I'm so sorry. I keep forgetting how hard things must be for your people back home." The others murmured their sympathy alongside him. Though Finn watched me curiously for some time after.

As for Meriel, she gave me a look of her own. *What was that about?*

I couldn't tell her here. But when I did, she'd understand what all this meant. I'd used an idol of Artha in the Weaver vault to call forth the Bear. The Fox had told me she had an idol somewhere of her own. *It's in Sligach, I think.* Turns out she was right—because I was pretty sure this Fox idol was the one that summoned her.

As if this gaff isn't insane enough, I thought. Well, I couldn't worry about it now. I wasn't going to go anywhere near that idol, that was for sure. Instead, the tour over, I followed the others out into the courtyard.

Spurred on by his wife, Aidan had taken Meriel's suggestion of a picnic seriously. He'd even brought along a few rail employees to prepare it. While we'd been wandering around the keep, they'd set up a pair of long tables in the grass with food and drink, and a canopy overhead to keep off the sun. The whole arrangement lightened the mood, and soon everyone was having a grand old time, like this was some holiday outing. I don't think any of them noticed the Riflemen on the walls, glancing down at the party with envy. Colonel Deavers, teetering on the edge of rudeness, declined our invitation, begging off with an apology that he really had to return to his duties. Superintendent Riley didn't mind seeing the last of him.

In a way, I was glad for the impromptu party. It would make Meriel's and my next gaff easier. Still, the whole thing struck me as ridiculous. Those poor prisoners inside, living a life of isolated torment, and here we were, having a picnic. It was almost obscene.

But I kept up my role, lounging about with the rest of them—at least for a while. Then I gave Meriel a prearranged sign—I scratched my nose with my left hand—and she excused herself from the other ladies.

She called up to one of the Riflemen standing guard on the wall. "Pardon me. Where might I find the facilities?"

He looked confused. "The what, miss?"

"The facilities. You know, the water closet."

"Oh." He looked a little embarrassed. "I'm, uh . . . afraid there isn't any proper water closet in the castle."

"Don't be silly," she said. "There must be. You gentlemen do still go, don't you? Or does the emperor train it out of you when you join the guard?" She giggled.

He turned beet red. "Er . . . yes, miss. I mean—no. We have—it's called a garderobe."

"A what?"

He really did not want to be having this conversation with an outrageously pretty girl. "It's a sort of . . . latrine."

I spared him. "I know what he's talking about, Scarlett."

"I'm glad someone does," she said.

"Where is it?" I said.

The Rifleman looked relieved to be off the hook. "You can use the one in the administrator's office, sir."

"Thank you, we'll find it." I escorted Meriel away from the rest of the party.

"What is a garderobe, anyway?" Meriel asked me when we were alone.

"It's a hole in the castle. Like an outhouse, but inside. You go, and . . . stuff . . . just drops into the water." Come to think of it, I didn't want to be having this discussion with her, either.

The second we were out of sight of the party, we changed direction. Instead of the administration office, we headed straight into the keep. The lack of guards inside was a huge stroke of luck.

I thought we'd have to dive and dodge around; instead we could work quickly.

There was a spiral staircase to one of the upper levels. I hid there, peeking out, while Meriel hurried to the guardroom where we'd seen Deavers collect the cell keys.

"Pardon me." Meriel knocked on the guardroom door, poking her head inside. "I think I'm lost. Is this the way to the garderobe?"

"No, miss," I heard the guard Greeley say. "You'll want to use the one in the administration office. It's the next building over."

"That's where I was supposed to go," she said, pouting. "I suppose that's why I'm lost. Could you show me?"

"Sorry, miss. I'm not allowed to leave the guardroom except for emergencies."

Shuna's snout. Time for plan B. I left my hiding place, hurrying down the corridor.

"But this *is* an emergency," Meriel insisted, switching to playing a spoiled girl.

"I'm very sorry," Greeley said. "I have strict instructions—"

"There you are," I said to Meriel. "Whatever are you doing in here?"

"I'm *trying* to find the *garderobe*," Meriel said.

"You're in the wrong building— *Look out!*"

While the guard's attention was on me, Meriel took a step backward.

Then she fell down the stairs.

CHAPTER 41

SHE WENT TUMBLING, head over heels.

"Scarlett!" I shouted.

Greeley stared in horror as Meriel rolled down the steps. He chased after her, panicked.

Coins tumbled from her pockets as she fell, jingling on the stone as they bounced. I followed, pretending to be panicked, too. "Scarlett!"

She hit the bottom, sprawled out, unconscious—or apparently so. I hoped she was faking. That fall had certainly looked real.

Meriel hadn't been pleased when I'd told her what my plan was for getting the key to the cells. If she couldn't pull Greeley from his station—and I'd suspected he wouldn't leave—then the only thing we could do was create a distraction.

"Those stairs next to the guardroom," I'd said. "Can you tumble down them without breaking your neck?"

"Of course," she said, grumbling.

"What's the matter?"

"Ardal trained me in acrobatics for years," she complained. "I can walk a tightrope with my eyes closed a hundred feet off the ground. Yet all you ever ask me to do is fall down."

"Sorry." But it really was our best shot at removing that guard from his post. He'd never just sit there if he saw her get hurt. I'd told Meriel to toss a handful of coins as she fell, too. The added distraction would buy us more time.

"Miss," Greeley said, kneeling down and shaking her. He looked terrified. This had happened on his watch. "Miss!"

"Where's your physick?" I grabbed his shoulder. "Your physick, man!"

That seemed to rouse him. "In the barracks. I'll—"

I cut him off. "I'll bring him. Stay with her!"

"But—"

Too late for him; I was already bounding up the steps. And Meriel had started moaning in pain. He turned back to her. "Miss? Can you hear me?"

Perfect.

I darted into the guardroom and closed the door. I didn't have much time. Carefully, so as not to make any noise, I lifted the key ring from its peg and placed it on the desk.

Now came the tricky part. We couldn't just steal the keys. It would be noticed that they'd gone missing. We'd have to copy them instead.

So I dropped my trousers. Strapped to the inside of my leg was a long metal box. Inside that was a key-copying kit from the Lemon Tree: ten pairs of wax blocks.

I took the first key off the key ring. Then I pressed it into one of the wax blocks and clamped the other block over it to squeeze them together. The wax, softened by the warmth of my body, gave enough for the key to sink into it, making an impression.

Gareth, who'd shown me how to do this, had told me just pressing the keys in wouldn't be good enough. To be sure all the finer details made an imprint on the wax, I'd need to squeeze each key between the blocks for a full minute to let the wax form around them. And there were four keys here.

So I counted seconds in my head. *One . . . two . . . three . . .*

It was absolutely nerve-racking. I'd watched very closely when Deavers had unlocked the empty cell. Assuming that was the key to all the cells on this floor, I started with that one. But with no guarantee, I'd have to do all of them.

Twenty-four . . . twenty-five . . . twenty-six . . .

I could hear voices downstairs through the door. Meriel had "woken." Now she'd have to keep the guard with her for at least four minutes.

Thirty-eight . . . thirty-nine . . . forty . . .

I'd told her to pretend at first to be insensible, incoherent. If Greeley tried to leave her, if he got worried that I hadn't come back, she'd need to grab him and hold him there.

Fifty-two . . . fifty-three . . . fifty-four . . .

Play the helpless little girl, I'd said. Guards were suckers for that.

Fifty-nine . . . sixty.

Careful, now, the Old Man said. Gareth had warned me not to pry apart the wax blocks too quickly. If I did, they'd break, and the blank would be ruined.

So I pulled on them slowly. So . . . painfully . . . slowly.

They came apart. Delicately, I removed the key and checked

the impression. It looked good, but I didn't have time to confirm it. On to number two.

I pressed the second key on the ring into a different pair of wax blocks. Then I held it.

One . . . two . . . three . . .

I heard a sound.

Someone was coming.

CHAPTER 42

I STOOD THERE, frozen, the count continuing in the back of my mind. The footsteps sounded like the drunk, doing his patrol. If he came in here, he'd see me with my pants down, the prison keys out, and me making wax impressions of them. Not even the Old Man could talk himself out of that one.

Fifteen . . . sixteen . . . seventeen . . .

"What's goin' on there?" a voice bellowed.

I cringed, and the blocks nearly slipped from my hands, slick with sweat. That voice had come from just outside the door.

Twenty-nine . . . thirty . . . thirty-one . . .

"Mullins!" the guard downstairs called. "This lady's fallen down the steps."

"I didn't do it!" Mullins protested. "I wasn't even here!"

"You idiot! Go get help. Her brother went for the physick, but he probably got lost. Hurry up!"

"Fine, fine." He paused. "Are those crowns on the stairs?"

"They're the lady's! Move your backside, or I'll tell Wilkins you sneak drinks from the beer casks!"

"All right, all right." Mullins stomped off, grumbling.

I could breathe again. But not for long.

Fifty-nine . . . sixty.

I pried the wax apart. Careful . . . careful . . .

Done.

Two keys down. On to the next.

One ... two ... three ...

I counted out the third key with no problem. But when I pulled those blocks apart, I was too impatient. One cracked, snapping off in my hands.

Shuna's sneezing *snout*. I'd have to do it again.

One ... two ... three ...

I counted the full minute. This time, I pulled the blocks more slowly, and they came apart with no trouble. One more to go.

One ... two ... three ...

I could hear Meriel talking downstairs. She was no longer pretending to be woozy.

Eighteen ... nineteen ... twenty ...

Time was running out. Come on, come on.

Forty-one ... forty-two ... forty-three ...

I heard footsteps. Someone else was coming. Oh no.

Fifty-four ... fifty-five ... fifty-six ...

They stomped past the guardroom, hurrying down the steps. The physick, I guessed, with Mullins.

Sixty.

I wanted to rip the blocks apart. But I'd already made that mistake once, and I was running out of time.

Carefully, then. Carefully.

And ... the wax pried apart. I was finished.

I stuffed the blocks back into the case. Then I tucked the case under the strap inside my leg and did up my trousers.

Now the keys. Put them back on the key ring—in the right

order. *Never miss the little details*, the Old Man always said. *The little details will rooker your entire gaff.* So. Four . . . three . . . two . . . one.

Done.

Key ring back on peg. Keys facing the right direction, too. The little details.

Done.

All done.

Just one problem. I was still trapped in the guardroom, with two guards and the physick downstairs.

Then I heard Meriel's voice. "Thank you so much," she said. "How clumsy of me. I'm so embarrassed."

"Nothing to be embarrassed about, young lady," the physick said. "Could happen to anyone."

"You're too kind," she said. "But—oh, Artha's heart, I've dropped all my coins. Could you help me collect them?"

Shuna love you, Meriel, I thought. For while they were all bent over, picking up the lady's crowns, I slipped out of the guardroom and hurried downstairs.

"I got lost," I said. "Scarlett! Are you all right?"

"She's perfectly fine, sir," the physick said. "Just a little bruised. I hope you're not too troubled about it."

"Well, my heart nearly stopped," I said truthfully. "But I'm better now."

CHAPTER 43

W E RODE THE train with the others back to Sligach.

The outing was a great success for everyone. All the guests were buzzing with the thrill of seeing the inside of Castle Cardogh and living to tell the tale. They'd lord this over their social circles at their next dinner party. Next several parties, probably.

Aidan, too, was delighted. He'd impressed three potential business partners with his train and his hospitality. They were already talking about bringing custom to Morrigan and Sons. A huge coup for the young Director of New Business.

He shook my hand. "I do hope this trip helped you make a decision," he said.

"Absolutely," I said. "I intend to give your firm the highest recommendation to my father when I return. Of course, the ultimate decision rests with the emperor, so ..."

"I understand. The wheels of empire grind slowly. In the meantime, I hope you'll keep in touch. I would hate to lose your friendship."

"Me too," I said, and I was surprised to realize I actually meant it. Inwardly, I sighed, and hoped one day I wouldn't have to gaff anyone anymore.

Superintendent Riley was satisfied as well, in his own way.

I shook his hand at the station and said, "Unfortunate trip for both of us, I suppose."

He shrugged. "Nothing useful to learn, true. But at least my curiosity is sated. Good day, Mr. Quinn. I wish you and your family well."

The others said their goodbyes, with much thanks for arranging it. "All thanks to Mr. Farrell," I told them, with the hope that he really would gain their business.

Finn Campbell was the last to shake my hand, a curious smile on his face. "You're an interesting one, Mr. Quinn. You and your sister both."

"Likewise, Mr. Campbell," I said.

"Best of luck on your adventure, then. I imagine I'll read about it in the newspapers soon enough."

My heart skipped a beat. "Adventure?"

"As I said, Mr. Quinn: you're an interesting one." He winked. Then he kissed Meriel's hand in goodbye, offered his wife his arm, and left the station.

"What was that about?" Meriel asked.

"He's rumbled us," I said quietly.

Her eyes went wide. "How?"

"Don't know. But I think he was lying about having never been to Garman. He must have recognized our accent didn't quite fit."

"But then he's known we were on a gaff since last week!" Worried, she stared at the exit he'd left through. "Will he turn nose?"

"On us? Not a chance."

"Why not?"

I smiled. "He wouldn't find it nearly as entertaining."

⌒◡

When we returned to our hotel, I handed the wax blocks off to Gareth. He inspected them and declared them good enough. We then told the others what we'd seen, both at the Sligach station and inside the Rose Garden.

For their part, Foxtail, Lachlan, and Gareth had made a pain of themselves in the city, all to draw away the Breakers. The three of them had cased different railway offices, safe manufacturers, and costumers, the same as they'd been doing since the start of the gaff to keep Sheridan off our trail. Foxtail, who'd shadowed us to the station, confirmed no one had followed us today.

That was it, then. On the ride back, I'd already formulated our plan for the escape. I'd still have to work out a few of the finer details, but for now, I told the others the main points. "We'll need to prepare. And Lachlan, let's get the keys made from these blanks right away. But don't go to the Lemon Tree. Even if Collins can't tell where they're from, I don't want to give him the chance to get curious. Go through Diana. Let her find a different fence."

He gave me a thumbs-up. "Righto."

"And while you're with her," I said, "tell her to prepare her own plans for escape. We're going in on the next train."

CHAPTER 44

I DREADED GOING to sleep that night.

I was terrified of running into Artha again. But I also kept thinking of what I'd seen in Castle Cardogh. As everyone turned in, I hung out in Gareth's room for a while, talking of nothing, until I finally said, "Shuna's summoning statue is in the prison."

He stared at me. "How ... I mean ... how do you ... ?"

I held up my hand, showed him the seven-banded mark. "This got warm when I approached it."

"Are you ... thinking of using it?"

I wondered if I could. There was obviously some magic inside the mark. Would it be enough to summon the Fox the way it had the Bear? I got this horrible image of my finger shattering like the ring. Made me doubly sure I didn't want to try it.

But that wasn't the only thing that had me thinking. "Another big coincidence, wouldn't you say?"

Gareth frowned, understanding. I'd already remarked how the only man who could tell us about the Spirits just happened to be in Sligach. And Shuna had told me she last saw her idol in Sligach—which, again, is where we just happened to need to go. Even more than that, it was in the Rose Garden—where the Hollow Man just happened to be. "What are the odds?" I said.

Gareth shook his head. "You couldn't . . . There's no way . . . Near zero."

"Right. Which means it's not a coincidence that idol is there. That's pretty much the only thing I know."

"Do you think Shuna l-left it for you?"

"Actually, no. She genuinely forgot about the idols until I'd mentioned them outside Carlow. It has to be that old trickster she mentioned."

But who was that? Bran? It would make sense, if the crow that kept leading me through Shadow really was the Crow. But "trickster" also made me think of the Adversary. And it was entirely possible it was neither.

"I wish you could just tell me who it was," I said.

Gareth looked guilty. "S-sorry."

"No, no. I didn't mean it like that. It's just . . . you're the smartest person I know. Except maybe the Old Man. And he and I don't exactly speak anymore."

Outside of my head, anyway. I really wished he would come back and help me. If there was one thing I knew, it was that I was trapped in one giant gaff. And no one knew gaffs like him.

Yet you don't seem to have much to say about it, I commented.

Much to say? he said, amused. *I told you to stay away from this mess from the start. Don't blame me, boy. It's you who was always the contrarian. How many times do I have to tell you? Fiddling with nature—*

"Is for fools," I said. "I know, I know."

Gareth blinked. "Pardon?"

I flopped back on his bed. "Wasn't talking to you."

As it turned out, I didn't see Artha—at least not that night. Or the night after that. Since we had a full week until the next train to Castle Cardogh, we spent our days preparing for the job. Lachlan had the keys made through Diana. He also arranged with her the clothes we'd need for the gaff. I had Foxtail go dig up our buried enchantments and bring them back; we'd need a few of them. The rest—the Dragon's Teeth in particular—she buried in a new hiding place north of the city. Unless things went perfectly in the Rose Garden, we'd have to flee Sligach immediately. And when had things ever gone perfectly for us?

Beyond that, we practiced over and over how we'd pull the prison break. As if that wasn't enough, we also had to keep up our fake gaff to convince Sheridan's tails that we were actually planning to steal the gold shipment from the trains. It meant a week without rest, with us constantly on our toes. By the night before the job, I hadn't even had time to worry about seeing the Bear in Shadow again.

Which meant, naturally, that's exactly where I ended up.

CHAPTER 45

I RECOGNIZED WHERE I was right away.

I was standing knee-deep in the grass. The creek I'd followed the last time I'd visited Shadow burbled past me, flowing down the beach into the river. And there, on its bank, was Artha.

She paced back and forth, hands clenched, sandals kicking up sprays of sand. She looked furious. She looked like she wanted to tear something apart. I was pretty sure that something was me.

I dove into the grass. The only thing that had spared me was that she hadn't noticed me appear. Yet.

From what I'd seen the last time, Artha had some control over what this prison her sisters had trapped her in looked like. But her control wasn't total. As she stomped through the sand, the air warped around her, like she was trying to bend it to her will. I caught brief flashes of different landscapes—different worlds, with strange skies and alien creatures—but she couldn't make any of them come forth. The land remained a peaceful, beautiful riverside.

Hoping she'd stay focused on that, I crawled through the grass back toward the woods, trying to keep out of sight. I'd just made it to the tree line when I heard a rustle.

I froze. Had Artha spotted me? I was too far from the riverbank to hear her there, but I couldn't see anything through—

bonk

An acorn bounced off my head.

Heart sinking, I looked up. The crow was in the branch above me.

caw

"Oh, not you again," I whispered. "Go away."

It cocked its head at me, as if wondering what I was doing hiding down there.

caw

"Are you trying to kill me?" I whispered. "She'll hear you. Go away. *Please*."

The crow flew off into the trees. With a deep breath, I laid my head on my arms, trying to calm my thumping heart.

Then I was hauled from the grass by my collar.

A strong arm tossed me across the field. I rolled, stumbling to my feet. I looked back to see Artha stomping toward me, eyes blazing.

I ran for my life. I made it as far as the beach, where my shoes sank into the sand, slowing me down. I tried to keep my footing, but I was going too fast. Arms windmilling, I sprawled headfirst into the dunes.

Panicking now, I turned, crawling backward. Artha followed, moving with incredible speed. She yanked me up by my shirt and shook me.

"YOU DARE?" she roared.

She threw me across the beach, then stomped forward to pick me up again. She didn't look any bigger than Meriel, but her strength was beyond human. She lifted me like I was nothing and tossed me along the bank.

I scrambled to my feet, my mouth full of grit. "Wait," I said, spitting out sand. "Please!"

"*Please?*" She grabbed me and shook me. "You mock me! You toy with me! You trap me in this prison then pretend to be my friend! And now you dare to beg me for *anything*?"

She slammed me into the ground at her feet. I cringed, pleading silently for Shuna to appear.

"I will tear you apart, human!" Artha shouted. "I will make you *pay* for what you've done to me! And then you will *beg* me for release!"

The air warped around her again. But this time, it was Artha herself who seemed to shift. Her form wavered, distorting into something much bigger. The Bear.

But she couldn't change. Each time, as the form of the Bear began to replace her, it vanished, returning to that furious girl. And as I watched each attempt fail, I realized something else.

I wasn't in pain.

Artha had tossed me like a rag doll. By now, I should be bruised, battered, broken. But other than the usual ache of my scars, I didn't feel anything. The worst I'd got was some sand in my mouth.

"You can't hurt me," I said, barely aware I was saying it out loud. "In this place . . . *you can't hurt me.*"

She stared at me, full of rage.

Then, suddenly, she burst into tears.

All of Artha's fury drained away. She fell to her knees, face in her hands, crying, shaking with great wracking sobs.

I sat there, not knowing what to do as she wept. She sobbed so hard, she could barely get the words out. "W-why do you h-hate me so much?"

Of all the things she could have said, that surprised me the most. "What? I don't hate you."

"Then why are you d-doing this to me?" she cried.

"I don't—"

"No one talks to me!" She wept, crying out across the water. "No one visits me! They stuck me here, all alone! Did Shuna send you? Did she send you to torment me?"

"I— No," I said, flustered. "I don't know why I'm here."

"Liar!"

"I swear to you," I said. "I don't know why I'm here. I didn't ask to come. All I know is that I don't hate you. I'm not your enemy."

She sniffed, wiping her eyes.

"I'm not your enemy," I said again, because she'd seemed to respond to that. "I'm not. And I never wanted to be. What happened in the Enclave, when I made fun of you . . . I didn't really mean it."

She sat in front of me, quiet, head bowed.

"I was lying, back in the vault," I said. "I called you those names because I was desperate. Lachlan was dying, and you were taking away the Dragon's Teeth, and I couldn't let that happen. I needed them. I needed them to save my friend."

"To . . . *save* your friend?" she said, head still bowed.

"He had primeval magic inside. It was destroying him. That's why I needed the swords. I needed the Eye and the Teeth to save him."

"Save him," Artha repeated quietly. "With the Eye and the Teeth."

"Yes," I said, confused. "What's wrong with that?"

She'd stopped crying. Now she just looked like a girl in despair, sad and vulnerable. "You don't know what you're doing," she said.

I paused. "What am I doing?"

She shook her head. "You're a fool, human. You're nothing but a fool. Just like me."

"I don't understand what you mean."

She curled up in the sand, hands under her head, like she was going to sleep.

"Go away," she said.

I awoke.

CHAPTER 46

Today was the day.

I didn't tell anyone about my trip to Shadow. I really wanted to talk to Gareth about Artha's strange reversal, but I needed him focused on the job. We had no time to talk, anyway, as Diana came to meet us before dawn. She'd arranged with the Breakers to take the job of tailing us today, so there'd be no one to report to Sheridan we were going to the Rose Garden. I warned everyone to keep a lookout for other tails, just in case. I didn't think Diana would double-cross us, but Sheridan could never be trusted.

Sully, the foreman for the work crew, was already at the station when we arrived. An oily sort of fellow, he watched over the crew captain, Blocker, and the workers as they loaded the cargo cars. Sully nodded to Diana with a curious glance at me, Meriel, Gareth, and Lachlan.

When Diana pulled him aside to give him the news—we'd be taking the place of some of the crew today—he frowned. I moved a little closer to listen in.

"It's odd, girl," he said. "Mr. Fox always says don't make no waves. 'Don't make no waves, Sully,' that's what he says, first when I met him, and every when since. So why's he sending new birds in, all surprise-like?"

"He's put fresh hands on your crew before, Sully," Diana argued.

"Sure, a one here and there, yeah. Slip this in, take this out. But not a whole team. Never a whole team. That makes waves, it does."

"Can't be helped. Mr. Fox needs 'em special for the snaffle."

"I hear you. I hear you. It's just odd, it is."

I didn't like the way he was looking at her. Diana had assured us getting Sully to let us on the crew wouldn't be a problem. Time for me to step in.

I was dressed as rough as I'd ever been. Baggy canvas shirt and trousers, worn leather shoes, with a split in the side of the left one. The absolute poor is what I looked like, blessed by the Spirits to have any work at all. I also had a bandage covering half my head, with makeup from our disguise kit used to give me blisters, like I'd been burned.

It was exactly the sort of detail the Old Man had always warned me to avoid. A half-bandaged face would stand out, and the last thing I wanted on this job was to stand out. But I didn't have any choice. I had to cover up my eyepatch. Though the guards at Castle Cardogh had seen me before, they weren't likely to recognize me in this getup. As the Old Man had taught me, *how* you're perceived—prince versus pauper—is given much more weight than what you actually look like. With my ratty clothes and dirt smudged on my face, the guards would never match me to that well-dressed, proper young noble who'd visited them the week before. But I couldn't do anything about my eyepatch. I had to wear it. And if they saw it again, they *would* remember.

So burn and bandage it had to be. As it was, this getup made me look a little fearsome. I used that, stepping up to Sully with a cold eye. "There a problem?" I said.

Sully shrank away a little. "No problem. No problem. Mr. Fox says you go, you go."

"Then stop wasting my time and send five of your crew home."

"Five?" He frowned. "Only four of you here."

I glared at him.

"All right. All right. You say five, five it is. They won't be happy."

"This will make them happy." I handed him five half-crown coins. "Happy *and* silent. Make sure they understand—if they want to keep their tongues."

He pocketed the coins. "No worries."

"And tell your head lad, Blocker, that we're setting the work assignments. He's not to argue. We say we're doing a thing, that's the thing we're doing."

Sully shrugged. "Whatever Mr. Fox wants."

I poked a finger in his chest. "One more thing, Sully. Those half-crowns go to the children we kicked off the crew. I find a single coin in your pocket—one you 'forgot' to hand over, say— I'll come visit you quiet-like."

He put up his hands. "No need for that, friend. I'll pass 'em along, you'll see."

The rest of the team was already helping the other crew load the cargo. Gareth and Lachlan rolled a beer barrel we'd brought with us into place at the back of the car. Meriel worked beside a young woman, piling the linens in one of the carts. I joined them.

Meriel needed her own disguise, because a girl who looked like her always turned heads, no matter what she was wearing. So, in addition to her raggedy brown dress, we gave her an ugly dye job, used makeup to change the contour of her eyes, put on a false nose and a fake wart from the disguise kit, and stuffed cotton in her cheeks to hide her cheekbones. I added a scar on her lip for good measure, and now she was unrecognizable as last week's Scarlett Quinn.

"Is he going to be a problem?" Meriel said quietly, nodding in Sully's direction.

"Yes," I said.

"D-do we w-walk away, then?" Gareth said, worried.

"Too late. It's this or nothing. Don't worry, I know how to deal with Sully." At least I hoped I did. "Lachlan?"

He wiped his brow, sweaty from lifting the barrel. "Yeah, guv?"

"Would Galawan recognize faces he's only seen once before?"

"Sure as Shuna's a fox. He's right proper clever, he is."

I left them to load the cars and stepped out back, where I'd told the little sparrow to wait for us, outside the station. When I whistled, he came down from the eaves, landing on my finger.

"Got a job for you, Galawan," I said, pulling out a letter. "I need you to pass along a message."

The bird tweeted a friendly little tune.

CHAPTER 47

WE DIDN'T GET to watch the journey into the prison this time.

The cargo cars had no windows. We crammed ourselves in with the other work crew as Sully shut the doors. One of the Riflemen overseeing the transfer then padlocked the car shut from the outside. Now only a guard inside Castle Cardogh could let us out.

It felt awfully claustrophobic in that car. The atmosphere inside was hot and sticky, and the only light—and air—came through the tiny grated vent in the roof. With the whole crew breathing, that vent wasn't big enough. If they left us in here for much more than an hour, we'd suffocate.

Fortunately, the trip across the river only took twenty minutes. We bumped and swayed with the motion—no first-class springs on this car—until we heard the whistle and felt the train slow to a stop.

A Rifleman opened the door—Mullins, that guard I'd seen last week, once again smelling faintly of alcohol—and we piled out, sucking in the floral air of the Rose Garden with relief. Blocker started issuing orders, a few of which I'd given him before we boarded.

"You two!" He pointed to Lachlan and Gareth. "Take the water to the barracks, and the beer and wine to the buttery. And you two," he said, pointing to me and Meriel. "Linen carts to the barracks. Then come back for the mops. Let's go, let's go! Train heads back at seven. You ain't on it, the soldiers'll find you a cell."

Mullins smirked at that. Lachlan and Gareth began rolling barrels down the ramp as ordered. Meriel and I began to follow with our cart.

"Boy."

The voice froze me in my tracks. I turned.

The officer who'd been overseeing the duties last week was here again. Captain Wilkins. "Come here," he said.

I went, looking humble, heart thumping underneath. Had he recognized me? Last week, he'd been so focused on his duties, I would have thought he'd barely remember the guests.

I put on a Sligach Low Quarter accent and kicked my voice to a higher register. "Yes, sir?"

He nodded at my head. "What happened to you?"

I put a hand to my bandage. "Caught in the fire, sir," I said. "In the Rowland blowup."

As I'd proved already this job, the best lies were always based on truths. There really had been an explosion last week at a warehouse in the Rowland district, when a lamp had fallen and ignited some barrels of whale oil. It had taken out half the building, leaving a pillar of smoke that had hovered over the city for three days. I was glad for it. If there hadn't been a fire, I'd have had to set one.

The officer stuck his thumb under my bandage and lifted it a little. I wasn't sure if he did that to test my story or whether he was just curious to see what the explosion had done. Fortunately, the Old Man had taught me well. I'd put the burn makeup on under the gauze, too. *If you're not going to play a gaff properly*, as he said, *there's no point in playing it at all.*

"Papers claimed no one died in that fire," Wilkins said.

"No, sir, not a one o' us. I was one o' the few what was caught when the tiles came down, but me mates pulled me out, they did. A true miracle, sir, and that's no lie. Blessing o' the Fox, it was."

The captain let my bandage go. I'd put ointment on my "burn"; he wiped his thumb off on his handkerchief with a slight look of distaste. "The Bear's the brave one, boy. Artha's the Spirit who pulls lads from fires. Make sure you leave her an offering next time you pass a shrine."

"Yes, sir. I will, sir. Thank you, sir."

He waved me away. Meriel and I pushed the cart down the ramp as I blew out a sigh of relief. Collins at the Lemon Tree might have been a pain in our backsides, but there was no denying it: the man sure sold good disguise kits.

Meriel and I met up with the boys in the barracks. They'd already put the beer barrels in the back of the storage area. Except for one.

"Open it," I said.

We pried the lid off. And out crawled Foxtail.

We'd dressed her as poorly as the rest of us. But she had something special with her, too: the enchanted cloth mask Gareth had stolen from the Enclave, the one that copied faces. Before we'd come here, we'd put the mask on Diana so it would look like her. Then we gave it to Foxtail before sealing her inside the barrel.

She put it on now. Like before, the enchantment of Foxtail's mask interfered with the cloth's magic. The visage of Diana was lifeless, more like a wax replica than the girl herself. It wouldn't stand up to scrutiny. But as long as Foxtail kept her head down, scrubbing away on floors and the like—she'd even taken her hair out of her ponytail so it would hang in her face, which was the first time any of us had seen her do that—she wasn't likely to be rumbled. The work crew were a familiar sight to the guards, and not a particularly interesting one, so they didn't pay attention to them anymore.

Foxtail had also brought in the rest of the enchanted items and thieves tools I thought we might need. She handed them out. "All good?" I asked everyone.

"Ready, guv," Lachlan said.

I nodded. "Then let's get to work."

CHAPTER 48

WE NEEDED TO time everything just right.

The train back to Sligach would leave at seven p.m., twelve hours from now. That was more than enough time to break out Cormac and the Hollow Man—*too* much time, in fact.

We couldn't start the escape right away. The earlier we removed the prisoners from their cells, the greater the chance their disappearance would be detected before the train left. Of course, we couldn't leave it too late, either. If seven p.m. came round and we hadn't finished our mission, the job was sunk. This gaff would be our most delicate balance yet. We were fighting the clock as much as the guards.

So we actually did get to work—proper work, right alongside the cleaning crew. We restocked shelves in the pantry, changed linens in the barracks, scrubbed floors in the administration office, and hauled garbage across the compound to dump it down the garderobe, to mix with the rest of the waste flowing into the Cardogh River. We didn't even approach the keep until the afternoon.

Even then, we stayed away from the prisoners at first. The keep had four floors, so we started at the top, where no one was held, scrubbing away at the stone. We set Meriel as a lookout to confirm the patrol patterns hadn't changed from before. They hadn't. There was still the one guard, Greeley, in the guardroom, and Mullins did the rounds past the prison cells, though he followed no pattern we could detect.

As the day passed, we grew more and more restless. We left the bottom floor until the sun was sinking. The encroaching darkness would help hide our gaff.

"Let's do it," I said finally, and the others sprang to life. After Lachlan and Gareth finished cleaning the guardroom, working around Greeley with his feet up on the desk, we all moved downstairs to the cells.

I set Lachlan and Meriel to mop the stairs, keeping a lookout. Foxtail joined them after bringing a linen cart filled with rags down to our floor. Gareth and I hurried down to the end, where Colonel Deavers had told us Diana's brother was kept. I sure hoped he was right.

We'd made four keys from those wax blocks I'd smuggled out. Gareth greased the keyhole, then tried all four of them, one after another.

None of them worked.

Gareth had warned us this might happen. The impression a key made in wax was never perfect, so the keys made by Diana's locksmith wouldn't be exact. We'd have to make some adjustments on the fly.

Gareth studied the keys. "Which one do you think?" I said, glancing about nervously.

"Th-this one." He pointed out some grease marks on the key.

"The pins in the lock made these. I need to f-file it away there."

He got to it, using a file Foxtail had smuggled in just for this. Gareth scraped away at the key where the marks were, then tried it again.

Still no go. He filed some more.

Lachlan had come closer, mopping the stone. "Can't keep scrubbing the same spot forever, guv," Lachlan whispered.

He was right, but we couldn't rush Gareth. The more nervous he got, the longer this would take. "Take your time," I said.

In truth, there was another risk here, and not just from Mullins coming round. Gareth had to file just the right amount off. If he scraped too much away, the key wouldn't lift the pins to the correct level. And then it would never work.

Meriel whistled from down the corridor, a cheerful tune. *Guard's coming*, that signal meant.

"Quit that, you," Mullins grumbled as he approached. Meriel stopped whistling and bowed her head.

Gareth tucked his file away and knelt on the stone, trembling. "Just scrub," I said quietly. "We're only doing our job."

Mullins strode by. "Out of the way, out of the way," he said.

We stood aside as he passed. He barely glanced at us.

Good. When he'd gone up again, Gareth resumed his testing. Try the key. File away the metal. Grease the lock. Try the key again.

And then—

clack

We stared at each other. Then Gareth opened the cell door to see the figure huddled inside.

It was a boy, a year or two older than us. He cringed in the far corner, holding his hand up to squint against the light pouring in from the hallway. His clothes—if they could even be called that, just sackcloth and thread—were rough and filthy. The smell hit us the instant the door opened. *They haven't bathed him since they put him in here*, I realized. That was what, two years ago? It was a horror.

He curled up even further as we approached. Deavers had claimed they never tortured the prisoners, but from the way Cormac cringed at our entrance, I had to believe a guard—Mullins, almost certainly—stopped by occasionally to administer a beating of his own.

"It's all right," I said reassuringly. "Diana sent us. We've come to get you out of here."

He stared at me, at my bandage, at my apparently burned face. "Diana?" he croaked.

I wondered when the last time someone even spoke to him was. "She hired us." I knelt beside him. With the stench, it was all I could do not to gag. "We'll get you out. But you have to change your clothes, all right?"

He looked around, dazed, as if this was some sort of dream. Gently, I took his arm. He flinched at my touch, but he did allow me to help him up.

We'd have to do more than dress him differently, though. I'd made a mistake.

Deavers had never opened a door with a prisoner behind it, so it hadn't occurred to me how bad the smell would be. Our clothes could disguise Cormac, but that reek would be a dead giveaway.

"Scrub him down," I said to Lachlan and Gareth. They stripped him, then scoured his skin with our brushes and mops until the smell was just unpleasant.

Meanwhile, I took off the top layer of my own clothes. Underneath, I'd worn a second shirt and trousers exactly the same as the first. Cormac was a little taller than me, so I unrolled the cuffs a bit. Then I dressed him in what I'd been wearing. For shoes, Foxtail had an identical pair as mine hidden in the linen cart.

Now for the final piece. I took the face-copying mask from Foxtail, put it on myself, then gave it to him. "Put this on."

Cormac shied away from it.

"It's all right, I promise," I said.

Reluctantly, he slipped it over his head.

And suddenly, I was staring at a mirror image of me.

I hadn't worn the mask before, so I'd never experienced this. It was the strangest thing, seeing someone else with your face. He—I—looked puzzled, and scared. Something about that made my stomach churn. *This isn't natural*, I thought.

You passed natural a long time ago, boy, the Old Man said. *No point in second-guessing now.*

Quickly, I finished the disguise. I removed the top layer of my head bandage—I'd doubled that, just like I'd doubled my clothes—and wrapped the extra gauze around his head.

Now he really did look like me. Mostly. He was an inch or two taller, and much gaunter in the limbs, though the baggy clothes covered most of that. He didn't walk like me, either, more hesitant, unsteady. Any gaffer would realize instantly this was a double. But most people only paid attention to the face, and the mask made the two of us a perfect match. He'd pass. I hoped.

Time to find out. "Get him to the train," I said to Lachlan, "and bring those clothes back with the mask." We'd leave Cormac hidden in one of the empty barrels in the cargo car and disguise the Hollow Man the same way once he was out.

Lachlan escorted Cormac away, giving fake-Cal a mop and bucket to hold, a distraction for the eye. "C'mon, mate," he said kindly. "You're almost free."

One down, one to go. We locked Cormac's now-empty cell back up. Then Gareth and I hurried to the other side of the hall, bringing Meriel and Foxtail as lookouts again.

"W-which one?" Gareth said, motioning to the cells.

The doors all looked identical. So I looked at the floor instead. There was only one door with recent scrapes on the stone where the food slat opened and closed. "That's got to be it," I said. "Try the same key."

Gareth slipped it in and tried to turn it. It didn't work.

Too much to hope for, I guess. So Gareth started in on the keys again. He greased the lock, found the most likely candidate from the other three from the grease marks the pins left on it, then got to filing. We had to stop when Meriel signaled the patrol.

Foxtail, her steel mask now exposed, had to hide under the rags in the linen cart as Mullins walked by again. Meriel's tune had apparently got in his head; the guard was whistling it now. He ignored us this time as we stood aside, but I detected a stronger scent of hops as he passed. He'd nipped into the beer barrels between rounds.

When he was gone, Gareth got back to the lock. Grease. Try. File. Grease. Try again.

Clack.

The key turned. I clapped Gareth on the back, then opened the door.

And the two of us stared in horror.

CHAPTER 49

WE'D FOUND THE Hollow Man.

There was no doubt this was the right cell. Both Sheridan and Colonel Deavers had told us the Hollow Man was Castle Cardogh's oldest prisoner, here for ninety-seven years. The man inside, slumped on the floor, certainly looked the part. Ancient, wrinkled flesh sagged over his bones. Long gray hair fell past the sunken cheeks of his weathered face, his eyes closed. His clothes were nothing but tatters, worn to the barest threads, faded to a dull gray. He was so dirty with stone dust, it was hard to tell the difference between his rags and his skin.

He didn't look like a danger at all. But whoever the Hollow Man was, he'd been singled out for special treatment. Because unlike Cormac, this man was shackled to the wall.

Rusted chains hung down from a spike driven into the stone. The chains ended at manacles equally caked with rust. *Ninety-seven years in this cell*, I thought. It was impossible for him to escape, yet they'd still kept him shackled. I wondered what he'd done. *Treason*, Deavers had said. Still, did the Hollow Man deserve *this* kind of punishment? Did anyone?

We didn't have time to ponder it. "Get him out of there," I said to Gareth.

The Hollow Man didn't react as Gareth approached him.

Though his eyes remained closed, I didn't think he was sleeping. He just didn't care we were there.

Gareth turned the manacles over, inspecting them. Flakes of rust stuck to his hands. He looked up at me, wide-eyed. "I c-can't."

My guts sank. "You don't have the right key?"

"There isn't . . . I mean . . . there *is* no r-right key. There's no keyhole."

At first, I thought Gareth meant the hole had rusted over. But when I inspected them, I realized what he was telling me. There was no visible keyhole because there was never a keyhole at all. After they'd put these manacles on him, they'd welded them shut.

My mind recoiled with the horror of it. They hadn't merely been keeping the Hollow Man in prison. They'd literally just shackled him in, ninety-seven years ago, not even allowing him enough chain length to reach the door of his own cell.

Who are you? I wondered again. *What could you possibly have done?*

Either way, we were in real trouble now. I ran outside to Meriel. "Get Lachlan back here," I said.

She hurried after him. Gareth and I locked the Hollow Man's cell back up, then stood around, waiting nervously. When Meriel returned, I was shocked to see Lachlan wasn't the only one accompanying her. I was with them, too—the fake me, Cormac in disguise.

"Why did you bring him back?" I said to Lachlan. "You were supposed to leave him on the train!"

Lachlan spread his hands in apology. "Couldn't get him there, guv. He got scared of the guards when I tried to go up the ramp. Had to take him back to storage and calm him down, I did."

Shuna's snout. I should have anticipated that. I'd seen the way Cormac had cringed when we opened his cell. His time in the Rose Garden had wounded his courage badly. My mind raced with what to do with him. We'd smuggled in our thieves' tools with Foxtail, so if worse came to worst, we could always knock him out with our snooze goo and try to hide him at the bottom of the linen cart. But he was really too big to go unnoticed. There was a more-than-good chance that would get us caught.

I took Meriel aside and told her the problem. "Treat him gently," I said quietly. "See if you can encourage him. But I can't have a duplicate of me running around until then. We'll need to put him back in his cell. And he won't want to go."

He didn't. Cormac began to panic when we told him. "No," he said, moaning. "No no no *no*—"

"It's all right," Meriel said, soothing him. "We came all this way to get you. I promise you, we won't leave you behind. We don't leave any of us behind. Not ever."

Lachlan reassured him, too. "Trust the guv, mate. We'll get you out, sure as Shuna's a fox. You got me promise as a Breaker. Until the earth takes me."

The motto seemed to calm him. "Until the earth takes me," he whispered, remembering. It was enough to get Meriel and Lachlan to walk him back to his cell. Which only left our bigger problem.

"How do we get the Hollow Man out of here?" I asked Gareth.

"We could . . . I mean . . . we could try to break them. The m-manacles."

"We'd have to chisel them off," I said.

Gareth nodded.

That would make way too much noise. Greeley, upstairs, would be sure to hear metal banging and check it out. We hadn't brought a chisel, regardless.

"Could you g-gaff the guards?" Gareth asked. "Get them to remove him from his cell?"

Given the way they'd shackled him in, not a chance. "The only way he's leaving here is if he's dead."

"We have the ... I mean ... what about the disguise kit?"

"Make him look dead?" I said.

I considered it for a moment, but that wouldn't work. Even if we could color his skin so he looked pallid enough, they'd never free this man without examining the body. They'd see he was breathing even before they checked his pulse. When Meriel and Lachlan returned, I told them the problem.

Lachlan chewed his thumb, thinking. "What if we gave him the weeping sickness?" he said. "Ain't nobody going near that."

Right—that ring Lachlan stole. If it looked like the Hollow Man had the weeping sickness ...

I cursed. I hadn't told Foxtail to smuggle all our enchantments in, just the ones I'd thought would be useful. "We don't have it with us."

Lachlan suddenly looked a little guilty.

"Lachlan?" I said. "What did you do?"

"Um ... I might've snaffled the ring again, guv." He reached under his belt and pulled it out.

I stared at the thing. "You took it back ... even though I *ordered* you not to?"

"It *is* mine," he said defiantly. "What's the point of being a thief if you can't even enjoy what you nick?"

I took him by the shoulders. "Lachlan," I said, "right now, you are my favorite person in the whole world."

He beamed at me. "See? I knew you'd come round."

CHAPTER 50

We sent Lachlan up to the guardroom. I followed, listening from around the corner.

"Hey," Lachlan said. "You. Uh ... sir?"

Greeley's voice echoed from upstairs. "Yeah? What do you want?"

"Got an emergency, mate."

"What's the problem?"

"Think one of the prisoners croaked it."

There was a pause. "What are you talking about?"

"Croaked it," Lachlan said. "Left the empire. You know. Dead-like."

There was another pause.

Then I heard a chair scraping. I ran back to join the others. Gareth had already locked the Hollow Man's cell up and wiped away the grease. Now the three of us stood back from the steel door, looking concerned.

Greeley came around the corner, Lachlan in tow. "What makes you think he's dead?" the guard said.

"The smell, mate. Stinks something awful round his cell."

Greeley stopped, rolling his eyes. "You idiot. They all smell like that."

"Nuh-uh," Lachlan said. "This is the rot, this is."

Greeley wavered. I could tell he still thought Lachlan had mistaken the stench of unwashed prisoners for the smell of decay. But he couldn't just ignore the boy's claim. A dead prisoner was something he'd have to check for himself. He resumed walking toward us, shaking his head.

Then he stopped.

His eyes widened slightly as he caught a whiff of the dead juice we'd bought from the Lemon Tree, sprinkled just behind the cell door. It smelled, as one thief had put it, "like a thousand corpses rotting slowly in the summer sun."

This was unquestionably the scent of death. Greeley glanced at us, worried now, as he approached. Hesitantly, he kneeled on the floor and slid back the locking bar on the food slat. Then he lifted it to look inside.

With the slat open, the full blast of the dead juice got him right in the face. He reeled away, retching. "Shuna's teeth," he breathed. But he was proper worried now. "Where in the twin moons is—Mullins! *Mullins!*"

The lazy soldier had just come around the corner, doing his rounds. "What?" he said, somewhat surlily.

"Get Captain Wilkins. Now!"

Mullins frowned, but he went. Greeley waited, standing back with the rest of us, not wanting to get close to that smell again.

Soon enough, Captain Wilkins marched down the steps and around the corner, Mullins behind him. "What's the problem, Greeley?"

The guard pointed to the door. "I think this one's dead, sir."

Wilkins slowed, just like Greeley had, when he got close

enough to smell the dead juice. He stared at the door. "Isn't that . . ."

Greeley nodded.

"You have the key?" Wilkins said.

Greeley ran back to the guardroom, returning with the jingling key ring. We got the full reek of the dead juice once more as the door creaked open. Wilkins made a face, but he steeled himself against the reek and marched into the cell.

The Hollow Man lay curled against the wall in his shackles, his back to us. Wilkins grabbed the prisoner's shoulder and turned him over.

Then he cursed. "*Artha's bleeding paws!*"

The captain backpedaled so fast he tripped over his own feet, landing hard on the stone. He crawled out, only half rising before making it through the door. He backed against the wall, eyes wide with panic.

The Hollow Man's flesh was seeping. There were boils all over his skin. They swelled, red and inflamed. Some had burst, sending streaks of horrid yellow pus oozing down his cheeks. His eyes looked sunken into his head, his lips cracked, his tongue swollen and purple.

The other guards, who'd been watching, reeled back, too. "That's the weeping sickness!" Greeley said in horror.

It certainly looked like it. Before locking the Hollow Man's cell back up, we'd put Lachlan's ring on him, dabbing his neck with dead juice. We'd also poured a decent amount of snooze goo down his throat to keep him unconscious. It wasn't enough to appear dead for this gaff. He had to act dead, too. We couldn't take the risk of him rousing and giving the game away.

There was still some danger here. The snooze goo slowed one's breathing, but it didn't stop it. If anyone watched the Hollow Man closely enough, they might see the subtle rise and fall of his chest. But the appearance of the weeping sickness ensured no one would look closely at *that* corpse. Even now, the guards had backed out of sight.

"Bring Colonel Deavers here with the physick," Wilkins ordered Mullins, still shaking. "Double-time. *Double* double-time."

We waited again, this time with both Wilkins and Greeley beside us. Wilkins had regained his composure, but I could tell he was more than worried. He'd actually touched the boil-infested body. He kept wiping his hand with his handkerchief, looking for any sign of the sickness.

I glanced at Meriel as Colonel Deavers and the physick came to join us. As she had with Greeley, she kept her face turned away, and so did I. Of all the people we'd met last week, it was these three we'd spent the most time with. If anyone was likely to recognize us, it would be them.

Fortunately, just as Greeley had barely glanced our way, as far as Deavers was concerned, we may as well not have been there. His only interest was the Hollow Man. Carefully, he approached the open cell door, a scented handkerchief already pressed to his nose.

With the Hollow Man's pus-dripping face now visible, the

warden didn't even need to ask his physick to step inside. I watched Deavers's eyes as he looked at his dead charge, and saw a complex wave of emotions. Fear. Wonder. Surprise.

And worry. Not just for his health but also his position. *How did that man get the weeping sickness?* he was thinking. And: *What will the emperor say?*

He'd never get an answer to the first question. And right now, he had a much more pressing matter on his hands. Deavers turned to the physick. "Check the men. Every single one of them. Make sure no one shows signs of the sickness."

The physick hurried off to get his examination kit. Wilkins motioned to the Hollow Man. "What about . . . ?"

"Dispose of the body. Burn it in the courtyard. And check on the other prisoners."

"Yes, sir." Wilkins hesitated. "And . . . if they're infected?"

"Take them outside," Deavers said. "And burn them, too."

CHAPTER 51

DEAVERS MARCHED AWAY, wrapped up in his thoughts.

"Take care of this," Wilkins told Greeley. "I'll muster the men outside for the physick. Hop to it."

Greeley paled with the instruction. "Y-yes, sir," he stammered. But when Wilkins left, he turned to Mullins. "You heard the man. Get that body out of there and burn it. Then check on the others."

"Me?" Mullins protested. "The cap'n ordered you to do it!"

"And now I'm ordering you. That's how rank works." He scurried away.

Mullins stood there, wide-eyed, teetering on the edge of refusing. Either way, I couldn't wait for his decision. I couldn't let him or any other Rifleman handle the body.

I positioned myself right in front of him. "C'mon, then," I said to Meriel, Gareth, and Lachlan. "Let's get out o' the man's way. Don't want to be anywhere near when he drags the body out, we don't."

Got him.

Mullins grabbed my arm. "Oi, oi, oi," he said. "Where do you think you're going?"

I put on a surprised look. "Cleaning's done here, sir."

"Oh, no, it isn't. There's that body to be tossed out."

"That's *your* job," I said, alarmed.

He cuffed me on the ear, hard. "And I'm making it yours. You two"—he pointed to me and Gareth—"carry him. And you"—he pointed to Lachlan—"you're with me. You'll check on the other prisoners." He seemed rather satisfied with himself for thinking of it.

"But the body's shackled," I protested. I cringed as Mullins raised his hand again. "We don't have no key."

"Ain't no key for that one," Mullins said. "You'll have to chisel 'em off. There's tools in the shed beside the barracks."

I bit my lip. "Can we wrap him in linens, at least? So the sickness don't spread through the hall when we carry him out?"

Mullins's eyes widened; he hadn't thought of that. "Yeah. Linens. Wrap him up. And you wrap him up good, you hear me?"

"Yes, sir." As Mullins left, dragging a protesting Lachlan by the collar, I said quietly to Meriel, "Bring another linen cart. Make sure it's as big as can be."

We chipped the manacles away from the Hollow Man's wrists as Mullins forced Lachlan to check on the other prisoners. Since we couldn't let Mullins actually open the cells—Cormac was still dressed like me and wearing my face—Lachlan suggested he just look through the food slats. "You know, so we get less bad air to breathe in the halls, like."

Mullins, lazy at the best of times, was perfectly fine with that. So Lachlan, on his knees, just pulled open the slats, calling out, "Hey, mate! You feeling daisy-like? Crackers and jam. That one's all right, he is." And they were off to the next.

It didn't take long to remove the manacles, degraded as they were with rust. Half a dozen blows with hammer and chisel and the shackles broke apart. By the time we were done, Meriel had returned with the linen cart. Foxtail had already climbed out of her hiding place; no one would be coming back to this cell tonight.

"Grab the linens," I said to them. "We need to make a body."

We began shaping the cloth into piles. Gareth made the head and arms. Meriel and I packed the torso. Foxtail formed the legs. When we had something roughly the right size and shape of a man, we took the rest of the linens and used them to bind the figure. When we were finished, it looked like a mummified corpse.

There were a few linens left over. "Don't use those," I said. "We'll need them to cover the cart."

That had been my plan, anyway: Use the linens to make a fake corpse, hide Foxtail at the bottom of the cart, stuff the Hollow Man in an empty beer barrel, and roll both back onto the train. Unfortunately, I hadn't anticipated one problem.

To sell the Hollow Man's death, I'd needed to dab his neck with dead juice. Now he stunk of it. If we tried to sneak him out like that, he'd smell. We'd never get past the Riflemen at the train platform with a barrel reeking of death.

"Can't we just wash it off?" Meriel said.

Gareth shook his head. "It only c-comes off with l-lemon juice."

Which we didn't have. My stomach dropped as I realized my terrible mistake.

"Then ... what now?" Meriel said.

Foxtail tapped her chest. *I'll get him out.*

"How?" I said.

She made a horizontal circle with her arms. Then she motioned downward. And then she pointed to a ... uh ... rude place. It took me a moment to understand what she was saying.

"You want to drop him down the *garderobe*?" I said incredulously.

She nodded, gesturing. *It's just wide enough for us to fit. I'll carry him down slowly.*

She mimed digging her shoes into the sides of the hole to slow their descent, so they wouldn't hit the water too hard. And as I thought about it, I realized the water below the garderobe would have to flow somewhere. So there had to be a secret exit under the island that led to the river.

That still left a big problem. "How will the Hollow Man survive? He's out with the snooze goo. He'll drown."

She waggled a finger at me. *No, he won't.* And she pulled Gareth's pouch from her pocket.

"The pearl," Gareth said, surprised.

Right. Foxtail had brought Gareth's pouch in with the enchantments and tools. One of the orbs—the pearl—let you breathe underwater. As long as Foxtail held the Hollow Man's mouth closed around it, he wouldn't drown.

"You've saved us again," I said to Foxtail, amazed.

She patted my cheek.

CHAPTER 52

GARETH AND I carried the corpse up the stairs. Since it was only linen, bundled and wrapped, it didn't have anywhere near the proper weight. "We'll have to fake it," I said.

I went first, staggering under the supposed load, arms wrapped around the chest. Gareth took the legs. I couldn't tell how well he was acting, and I didn't dare turn to look. All eyes were on us now.

The Riflemen had started a bonfire in the courtyard, the biggest I'd ever seen. Word of the weeping sickness had spread like the contagion itself. Everyone in the prison—absolutely everyone—was watching as we made our way outside.

The good part was that no one came near us. And since the sun had gone down, the only illumination in the courtyard was coming from the bonfire, the lanterns, and our twin moons' light. No one was close enough to see that the body didn't look quite right. They all just watched, worried, as we carried the corpse to the fire.

We got as close as we could. The heat was scorching. "Remember," I said under my breath, "this body's heavy. On three." We began swinging it back and forth. "One . . . two . . ."

We tossed the bundle into the blaze. The linen caught quickly, adding to the smoke and the flame. I was grateful they'd built the fire so big. It would disguise there wasn't actually a person inside.

As it was, we had to get out of here. The presence of plague had got everyone nervous, and the train conductor was insisting we leave. Blocker called down to us. "You two! Collect your gear. We're leaving in twenty minutes. If you're not on board, that's your bad luck."

I was pretty sure he meant it this time. We hurried back inside the keep, joined by Lachlan. Meriel had already pushed the cart back and forth to the barracks twice, once to carry Foxtail, the second time with the Hollow Man.

"There's nothing for it," I said quietly. "You two have to get Cormac to the train."

We returned to Cormac's cell and unlocked it. He'd slumped back in the corner, rocking to try to comfort himself. He stood, frightened, when we came in.

There was no time for coddling now. "Do you want to see your sister again?" I said. He was too nervous to hear me. I got in his face. "Cormac! *Do you want to see your sister again?*"

That got through. "Yes," he said softly.

"Then you have to go. Do you understand? All you have to do is walk out of here with that mop, up the ramp, and step onto the car. No one will stop you." I took him by the arms. "You can do this. You stole the emperor's scepter. *You can do this.*"

He stared at me. For a moment, I thought he'd balk.

"Until the earth takes me," he whispered. "I can do this."

"I know it," I said. "Shuna will walk with you."

He blinked. And he seemed to come to life. "Thank you."

"Go on."

He went out, sandwiched by Gareth and Lachlan. "What about you?" Gareth said, worried.

"We can't have two of me in sight at the same time," I said. "So get him right on that train. I'll follow in a couple minutes. *Hurry.*"

They escorted Cormac up the stairs while I collected the remaining rag cart. But when I got to the entrance to the keep, I didn't step out, not yet. I waited inside the door, watching. I couldn't go until Cormac had boarded.

Even this was playing with fire. Normally, I'd hide somewhere for another ten minutes at least, so everyone would lose track of where "I" had gone. But we didn't have that kind of time. It was very likely some of the work crew would notice the double. Certainly Blocker would. He was up on the platform, keeping track of everyone coming past, checking the equipment against a list and counting the crew.

That didn't worry me. Blocker thought we worked for Mr. Fox, and there was no chance he'd cross the Breakers. Neither would the rest of the work crew, who owed their jobs to the charity of the thieves' guild. No, what I was worried about was the guards. I had to hope that the Riflemen were too flustered, too concerned with their own hides in the wake of a weeping sickness outbreak to notice an extra me.

So I waited. Gareth and Lachlan escorted Cormac up the ramp.

Then I spotted Mullins coming down.

What's he doing up there? I watched, pleading with Shuna in my mind. *One time. Just let him not notice one time.*

They passed him—

And I breathed a sigh of relief. Muttering to himself, Mullins barely glanced at them as he walked by. Cormac's disguise had passed.

All right. Now I just had to wait for him to board the train—

Oh no.

I should have kept watch on Mullins, not my friends. The guard was coming back to the keep.

Our eyes met.

He blinked.

Oh *no*.

I ran back toward the stairs to the cells. I risked a look behind me as I went.

Mullins had entered the keep just before I turned the corner. He stared at me, confused. "How . . . ?" He looked back at the platform, then once more at me.

I ran down the stairs.

"Hey!" he called from behind me.

I kept going. But now I was trapped.

"Hey!" he called again. "Come back here!"

Greeley had locked himself in the guardroom. He cracked the door open to say, "What's wrong?"

"Did you see— Hey!"

Greeley didn't know what was going on and, frankly, didn't care. He shut himself in again as Mullins chased me down the hall. But even with just one guard after me, I was still trapped. There was only one staircase up from this level.

Think, Cal, think. Could I hide? Lock myself in a cell?

That wouldn't do any good. Even if Mullins didn't see me shut the door behind me, the train would leave in a few minutes. And if it stayed, I'd still have to explain myself when I got out.

I was rumbled. Down here all alone.

But you're not alone, the Old Man said suddenly.

You're only in my head, Old Man, I said. *You're not actually here.*

He snorted. *I wasn't talking about me.*

Then what—

Aren't you the one who keeps going on about coincidences? he said.

I paused. *No.*

He raised an eyebrow. *Do you have a different gaff up your sleeve, boy? Now that you're so keen on having friends, you may as well use them.*

He was right. Mullins was closing in. There was only one play left.

I ran down the spiral steps to the shrine room. The Bear's idol had a few offerings inside its bowl, waiting for the next time the Spirit acolyte returned to the prison. After my gaff with the weeping sickness, Deavers would have to call the acolyte in early. That bowl would be overflowing before sunrise.

But I wasn't here for the offerings. I placed myself between the shrines and waited.

Mullins ran in, skidding to a stop when he saw me.

He looked incredulous, and scared. But most of all, angry. He'd been terrified by the weeping sickness, but I'd pegged his character from the start. He wasn't just a layabout. He was, at his heart, a bully. And here was someone to punish to make himself feel strong.

He was still confused by what he'd seen, though. "Why are there two of you?" he said.

If I was going to play this gaff, it was now or never.

"There are *more* than two of me," I said, dropping my voice low. "We are legion."

"You're what?" He was getting angrier now. "You come here—"

"We are the messengers of the Spirits," I intoned, pointing at him. "The weeping sickness was only a warning. For your mistreatment of these prisoners, you shall face our *true* wrath."

For a moment, he recoiled, genuinely frightened. Then he realized how ridiculous what I'd said sounded. He stomped toward me.

"Boy," he said, "I am going to beat you until—"

"*Look upon your doom*," I snarled.

And I touched the idol of Shuna.

My finger, already burning so close to her statue, flared. The pain seared almost as bad as the shattering crystal ring.

But my finger didn't break apart. Instead, a sound grew in the room, like a whisper, the breath of a gentle breeze. When I'd touched the idol of Artha in the vault, there had been a terrible gong, a bell echoing through the Enclave. Now I heard only a soft chime in my own head as the ring's magic, trapped inside me, resounded with the power.

And then a fox appeared.

"What the—" Shuna said.

Mullins froze in his tracks. He stared at the animal—the *talking* animal—that had suddenly appeared before him.

"*Behold . . . THE FOX!*" I thundered.

Shuna stared at me in alarm. "Cal? What are you . . . ?"

Mullins's mouth worked, but no sound came out. A patch darkened on his trousers. He'd wet himself.

"*For your cruelty,*" I boomed, "*the patron Spirit of prisoners has come for your SOUL!*"

Mullins fled.

Panicked, he smashed into the doorjamb. It left a welt on his forehead, but he didn't notice. He just ran away, mewling like a kitten.

Shuna glared at me. "Behold the Fox? His *soul?*"

I smiled weakly and shrugged.

Her eyes narrowed. "You are in *such* trouble," she said.

Then she vanished.

When I went back upstairs, Greeley was half leaning out of the guardroom, staring toward the exit to the keep, where Mullins had fled.

"What in Artha's name was that idiot on about?" he said as I passed.

"Don't know, sir," I said. "Perhaps the fear of the sickness has driven him mad."

"The drink, more like," Greeley muttered, and shut himself back in.

I hurried up the ramp with my cart. There were three Riflemen there, standing with Blocker. One of them waited impatiently with a padlock by the cargo door.

Blocker was pacing, angry. "I thought I told you . . ." he began.

Suddenly, he trailed off, puzzled. He looked at me, then at the open cargo car, then back at me again. His eyes went wide. "Didn't you just—"

I cut him off. "Yes, sir, I'm the last."

He opened his mouth to say something more. Ever so slightly, I shook my head.

He swallowed. "Get on, then," he said, voice shaking.

I pulled myself up into the cargo car, scanning the crowd inside. I was relieved to see Meriel, Gareth, and Lachlan there—and no other me. They'd hidden Cormac safely. I cocked my head at Meriel, a question. *Foxtail?*

Meriel nodded. *She's all right. She's gone.*

None of the other crew would look at me. In fact, none of them were looking at any of us. We'd got plenty curious glances on the way here. Now, with the news there was weeping sickness, whatever we'd done, they wanted no part of it.

Blocker knew enough to keep his mouth shut, too. He hopped inside and banged on the door. "Ready to go."

"All clear," the Rifleman said, and he began to slide the door closed.

"Stop!"

The voice came from down the ramp.

My heart sank. It was Captain Wilkins. Mullins, looking absolutely white, was right behind him, marching up the platform.

"Where's the boy with the bandage?" Wilkins demanded.

Blocker didn't say a word. He just moved aside as Wilkins looked into the car.

The captain spotted me. "You. Out here. Now."

I stepped out, a puzzled expression on my face. "Yes, sir?"

Wilkins pointed to me. "Well?" he asked Mullins.

The guard shrank back, nodding. "That's him. That's the one."

Captain Wilkins looked from him, to me, then back to Mullins. "Tell me again what he said to you."

"But I already—"

"*Again.*"

Mullins's voice trembled. "He said he was the messenger of the Spirits. He said he'd brought the weeping sickness to the castle as punishment. He said he'd take all our souls."

Wilkins watched me carefully as Mullins spoke. "And then what did he do?"

"He summoned the Fox!" Mullins cried.

"The Fox. Shuna the Fox."

"The very same, I swear! She knew him, Cap'n. She called him 'Cal'!"

"Cal," Wilkins repeated.

I stared back at him, totally confused.

"Turn around," he said.

Still looking puzzled, I started to turn.

"Not you," Wilkins said. "You."

"What?" Mullins said.

"Turn around. Face the other direction."

Hesitantly, Mullins turned.

Wilkins kicked him so hard in the backside, the Rifleman's feet actually left the ground. "*Aaaggghhh!*" Mullins screamed, clutching his bum.

"What kind of a fool do you take me for?" Wilkins screamed back. *"You think I can't smell that beer on your breath? You get back in that keep and you scrub that cell until it shines! Then pack your kit—I'm shipping you out on the next train! And if I hear one more word from you about the Fox, I'll make sure your next posting has you guarding the frozen wastes of Absalor! In* WINTER!*"*

Mullins scurried off. I just stood there until Captain Wilkins turned and said, "Why are you still here? *Go!*"

I scampered back onto the train. The Rifleman shut the cargo door, then padlocked us in.

No one said a word.

CHAPTER 53

THERE WAS NO time to celebrate.

The gaff wasn't finished yet. It had been clear this morning that Sully, the foreman, knew this job was too strange. I'd worried something like that might happen. That was why I'd had Lachlan tell Diana not to inform Sully we were coming. That way he wouldn't be able to check with Sheridan before the train left.

But after . . . I was certain Sully would send a runner to confirm with Mr. Fox that he had indeed sent the orders to smuggle us into the Rose Garden. And since he hadn't, there'd be trouble on our return. Big trouble.

I'd warned Diana of this before we left. *As soon as our train leaves the station*, I'd said, *you scarper. Grab anything you want to take with you and get out of town.* If she waited even an hour, she'd end up floating down the Cardogh. Whether we succeeded or failed, her time with the Breakers was done.

Diana had the luxury of fleeing. We didn't. We were trapped on this train until it pulled into the station. And Sheridan would surely be there to greet us.

So, as the train slowed, it was time for one last disguise. I'd told Foxtail to give Gareth the light orb before she took the Hollow

Man away. He held it up for me now, so I could change inside the car.

The rest of the work crew shifted nervously as I stripped off my baggy clothes to reveal my final set of togs underneath. I was now sporting a form-fitting silk shirt and pants, highly fashionable. I also pulled the bandage from my head. Wetting the gauze with her saliva, Meriel wiped the burn makeup off my face.

The only thing I couldn't wear underneath were new shoes. Those I'd given to Foxtail to smuggle into the prison inside her barrel. We'd then carried them back on the train at the bottom of the nearly empty linen cart. I put those shoes on now, while Lachlan and Gareth helped Cormac from his hiding spot, removing his bandage and the face-copying mask.

"Sheridan will r-recognize him," Gareth warned me.

"Doesn't matter," I said.

At least as long as the final piece of our gaff played its part.

We let the work crew get off first.

Their job wasn't done. They still needed to remove the empty barrels, boxes, and carts from the cargo car and clean it for the next run. They shuffled out as quickly as possible. They could smell it: trouble was coming.

I stepped out behind them, glancing around. And there he was.

Sheridan waited inside the station, chatting casually with his lieutenant, Byrne. All the exits were blocked by Breaker goons. When Sheridan spotted us, he signaled to the others not to let anyone through. Then he and Byrne came toward me.

I moved away from my friends. The goons would block them from leaving, but that wasn't my issue. There was no good reason a young noble—as I was now dressed—would be standing around with this raggedy bunch. So I hurried down the platform, near one of the exits.

It must have looked to Sheridan as if I was trying to flee. He smirked, changing direction to meet me, but he was in no hurry. I had nowhere to go. I found a spot on the wall to fold my arms and lean against, as if waiting for someone.

Sheridan looked back at the train as he and Byrne joined me. "Cormac," he said, spotting the boy standing with my friends. "You actually got him out."

I nodded. "My team's a lot better than you thought, eh?"

"It is impressive," Sheridan agreed. "Too bad it was all for nothing. I'm going to send him back on the next train. His breakout won't even make the newspapers."

I frowned. "He's one of your own. Why would you send him back to that hell?"

"You know why. I already told you I want no trouble with the emperor. My returning him will assure His Imperial Majesty that I had no hand in any of this. And, as you point out, Cormac *is* one of mine. Which means I do with him as I please."

Byrne's expression didn't change. Yet from the way he shifted, I could tell he didn't like that. The lieutenant wouldn't begrudge his boss's prerogative to rule as he saw fit, and Byrne was certainly not the squeamish type. But one of their own had just broken out of the Rose Garden. It was a matter of pride—which Sheridan would now throw away. I wondered if there might be a struggle between these two sooner than I'd thought.

Well, if there was, it would come too late to help me. At the moment, Byrne was Sheridan's man. He'd probably be the one ordered to kill me. Assuming Sheridan didn't save that pleasure for himself.

I shrugged. "What you do with Cormac is not my problem. You want to send him back in, go to town. I only brought him out as Diana's payment for my end of the deal."

"Ah, yes. That one," Sheridan said. "I don't suppose you know where she's hiding?"

"You don't suppose right."

Sheridan smiled. "Well, one way or the other, you'll tell us soon enough." I imagined he was looking forward to the torture. "Still, you speak of deals. What about ours?"

"Come on," I said. "You know we never had a deal. That was just part of my gaff. It's not my fault you fell for it like a common mark."

I probably shouldn't have said that. There was no worse insult you could offer a gaffer than to call him a mark. Sheridan took it in stride, though I could tell inside, he was seething.

"And what of the Hollow Man?" he said. "I don't see another escaped prisoner."

"Why would you? He's dead."

Sheridan's eyebrows shot up. "You killed him?"

"Check with your contacts inside if you don't believe me."

Sheridan weighed what I'd said. He hadn't pegged me for an assassin. Though he clearly realized by now that he'd misjudged us badly. He shook his head, as if regretting what he now had to do.

"I did warn you, Callan," he said. "Now I have to keep my word. A shame; I think we could have been friends."

We both laughed. That was a gaffer's joke: gaffers don't have friends. Though deep inside, I was so happy I'd proved that wrong.

"Come along, then," Sheridan said.

I stayed where I was. "I'll pass."

He looked disappointed in me. "You're not going to make a scene, are you?"

"No scene. I'm just not going."

"And how will you stop me from taking you?"

"I won't," I said. "*He* will."

Sheridan looked where I pointed. The Breaker goons had moved away from the main entrance. Now they were standing around nervously, looking askance at who'd just come in.

Chief Superintendent Phelan Riley, head of the Stickmen, entered the station. Galawan was with him, tweeting pleasantly from Riley's hand. A squad of Stickmen were with him, too, carrying scatterguns instead of nightsticks. On the superintendent's orders, they spread out.

I don't think I'd ever been so happy to see so many Stickmen at once. In fact, I don't think I'd ever been happy to see a Stickman at all. Certainly the Breakers weren't; they took one look at those guns and made themselves scarce.

As soon as the exits were free, Meriel, Gareth, and Lachlan fled, Cormac huddled between them. Sheridan watched them go, that smile never leaving his face. When he spoke, however, his voice was the coldest I'd ever heard. "Nicely played."

I gave him a friendly salute. "I'll pass your compliments to my crew."

His lips tightened. "You do understand that you've made an enemy today?"

I knew I should keep my mouth shut. There was no value in provoking him. But I'd had a hard day—a hard year, really—and I was tired of being pushed around. So I said, "No offense, Sheridan, but considering the enemies I've made recently, you don't even crack the top five."

∩∪

Sheridan walked away, never dropping that smile. Byrne had a small smile, too. He nodded to me. I nodded back. He was a good lieutenant.

As Sheridan left, I whistled for Galawan. The little sparrow flew out of Riley's hand to join me, landing on my shoulder with a tweet hello. The superintendent came over, staring at the departing Sheridan's back.

"Mr. Quinn," Riley said.

I shook his hand. "Thank you for coming. You got my note, then?"

Riley held up the letter he was carrying. "Indeed I did. And just in time, it seems. How did you come by it?"

"My father has arranged some . . . special security . . . to protect my sister and me while outside Garman. The note was theirs. I'm not exactly sure what it means."

Riley unfolded the letter—which, in anticipation of Sheridan finding out about our prison break, I'd prepared last night for Galawan to deliver. At the top, I'd written:

Superintendent—
I think there might be trouble brewing. Please see below.
A.Q.

The proper note, I'd had Gareth write, all in block capitals:

CAUTION.
POSSIBLE TARGET: MORRIGAN AND SONS
RAILWAY COMPANY.
TRUSTED INSIDER REPORTS POSSIBLE PLOT TO
SABOTAGE RAILWAY LINE TO CARDOGH PRISON
TODAY AFTER TRAIN'S RETURN.

"I understand business here is somewhat cutthroat?" I said.

"Quite literally, on occasion," Superintendent Riley said.

"That's why I sent you the note," I said. "I suppose I should have stayed away and let you handle things, but Mr. Farrell has been most decent. Ignoring such a warning would hardly be the honorable thing to do. Regardless, I apologize for bringing you all the way out here. I haven't seen any trouble at all. It appears the information I was passed was wrong."

"On the contrary," the Stickman said. "Do you know who that was you were just talking to?"

"Said his name was Sheridan. A businessman of some sort, if I recall."

Riley scowled. "He's no businessman. We believe that's Mr. Fox, the head of the thieves' guild in Sligach."

"You're joking." I stared at the exit Sheridan had left through. "Artha's heart. I had no idea. He seemed a most pleasant fellow."

"That's his specialty. He's a gaffer by trade."

"A gaffer?"

"A con man."

"Ah," I said. "Well, if they were planning a heist, the train to Castle Cardogh seems a poor choice. Why would one rob a train for such meager supplies?"

"The supplies aren't what's of value in Cardogh, Mr. Quinn. The *prisoners* would be the prize."

I looked at him, as if startled. "You think this Sheridan blackguard was planning a prison break?"

"I don't see what else he could be doing here," Riley said. "Though I admit, I find it hard to believe. You saw the castle's security. An escape attempt would be madness."

I nodded with feeling. "Indeed, Superintendent. I quite agree."

CHAPTER 54

I REMAINED WITH Superintendent Riley for quite a while.

Certain that Sheridan would leave someone behind to tail me, I stuck with the Stickman as his men inspected the train, then traveled with him in his carriage all the way to their main head-quarters. I spotted the tail as soon as we left the station: a youth dressed as a rail worker. Riley was no fool; he rumbled the boy, too. With a curt nod to one of his men, he sent the thief running as a couple of bluecoats began marching his way.

Once at Stickman headquarters—*If the Old Man could see me now*, I thought—I took my leave of the superintendent as soon as politeness allowed it. Then I found an empty office and fled through the window. I'd had more than enough of both Stick-men and Breakers to last me a lifetime.

I headed straight for the sewers. In anticipation of our getting caught by Sheridan, Foxtail had scouted the area the day before and told me where the closest out-of-the-way manhole was. With Galawan safely tucked away in my jacket pocket, I pulled aside the grate and climbed down.

Foxtail had left a package for me behind the pipes. In it was a map of the sewers on which Gareth had drawn the route I should take, a bullseye lantern, and a pistol. Like all gaffers, the Old Man had frowned on weapons. *If you need one*, he'd once said, *then you've already made a big mistake.* I didn't disagree with him. But if Sheridan's men—who were no doubt scouring the city for me this very moment—came for me, I didn't intend to go down without a fight.

Still, that was a last resort. My first and best plan was to hide if anyone showed up. And for that, I had the greatest early warning system on Ayreth: the Eye. As I lifted the patch, I got the sense of it filling my mind.

what is it now, foxchild? it said impatiently.

I thought about asking it something silly, just to annoy it. But for the first time since we'd come to Sligach, I could finally give it a better answer. And I wanted all this to end.

"We broke the Hollow Man out of prison," I whispered.

The excitement in the Eye's voice was palpable. where? where is he?

"The others smuggled him out of the city. I'm going to join them now. But I need you to spot anyone who's coming for me."

you may rely on me, foxchild. as I promised you long ago, I will keep you safe.

There was something in its voice, something sardonic. I wasn't sure why. I knew the Eye wasn't lying: it *would* keep me safe; it needed me. But there was a tinge of humor in its words I didn't understand, and it set me on edge.

Foxtail and Gareth had laid out my escape route. I was to follow the outflow through the sewer until the end, turning where they'd marked on the map. I moved slowly, lantern in one hand, pistol in the other, Eye out to search for any signs of life. Every so often, I'd see a brownish-red glow: a rat. Once I came upon a whole colony of them. I shuttered the lantern and stayed absolutely still, watching their lifeglows scuttle past until they were gone.

Otherwise, I encountered no one. Or, I should say, the Eye saw no one. Because though there was no lifeglow, a figure suddenly appeared in my lantern's spotlight.

"Shuna's sniffling snout!" I cursed.

It was Foxtail. Her mask prevented the Eye from seeing her, so I'd had no advance warning she'd appear. I bent over, pushing my eyepatch back down, trying to quiet my thumping heart. "Stop *doing* that," I said. "I nearly shot you."

Foxtail gestured, amused. *I was worried you'd get lost.*

Near apoplexy aside, I was glad she'd come. She was a lot better company than the Eye. And I didn't need to keep consulting the map anymore, as she already knew the way out. "Where are the others?"

Safe. Everyone's waiting at the camp.

"And the Breakers?"

She waved a hand dismissively. *Far behind.*

We moved faster now, until we reached a giant grate where the sewer's contents dumped into the Cardogh River, downstream of the city. A rowboat waited on the bank, Lachlan sitting on its bow.

"Guv!" He sprang up and gave me a big hug. Already jubilant at our victory, he was even more delighted to get Galawan back. The bird sang a happy melody as we climbed into the boat and pushed off.

"Never thought I'd work *against* the Breakers," Lachlan said as he and Foxtail began rowing across the mile-wide river. "There anyone in the empire who ain't peeved at us by now?"

Exhausted, I let the two of them do the work. "If there is," I said, "I'm sure we'll enrage them soon enough."

Our camp was on the north side of the river, inside the woods. Diana was there with the others. I'd missed the reunion with her brother. "Thing of beauty, it was," Lachlan told me, a tear in his eye.

It did feel good to do something nice for once. Even now, Diana clung to her brother, his arm wrapped around her in response. He still seemed dazed, but it was a happy sort of dazed. Like someone had offered him a brand-new life, and he was just starting to realize it. Which wasn't too far from the truth.

They stood as we arrived. "Thank you," Diana said seriously, and he repeated the same. "Thank you. I—"

"Don't worry about it," I said. "Have you got someplace to go?"

"No," Diana said. "I never..."

I already knew what she'd say. She'd never been anywhere other than Sligach. And she hadn't actually dared hope we'd pull it off.

It didn't matter. "Head east," I said. "Follow the river upstream. Stay off the roads until you come to a stagecoach inn about forty miles that way." Meriel gave them some provisions we'd stored, plus several hundred crowns. "Once you get there," I continued, "buy a ticket to Redfairne. When you arrive, go to Grey's Fine

Clocks in the Water district and talk to the owner. Tell him Cal sent you. He'll set you right."

Cormac shook his head. "We can't . . . How can we ever repay you?"

"Just help Grey out around the shop for me, will you? He's been sick, and he's still recovering. Go on; it's best you travel at night."

With handshakes all around, we sent them on their way. "And where do we go?" Meriel asked once they were gone.

Good question. It was time to find out.

The others had already made a fire. The Hollow Man was curled up beside it, still unconscious from the snooze goo, covered only by his tattered clothes. Even after Foxtail took him through the river, the stain of the rusted manacles hadn't washed off. His bony wrists and ankles were a rusty brown.

This was what everything we'd done in Sligach was for. This . . . man. It was hard to think of him as that, and not just because he looked so frail that if you handled him roughly, he might break. Who was he? Was he really two hundred years old, as Sheridan had thought? What magic could keep him alive all that time, just to leave this husk behind?

There was only one way to know. I stood apart from the others, then lifted the Eye.

I wasn't sure what I expected to see. Some extraordinary shine of magic, maybe. Something that would explain what was so important about him. Why the Eye wanted him so badly. Why he'd been locked up for ninety-seven years.

What I saw instead was nothing special. The Hollow Man

had the same red glow all people had, if a little darker. It was also much dimmer, like he didn't have much life left. Not surprising, I guess, considering he'd spent the last century in chains, eating one meager meal a day, never seeing the sun. When I looked a little closer, I thought there might be something else on his skin—symbols, maybe? Tattoos?—but they were too faint for me to make out.

Whatever he looked like to me, he was obviously precious to the Eye. The moment it saw him, its exultation filled my mind. I'd only ever felt that joy once before. When it had first seen the Dragon's Teeth.

YES, the Eye said. YES.

"What now?" I said, dreading the answer.

you have done well, foxchild. now you may rest.

Was it finally letting go of me? "What do you mean?"

rest. you will need your strength. the hollow man will need his as well.

"What do we do with him?"

feed him. feed him as much as you can. in the meantime, begin to travel that way. A faint trail appeared in front of me, glowing, leading north.

"Why?" I said. "What's to the north?"

The Eye laughed with delight.

our freedom.

CHAPTER 55

I WAS SO tired.

My body ached in places I didn't know muscles existed, so much that I barely even noticed my scars. My mind, in a way, ached even worse. A long gaff was a strain: days, weeks, months of pretending, scheming, lying. It wore on you. When it was over, I always felt more relief than joy. *It's done. Good job. Now I can sleep.*

So when we lay beside our fire, Foxtail keeping watch, I pleaded in my mind with Shuna, Artha, the Eye, the Adversary, the universe, and the seven-banded mark on my finger to leave me be. For one night, just tonight, let me sleep a dreamless sleep. But whatever was out there either wasn't listening or didn't care, because the minute I closed my eyes, I was back on Artha's beach.

The Bear—the girl, really, though it was hard to think of her as that, even though that's all she appeared to be—still lay curled on the sand by the water, her back to me. Somehow, she seemed more weary than I was.

"I know what you are," she said without turning.

"What's that?" I said.

"My punishment. You're part of my punishment."

I sighed. "If you're being punished, then so am I." I stared into the water. It really was pretty here. "What did you mean before," I asked, "when you said we were both fools? I mean, I get that I'm a fool. I know I'm being played. And so are you. I just don't have any idea how."

"What difference does it make?"

"I honestly don't know."

Now she sighed. "Why do you keep coming back, human? Why are you here?"

"My name's Callan. Cal, to my friends."

She ignored that. "Why are you here?"

I sat beside her on the beach. "I think I'm supposed to find a secret," I said. "That's what happened every other time I was brought to Shadow. First I learned about Meriel's past. Then I saw the Dragon's Light. I don't know why I was shown that. But now I'm supposed to find a new secret. And I think I've been sent here to trick you into telling me."

Artha rolled over, propping herself up in the sand to look at me.

"I'm a gaffer," I told her. "Tricking people is what I do. It's all I really know how to do. So whyever I'm here, whoever brought me, there's only one reason to send someone like me. You know something, and I'm supposed to find it out."

I shook my head. "But I'm so *tired*," I said. "I don't want this life anymore. When I took the Solomon job, I was just trying to find a way out. Now something's caught me in its gaff, and just like I'm its mark, you are, too. I'm here to trick you. But I don't want to trick you. I don't want to."

Artha studied me a moment. "If you really don't want to be here," she said, "then why do you keep coming?"

"I'm pretty sure it's this that drags me here. I just wish I knew why." I held up my hand with the seven-banded mark.

She sat up, staring. "Where did you get that?"

"It used to be a ring," I said. "A crystal ring the Old Man swiped from some Weaver. Shuna—" It felt kind of awkward mentioning the Fox to her sister. "Shuna thought it came from some old trickster. Why?"

"Because that's your answer," Artha said. "You *are* supposed to trick me." She stood. "Come on, let's go."

I looked up at her, confused. "Go where? And . . . why?"

"You don't need to trick me," she said. "This secret you want? I'm going to tell you anyway."

CHAPTER 56

WE WALKED ALONG the beach.

"You call us Spirits," Artha said, gazing across the water. "I suppose that's as good a name as any. The truth is, we never really had a name for ourselves. It wasn't the sort of thing that mattered. What we were was what we did. And what we did was explore.

"We were explorers," she said. "Our only purpose was to go to new places and see what was there. Other worlds. Other realms."

And she showed me.

The landscape around us shifted. The beach shimmered

and then we were standing on a grassland—if it was, in fact, grass. It rose all the way to my neck, a strange turquoise sheen to it. Nearby, a herd of tall, thick, cow-like creatures ripped giant mouthfuls of the grass from the ground, blowing deep, heavy breaths as they chewed.

"What the—" I began

and then we were on a rocky, craggy plain. It was nighttime, but though there were no clouds in the sky, there were no stars, either. I heard an angry buzz, and then a cloud of—insects? I'd never seen the like before—came swarming toward us. They had bulging, blood-red eyes and gossamer wings and a long needle where their mouth should be. I smelled the stink of rotting meat

and then we were floating in the air. There was no ground,

only sky. It was purple, a bright, vivid glow, with puffy green clouds in the distance. Great gassy bodies floated all around us, translucent, the organs visible, pulsing within. Small flat creatures with streaks of orange and black flew among them, biting off tiny chunks. The gas-beasts didn't seem to notice.

"Where are we?" I asked, breathless.

"Another realm," Artha said. "Where the rules of their universe are upside down."

And as she said that, I had the strangest sense that *I* was upside down. My head began to spin. This place was wrong. It was *wrong*.

I'm falling, I thought, starting to panic. *I'm falling I'm falling I'm falling—*

"Steady," Artha said. She grabbed my arm

and we were back on the beach again. I fell to my knees, dug my fingers into the sand. The grains scratched my skin. It made me feel real once more.

Artha kept a calming hand on my shoulder until I stood. Despite my dizziness, I said, "That was . . . amazing. Wherever that was . . . were we actually *there*?"

"No," Artha said. "That was only Shadow."

"The realm between realms," I said.

"That's one way to think of it. But it's more than that—and less. Shadow is the *path* to other realms, but it's also an *echo* of those realms. If a world *can* exist, then somewhere, in some realm, it *does* exist. Shadow, then, is a place of probability—and therefore, possibility. If a thing exists, you can find it through Shadow. And Shadow will copy it in return."

I tried to wrap my mind around it. "Like . . . dreams. The odd places you sometimes see. Or how you might be able to fly?"

"Yes," Artha said. "In your realm, no human can fly. But there are realms where they can. And so you might dream and touch that echo. But it is *only* an echo. Do you understand?"

She pressed that point, like it was somehow important I got it. "Shadow is *not* the place itself," she said. "It carries the shape of the thing but not its weight. You humans can see those realms in your dreams, and maybe even experience them. But you never actually travel to those realms, because while you have the ability to move *into* Shadow, you don't have the power to move *through* it. We Spirits do." There was suddenly a profound sadness in her voice. "Or at least we did."

Artha sighed. "What you just glimpsed was what our life was like," she said. "We explored, not merely seeing those creatures but *being* them." Artha held her arms out. "This isn't what I look like. It isn't my real form. I'm not a bear, either. Just like Shuna isn't really a fox."

I was too curious not to ask. "What *do* you look like?"

"It depends on how much of the light spectrum you can see. To you—to human eyes—we'd look like mist. But our true forms don't really matter. Being ourselves was never the point. We took *their* forms—*your* forms—lived in those bodies, just to experience the wonders they saw every day. And so we traveled the realms. By your reckoning . . . I don't know how long. Time doesn't flow the same everywhere. A hundred thousand years? A million? It was eons. A life full of play, richness, and wonder."

There was such loss in her voice. "What happened?" I said.

"We were on a world," she said, "very similar to Ayreth, where humans lived. We took their forms and lived among them for a while—a hundred years or so, maybe—but then we got bored with that, so we shifted, each of us trying different animals. I liked being a bear; it fit me."

Like it fit Shuna being a fox, I thought. She did make a pretty good fox.

"But then one of my sisters, Lila—you think of her as the Rabbit—came to us and told us she'd discovered something terrible.

"We'd never met another being that could travel through Shadow like we did," Artha said. "We'd begun to think nothing else like us existed. But there was . . ." She shook her head. "Not like us, exactly. It wasn't a shapeshifter. And it wasn't an explorer. It was a destroyer."

"The Adversary," I said, surprised.

"More than that," Artha said. "So much more. You would call it a dragon. We called it the Devourer, because that's what it did. Every bit of life it saw, it consumed. Not just plants and animals. It fed on entire *worlds*. There was nothing that could stand against it. It would arrive and then feed, stripping all life from a planet until nothing was left but a barren husk."

"And this dragon," I said, alarmed, "Adversary—Devourer—could travel through Shadow? To *any* world?"

"Travel through Shadow, yes. But not to any world. It had the ability to enter Shadow but no power to leave on its own. It could only go through when something led it to an exit."

Realization dawned. "And you . . . you Spirits . . ."

Artha nodded, miserable. "*We* provided the exit. Our travels through Shadow left behind what you might think of as a doorway. An opening, which the Devourer could find and use. That's what it had been doing. Every world we'd traveled to, every wonder we'd seen, every creature we'd lived as . . . they were all gone. The Devourer used our paths, followed in our footsteps, to consume every world we'd ever loved. Billions of dead. *Trillions*. Because of us." She sounded stricken.

"You can't take the blame for that," I said.

"Can't we?" Artha said bitterly. "It was our travels that opened the way. We never intended harm to anything, ever. But we were the cause of it nonetheless. Whether we knew there was something evil like that out there or not, it was our responsibility to watch for it. But no. We were too wrapped up in ourselves to imagine anything else."

I couldn't imagine the weight of that pain. It must have been crushing.

"There was nothing we could do about the past," she continued. "But there *was* something we could do about the future. We hatched a plan." She looked at me. "We were going to trap and kill the Devourer. Even if it killed us in return."

CHAPTER 57

"WHAT DID YOU do?" I said, riveted.

"Lila had discovered," Artha said, "that our doors through Shadow shone like a beacon to the Devourer. So we made the biggest beacon we could. My sisters tore open the portal to the world we'd been living on. Meanwhile, I and"—she paused—"someone else built our trap. We opened a second portal *from* that world, and we waited."

Her eyes had hardened when she said *someone else*. She'd refused to even mention their name. *One of her sisters?* I wondered. *Or Bran the Crow?* The look on Artha's face stopped me from asking.

"Like a moth to a flame," Artha said, "the Devourer came. It swooped through the portal my sisters had widened, ready to plunder that realm. That's when we sprang our trap.

"We took a chunk of that world—my sisters and the Devourer included—and flung it through Shadow to a new realm. This new world was barren, completely devoid of life except for that little pocket we carried with us. And that lifeless world was where we made our stand."

Artha grew quiet, remembering. "We weren't prepared for the fight. We'd never met anything else like us before, but since the

Devourer could travel through Shadow, we imagined it would be as strong as we were. We were wrong. It was much, much stronger.

"The battle was terrible. The clash of magic. The Devourer's fury . . ." Her voice faded. "It was monstrous. Even as we chipped away at its essence, it hammered us. Nuala, the Wolf, charged in, shredding the dragon's heels. She was the first of my sisters to die. Lila, the Rabbit, should never have been in the fight at all. She was too young, too inexperienced. She fell next."

"And Kira," I said, finally understanding what could kill a Spirit. "She was killed, too."

"Yes." Artha's grief was overwhelming. "I don't think you can understand what it means for one of us to die. We don't have bodies like you do. All we are is carried in our souls. The Devourer consumed them until there was nothing. The life we'd lived, hundreds of thousands of years of joy and memories and love . . . all gone. Nothing to remain."

"But . . . Kira *did* leave something behind," I said.

"What do you mean?"

I told her what had happened in the cave below Lake Galway, of Kira's blessing. "She helped us," I said. "I thought . . . maybe you'd want to know that."

"I do," Artha said, and the idea seemed to give her some peace. "Thank you for telling me, hu—" She paused. "Callan."

She glanced at me, then looked away, as if embarrassed. "I suppose I shouldn't be surprised," she said, "that Kira was able to leave some remnant of herself. She'd studied our powers more than any of us. In fact, it was she who really saved us.

"You see, the Devourer had one weakness—only one. The more we injured it, the more it needed to heal itself. To do that, it needed to feed."

"The barren world," I said, finally understanding the Spirits' gaff. "That's why you opened the door to there. *Because there was nothing to fuel the Devourer's power.*"

Artha nodded. "It couldn't fix itself. It killed Nuala and Lila, and then it killed Kira, battering through the shield she created to protect us. But as the Devourer took her down, the rest of us came in on its flank. Bit by bit, we weakened it, just enough. Then we closed in. And we tore it apart."

This she remembered with satisfaction. "We ripped the Devourer into pieces, most of which decayed into nothing, as there was nothing to hold them together anymore. Its blood ran down, so much blood, seeping into the cracks of that lifeless world."

I stared at her. *Seeping into the cracks*, I thought.

"That blood," I said slowly. "You're talking about the primeval magic."

"Yes," Artha said. "What you call the primeval *is* rich with magic. For it is the dragon's blood, the life it stole from countless worlds."

"That would mean . . ."

"That barren world is now your world. Lifeless no more."

"But *we're* here," I said. "People, I mean. How . . . ?"

Artha suddenly looked defeated. "I told you the trap to draw the Devourer here was my design. But we had little time to put it together. In my haste, when I flung a chunk of that world through Shadow, I reached out too far. I caught a human village in my wake and brought it through.

"It wasn't many. Three hundred or so people. But we'd brought them here, and once the fight with the Devourer was over, there was nothing for those people to survive on. Accident or not, they were going to die. Once again, our fault.

"Those of us remaining decided we couldn't bear that guilt any further. We couldn't do anything about the lives that had been lost. But we *could* save these people. With the power of the primeval, and with the three remaining pieces left of the dragon, we could build a new world.

"So we did," she said. "The Dragon's Heart anchored the primeval—the blood—to the world. The Teeth still held the Devourer's powers, the ability to consume that energy, then reshape it as we needed to. And the Eye gave us the focus to do it. With these, we brought life to that rock—this world you call Ayreth. We grew the grass and the trees, and we filled them with the creatures your ancestors knew from their original home: foxes and bears and fish and birds ... everything. All made in the image of that old realm, to which they could never return. We did that for your ancestors so they would live. No more would die at our hands."

I wished Gareth were here to hear this. "So all the stories," I said, stunned, "they were true. You really did create Ayreth. And the dragon's blood is the primeval magic. And all life here contains magic ... *because it was born from magic.*"

Artha nodded.

"But why is magic in us?" I said. "You didn't create us—our ancestors."

"No. But your ancestors ate the animals, and grew the crops to eat them, too."

And so we took the magic inside us, I realized. *Then passed it down to every generation thereafter.*

It was an incredible story. But Artha looked so sad. And not, I thought, just because she was remembering her fallen sisters. "You killed the dragon," I said. "Why don't you consider that a victory?"

"You didn't ask the right question," Artha said.

"Which is?"

"Why are we still here?"

"You mean . . . you Spirits?" I said.

"Yes. We saved your ancestors by building this world for them. They didn't need us after that. So why are we still here? We were explorers, remember? Why did we stay?"

I had no idea. "Wasn't the dragon gone?"

"*That* dragon was," Artha said. "What about the others?"

I stared at her. "There are *more* out there?"

Artha shrugged. "We don't know. That's the problem. For so long, we were fools. We traveled from realm to realm without ever asking: *Is there any danger in this?* Now we knew the answer. Yes—and maybe even still. The only way to know if there was more than one Devourer would be to search through the realms to find it. And if we did that . . ."

"Then you'd open more doors for it," I said, understanding. "And possibly destroy more worlds."

She nodded. "So we knew what we had to do instead. We took forms your ancestors would understand—Bear, and Fox, and so on—then helped them find their feet, pointed them on their way. Then we left them alone. And so we'd never be tempted to do anything that would destroy their world again, we swore a pact."

"No more interaction with people," I said.

"Oh, it was much more than that." Here Artha's voice grew hard. "We didn't just cut ourselves off from you. We hid the truth about the Devourer and Shadow, so you wouldn't be tempted to call on those powers, to damage your own world like we had. And—much greater than that—we sealed *ourselves* off from traveling through Shadow. We bound our souls so we could enter Shadow but never leave through any other door. For us, it was Ayreth or nothing. Forever."

I could see how that would be painful for the Spirits, who'd lived to travel through the realms. But... "Can't you still see those other places?" I asked. "You said it yourself: If a thing can exist, it does exist. And somewhere in Shadow is its echo. So you could still explore the echoes—"

Artha cut me off angrily. "You don't understand. When you look at this beautiful beach, you don't know where you are. Because you don't *see* Shadow. To you, this is real. This sand running through your fingers. This water wetting your feet. It looks real, feels real, smells and sounds and tastes real. To you.

"But not to me," she said. "I can see what this is. It's Shadow, and that's nothing but a pale imitation of the real thing. To me, all of this . . . this *beauty* . . . looks like little more than what your friend's shadow might look like on a sunny day. It carries the *shape* of your friend, but it *isn't* your friend. You can't hold a shadow."

A pit grew in my gut as the truth of that sank in. How awful it would feel to live in a world made of nothing but shadows. How empty.

"I'm sorry," I said, and I meant it. The Spirits had sacrificed everything for us. And not just us. "I know you couldn't save those who were already killed by the Devourer. But you did save all the other realms it never found."

"You still don't understand," Artha fumed. "We saved nothing. All we did was delay the inevitable."

Though I was afraid to make her angrier, I said, "But you killed the Devourer."

"No. *No.* We killed *nothing.*" Artha's fury was growing. "The Devourer isn't like you. If I tear your body apart, you die. That doesn't happen with beings like us. Our bodies don't matter. It's our soul, our *essence*, that is our life. Lila and Nuala and Kira didn't die because the dragon broke their bodies. They died because it consumed their souls."

"Except . . . Kira saved herself."

"A piece. A fragment of what she was. Enough to linger until her final task was finished. But now she's gone, because there's nothing left to anchor her to this world. Unlike the Devourer. Do you see now? *That's what the Devourer did.*

"When it realized it was losing," she said, "it retreated. As we tore its body apart, as its blood bled into the ground, it saved itself by hardening the parts that could anchor it. There were three pieces of that dragon we couldn't destroy, even with all our power. The dragon fled *into* those pieces. It sent its soul into its Heart. Its abilities went into the Teeth. And its mind, its consciousness, hid inside—"

"The Eye," I whispered in horror. "The Eye . . . *is* the Devourer."

"Yes," Artha said. "*Now* you understand. Everything you've done for the Eye, you've done to serve the Devourer. And it wants only one thing: to re-form the body that we destroyed, to begin its life anew.

"That's what the Eye has been working toward," she said. "That's what *you've* been doing. The dragon plans to return. And when it does, everything on Ayreth will die."

CHAPTER 58

I FELT LIKE throwing up.

There was the gaff. The one the Eye had been playing all along.

There's a . . . let's call it a set, Mr. Solomon had told me when I'd brought him the jewel. *The Eye, no doubt, wanted to join with its brethren.*

The Dragon artifacts. The pieces that remained, that contained everything the Devourer was. Eye, Teeth, and Heart: mind, power, and soul. The Eye wanted to put them back together.

It had used me to gain its freedom from the cavern where it had been imprisoned by Shuna. Then it had used me to find the Teeth, which held its power. It had even manipulated me into feeding those blades, to reawakening them and filling them with life, framed as the only way to save Lachlan.

Now it had sent me to free the Hollow Man. And while I was certain he wasn't the Dragon's Heart, I was sure his only purpose was to lead us to it. And then the Devourer would return.

come for me, the Eye had said. agree to this willingly, and you shall not die.

Ever? I'd asked.

possibly.

What a mark I was. I told Artha what it had told me.

"Now you understand what it meant," she said. "It wasn't

lying. You would live forever. As part of it, after it consumes your world."

The despair was overwhelming. Everything I'd done. Everything *we'd* done. I just wanted to lie down and die. "I'll stop," I said. "I'll stop now. I won't do anything else it wants."

"That won't make any difference," Artha said. "No matter what you do, Ayreth is doomed."

"Why?" I said. "If we just don't let it—"

She put her head in her hands. "How can you be so blind? The signs are all around you, and you still don't see."

"See what?"

"Why are the volcanoes erupting?"

"The . . . volcanoes?" I wasn't expecting that. "Well, I don't know about Bolcanoig, but Bolcanathair blew because Mr. Solomon cracked the earth with that dragon staff. The primeval . . ." I trailed off. "The *primeval*."

"Yes," Artha said. "If the answer to keeping the Devourer down was simply to lock its pieces away forever, don't you think we'd have done that? In fact, Shuna *did* do that. She sealed the Eye in that cavern thousands of years ago. All it did was delay the inevitable. Because as life flourished on Ayreth, it wasn't just life that grew. *The primeval grew with it, too.*"

I remembered feeling the primeval's power—even its basic consciousness—when it had flowed through me as I was holding the Teeth. **GROW EAT GROW EAT GROW EAT GROW.** The dragon's blood, still alive under the earth after all these millennia.

"There is immense power in the primeval," Artha said. "And

its tie to the Devourer's soul has made it unstable. Even if you could prevent the dragon from re-forming itself, the primeval will continue to grow. The strain is already making the volcanoes erupt. Soon, it'll crack the whole planet apart. The only way to stop this is to sever the primeval from the Devourer once and for all. To do that, you'd have to kill the Devourer. *Truly* kill it. And you can't. We tried. We tried as hard as we could. We'll never get that chance again."

"But maybe we could find a way," I said. "You stopped it once before—"

"By luring it to a barren world!" she shouted. "It won't fall for that trap a second time. And even if it did, we couldn't fight it. It took my whole family to tear apart that dragon. With three of us lost, we're dead.

"So there you are, Callan," Artha said bitterly. "There are the secrets you were sent to my prison to find. The Eye is the Devourer. The primeval is its blood. It's going to re-form. Your world is going to end. You've been doing nothing but serving it all along. Just like me. And *that's* why we're nothing but fools."

CHAPTER 59

WHEN I AWOKE, I lay there, on my blanket beside the fire, for a long, long time.

Lachlan had taken the second watch from Foxtail. I could hear the flapping of metal wings; he was playing with Galawan. As the sun began to rise, he set a pan to heat in the fire. We had bacon in our packs; the sizzle and smell roused the others. They talked and laughed among themselves as they ate.

I just lay there.

"Food, guv," Lachlan called.

"I'm not hungry," I said, my back to them.

Meriel came over to check on me. "Are you all right?"

"I'm fine. I said I'm not hungry. Good enough?"

She paused. "Okay." She returned to the others, but the morning's chatter quieted.

I wanted to scream at them. *Do you think I can't tell you're all looking at each other now? Do you think I don't know you're all wondering, 'What's wrong with him?' Do you think I can't read every single one of you as if your minds were shouting every little thought out loud? I'm a gaffer! I know!*

But I didn't know, did I? Turned out I didn't know anything at all.

I rose. "Finish eating and pack up. We're leaving."

Silently, they popped the last bits of bacon into their mouths, then rolled up the blankets while Lachlan scrubbed the grease into the river.

Why are you blindly doing what I say? I wanted to scream. *Do you just wait for me to tell you everything? Don't you have minds of your own?*

Gareth was looking at the Hollow Man. The withered figure was still asleep. I knew Gareth wanted to ask, *What about him?* but my mood made him too afraid to speak.

I wanted to shake him. *Can't you just say what you want to say? Can't you grow a spine for once?*

Meriel spoke instead. "Why's he still sleeping?" she said, nodding toward the Hollow Man. "Did we give him too much snooze goo?"

"No way," Lachlan said. "Dosed him proper, I did. If there's one thing I know, it's snooze goo." He scratched his head. "Should be awake, though. He ain't dead, is he?"

He wasn't. His chest was rising and falling. "We can't wait for him," I said. "Foxtail, pick him up."

Foxtail didn't protest. She just lifted him, carrying him over both shoulders. It looked a little awkward—the Hollow Man was much taller than she was—but he was also old and frail, and as we'd seen before, Foxtail was stronger than she looked.

Not that you'll tell us why, will you? I wanted to say. *Got to keep those secrets, after all.*

She looked back at me calmly, waiting.

"Let's go," I said. I started marching west, following the Cardogh downstream.

"Didn't you say it were that way?" Lachlan said, pointing north.

"Well, now it's this way. I was wrong. I'm wrong sometimes, you know?"

"Everybody is," he said cheerfully.

I wanted to smack him. I just walked away, following the river.

We hiked for a full ten minutes before the Old Man started up in my head.

Well, this is productive, he said.

Shut up, Old Man, I snarled.

Oh, no, boy. The others may stay silent. But I'll never keep quiet.

And why is that? I said. *You're gone. You abandoned me. Why won't you leave me alone?*

Didn't you already ask that? he said. *You tell me. It's your head, after all.*

Is everything just a joke to you?

Most everything, yes. Now stop being a fool.

I laughed, a bitter sound in my head. *Didn't you hear Artha? Being a fool is what I do best. Why would I stop now?*

You can't do anything about the past, he said. *But just like Artha and her sisters, you can do something about the future.*

Oh yeah? Like what?

The Eye's been snaffling you, he said. *Maybe it's time you started snaffling it back.*

I wanted to rage at him, like I wanted to rage at the others. But even before I started to, the rage in me broke.

I *was* being a fool. I knew it. And that thought washed away the rage and replaced it with something worse. The something I'd been trying to avoid. Despair.

I don't know how, I said, just wishing I could die, that this could all be over. *Please tell me how. Please.*

I can't, the Old Man said gently. *I'm not really here. But you have friends who are, don't you?*

I'm the gaffer, I objected. *What can they do?*

But even as I thought that, I saw the Old Man raise his eyebrow. And I saw the past. *Our* past.

Gaffing Padraig to give up the keystone.

Snaffling the real Eye from Mr. Solomon and replacing it with the fake.

Solving Veran's riddle under Lake Galway.

Sneaking into the Weaver vault.

Breaking the Hollow Man out of the Rose Garden, under the nose of Mr. Fox, Colonel Deavers, and Superintendent Riley all.

What can your friends do? the Old Man said. *What can't they do? What can't you all do when you're together?*

It cracked my despair. Just a little.

But that was enough.

I stopped. "Put him down," I said to Foxtail.

She slumped the sleeping Hollow Man against a nearby tree.

"What's up, guv?" Lachlan said.

I sighed. "I think we'd all better sit for this."

I told them everything.

I told them what Artha had said. I told them about the other realms, and the Spirits, and the Devourer dragon, and the Eye. There was nothing I left out, nothing I didn't lay bare.

I should have told them right away. I didn't because I was

ashamed. Callan the gaffer, a mark in someone else's gaff? Even though I'd known it was happening, it was still humiliating to discover just how thoroughly I'd been played. I told them that, too. I asked them to forgive me.

"Naw, guv," Lachlan said. "Ain't your fault none."

"We made our own choices," Meriel said. "We didn't have to do what you asked. We chose to." I blamed myself for that, too. They waved that away.

But the weight of what I'd told them, it did nearly knock them flat. Lachlan finally summed it up best: "Artha's fuzzy bum," he said.

An accurate a thought as any, I supposed. It actually made me laugh. The others, too. What better way to face the end of the world?

"We can always count on you, Lachlan," I said.

"Course you can, guv," he said, though he seemed a little puzzled as to what he'd actually done.

"So that's why you said go west?" Meriel said. "We're just trying to avoid what's coming?"

I nodded. "Stupid, I know. Running away won't help."

"Why not? Why not just abandon it all?"

"We c-can't," Gareth said. No surprise, he'd already grasped the full implications of what Artha had told me. "If the primeval is still growing . . . I mean . . . it will eventually tear Ayreth apart. To stop it, we'd have to actually kill the Devourer. For good."

No one asked how we might do that. They already knew the answer: we couldn't.

But that wouldn't stop Gareth from thinking about it. "Though ... I mean ... maybe we could slow down the Eye's plans. If we can. It could give us time. To come up with something."

"How could we do that?" Meriel said.

"Well . . . him." Gareth indicated the Hollow Man. "He obviously has some purpose. So if we ... you know. S-stopped him."

What Gareth suggested made everyone go silent.

Meriel was the first to speak. "I could," she said quietly.

She showed us the throwing knife in her hand, even as she looked unhappy at the idea, at killing another person in cold blood. I shook my head, and not just because I wanted to spare Meriel the grief. I simply didn't think it would help.

"We don't know what the Eye wants with him," I said. "For all we know, it might *want* him dead. He could be a sacrifice, like how the Dragon's Light sacrificed me in that Shadow vision, to awaken the dragon statue. Maybe the magic to free the Devourer is in his blood, and spilling it is what brings the dragon back."

Or a million other things. "That's the problem," I said, "when you find out you're in a gaff. You can't trust anything anymore. A good gaffer will have set everything up so you'll do what he wants without even knowing it. And there's our problem. What does our gaffer want? The Hollow Man alive? Or dead? Who says he didn't predict this very discussion? It's what I would have done."

And it was even worse than that. "We don't even know who's running the gaff," I said. "The Devourer? Artha? Shuna? That crow? Or something we don't know? Everyone's playing their parts, thinking they're in charge. That's how the best gaffs work. You make your marks think all their ideas come from them, when in reality, you've been stringing them along the whole time. There's just nothing and no one you can trust."

What could anyone say to that? We sat in silence again. Lachlan was frowning.

"What is it?" I asked him.

"Huh? Oh, nothing, guv. Just thinking it was strange, that's all."

"Us being snaffled? Even gaffers fall for it sometimes, Lachlan. The Old Man tried to teach me that. No matter how good you are at manipulating people, there's always someone better."

"Naw," he said, "that ain't what I mean. I was just thinking . . . two months ago, I didn't know none of you. Now I'd do anything you asked. I'd die for you. Come to think of it, I have, twice. And what're the odds of that? Not dying, I mean. I'm saying the odds of finding mates like you lot, just before the end of the world, when you never had nothing before?"

He shook his head. "I ain't complaining," he said. "I'm proper glad for it, I am. I'm just saying I trust you. All of you, I do. Whatever you decide, I'm in."

Foxtail laid her hand on her chest. *Me too.*

Gareth nodded. I looked at Meriel.

"I left someone I loved behind once already," she said, sounding sad. "It might have been the right decision. But I'm never doing that again. We'll fight whatever comes. Together."

My heart swelled. And with that, I started to feel the tiniest sliver of hope. Not a lot. But enough.

Either way, I couldn't just do nothing. They mattered too much. "All right," I said. "But if we're going to fight the Devourer, then I think we'll need some help."

Foxtail spread her hands. *Where are we going to get help?*

"In Shadow," I said. "I need to talk to Artha once more."

CHAPTER 60

IT WAS A nice sentiment. I even believed it. There was only one problem.

I couldn't dream anymore.

For the last few weeks, dreaming was the last thing I'd wanted. Every single night, I'd dreaded closing my eyes, worried I'd wake up in Shadow. Yet now that I actually wanted to go, I couldn't.

The crow wouldn't allow it.

I'd close my eyes, relax, feel myself start to drift off. And every single time, as a dream began to take form, that crow would appear, flying straight at my face, flapping his wings, claws ready to tear at me.

caw! caw! caw!

I reared back, trying to protect my eyes, but the dream always shattered before the crow reached me. My fear shook me awake.

I lay there each time afterward, breathing deeply. *It's just a dream*, I told myself. But another part of me kept asking, *Is it? Remember what Keane said about Shadow. The things that live there can tear mind and soul apart.* And I remembered the Dragon's Light stabbing me, and the way the pain had lingered, and then I just couldn't control my fear. The crow chased me away every time.

I spent a fitful few hours that night trying to doze off. Finally,

I accepted I wouldn't succeed and relieved Meriel at watch. If I couldn't sleep, no point in anyone else staying awake.

I sat up the rest of the night, feeding the fire, munching some walnuts Foxtail had foraged, and playing solitaire with Gareth's deck of cards until the sun began to dawn over the horizon. I pulled the pan out of Lachlan's pack, preparing to start breakfast. It was when I turned back toward the fire that I realized: I wasn't the only one awake.

The Hollow Man was staring at me.

I jumped back, startled. He sat slumped on the other side of the fire. "Food," he croaked.

I tried to still my thumping heart. "I'm about to fry some bacon—" I began.

He grabbed the pound of smoked pork belly I'd placed near the fire and tore a chunk of it out with his teeth. Raw.

". . . or you can just eat it like that," I finished weakly.

Unnerved, I studied the Hollow Man as he wolfed down our food. Again I was struck by how he looked less like a man and more like the shell of one. There was something about him . . . I couldn't place it, but the way he moved made me feel like he was once big and strong, like a soldier. But time—and a century in the emperor's dungeon—had wasted that away to this emaciated husk. He looked like a walking corpse.

Except for his eyes. As he tore chunks from the bacon, his eyes burned, watching everything. They flicked from me to my friends, still sleeping in their packs. He glanced at the woods around him, then brought his gaze back to me again. There was a sharp intellect in there, undulled by his lifetime of captivity, and it made me more than wary. For some reason, it chilled me to my bones.

The Hollow Man finished the bacon. "More," he croaked.

All we had left was some beans, plus our iron rations, which would only last a few days. I hadn't really expected a long stay in the wilderness. We'd have to start hunting soon or send Foxtail back to Sligach to snaffle some food.

"There'll be more later," I told him. He seemed to accept that answer. "What's your name?"

His voice was rough and gravelly, like he hadn't used it in a long, long time. "I don't have one."

"What do you mean?"

"My name was taken from me long ago. I gave it freely."

"Why?"

"So I might serve."

I knew what he meant. *Serve the Eye.* No name, I thought. Was this why they called him the Hollow Man?

"You must have had a name before that," I said. "The name you were born with. What was it?"

"I ..." He trailed off. "I don't remember. I haven't heard it in so long ... so long."

The strangest thing was, I believed him. Sheridan had suggested the Hollow Man was nearly two hundred years old. I was starting to think he was much, much older than that.

"Why have you freed me?" he asked.

I considered lying, making up a story. But I didn't see the point in that. I had a feeling he'd see through it, anyway. And besides, maybe he could tell us something about the artifact. After all, our only chance to stop what was coming was to learn all we could.

"The Eye needs you," I said.

He paused. "Where is it?"

I didn't want to show him. *It's not just the Eye to me anymore*, I thought. *I know what I'm really carrying around inside. The Adversary. The Devourer. The enemy of every living thing is in my head.*

I'd avoided facing it since Artha had told me the truth. I knew I couldn't avoid it forever. At some point, I'd have to free the Eye again and hear its voice inside my head. I dreaded it. I dreaded it more than anything I'd ever been afraid of.

But I had to.

I could feel the Old Man watching me, an unspoken warning on his face.

I know, Old Man, I said. *If I'm going to gaff this thing—if that's even possible—then I have to pretend I don't know it's really the Devourer. I have to treat it no differently than before.*

He nodded, watching carefully.

I steeled myself and said, "Here."

I lifted my patch.

The Hollow Man stared. The shine in his eyes blazed with passion and joy. As for the Eye itself

(the Devourer the enemy of all living things don't say it don't say it don't even think it)

it reveled in the sight of the living skeleton before it.

excellent, foxchild, it said. but he is still weak. you must feed him. give him all that he needs.

I couldn't take any more. I slipped the patch back down, and the Eye went silent.

The Hollow Man looked upon me with a new respect. "Emissary," he said reverently.

Emissary. That's what Bragan had called me when he'd seen the Eye. I thought of the Dragon's Light stabbing me. I remembered the pain as those blades pierced my flesh. It almost felt like that pain had returned.

"And the Teeth?" the Hollow Man said. "Where are they?"

It rattled me that he mentioned the swords just as they'd entered my mind. "We have them," I said, though I didn't go into Foxtail's pack to pull them out.

He gave a great sigh of satisfaction. "You truly are the Emissary."

"What does that mean to you?" I asked.

"That I serve you, too." He shook his head in amazement. "I had begun to doubt this time would ever come."

I didn't respond to that. Instead, I said, as casually as I could, "The Eye . . . Do you know what its plans are?"

"For me? Yes. I am the path. I am *your* path."

My path? "What does that mean?"

Slowly, as if his bones might break, he rose. Then he removed the tattered remnant of what had once been his shirt and opened his arms.

"Uh . . . Cal?" Meriel said.

She'd woken. Now she sat, blanket still covering her legs, startled at the sight of the Hollow Man standing nearly naked by the fire. A knife was already in her hand.

The others had woken, too, and were staring alongside her. I held out a hand. *Wait.*

"Look," the Hollow Man said.

He was painfully thin, the bones of his rib cage cutting deep ridges in his skin. It was almost impossible a man in this state was still alive.

"Look," he said again. *"Look."*

Suddenly, I knew what he meant. Fingers trembling, I lifted my patch once more.

And his skin came alive with light.

The first time I'd seen him through the Eye, his lifeglow had been dim, the faint haze of a dying man. The food he'd just eaten had rejuvenated him a little. His flesh now glowed a touch brighter, though still a deep, dark red.

That wasn't all the Eye saw, however. Before, I'd got the faint sense that there was something marking his skin. Now I saw them. They were still faint, but they were there.

Tattoos. The Hollow Man was covered with tattoos.

They weren't made of ordinary ink. These tattoos were enchanted, the same as I'd seen on Bragan. But the Hollow Man carried some different symbols, as well. I could make some of them out.

"What is this?" I said.

"It is the path," he said. "Marked on my flesh by the Dragon's Light, carried through the generations, unchanged. In it are secrets. In it, you will find the truth. Look, Emissary. For my path is your path, too."

Secrets? The truth? What did that—

Wait.

Was that . . . ? It looked like . . .

"A mountain," I said. "With an arrow on it."

Gareth gasped.

"What is it?" Meriel said to him.

"That's Bolcanashach," Gareth said. "I mean . . . the Seven Sisters volcano. North of Sligach. It has a rock formation in the shape of an arrow on its slope. What else do you see?"

"There's . . ." I tried to make it out. "It looks like a settlement, maybe? Below the mountain. And a line . . . No, a curve. It leads from the settlement to the mountain, then around it, on the side where the arrow points."

Gareth rustled through his pack and pulled out his map, unfolding it on the grass. "What else?"

The Hollow Man remained still as I studied him. "The curve goes up," I said, "until it reaches seven . . . I don't know what those are. Pillars? Standing stones, maybe? Then it goes left . . . over a road? Oh—that's water; it's a river. Then through hills. And it comes to a stop at . . . a tree."

Gareth traced his finger along his map, mumbling to himself. "The settlement. The settlement is . . . Sligach? From Sligach . . . around Bolcanashach . . . to the Standing Stones of Weyring. Then left . . . west. Across a river . . . the River Goul . . . and then into hills. The valley . . . the Valley of Kildinan."

He looked up, amazed. "It matches," he said. "It's a map. His body is a *map*."

CHAPTER 61

WE ALL LOOKED over Gareth's shoulder as he retraced the route on the paper. He drew it exactly as I'd described, marking an X where it ended.

"The Valley of Kildinan," Meriel said, reading off the map. "What's there?"

"Nothing," Gareth said. "I mean . . . no one lives there. No one ever has."

"So what's all this about, then?" Lachlan said.

I looked over at the Hollow Man. He'd put his tattered shirt back on after I'd put the Eye away. Now he sat again by the fire, staring into the flames.

I kept my voice low, so he wouldn't hear me. "Artha mentioned a third artifact. The Dragon's Heart." *Where the Devourer secured away his soul.* "I'm guessing the Heart is in that valley."

Foxtail gestured. *Do we go?*

My first thought was *No, absolutely not.* But if we didn't, the Eye would realize something was wrong. And I couldn't take the risk of letting it know I knew what it really was. Not yet.

"How long would it take to walk there?" I asked Gareth.

He spaced out the route on the map with his fingers. Around the mountain and into the valley. "About a w-week and a half."

"Will he even make that trip?" Meriel said, nodding toward the Hollow Man.

He did look too frail for a long journey. But the way the bacon had brightened his glow made me remember the Eye's command. *Feed him.*

"We'll have to start hunting," I said. "Anyone know how?"

Meriel looked at me oddly, like I'd just asked them if they'd ever heard of the sun. "Of course," she said. Foxtail tapped her chest, too.

"Then we may as well get going. Just, um . . . no need to rush."

They knew what I meant. Unless we came up with a plan to defeat the Eye, we were only marching to our deaths.

And the end of all of Ayreth, I thought.

The girls, it turned out, were very good at hunting indeed.

Lachlan, Gareth, and I stayed with the Hollow Man, who was now dressed in proper, if overly baggy, clothes. Anticipating we'd need garb for our escaped prisoner, Foxtail had brought some things from Sligach in her pack. When I'd first offered them to the Hollow Man, he just shrugged, as if they were unimportant.

"It'll be cold at night," I pointed out.

He shrugged again, but said, "As you like, Emissary," and put them on.

As we marched toward Bolcanashach, Meriel and Foxtail ranged through the woods, looking for game. Meanwhile, I tried questioning the Hollow Man some more, hoping he could give me information about the Eye without me revealing what I knew in return.

At first, I just asked him about himself: where he was born, how he grew up, and so on. Some things he claimed, as he had with his name, that he couldn't remember. To others he said, "Such matters are unimportant, Emissary. That life, I left behind."

It sounded like something the Eye would say. It gave me the shivers. "So why did the emperor imprison you, then?"

"He didn't."

I frowned. "You were in Castle Cardogh. Only the emperor sends people there."

"Conalthan signed the order, yes. But he was merely a puppet, doing the bidding of his master."

"His master?"

"Kainan."

So far, Gareth, intimidated by the Hollow Man, had kept quiet. But now he stared at him and said, "Kainan . . . IV?"

The Hollow Man nodded.

"Who's that?" Lachlan said.

"The High Weaver," Gareth said. "From a c-century ago. Conalthan was his emperor."

Professor Keane had told us the Weavers had had the dragon cult outlawed. While remnants of it had obviously survived, it seemed, after nearly four thousand years, they'd finally caught the Hollow Man. It was almost impossible to comprehend.

"Why didn't the Weavers just kill you?" I said.

"It would not have served their purpose."

"What does that mean?"

He didn't answer. But I began to suspect they'd interrogated him. Run tests on him. Tried to learn what he knew. Tried to learn his magic, discover how he'd stayed alive all those millennia. Then, after they were done with him . . . had they just left him in prison to rot, drained of his power? A punishment, for the cult's endless, bitter defiance?

Lachlan was amazed. "Shuna's paws. You really thousands of years old, then?"

The Hollow Man stared into the distance. "Is that how long it's been?" he said quietly.

I believed it, even if it was still hard to imagine. Regardless, details of his past weren't what I really wanted from him.

"And the Eye?" I said. "You told us what its plans for you were. What about me? Or what it intends to do, when all this is over?"

He shrugged. "I cannot say, Emissary."

The way he said it, it sounded like he didn't know. This, I didn't believe. But even if he was lying, it didn't matter. He wasn't going to tell me either way.

∩∪

When we stopped for the day, Meriel was the first to return to our camp. She had a pair of rabbits slung over her shoulder.

"Crackers and jam. I love rabbit," Lachlan said, and he began setting the fire while Meriel skinned her catch. She paused as Foxtail returned, dragging a much bigger prize behind her.

"A deer!" Lachlan said. "Shuna's fluffy tail."

Meriel looked a little put out to be shown up like that. "How did you catch that?" she said. There didn't seem to be a mark on the beast.

Foxtail gestured. Meriel tried to follow what the girl was saying as she skinned and quartered the carcass. Lachlan called out to our traveling companion as the fire began to blaze. "Hey, Mister . . . um . . . Man," he said. "You want to choose your piece? Uh—"

The Hollow Man snatched one of the deer's skinned legs. As he had with the bacon, he tore chunks from the flesh with his teeth, eating it raw.

"I ain't sitting next to him no more," Lachlan whispered to Gareth. "Likely to end up as dessert, I am."

The Eye had said the Hollow Man would need to feed, and so he did. He ate most of that deer by himself, which I wouldn't have thought possible. I peeked at him later with the Eye and saw his glow had brightened considerably. The tattoos shone brighter, too. I no longer had to peer to see them.

yes, the Eye said. yes. I tucked it away, more worried than ever.

Like everyone else, Meriel had watched him during dinner. Now, as I glanced at her, she surreptitiously showed me the knife in her palm. I shook my head. The plan hadn't changed. We still didn't know what killing him might do.

And it was more than that now. As I watched his tattoos grow brighter, I thought of the symbols inked on Bragan and Mr. Solomon. The Hollow Man wasn't just feeding to replenish his own body. He was also replenishing the magic in those enchantments, drawing on the life force of the animals to fuel them.

And he was covered in tattoos, most of which weren't part of the map. I suspected at this point that even if Meriel did try her knives, they wouldn't make a scratch. If we were supposed to kill him, I was pretty sure we'd already missed our chance.

We spent the night at the foot of Bolcanashach, that strange natural arrow which marked the rock looming a half mile above us. And for the second night in a row, I couldn't sleep.

The crow stopped me again. It flapped into my face, cawing, jolting me awake every time. Already exhausted, it left me feeling like my head was stuffed with cotton the next day as we rounded the volcano, then camped, the Hollow Man devouring almost another whole deer.

The crow came back the third night, too. By now, I was so tired that I did manage to catch some sleep anyway. But I still couldn't return to Shadow. I had wild dreams, yet no control over them, and no sense of being alert. Every time I started to recognize I was dreaming, the crow would appear to frighten me awake.

That bird was working hard to keep me from seeing Artha again. I still didn't know why, or even if it was doing it on its own. I conferred with Gareth, in the desperate hope that he might think of an answer.

"It showed me the door to find Artha," I complained. "Now it doesn't want me to speak to her anymore? What's it up to?" But Gareth had nothing to tell me.

The next day, I only half remembered walking. I recalled moving through some heavy brush, breaking the branches aside, while I trudged alone, staring at the ground, barely conscious. Just one foot after another. One foot after another. One foot after anoth—

The crow suddenly appeared right in front of me.

"Ahh!" I shouted, and startled, I stumbled. Off-balance, I fell into a bush of spiny brambles.

Then I really shouted. "*Aaarrrggghh!*"

The others ran to help me. "W-what happened?" Gareth said.

"He tripped over his own feet," Meriel said.

She and Lachlan pulled me from the thorns. "It was not—*ow!*—my own—OW!"

Lachlan made a face. "Sorry, guv."

They finally managed to tug me out. I felt like I'd been pierced by a thousand needles. From the little dots of blood all over my shirt, I wasn't far off. Well, I was awake now, that was for sure.

"Let's camp here," Meriel said. "It's getting too dark to walk, and Cal can barely stand anymore. The last thing he needs is to fall into more brambles."

"I didn't fall," I insisted as Lachlan began preparing the fire. "I was tripped."

"By what?"

"That crow."

Meriel looked at Gareth. "What crow?"

"The crow! The crow! The blasted, Spirit-cursed crow!" I said. "Didn't you see it?"

Now Meriel looked worried. So did Gareth. "Th-there was no crow," he said.

"Of course there was! How could you miss it?"

"Cal," Meriel said, "we were right behind you. I promise you, there was no crow."

"But . . ." I trailed off. Had I dreamed it? Had I fallen asleep while walking?

It was possible. But I was sure I'd been awake. Whether they saw it or not, that crow had been there. It had deliberately sent me sprawling into those brambles.

And they sure were painful. I flinched as Meriel removed my shirt. Several thorns were still stuck in my skin.

"This is going to hurt," she said as she began pulling them from my chest.

"*Ow!* You think?" I yelled.

"Don't be such a baby."

I bit back a retort. The truth was, I was sort of used to that kind of pain. My scars always ached. And they'd been aching a lot more lately.

When Meriel was done with the needles in my chest, she dabbed some ointment from the first aid kit we'd bought from the Lemon Tree.

"I still got that healing ring," Lachlan offered.

"Forget it," I said. I'd had enough of magic to last me a lifetime. This was just a few pinpricks. Well, a lot of pinpricks.

The front done, Meriel moved to my back. "I need some light," she said. "Can you bring your orb, Gareth?"

He stepped over to her obligingly, pulling his light orb from his pouch. He held it up.

And he gasped.

Meriel scrambled back in alarm. "Shuna's snout!" she said. "What is *that*?"

"What?" I said, fingers running over my back in worry. All I felt were my scars.

"There's marks on your back, guv," Lachlan said, puzzled. "They're *glowing*."

I froze. "Glowing?"

"They're not . . . I mean . . . they're not just marks," Gareth said, breathless. "They're magic. The orb is making them glow. And they're *words*."

I looked over at the Hollow Man, but he hadn't moved from beside the fire. My skin prickled with goose bumps. "What do you mean, words?" I said.

"It's the Old Tongue," Gareth said. "Someone's written a message in the Old Tongue on your back."

I could barely breathe. "What does it say?"

"*Ní goinéch a fadesín sét*," he said.

"Which means?"

"Only like kills like."

I turned to stare at him.

Meriel was shocked. "That's what my father used to say!" When the others looked at her, she explained. "Whenever he got sick. He'd go on about birds and beasts, and he kept repeating that phrase. 'Only like kills like.'" She looked at me sharply. "Wait—that's what I was dreaming when you were there. Ardal said it, too."

"What's it mean?" Lachlan said, confused.

Only like kills like. "It means I'd better talk to the Bear again," I said. "I need to dream."

"I thought that crow won't let you," Meriel said.

"I'll have to force my way past it."

"How?"

"It keeps scaring me awake," I said. "So what I have to do is not wake up, no matter how scared I get. Lachlan, do we have any snooze goo left?"

"Enough to treat a horse to a serious nap," he said. "You want to take it?"

"Unless one of you would rather bonk me on the head."

Meriel left that alone.

"Are you s-sure that's a good idea?" Gareth said. "If you can't wake up . . . I mean . . . what if you get trapped?"

Terrorized, he meant. *Just like Keane's poor Weaver friend.*

It made me shudder. But what choice did I have? "I'll have to take that chance," I said.

And hope that this time, the odds were with me.

CHAPTER 62

IT WORKED.

Lachlan fed me a heavy dose of the snooze goo. I was surprised at the lack of taste. The thick, straw-colored syrup had only the faintest flavor, a bit like honey. "This'll put you right out, guv."

The aches from the brambles' pricks faded as I became woozy. As I drifted off to sleep, I worried that the snooze goo would keep me groggy, even in Shadow. Instead, for the first time in days, my head was clear, alert—and ready to fight off that stupid crow.

To my surprise, the bird didn't come at all. I don't know whether it was the sleeping draught or whether the crow had just given up, but when I opened my eyes, I found myself on the beach again, Artha sitting on the sand.

She shook her head as I approached. "Haven't you had enough?" she said, sounding tired. "Why do you keep coming here? I have no more secrets for you."

"Actually," I said, "I might have one for you. Did you write on me?"

"*Write* on you?"

"Yeah."

She waved a hand in dismissal. "I don't know what you're talking about."

"Someone wrote on my back. With invisible magical ink. In the Old Tongue."

"Humans haven't spoken the Old Tongue for two thousand years."

"I know. Which means it wasn't put there by a human."

Artha frowned. *The Bear is curious*, Daphna had once said to me. She'd got that right, at least. Because even as Artha sat there, wishing I'd stop bothering her, she couldn't help but ask, "What does it say?"

"'Only like kills like,'" I said.

"I have no idea what that means."

"It's similar to one of the gaffer tricks the Old Man taught me. *Nothing makes a job easier than an inside man.*"

"I'm not a gaffer, Callan. Why should I care?"

"Because I keep hearing that phrase in Shadow. When I saw Meriel's past, her father said it over and over again. He even made me repeat it."

Artha shrugged. "There are many strange things in Shadow. That's what Shadow is."

"Sure. But it got me to thinking: Every job we've done with the Eye, we used that same trick. We gaffed Padraig to get into the High Weaver's mansion. We used Daphna to get into the Enclave. We tricked Aidan and Sully to get into Castle Cardogh. Every time we needed a new piece of this puzzle, we used an inside man to get it."

"So?"

"So maybe that's the secret to beating the Eye—the Devourer. An inside man."

"You can't defeat the Devourer," she said wearily.

"Not in a straight-up fight. But if we could gaff it somehow... Does Shuna know everything you can do?"

Artha's eyes hardened. "Why?"

I spoke carefully, trying not to make her angry. "You said you're not a gaffer. But Shuna is." A pretty good one, actually. I didn't dare point out how many times she'd snaffled the Bear. "I was just thinking maybe she'd have some insight into this. If we could talk to her."

"My sister doesn't know a fraction of what I can do," Artha snapped. "None of them do. Even if you put all of them together, they wouldn't match my strength or knowledge of magic. The only one who did was Kira, and she's . . ." Her anger faded. "She's gone."

"All right," I said. "You know magic. But Shuna knows tricks. And she knows the Eye—the Devourer—too. Doesn't she?"

I thought Artha would get angry again. Instead, she bowed her head. "Yes, Callan. Shuna knows the Eye. Better than I ever did."

"What do you mean?"

"I tried what you're suggesting already." Now there was shame in her voice. "I thought I could outsmart the Eye. We'd just defeated it, after all, and used it to shape Ayreth. I thought I could keep it. Continue to unlock its power. Use it for our own purposes.

"But the Devourer tricked me. It *wanted* me to use it. Because the more I did, the more I fell under its sway. It corrupted me. It took what I was—arrogant, prideful, oh so clever—and used it to twist my mind. Until I was even against my own family."

Sorrow bled from her. Sorrow and deep, deep regret. "We were so close back then, Shuna and I. She saw what was happening before any of the others. She tried to reason with me, tried to stop me. But what did I need her for? I had the power of the Eye.

"So I struck her down. I nearly murdered my own sister, Callan. Only like kills like? How well I know. The Eye already used me against Shuna. It's futile to fight it."

I could only imagine the magnitude of her shame. I remembered how, back in Veran's cavern under Lake Galway, the Eye's rage had taken me over, and I'd hit Lachlan when he tried to hold me back. It was just a punch, but I'd felt so guilty afterward. How much worse would it have been if I'd tried to kill him?

And yet I couldn't accept we were finished, either. "The Old Man told me something, long ago," I said. *"There's always a way out.* That's been true so far, even when I believed otherwise. Shuna believes it, too."

Artha shook her head. "She always had hope. What good has it done?"

"Well, I'm still alive, when I should be long dead. Shuna's been playing some gaff; I know it. Some of this, she's planned. She must have a reason. The thing is, I'm pretty sure she's right—and that *you* have the answer she's looking for. Even if you don't yet know it."

"That's just wishing," Artha said.

"It isn't," I insisted. "If it is, why did that crow try to prevent me from speaking to you?"

Artha went very still.

"Crow?" she said. "What crow?"

"In Shadow," I said. "Even on Ayreth. It keeps showing up. Is that Bran?"

Artha was looking at me intently now. "When was the first time you saw it?"

"The first—no, the second time I visited Shadow. It led me to a door in the forest. Meriel was behind it—"

Artha stood. "Tell me everything," she said. "Start from the beginning. The first time you came to Shadow. Leave out nothing. *Nothing.* No matter how small or irrelevant you think the detail is."

The intensity of her gaze rattled me, but I did as she said. I told her about rescuing that fox, and how the next time, the crow led me to Meriel's past. I told her everything I'd learned in Shadow Torgal, and how Meriel's father could see me. I told her of our escape the night Meriel's uncle came, and how the cart we fled on brought me to an ancient place with singing girls and the Dragon's Light.

Artha interrupted me there. "The Dragon's Light," she said. "He stabbed you with the Teeth? And that's what brought the dragon statue to life?"

"Yes."

She paused, thinking. Her eyes widened slightly. "Go on."

I told her how the crow had led me to her prison, then stopped me from hiding when I'd returned. Then how it had prevented me from dreaming, and tripped me afterward into the brambles.

"So," Artha said slowly, "the crow stopped you from dreaming … but *only* until you fell into the brambles. Which it made you do."

"Yes," I said.

"And that's how you found the writing on your back."

"Right. Then I came here."

Artha's eyes widened further.

I started to ask a question. "Is there—"

"Be quiet."

I shut up as Artha began to pace along the riverbank. She moved faster, thinking, gesturing, muttering to herself. "Only like kills like," she said. "Nothing makes a job easier than an inside man."

She stopped.

"Is it possible?" she whispered. "Is that the answer, you miserable old crow?"

She stared across the river.

Then she turned to me.

"I think I can help you fight the Devourer," she said.

"You can?" I said. "How?"

"First you have to do something for me."

"What's that?"

"Get me out of here."

". . . What?"

"Break me out of this prison," she said. "Help me escape, and I'll help you."

"I . . . wouldn't even know how to do that."

"I do. I'll tell you."

I looked at her, wary. "If you already know how to leave," I said, "why are you still here?"

"The only one who can't come and go freely from this prison is the one who gets placed inside it."

"How would you know that?"

"Because *I'm* the one who built it," she said, exasperated. "It was a prank on Shuna. I made this place out of Shadow and stuck her in here, ages ago. Took three weeks before Kira realized she'd gone missing and went looking for her."

A Spirit prank. That was just crazy enough to be believable. Which made me even more wary. "Why don't you tell me what your plan is first?" I said. "Then I'll let you out."

"I won't do that," Artha said. "Even after you let me out, I won't tell you."

"Why not?"

"Because the Eye's in your head."

"What's that got to do with anything?"

"How do you know it isn't listening?" she said.

I paused. "It can't hear us. My eyepatch is on."

"How do you know that stops it?"

"Well . . . it's never been able to see the world through it before. It kept getting mad when I tucked it away, because it didn't know what was happening."

"That's what it told you."

"No," I said, "that's what I felt."

"Maybe," she said. "Or maybe that's what it *allowed* you to feel. How do you know that wasn't a trick? You've already discovered how badly it gaffed you. How it gaffed me. It's arrogant, Callan, much more than I ever was—but it's also incredibly clever. Even if you're right, and it can't hear you through that patch, how do you know it can't pluck thoughts from your mind every time you let it free?"

I realized, with horror: She was right. I didn't know. I couldn't. So she really *couldn't* risk telling me her plan. The Eye needed to be our mark. And you have to keep your mark in the dark.

But what if *Artha* was snaffling me now? I knew she wanted the Eye—or at least she had, once. And she was plenty clever, too. Maybe this was her plan to escape what her sisters had done to her. Maybe Artha was running the gaff . . . and had been all along. Like I told the others, that's the problem with great gaffs. They make you think you're steering the ship, when you've actually been the pigeon from the start.

"I don't know," I said.

She shrugged and sat on the sand. "Come back when you do."

CHAPTER 63

I AWOKE MORE confused than ever.

The others were already up. The Hollow Man had eaten the last of the bacon days back, but Foxtail had managed to scrounge up some eggs—I didn't think they were from a chicken—which Meriel was frying over the fire. I just lay there, listening to them talk, not wanting to get out of bed.

The weight of this decision. It was overwhelming.

And I couldn't make it. Not yet.

Lachlan noticed my eyes were open. "Eggs, guv?" he said, holding out a plate.

I took them, though I wasn't hungry.

"Snooze goo work all right?" he asked.

"Yeah."

"So?" Meriel said.

They were all looking at me expectantly. "Can I think on it for a bit?" I said.

Meriel was surprised, but she said, "Of course."

"Take yer time, guv," Lachlan said cheerfully. "Ain't no rush. Well, maybe a bit of rush, eh?" Meriel whapped him on the arm. "Sorry, guv. Er . . . take yer time."

Time wasn't what I needed. Help was. I glanced over at Foxtail.

She seemed to understand. She walked away from the group. I joined her.

"I need to talk to our friend," I said.

She nodded and put a hand on my arm. *I'll try.*

We continued on like before. Gareth, using his map, his pocket watch, and the position of the sun, kept us going in the right direction.

We'd reached the Standing Stones of Weyring yesterday afternoon: seven cracked pillars of rock jutting from the earth. Gareth said they were a natural formation, though no naturalist had ever discovered the process that made them. From there, we'd turned west. Now we were on our way to cross the Goul, a long, meandering river that drained into the Cardogh where Tullagh province bordered the principality of Westland.

Only Foxtail hunted for us now. The deer she managed to snare each day kept us more than fed, even with the Hollow Man taking the lion's share of it. But that wasn't really why Meriel didn't go. She didn't want to leave us alone with him anymore.

With his feeding—it was too savage to call it eating—the Hollow Man had transformed at a shocking rate. Gone was the frail old man on the cusp of death. Now he was a brute. He still looked old, his gray hair shaved off, his face lined with wrinkles. But his build had grown like a soldier's. He stood now like a weathered general, a grizzled veteran of countless bloody wars. When we'd started out, he'd practically disappeared into the clothes Foxtail had brought for him, so baggy they'd looked ridiculous, like the costume of a carnival clown. Now his muscles strained the fabric so tightly that he was near to tearing the stitches.

He could probably snap the whole bunch of us in two, I thought. I wanted to peek with the Eye to see his glow, but I didn't dare. After what Artha had told me, I was terrified to free the jewel, in case it really could read my mind.

As nightfall approached, we reached the east bank of the Goul. We camped there, planning to cross the river in the morning. Foxtail returned, a successful hunt once more. As the Hollow Man fed and Lachlan built our fire, she caught my eye—and nodded toward the woods to the south.

Quietly, I took a lantern and headed off. The others only glanced at me briefly, assuming I was answering the call of nature. The Hollow Man didn't look up from his meal.

I didn't have to go too far. Shuna was waiting just a few yards beyond the tree line. She looked the same as always, a magnificent red fox with a white underbelly. I thought of Artha—the girl, not the bear—and wondered: What would Shuna look like as one of us?

She watched me approach with a critical eye. "That was a very naughty trick you pulled back at the prison," she said.

"I didn't come here to talk about that," I said shortly.

"I know." Shuna sighed. "You're angry with me."

I was. Though I hadn't realized how much until she said it. "Shouldn't I be? With the secrets you've been keeping?"

"Everything I hid was for good reason."

"This wasn't a secret you had a right to keep!" I said. "We deserved to know the truth!"

"And what would you have done if I'd told you?"

"What?"

"If I'd told you," Shuna said. "If I'd come to you beforehand and told you about the Eye, and the Devourer, and the primeval magic ready to tear the world apart from below, what would you have done? Would you have taken Mr. Solomon's job? Would you have freed the Eye from its cavern? Would you have pressed it to your head and gone searching for the Teeth? What would you have done?"

"I . . ." I hesitated. "I would have taken care of my friends."

"But you didn't have any friends," she said. "None of you knew each other at the start. So if Mr. Solomon's letter had arrived, and I'd shown up at Grey's that night to tell you what was coming, would you still have got on that airship?"

I didn't answer. Which was, I suppose, an answer in itself.

"I did what any gaffer would do," Shuna said. "I told you exactly what you needed to hear so you'd do exactly what you needed to do. And you've done it brilliantly so far."

"And what good has that done us?" I said, getting angry again. "Has it stopped the Eye's plans? Will it prevent the Devourer from returning? All we've done is bring the world closer to its death. Is that what you wanted? Don't you even care about us?"

Shuna's ears went back, her tail low. "How can you ask me that?" she said quietly. "We sacrificed everything for you. For your ancestors, so your people would continue to live. We gave up everything we were, everything we loved doing, just for you. And our sacrifice tore my family apart."

I could hear the grief in her voice. I could see the sorrow in her face. And something else there, too. Guilt.

And suddenly, I understood.

"*That's* why they're angry," I said. "Artha became furious with you. And Cailín won't talk to you anymore. They blame you . . . because the Pact was *your* idea."

"Yes."

"And . . . you knew, didn't you? You knew what the Pact would do to your family."

Shuna slumped. "Yes."

"But you did it anyway. Why?"

"Because I knew what would happen if we didn't." She looked sad and wistful. "Artha loved our life, Cal. Traveling, exploring the realms . . . she loved it more than any of us. Learning about new creatures, new places, new powers. I knew she'd grow restless, want to move on. That she'd be willing to take the chance there wasn't another Devourer somewhere out there.

"As for Cailín," Shuna said, "she was always the most independent. Fiona would follow the rules; she always did. But, like Artha, eventually Cailín would want to leave, too. I couldn't take the risk.

"So I went to Artha first. We were best friends, so she trusted me. I convinced her we needed to bind ourselves to this world, and the two of us convinced the others. And so the Pact was sworn."

Shuna looked miserable. "I was right. Artha grew restless. It bothered Cailín, too, but our rules chafed on Artha the worst. Over time, she became obsessed with getting out. Of all of us, she understood the nature of magic the best. So she began to study the Eye, trying to harness its power. Not for any bad purpose, not at first. She was trying to learn how the Devourer had tracked us. If she could discover that, then maybe we could guard against it and travel freely to other realms again.

"I warned her the Eye couldn't be trusted. She insisted she had it under control, that she was learning so much about the Devourer's true nature and its powers. She admitted the Eye whispered thoughts into her mind, but she promised she was strong enough to resist them."

Shuna shook her head. "If Artha hadn't been so desperate, maybe she wouldn't have fallen for its lies. But she let it in too deep. And it wormed its way into her mind and corrupted her.

"That's the Bear you met in the vault," Shuna said. "That wasn't my beloved sister. That's what the Eye did to her."

I remembered how Shuna had pleaded with her. *The Eye was never yours, Artha. Can I not make you understand? You can't own it. But it can own you. Won't you listen to me? Won't you remember who you were? Please?* After I'd met Artha in Shadow, I'd told Gareth how different she seemed from back in the vault. That she'd been playful, friendly, like in the early Fox and Bear stories.

Won't you remember who you were? It seemed that, free of the Eye's influence, she had—

"That's it," I said, staring at the Fox. "It was about *Artha*."

"What was?"

"All of this. You manipulated Artha into breaking the Pact so you could trap her in that prison—where she'd finally be free of the Eye's corruption. So she *would* remember who she was. Your gaff ... I thought it was on me. But this whole time, the real target of your gaff was your *sister*."

"Yes."

"Because of all of you, she's the only one with deep knowledge of the Devourer. So only she might figure out how to defeat it."

"Yes," Shuna said. "That was my gaff. I needed her to be who she really was. Because, Cal, I don't know how to beat the Devourer. I just don't know."

My heart was pounding. "Artha says she's figured it out."

Shuna perked up. "She has? How?"

"She won't tell me." I explained how Artha believed the Eye might learn her plans. "She wants me to help her escape."

The Fox went very still. "Did you let her out?"

"Not yet. That's really why I wanted to talk to you. To ask if you think she can be trusted."

Shuna stared off into the distance, troubled. "I ... I don't know how to answer that. If she's truly Artha again—my sister, the way she used to be—then yes. But if the Eye still has any hold on her, even the tiniest piece ... she's clever enough to fool both of us into thinking she's free."

"Is there any way to tell if she's herself again?"

"No." Shuna sighed. "And I love her too much to say she isn't and doom her there forever. I can't make that decision. I can't trust what I'll say."

"Oh, and *I* can?" When the Fox shrugged, I sat in the grass and buried my head in my hands. "Why me? Why is it always *me*?"

"I don't know," Shuna said seriously. "Sometimes there is no reason. Not everything's a gaff. Sometimes you're just in the right place at the right time."

"Or the wrong place at the wrong time," I muttered.

"That, too. But look . . . when I first came to you, it was because we were out of time. Choices had to be made, so I could only hope you'd make the correct ones. I know it hasn't been easy. No one's paid the price for this more than you. But you've been pretty good at making decisions so far. So trust your heart, as always, and I believe you'll make the right choice again."

"And if I don't?" I was so scared. "I'll be dooming the whole world."

Shuna sat next to me and placed a paw on my arm. "I don't have much left to promise you," she said. "But this I do promise: if the end comes, I'll stand by you, no matter what."

We stayed there a while, just sitting together in silence.

CHAPTER 64

I WALKED BACK to camp alone.

Though . . . I wasn't truly alone, was I? Sitting with Shuna may not have given me an answer. But I knew now I didn't have to struggle with the question by myself.

I stopped outside of our camp. Foxtail, always alert, saw the swing of my lantern approaching. I waved for her to come and bring the others. I didn't want to have this conversation near the Hollow Man.

They joined me just inside the woods. There we sat, and I told them everything Artha and Shuna had said. I laid it all out for them, along with the truth. "I don't know what to do."

"You can't possibly trust Artha," Meriel said, alarmed. "She's been after the Eye for thousands of years. She'd say anything to get her hands on it."

"You might be right," I said. "On the other hand, if I don't trust her, what chance do we have?"

"Maybe she'll make things worse."

"What's worse than the end of the world?"

"Nothing," Meriel said. "But we don't know *when* that's going to happen. It could be months, even years, until the primeval grows enough to crack the earth. Right?"

"Could be," I agreed.

"So maybe we should stop right here. Stop the Hollow Man, then go somewhere until we're really out of time. Maybe someone will think of something else by then."

That struck me as a genuine option. "Gareth?"

This kind of decision made him squirm. "Meriel could be . . . I mean . . . she could be right. But if Artha has an idea . . . she's the best one to stop the Eye." He struggled, wanting to be able to answer this for me, but he couldn't. "I don't . . . I don't know."

I looked to Foxtail. She shook her head and shrugged, then pointed at the rest of us. *I don't know, either. Whatever you decide, I'll be there with you.*

Before they'd joined me in the woods, Gareth had been reading to Lachlan from the Fox and Bear book I'd given him. Lachlan sat there now, the book clutched to his chest. "What do you think?" I said.

"Me?" He seemed surprised to be asked. "I ain't all that clever, you know."

"You're as important as any one of us. You get a say, too."

"I know. But . . . I dunno. I been thinking about these stories, right?"

He laid his book on his lap, ran his hand gently over the binding. The cover plate showed Shuna and Artha when they were still friends, standing atop a mountain, gazing over Ayreth below and grinning.

"The one Gar was just reading," Lachlan said, "was the Fox, the Bear, and the Twin Serpents. You know, where Shuna almost dies? But Artha comes in and saves her."

"I know the story." The Old Man had told it to me many times.

"When the snakes go to bite the Fox, the Bear jumps in front of her and takes the bites instead. So Artha gets poisoned instead of Shuna and stays sick for years after. And I was just thinking, she didn't have to do that, you know? She could have let Fox get sick instead, but she cared about her too much to let that happen. I guess I'm just saying . . . Artha was good once, before the Eye. Maybe we should help her be good again."

I reached out and pulled him into a half hug. "You're really the best of all of us, you know?"

"Aw, c'mon," he said, embarrassed. But he looked proud.

We returned to our camp, where the Hollow Man lay on his blanket, sleeping. We chatted a while, let Gareth read one final bedtime story from Lachlan's book, then lay down under our blankets.

I didn't close my eyes. Not yet. There was one more person I wanted to talk to.

I was wondering when you were going to get to me, the Old Man said.

I'm surprised you haven't already given your opinion, I said. *Whether I wanted it or not.*

Well, if you don't, I'll just be quiet.

I smothered a smile at the joke. The Old Man not offering an unasked-for opinion? Impossible.

He grinned. *You don't need me to tell you, boy. You already know what the gaffer's answer is.*

Trust nothing, I said. *Trust is for marks.*

Exactly. Most of the bad things that happened in your life were born from trust.

He was right. Every time we'd been burned, it was because we trusted someone else. Mr. Solomon. Daphna. Even the Old Man, when he left me behind.

But the opposite is true, too, Old Man, I said. *All the good things in my life also came from trust. My friends. Grey. Even you.*

It hurt me when you left, I told him. *It hurt me deeper than my scars ever could. But you'd taken care of me for years, long after you needed to. And as angry as I was, I loved you. I still do. And I wouldn't change that for the world.*

So, he said softly. *What's your answer?*

I'm not going to tell you, I said.

Why not?

I don't think you'd approve.

He laughed.

I closed my eyes. When I opened them, I was on the beach. Artha was sitting by the river, drawing strange, alien symbols in the sand with her finger. She looked up at me.

"I guess it's time to break you out of prison," I said.

CHAPTER 65

SHE STOOD, CALMLY. I thought she'd be more eager.

"What do I need to do?" I said.

"Take my hand."

Artha's fingers slipped into mine. She had the softest skin I'd ever touched. Like nothing in her whole life had ever marred it.

"Close your eyes," she said.

That made me pause. "Do I have to?"

"No. But you're not used to traveling through Shadow, so it'll be easier if you do."

If you're going to trust her, I told myself, *then you may as well actually trust her.* I closed my eyes.

"Now walk with me," she said.

We strolled along the beach. Her hand felt warm in mine.

"I want you to remember," she said. "I want you to think back to the last time you were happy."

"Shouldn't be hard. There aren't too many of those." I said it as a joke, but the fact that it was true made me sad.

Gently, she squeezed my fingers. "Concentrate. The last time you were happy."

I cast my mind back to find it. Little moments flitted through my memory. Lachlan playing. Foxtail twirling. Gareth reading. Meriel smiling at me.

But they only came and passed. And each time, I felt that pressure. *How are we going to pull off this gaff? What if this doesn't work? What will the Eye do to me?* My shoes sank into the sand.

"Keep going," Artha said. "Push your dark thoughts aside. The last time you were truly happy."

I traveled further backward in my mind.

We arrive at Sligach. We are traveling to Sligach. We are boarding the stagecoach in Stonewall. We are fleeing the Weaver Enclave.

Lachlan is alive.

Yes. I remembered. We'd saved him.

Aw, he said. *I ruined another shirt.*

My shoes scraped on stone.

I was walking on stone now. It echoed, like I was in a hall, the sound familiar. *That's the floor of the Weaver dungeon,* I thought. *Am I back there?*

I began to open my eyes—

"Keep them closed," Artha said. "Keep walking. Go back. Another time you were happy."

I pushed away the sound and searched again. I didn't have to go back too far.

It is the night before our vault job. We've put aside our worries and are just spending time together, playing games and stuffing our faces around the fire. I give Meriel her dragon pendant, and she looks at me with those beautiful eyes.

The ground changed again. Gone was the stone. Now the dirt was soft under my feet. A fire crackled beside me, the air filled with the sweet scent of roast pig.

"Keep going," Artha said.

She was holding my hand. The memories came faster now.

I am on the Malley, *my first ride on an airship. This is where I belong, I think.*

I stepped onto varnished wood. The floor swayed. I heard the *whoom-whoom-whoom* of the *Malley*'s propeller, felt the gentle rush of air over my face.

Faster now. Farther.

I am in Grey's shop, many years ago, under the clockmaker's workbench. I am playing with Lopsided the cat. Grey has just brought him home, payment from a Weaver for a job, though Grey doesn't tell me what. He's a silly thing, Lop, but I adore him from the first time he leaps into my arms.

Floorboards creaked under my feet. I smelled the fishy stink of burning whale oil. And over that, the rich smell of tobacco smoke.

The Old Man's pipe, I thought.

And then I am with him. We are camped by the fire. I can't see him on the other side of the blaze, but I hear him. He is telling me a story. Fox and Bear.

The floorboards changed to dirt again, twigs snapping underneath

and then I was walking on floorboards once more.

"We're here," Artha said.

I opened my eyes.

CHAPTER 66

I WAS ON an airship.

Artha and I were high in the sky. Puffy white clouds drifted lazily beneath our hull. Far below them was Ayreth. I saw its green grasslands and craggy mountains and wide rivers streaming into vast lakes. Above us was nothing but blue, glorious blue, the sun shining bright.

This airship was much smaller than the *Malley*. The helion looked to be only a fifth the *Malley*'s size, with small twin propellers softly *whirr-whirr-whirr*ing at the rear. The main deck was much smaller, too, with fewer central cabins and a smaller deck above, underneath the helion's skin.

And we weren't alone. My friends were there. Meriel and Lachlan crouched near the prow, tossing dice over a pile of septs and cheering—or groaning—at the result. Gareth sat nearby, nose buried in a book. Above them, legs dangling from the upper deck, was Foxtail, enjoying the cool, gentle breeze.

They weren't the only ones here, either. I heard singing coming from the upper deck. *That song*, I thought.

That song.

Memories washed over me like waves. I remembered the girl who'd taken care of me when I was little, the one I'd called Mum. That was her song.

That was her *voice*.

Before I could run up the stairs, a door to one of the cabins creaked open. It was Lop, slipping through, going inside. Puzzled, I pushed the door all the way open.

Grey's workshop was on the other side. The clockmaker—a younger version of him, the way he'd appeared when I first met him—looked up from where he tinkered at the bench. "Will ya close that blasted door already, boyo?" he said. "Can't hear myself think with all that racket."

Grey? What was he doing here?

And then I smelled the pipe. *His* pipe.

The faint scent of tobacco wafted from the next cabin over. That door was closed. I went to it, put my hand against the wood.

He's inside, I thought. *The Old Man really is inside.*

Artha stood beside me. "What is this place?" I whispered.

"This is your soul," she said. "The core of it. The deepest, most secure place inside you. Where there are no worries, no pain. Where you keep all the things you love."

No pain, she'd said. And as she spoke, I realized: I really *did* feel no pain. I lifted my shirt.

My scars were gone.

My skin was smooth, as if the Stickman's whip had never lashed me. I touched my face, searching, and discovered my eye was back, too.

"This is the place that makes you," Artha said. "No one, nothing, can choose to come here except you."

"But you're here," I said.

"Because you brought me inside. If you hadn't, all my powers couldn't have breached its walls."

I looked around in wonder. I'd never felt such peace.

When Artha spoke, it was as if she'd read my mind. "You can't stay. You have to leave."

"Why?"

"This place is dangerous for you. The longer you remain, the more it will hold sway."

I couldn't stop staring at everything around me. To always feel this peace? "What's wrong with that?"

"If you don't leave soon, you never will. Your mind will bury itself here. To the outside world, it will look like you're asleep. But you'll never wake up. Your body will waste away and eventually die."

Somewhere in the back of my mind, I knew she was right. I was already starting not to care what happened to me outside.

But the peace . . . the peace.

I'll just open this door, I thought. *Just this one. See the Old Man again—*

"Callan."

Artha's voice was sharp. It brought me back.

"All right . . . all right." I shook my head to clear it and remembered why we'd come here in the first place. "So it worked, then?" I said. "You're out of prison?"

She nodded. "We left the prison a while ago, when your mind first stepped into the Weaver vault."

"But we're still in Shadow."

"No. We're back in your realm now. That's where your soul is, inside you."

I didn't really understand. But I was feeling that pull to stay again. "What now?"

"You go," Artha said, "and you leave me behind."

"You want to stay in my *soul*?"

"In here, at its core, yes."

That didn't sound like a good idea. "Won't that leave me exposed? At your mercy?"

"Yes."

"So . . . you could hurt me if I left you here."

"More than that," she said. "I could tear apart all that's good inside you. It would leave you a miserable, vicious husk of a person. There's nothing worse that could happen to someone. Death would be preferable."

I stared at her, horrified. At least no one could say she wasn't being truthful. "Then why would I let you stay?"

"It's the only way to trick the Eye. If I just remain inside you like the Devourer is inside you, it will sense me. It'll know I'm there. And my plan won't work. We have to take it by surprise. Your soul core is the one part of you we can be absolutely certain the Eye can't see into. It's the one place within you I can truly hide."

"But *I'll* know you're here," I objected. "If it can read my thoughts . . ."

"You won't remember this."

"Why not?"

"I'm going to alter your memory before you leave. All you'll know is that you freed me from my Shadow prison, and I promised I'd come help you when you needed it."

I didn't know what to think. On the one hand, it was madness. Leave the Bear—not exactly my closest friend—inside my soul core? On the other hand, she was being brutally honest with me. It made me inclined to trust her. *Which is how the gaff works*, I thought.

Yet looking around this place . . . it was hard to feel anything but secure. Maybe that was part of the gaff, too. But I supposed I'd already made my decision, hadn't I? In for a sept, in for a crown, as the Old Man liked to say.

"What do I do?" I said.

Artha nodded toward the brass railing. "Jump over the side."

"You're joking."

"It's the simplest way to jolt your mind out of this place." When I hesitated, she said, "I can throw you off, if you'd like."

"Er . . . no, thanks. I'll do it myself." I climbed over the rail and gave one long, lingering look at what I was about to leave behind. "Could I just stay one more—"

Artha placed her palm on my forehead and shoved.

I lost my grip. And then I was falling

falling

falling

I

am.

Who

am

I?

. . .

I awoke with a grunt.

I sat up, pressing my temples. "*Uhhgghh.*"

Meriel, keeping watch over the fire, hurried over and kneeled next to me, a hand on my shoulder. "What's wrong?"

"My head hurts," I said. That didn't really do it justice. It felt like it was *splitting*.

"Here," she said. She wet a cloth in the river and placed it gently on my face. The coolness of it helped soften the pain, until it faded to a dull throb.

Meriel glanced over at the sleeping Hollow Man. "Did it work?" she said quietly. "Did you see her?"

I nodded, pressed the cooling cloth against my neck. "She's out."

"So where is she now?"

"She's . . ." I trailed off, frowning.

"What?" Meriel said.

I blinked. "I can't remember."

CHAPTER 67

It took us five more days to reach the valley.

"That's it," Gareth said as we came over the rise. "The Valley of Kildinan."

High hills surrounded the green. Most of the valley was bordered with plateaus, platforms of craggy rock with steep cliffs overlooking the expanse. Far below was a grassland, with low, rolling hills among it. From here, I couldn't see anything of interest at the bottom. Though maybe in the very center . . . was that—

"We must prepare," the Hollow Man said.

His voice made me jump. It was the first time he'd spoken in a week. "What?" I said.

"We must prepare." Even his voice had become stronger. "Everything must be made ready, Emissary."

"How do we do that?"

"Bindings must be inscribed. Your assistance will not be required. Though of course, you may accompany me to witness."

I figured we'd better. Though at this point, if we didn't like what he was doing, there wasn't much we could do to stop him. Meriel palmed a pair of knives, and Foxtail looked ready to spring, for all the good that might do.

I'd assumed he'd take us into the valley. Instead, he stared for a while at the surrounding hills. "There," he said, pointing. "I will place the first binding there."

We followed him over the rocks to one of the plateaus overlooking the expanse. It was strangely quiet around here, in a way I couldn't put my finger on but found unsettling nonetheless. When we reached the place the Hollow Man had marked, he turned to Meriel. "May I use one of those knives?" he said.

I supposed I shouldn't have been surprised we hadn't fooled him. He didn't seem to take offense that we'd tried. When Meriel looked to me, I shrugged, and she handed over one of the blades.

"This will dull the edge," he apologized, then kneeled on the stone. From there, he began scraping a large symbol into the rock. It looked similar to the tattoos he had on his body, and the ones we'd seen on Bragan, too. Overlapping lines, angular; crude compared to the flowing Weaver runes.

When he finished with the large symbol, he carved smaller ones around it in a many-branched spiraling pattern. Though I really didn't want to lift my patch again, I had to know. I peeked with the Eye as he worked.

There was no glow to the markings. "What are those?" I asked the Eye quietly.

did he not tell you? the Eye said.

"All he said was that he needed to prepare."

The Eye sounded amused. and so he does.

"Prepare for what?"

I would not like to spoil the surprise, the Eye said. do not worry, foxchild. it will be completed soon.

Soon was relative, I supposed, because it took a couple of

hours for the Hollow Man to finish. Once he'd completed marking the stone, he placed his hands on it, breathing deeply. Again I peeked with the Eye. This time, the runes did start to glow. The Hollow Man was enchanting them, using nothing more than the energy contained in his own body.

As I'd seen happen before during enchantments, I expected the Hollow Man's light to dim as he bound the runes. But his glow remained more or less the same. It appeared that his feeding over the past week had filled him with a reserve of energy much greater than what he was using. I wondered just how much he had left.

With that symbol finished, we moved on. He did the same thing three more times on different plateaus surrounding the valley. Gareth paid close attention, not only watching what the Hollow Man was carving but also marking the runes on our map. As the Hollow Man worked on the fourth symbol, Gareth pulled me aside.

"It's a square," he said, and he showed me the markings on the map. "The runes form the corners of a s-square around the center of the valley."

I asked the Hollow Man again what all this was for. He just said, "It is necessary, Emissary," without stopping his carving. I thought of using my position as Emissary to challenge him—or question the Eye—but what was the point? I didn't know anything about enchantments. Whatever they told me, I'd have no way of knowing if it was true.

I did learn the Hollow Man's energy wasn't boundless, however. By the time he finished the final symbol, his glow had dimmed—not by much, but enough for me to notice. He looked pretty tired, too. "I need to eat," he said.

I'd assumed we'd finish this now. But it had taken the Hollow Man all day to complete his work, and the sun was already beginning to set. So we made camp. The Hollow Man sat by the fire, scratching new symbols into round, flat stones roughly the size of his handspan, which he'd collected as we'd made our way around Kildinan. As Foxtail left to hunt, he looked up from his carving and stopped her.

"Do not search for prey in the valley," he said.

"Why not?" Meriel said, suspicious.

"You will find none. All creatures avoid it."

That was what was bothering me. Since this morning, I'd found the quiet unsettling. Now I realized why. We hadn't heard a single animal's call. No birdsong, no rustling in the grass, nothing. Just Galawan's occasional tweet as Lachlan played with him.

Gareth hadn't said a word to the Hollow Man since the day he awoke. His curiosity finally made him pipe up again. "W-what is this place?" he asked.

"An ancient battlefield," the Hollow Man said. "The resting place of the greatest struggle this realm has ever known."

"A battlefield, eh?" Lachlan said. "Would we find old stuff if we go digging, then? Swords and skeletons and the like?"

"None that you would recognize, little one."

I knew why. He wasn't talking about a clash of armies. This was where the Spirits had fought the Devourer.

I stared down into the valley, awed. Nuala the Wolf and Lila the Rabbit had died here. Kira, too, spiriting away just enough of her essence to linger on, so she could help us four and a half thousand years later under Lake Galway. This was also where the Devourer had fallen. And where Artha and Shuna and Fiona and Cailín had picked up its eye and teeth, turned them into the Eye and the Teeth, and used them to bring life to the previously barren globe. Everything Ayreth was, everything that had ever happened on this world . . . it had all started here.

Gareth had put it together, too. He walked to the edge of the cliff and stood over the valley for a long time. We had to call him over to come eat.

Dinner was a mostly quiet affair, made from the last of our provisions. Even Lachlan had little to say. The gravity of what awaited us tomorrow weighed too heavily.

When we finished, the Hollow Man curled up beside the fire to sleep, no different than any other night. But everyone else was restless. Lachlan flipped through his Fox and Bear book, looking at the illustrations. Gareth stared down into the valley again. Foxtail wandered off into the darkness. Meriel wandered away, too, toward the edge of the cliff. But she kept looking back at me.

I went to her, far enough from the others to be out of earshot. She looked nervous, rubbing the dragon pendant I'd given her between her thumb and forefinger. Like she wanted to say something to me but wasn't sure how.

I didn't press her. I just sat at the edge, legs dangling over the side, and stared up at the sky.

"Stars are pretty tonight," I said.

"They are."

I waited.

"Do you think we're going to make it?" she said.

If it was Lachlan or Gareth, I would have reassured them. But I didn't want to lie. Not to her.

"Probably not," I said.

She nodded and sighed. "What do you think happens after? I mean . . . after we die."

"I don't know. I asked the Old Man about it once."

"What did he say?"

I did a fair imitation of his voice. "'How would I know, boy? Ask me when I'm dead, I'll tell you then.'"

She gave a small, sad smile as she gazed across the valley. "My father always told me we go somewhere nice after we're gone. Somewhere kind of like this. But we get to do things over. We get the chance to fix all the mistakes we made in this life. To live in warmth and peace. To make a better place for everyone we—" She paused. "Everyone we care about."

That sounded pretty good to me. "I hope he's right."

She bit her lip. "If there is another life . . . after," she said. "Will you come look for me?"

I met her gaze. "For however long it takes," I said.

She flushed and looked away. Then she rooted around in one of her pockets for something. When she took it out, she held it tight for a moment, as if she wasn't sure what to do with it.

Then she shook her head, like she was being stupid, and held it out. "Here."

It was one of her knives. But it was one I'd never seen her use before. The blade was silver, the grip inlaid with a crisscrossing pattern of gold bands. Its surface was finely polished, its edge sharpened to a needle's point.

My first thought was *I don't think that's going to do anything to the Hollow Man. His tattoos will prevent us from hurting him.*

But as I watched her, I didn't think that was why she was offering me the knife. It was too fine to just be a weapon. And the way she held it out to me, with both hands, the blade flat on her palms . . . It wasn't a casual thing.

This wasn't for protection. It was a gift. A gesture.

A promise.

I stood.

Meriel watched me, eyes wide and uncertain. I took the blade from her hands. But I didn't tuck it away in my pocket. Instead, I slipped it in my belt, near my side. Where everyone could see it.

She looked pleased—and relieved. I could only guess what this gesture meant for a girl from Torgal, but I thought I'd got it right. She nodded, blushing, then turned to go.

"I was going to stay awhile," I said, "and look at the sky."

She sat at the edge of the cliff. I sat, too, and put my arm around her. She leaned against me, head on my shoulder, and together, we watched the stars.

CHAPTER 68

It was a fitful sleep that night. I didn't know whether it was because there was some lingering magic in this valley or whether it was just the anticipation of what was coming, but I had strange, wild dreams. I didn't think I ever drifted into Shadow, though it did leave me wondering for the fifth night in a row what had happened to Artha.

I'd spent a lot of time staring into the darkness, trying to recall where she and I had gone after I'd walked her out of her prison. *I was holding her hand. Her skin was so soft. We went . . . to a dungeon? There was stone . . . and—*

I pressed my hand to my head. It had started to hurt again. As the pain faded, I thought I could smell the faintest hint of . . . smoke? I couldn't remember.

In the morning, the others looked as rough as I did. Like me, they'd tossed and turned all night, except for the Hollow Man. He seemed the same as ever. And when the sun rose in the sky, he said, "It is time."

We followed him into the valley.

There was something in the center.

From the surrounding plateaus, I hadn't been able to make it out. Now, as we approached, at the top of a gentle hill, I saw a tree. It was an oak, an ancient one, its bark weathered, thick branches stretching from its giant trunk, springing forth with countless bright green leaves.

Near the base of the oak was a rock. It was rough and misshapen, eight feet high and wide. The rock was made of pure black stone, a kind I'd never seen before, that seemed to absorb all the sunlight that shone upon it. My skin prickled as we got closer. Even with the Eye covered, I could feel the stone's power.

Lachlan held his arms to his chest and rubbed them as if he was cold. He could feel its power, too. "Shuna's sneezing snout. What is this?"

"The end of our path," the Hollow Man said. "The Dragon's Heart."

I'd already known it, but hearing the words seemed to make it more real. My own heart thumped as we approached it.

The Dragon's Heart, I thought. *Where the Devourer hid his soul. Shuna—and Artha—please help me.*

"W-what's it m-made of?" Gareth asked.

"I do not know," the Hollow Man said. "I only know it is impervious to all things. All but one."

I froze.

There were three pieces of that dragon we couldn't destroy, Artha had told me, *even with all our power.* The Spirits had tried to crack the Eye, the Teeth, the Heart, to penetrate them, to get to the Devourer's soul as it escaped, but they couldn't. Now the Hollow Man had just let something slip.

There *was* a way inside.

If we could figure out what that was . . . *Artha? Shuna? Are you listening?* I couldn't remember where Artha had gone

(my head hurts why does it hurt?)

but she said she'd help me when I needed it. Well, now *I* could help *her. Artha? Where are you?*

Maybe she was waiting for the Hollow Man to reveal the answer. "What could get inside that?" I said, as if disbelieving.

"Patience, Emissary," he said. "We have yet to finish our preparations."

I didn't want him to grow suspicious, so I didn't press him. I just said, "What do you need to do?"

"This time, I will require everyone's assistance."

He pulled the stones he'd been working on last night from his pocket. There were four of them, each marked with a different design.

The runes he carved yesterday, I realized. *The big ones, in the center of the spirals, around the valley. They match the runes on these stones.*

He handed one to each of the others. "You will need to hold these," he said to them, "and stand between the platforms I carved and the Heart." He directed each of them to a different spot around twenty yards from the stone.

Lachlan turned to go immediately. Meriel stopped him. "Why should we?"

"It is necessary," the Hollow Man said simply. "It will not harm you in any way, I promise."

I'd found the man nearly impossible to read from the start. Yet I didn't get the sense that he was lying. "It's all right, Meriel."

She took her place, stone in one hand. I could tell she had a knife hidden in other her palm—and I believed the Hollow Man knew, too. He still turned his back on her, as if he just didn't care.

The others accepted their own stones and took their places, Gareth looking worried. He caught my eye and looked off into the distance. Like me, he'd noticed the symbols matched. When they'd taken their spots, they were standing in a perfect square, the Dragon's Heart at the center.

"I don't get a stone?" I said.

"I need you with me, Emissary," the Hollow Man said. "We will require the Eye and the Teeth."

We'd kept the swords bound in Foxtail's pack. I took them out and handed them to him. He held the blades reverently, almost lovingly, for a moment. Then he began cutting into the earth with them near the base of the stone, drawing new designs in the grass.

"Should I take out the Eye?" I said.

"Not yet." He continued his drawing. With the Eye covered, I couldn't see enchantments, but from the way he used the Teeth—cutting, then pausing; cutting, then pausing—I suspected he was transferring some of the magic in those blades to enchant the runes he was carving. Soon enough, I didn't have to guess.

Tiny flashing lights, dancing around like fireflies, rose from the grass. They winked different colors, floating outward to sur-round us.

I stepped back. "What are these?"

The Hollow Man grunted. Whatever he was doing was taking a toll on him. "A moment, please, Emissary," he said, his voice strained. He continued cutting until the air was alive with the lights. "There."

"So what are these?" I asked again.

"A distraction," he said.

Suddenly, he bent down and punched his fist into the ground. The lights—which the others were watching as warily as I was—winked out.

Then Meriel, Gareth, Lachlan, and Foxtail vanished, too.

CHAPTER 69

"WHAT DID YOU do?" I said, voice tight. "What did you do to my friends?"

"I dismissed them." The Hollow Man sounded apologetic. "They would only have got in our way."

"Did you . . . did you kill them?" My heart rose in my throat. "Where—"

"The platforms." He pointed with one of the swords—Belenoth, with its bright white pommel—toward the distant plateaus. "The binding on the stones they held transported them there. As promised, they are unharmed." He tucked the Dragon's Teeth in his belt. "Though why such things matter to you, Emissary, I do not know. Regardless, all will be made whole soon."

"What do you mean, made whole— Stop. Stop!"

The Hollow Man stalked toward me. I tried to back away, but he was moving so fast.

"Stop!" I shouted. "I command you—"

He grabbed me by the throat, cutting off my breath. "We both follow a greater command than yours, Emissary."

He lifted me from the ground by the neck. I clawed at his arms, kicked at his legs. He ignored my struggles, even when I tried slashing him with the knife Meriel had given me, which bounced harmlessly off his skin. He only slapped my hands away when I reached for the Teeth.

"Your ways are strange," he said, studying me like an insect. "You care for things that are small and unimportant. Yet our master chose you as his emancipator." He carried me toward the Heart. "I do not question, you understand. But I do find it curious. Perhaps there is a lesson here. All serve, whether they comprehend or not."

He slammed me against the stone. My skin crawled now as the power in the Dragon's Heart ran over me, like a million tiny spiders seeking prey. I tried to scream, but it only came out as a cough. My hands wrenched at his, trying to pull his fingers from my throat.

"Artha," I croaked. "Shuna—Artha—*help*—"

"You call to the Spirits?" the Hollow Man said, surprised. "Surely you know they can do nothing. They trapped our master, true, but they were seven then, and the world was bare—and even so, they could not truly defeat him. Now they are four, and the world is alive. The Spirits' time is over. But ours, Emissary, has just begun."

He drew Camuloth from his belt. Its jewel was nearly a match for the endless black of the stone he pressed me against.

"Wait—"

"He has already waited," the Hollow Man said. "He has waited for four and a half thousand years. Now you will guide him back."

And he stabbed me through the chest with the blade.

Pain. Nothing but burning pain as Camuloth pierced my flesh. It drove through my lung—and then into the Heart behind me.

The Dragon's Heart. Impervious to all things, the Hollow Man had said. All but one.

The Dragon's Teeth themselves.

Through the agony, the words rang in my head. There was the answer.

Only like kills like, I thought.

And then Camuloth began to work.

I felt myself—my soul—draining into the unholy blade. As the sword held me pinned to the Heart, the Hollow Man ripped off my eyepatch, and the world came alight with the glow of life and magic.

So *much* magic. I looked down at the sword in my chest. It was turning carnelian red as my soul drained into it.

YES

the Eye thundered.

Now the Hollow Man drew Belenoth from his belt. Its pommel shone bright in the sun.

"I envy you, Emissary," the Hollow Man said. "You will be granted eternal life above us all."

YES

the Eye thundered again.

And then the Hollow Man stabbed me through the heart.

I barely felt the pain this time as the sword plunged through my body and into the stone behind. My soul, already draining into Camuloth, ran across to its sister blade, turning Belenoth the same carnelian red. And I felt myself drawn away

away

away.

Then all was black.

CHAPTER 70

I STOOD ON an empty plain.

Everything was gone. Nothing surrounded me but that pure black stone, utterly flat and perfect, stretching away forever. The plain was illuminated by a faint light, almost like it was dusk, but there was no sun, no moons, no stars in the sky. Nothing.

No. Not nothing. A figure began to form in front of me. Smoky wisps curled from the air, thickening to coalesce into a shape, beyond huge. It had a long, sleek body, two leathery wings, and a head and a tail.

A dragon.

The Devourer, hidden inside the Eye. It had come through the Teeth with my soul, drawn out by Camuloth, sent forth by Belenoth, the blades penetrating the Heart to let the dragon's mind rejoin its essence once more. Together, they formed and grew and rumbled.

YES

the dragon said.

Its voice boomed across the obsidian plain. No longer just in my head, but everywhere. The dragon twisted, writhing in pleasure at the rejoining. It reared its head and trumpeted its victory, its joy making me tremble to the core.

The Devourer's head turned. It looked down upon me from a thousand feet high, its eyes amber jewels against the pitch-black sky.

foxchild, it said. we have succeeded. I have waited for ages to re-form. my mind joins now with my soul. and when it is complete, I will rebuild my body in your world.

My mind was already reeling at the sight of this magnificent, terrible creature—and at my death, my soul severed from my own body by the Teeth. Yet I couldn't help thinking of the people I'd left behind.

"And what will happen to my friends?" I said. *And to me?* I wondered.

I didn't know if it could read my mind in this place, but that was the question it answered. you will join me. already you lie within. I will keep you intact so you can witness my glory. I shall reclaim my blood, the lifeblood of your world, and devour this realm. then I shall find somewhere anew. as it ever was.

The dragon laughed. this is your promised reward, foxchild. is it not fitting? that we should see such things together, you and I?

Suddenly, I felt something stirring next to me. On the endless plain, something else began to form. A . . . girl? In a brown tunic, with sandals—

I remembered.

The walk through Shadow. My soul core. I'd left her there.

I *remembered*.

And now Artha stood beside me.

what is that? the dragon said. It stared, amber eyes high above us.

Then those eyes widened.

you, it said in surprise. how did you find your way inside?

I remembered. The gaff. Artha had hidden inside my soul. In the core, where the Eye couldn't see her. So when the Teeth had drawn me and the Eye into the Heart . . . *Artha had come through with us.*

I stared at her. She smiled.

"Like you told me," she said. "Nothing makes a job easier than an inside man."

And finally, finally, after all those gaffs . . . *I* was the inside man. I wished the Old Man were here to see this. He would have laughed.

The Devourer certainly did. Its mockery boomed across the plain. is this your plan, foxchild? did you bring the bear here to thwart me? fool. this changeling spirit only bested me with the help of its kindred, on a planet barren of life, where I could not rejuvenate. now it comes alone, after eons, when my lifeblood has grown, and fed, and blazes with power. it cannot defeat me on this world.

"*That* world," Artha said.

The dragon paused. what?

"You meant to say *that* world. On Ayreth. Where your blood runs under the earth and the life that grows could feed you. But we're not in that world, you abomination. We're in *this* world. We're in *your* soul. Where you have no extra power to draw on."

Artha bared her teeth. "There's nothing to help you here, creature," she spat. "There's nothing but you and me. And I've been waiting for this for a long, *long* time."

Then, suddenly, Artha was no longer the girl. She was the Bear—THE BEAR—a thousand feet tall to match the dragon.

The Devourer roared with rage. TRAITOROUS FOX-CHILD! I WILL SLAUGHTER THIS CHANGELING! THEN I WILL PIERCE YOUR HEART AND FEAST! YOUR SOUL WILL WRITHE IN TORMENT FOR ALL ETERNITY!

And then the Bear fell upon him.

CHAPTER 71

THE BATTLE RAGED across the plain.

The dragon clawed at the Bear. The Bear pounded the dragon. Madly, already knowing I was dead, I rushed in, as if I could even distract the Devourer with my puny fists. Artha saw me coming and swatted me away, a backhanded paw that sent me tumbling. "Don't be an idiot," she growled.

That's good advice, the Old Man said. *If I were you, I'd listen.*

I stayed back after that. It was a fight far beyond me, anyway. It happened on levels I couldn't comprehend. With my eyes, I saw the dragon and Bear tear at each other. With tooth and claw, with brute strength and tactical cunning, they fought, ripping great chunks from each other's souls.

The dragon bled black, the utter black of the void. The Bear bled red, bright and raging. Some of their wounds healed, the wisps that leaked out solidifying to re-form their souls. But some of their essences—more and more, as the fight went on—simply curled and blew away, gone forever.

Magic tore across the plain, too. The dragon called down great bolts of lightning from the empty sky. Jagged arcs struck the Bear over and over again, and Artha roared in pain. But she swiped back with one great paw, and suddenly waves of fire washed over the Devourer, burning the terrible creature in agony. And more magic came: beams of light; ghostly spears; dark, writhing forms. I cowered as the magic ripped the emptiness apart.

And something happened beneath that, too. Beyond the mind, deep in a place I didn't understand. I caught a glimpse of it as the titans clashed, not in my mind but in my soul, and the strange things I saw made my essence scream and threaten to burst apart. I had no words to describe the horrors. But I understood that there, in the layer below, the battle raged as well. And in another layer below, and a layer below that, and another layer and another layer and another and another and *another*

Something cuffed me on the back of my head. *Snap out of it, boy*, the Old Man said. *Didn't I tell you fiddling with nature is for fools?* I caught a fleeting image of him in my mind. Then he was gone, and I couldn't see those deeper layers anymore. But my head was spinning now, and I was falling

falling

falling

I lay on the plain.

I didn't know how long I'd been lost in my mind. But when I awoke, the Bear had the dragon's body wrapped in her arms. The Devourer clawed at her, ripping Artha's soul-flesh into tatters, yet somehow the Bear held on. And as the magic burned and battered her, the Bear took the dragon's neck between her jaws.

YOU CANNOT DEFEAT ME! the Devourer raged. I AM GREATER THAN YOU!

Artha clamped down harder. Her teeth sank deep into the dragon's flesh. And then that inky void began to curl away, disappearing into the starless sky.

TRAITOROUS FOXCHILD! the dragon shouted, its voice nothing but fear and rage. YOU WILL NEVER—

The Bear bit through.

And with one great tear, she ripped the dragon's head from its body.

The Devourer curled into wisps, evaporating. Its form wavered, then burst apart. A million billion pieces rose like dust, a million billion particles sparkling in the twilight, then vanishing into nothingness. And as it died, the Devourer saved the last of its hate for me.

traitorous foxchild, it whispered.

Then it was gone.

CHAPTER 72

ARTHA COLLAPSED ONTO the plain.

She was no longer THE BEAR, a thousand feet tall. Now she was just the Bear, as I'd seen her in the Weaver vault, when she'd still been under the influence of the Eye.

And she was terribly, terribly hurt.

I ran to her. Her chest was heaving, her fur matted with blood. There were so many wounds, so *many*, flesh bleeding and stripped to the bone where the dragon's claws had ripped at her as she'd held on for the killing blow. Her breath was ragged, shaking with the *huh-huh-huh* of the dying.

She needed help. Desperately. I tugged at her paw. "Come on," I said. "Get up."

Artha's voice was barely a croak. "I can't."

"Yes, you can," I said. "Look, we saved Lachlan. We can help you, too. If we can get back to Ayreth, I'm sure Shuna will come—"

"Shuna doesn't have the knowledge to save me. I'm too injured."

"Don't say that," I said, near shouting. "Don't say that!" I tried to drag her. I may as well have tried to lift a mountain. "Listen . . . Artha, please listen. You need to turn back into the girl. I'll carry you out—"

"Be at peace, Cal," she said. "I knew from the start that this was the end."

"No. *No.*" I tugged at her paw. "It's not *fair.*"

Even through what must have been horrible pain, the Bear smiled. "We tricked the Devourer well enough to kill it. Kill it forever. This trade is more than fair enough." She coughed. "Now you must go."

"Why?"

"This place is collapsing. It was a construct of the Devourer's soul. It won't hold together with the monster gone."

I looked around—and saw, with horror, that Artha was right. In the distance, the plain's horizon was getting closer. Like we were trapped inside a shrinking bubble.

My first thought was pure panic. *Get out!* And I wanted to.

But I couldn't.

I thought of all those times with the Old Man, listening to stories of Fox and Bear. I thought of Lachlan with his book, and how much he loved the Spirits. I thought of Artha, and how much she'd sacrificed, just for us. And I thought of Shuna, and how devastated she'd been when I told her I'd seen Kira. How deeply she loved Artha, even after all that had come between them. How could I go back without her? How could I tell the Fox that I'd just left her sister to die?

I wanted to run. And I knew Artha would resist my trying to help her. But even as my stomach fluttered, I was still the gaffer the Old Man had taught me to be. So I knew how to use this against her.

I sat next to the Bear and waited.

"What are you doing?" she said.

"You called me 'Cal,'" I said.

"So?"

"I told you, Cal's what my friends call me. And we don't leave our friends behind."

She was getting angry. "Do you not understand? You're throwing your life away. Shuna doesn't have the power to heal me. Even if you manage to take me from this place, I'll still die."

"Maybe," I said. "But at least you won't die alone."

The Bear gave me a look of exasperation. "You're just like her," she grumbled.

But grudgingly, she held out a paw.

I leaped up and took it. "Now change. Please? So I can carry you?"

"I can't. I simply can't, Cal."

To my dismay, I believed her. More of her form was curling into smoke, faster now. Even the act of lifting her arm had made things worse. My heart sank as her eyes fluttered.

"But this isn't my body," she said. "It's my soul."

"I don't know what that means," I said.

"Hurry." Her voice had grown so weak, I could barely hear her. "You must hurry. Go. Go."

"Go how? Where's the exit?"

"The only way out . . . is through the things that matter to you. Look for them. They'll help."

"I don't know what that means, either," I said, desperate now.

"Tell her . . . tell her I'm sorry," she said.

"Artha. Artha!" I shouted at her, but she was already unconscious. I yanked at her paw, but I couldn't move her. "Artha!"

And as it had so many times before, the Old Man's voice cut through the panic. *Would you listen for once, boy?* he said, sounding just as exasperated as the Bear had.

"She's too heavy," I said, helpless.

Oh, is she? he said. *And just how much does her soul weigh?*

Her . . . soul?

That's what Artha had said. *This isn't my body. It's my soul.* But if this wasn't her body . . .

In Shadow, the rules could be bent—like in a dream. I wasn't sure if this was Shadow or somewhere else, but maybe, just maybe . . . could the rules be bent here, too?

I closed my eyes. *She weighs nothing,* I thought. *Light as a feather. Lighter than air.*

I pulled.

She didn't budge.

This is just like a dream, I thought. *She weighs nothing, nothing at all. I'll pull on her, and she'll float. Just like in a dream.*

I pulled.

She moved.

Barely. It was like shifting a sack stuffed with lead. But she moved. And I dragged her.

I can leave, I thought, excited. *I can do this.*

The question was: How? The plain was collapsing. And where was the way out?

The only way out is through the things that matter to you, the Bear had said. But where were the things that mattered to me? There was nothing here. The plain was empty—and disintegrating faster by the moment. I couldn't see it. I couldn't *see*.

Because you're thinking about your body again, the Old Man said. *This is* your *soul, too. The things that matter are inside it.*

. . . Inside it?

Yes. I understood.

I closed my eyes. I remembered my soul core. The creak of the floorboards. The breath of the wind. The smell of the Old Man's pipe. And

"Cal?"

I blinked. Meriel had appeared right in front of me.

They all had. They were together, forming a chain with their hands. Meriel reached out for me. Holding her other hand was Lachlan. Then came Gareth, struggling with the strain. And holding on to him was Foxtail. I could only see her arm. It looked like it was coming from a wavering portal, flashing and sparking with light.

"Could you hurry up, guv?" Lachlan said. "Can't hold this forever, you know."

Dragging Artha's body with all my will, I struggled forward. Then I took Meriel's hand

and suddenly I was lying back in the valley.

Pain returned. Agony wracked my body. The Dragon's Teeth still pierced my chest, with Artha bleeding beside me.

But I wasn't pinned to the Heart anymore. The stone had cracked, splitting in two, the remnants dulled to a dead gray. I couldn't see the glow of magic anymore, either. The Eye—that cursed jewel that had carried the dragon's mind within it—had finally fallen from my skull. It lay on the ground beside me, the amber in fragments. Shattered with the death of the Devourer.

The Hollow Man was dead, too. All the life he'd taken in, the magic that had made him strong, kept him alive all these years, was gone. His corpse lay on the ground, nothing but a desiccated husk. Even now, as I looked at it, it withered away. It crumbled into dust and blew apart in the breeze.

But the Teeth . . . the Teeth held neither consciousness nor life. All they held was power. I felt that power now, even through the pain, held together by my own soul. The two swords seemed to be fighting each other. Camuloth draining me, Belenoth putting it back.

I thought of Lachlan. *We brought him back to life.*

Struggling against the agony, I let go of Artha's paw, grabbed Camuloth's hilt, and pulled. I screamed as the sword slipped from my flesh, then fell from my hands to stain the grass with my blood.

Belenoth remained. And with its twin brother removed, Belenoth's magic began working inside me. I let it stay until I just couldn't take it anymore. Then, with another shriek of pain, I pulled it out, too.

And though I wouldn't have thought it possible, now the pain grew worse, even as my body began to repair itself. Just like it had in Lachlan, I saw the wound in my chest begin to close.

My mind spun, lightheaded. *Shuna's sneezing snout*, I thought.

Then I passed out.

CHAPTER 73

SOMETHING BOUNCED OFF my forehead.

It woke me. I opened my eyes, squinting at the sun overhead, its rays shining through the branches of the old oak tree. The sky beyond was clear blue, the breeze warm and gentle.

It took me a moment to remember where I was. When I did, I sat up in near panic, lifting my shirt.

My sword wounds were gone. Fully healed. I was fine.

No. I was *more* than fine.

I stared at my stomach, trembling. My scars. My scars were gone, too. Not quite able to believe it, I ran my hand over my flesh, my sides, my back.

Smooth.

They were gone. All gone. My scars really had been healed. And with them, the pain I'd lived with for eight years had disappeared, too.

Barely daring to hope, I touched my face.

My eye. My eye was back.

Belenoth had fixed me completely. I remembered what I'd looked like in my soul core—unscarred, with both eyes—and I realized: that was the template the blade had used to rebuild me. When I'd transmuted the energy to heal myself, Belenoth had fixed it all.

The sword lay next to me on the grass, blade crossed over its twin. I stared at the Dragon's Teeth, not touching them, not wanting to break the spell. But there was no spell. I was back on Ayreth, whole once more, and the Devourer was dead forever. I just sat there, joy and relief washing through me, almost unable to believe it.

Yet something—some*one*—was missing.

Where was Artha?

Had I left her behind in the Dragon's Heart? A pit grew in my gut until I remembered: I'd brought her back with me. I was sure of it. I even remembered letting go of her paw to grab the—

bonk

Something bounced off my head again. It fell to the ground, plinking off Camuloth's hilt, rolling to a stop in the grass.

It was an acorn.

I groaned. "You've got to be kidding me," I said, and I looked up into the leaves once more. Directly overhead, perched on a branch, was that crow.

caw

I frowned. This was Ayreth, I was certain of it. So this crow wasn't in Shadow, or even in a dream. It was really here. And I was equally sure it hadn't come all this way just to hit me with acorns.

"You're not an ordinary crow, are you?" I said.

The crow laughed. "No, I'm not."

"You're Bran. Bran the Crow."

He did a funny little bow, one wing folded in front of his stomach, one behind his back. "Pleased to meet you."

"If you've come to watch the fireworks," I said, "you're too late."

"Oh, I saw them."

"Of course. You know, if you were there, you could have helped."

The crow sounded indignant. "Who says I didn't?"

"I suppose you did, didn't you?" I said. "You led me to those doors in Shadow. To Artha's prison."

"Uh-huh. And long before that, too. I've been helping for thousands of years."

I thought about that. "Were you the one who made the idol of Artha immovable, in the Weaver vault?"

"Technically, one of the High Weavers did that. But I tricked him into doing it, so . . . yes."

"And . . ." I looked at my finger. The seven-banded mark remained. Though every other part of me had healed, Belenoth hadn't changed this. "My crystal ring. You manipulated everyone so it would end up with me. So I could use it to summon Artha. And then its magic, once inside me, would pull me into Shadow."

"Better than that," the crow said. "I *made* that ring."

"So . . . all of it," I said, amazed. "Me, the Weavers, Shuna, Artha, even the Eye . . . you conned everyone from the very beginning. The longest gaff in history. Played out over thousands of years."

The crow spread his wings. "Impressive, eh?"

Part of me was annoyed at how completely I'd been tricked. But the gaffer in me couldn't help but stand in awe. The intricacy of it. The sheer skill and daring to pull it off. I nodded grudgingly. The crow did a happy little dance, then took another bow.

"So what happened to Artha?" I said.

"She's right over there."

The crow nodded toward the base of the tree. I stood, confused. There was nothing—

No—wait. Something lay nestled against the trunk, where the roots sank into the earth. I walked over to find . . . I didn't know what it was. It was a foot and a half wide and spherical, like a ball, but made of mottled brown and beige plates. It looked a bit like a turtle's shell, fitted together in an odd pattern of shapes.

"*This* is Artha?" I said.

"Yup."

I picked up the ball—or at least I tried to. It was so heavy, I nearly threw out my back. "I don't understand," I said. "What is this thing?"

"It's called a gulu," the crow said. "They're amazing animals. And really quite good-natured. When they get injured, they form those shells around themselves and regenerate."

This must have been one of those creatures from the worlds the Spirits had visited before trapping themselves on Ayreth. "Does that mean . . ." My heart leapt. "Will Artha survive?"

"I believe so. She'll have some scars on her soul, but one can live with such things. As you well know."

Except I wouldn't have to anymore. I rested my hand on the gulu's shell—or rather, Artha's shell, overjoyed. "She told me she didn't have the energy to change forms," I said. "And that Shuna didn't have the power to save her."

"She was right," the crow said. "Artha was too wounded to shift, and Shuna couldn't have helped. But *I* could. I just had to give up some of my own power to mend her soul; enough to help her change and keep her alive. A price I paid gladly, and would pay a thousand times more."

"Then you saved her!"

"Uh-huh. Couldn't have done it if you hadn't brought her out of the Dragon's Heart, though. So thanks for being so stubborn."

This really was amazing. My head was reeling, trying to make sense of it all. "There's still a couple things I haven't figured out," I said.

"Ask away."

"Who wrote on my back? The 'only like kills like.'"

"I did," the crow said.

I frowned, thinking back through all the times I'd met the bird. "When did you do that?"

"Oh, years ago. You didn't notice because you were unconscious at the time. And afterward, nobody looked at your back with magical sight. Sorry about tripping you into the brambles, by the way. I couldn't let you return to Artha until you'd seen the message. I really thought Gareth would have used his orb around you earlier."

So that was why it kept scaring me awake: I hadn't yet seen the writing on me. I tried to imagine how anyone could even set up a gaff so Gareth would take the light orb from the vault, then use it behind my exposed back, just so I could ask Artha about it . . . and so she would realize what it meant, and how she could kill the Devourer. The whole thing made my brain hurt.

And I *still* couldn't wrap my head around it. "If you did all this—gaffed everyone for so long, so we'd end up here—then you must have known for millennia how to beat the Devourer. That only the Teeth would penetrate the Heart. And that only a Spirit could face off against the dragon's soul inside and kill it for good. So...why go to all this trouble if you had the answer? Why didn't you just tell someone? Or do it yourself?"

"Ah. Well, to start with, I *didn't* have the answer. Not at first. It took me about a thousand years after our battle to work it out. And by then, things were a little tricky."

"You see," the crow said, "we Spirits don't all have the same abilities. Some of us are better at certain things than others. Me, for example. I'm very good with particular kinds of magic. It's why I could save Artha, while Shuna couldn't. But I don't have anywhere near the strength needed to fight the Devourer in its soul. None of the girls did, either—except for the Bear. She was the only one who could face it down inside the Heart and have a chance to succeed. The problem was, by the time I'd worked it out, it was too late to tell her. She'd already fallen under the sway of the Eye. She wouldn't have listened, anyway. She was too angry."

"With you?" I said. "Why?"

"Artha blamed me for taking her sister's side. When they began fighting over her using the Eye, I agreed with Shuna. It was far too dangerous to experiment with. Artha got upset at that and stopped speaking to me entirely."

He shook his head in dismay. "She always was the most willful of the lot," he said. "But I knew good still lived inside her. If she could just find her way back to who she was before the Eye destroyed it all ... That's why I gaffed everyone this way. I believed in her until the end."

"It worked," I said. "She listened to you, eventually. She finally realized what 'only like kills like' meant when I told her I kept meeting a crow."

"Thank you for telling me." He seemed genuinely delighted that Artha had found herself again.

Thinking of Artha made me think of the other Spirits—and one in particular. "Where *is* Shuna?" I said. "She told me she'd be here."

"That's my fault," the crow confessed. "I put up a barrier to keep her out. Even now, she's trying desperately to find a way through it."

Slowly, I took a step backward. "Why would you do that?"

"It's nothing bad. I just wanted to talk to you alone first. Besides thanking you for saving Artha, I had two more things to say, and I wanted to say them only to you."

"Which are?" I said, still wary.

"First of all, congratulations. What you've done—all of you: Gareth, Meriel, Lachlan, and Foxtail—is extraordinary. You saved the world, but no one's ever going to thank you for it, because no one's ever going to know it happened. Except me and the girls, of course. So: thank you."

"Um . . . you're welcome," I said, surprised. "And the second thing?"

Suddenly, the crow sprang from his perch. And as he fluttered down, his form began to change. His wings elongated, his body stretched out, until his feet landed on the ground—human.

I stared at him, trembling, as the man walked toward me. He cupped my cheeks in his hands. Then he leaned down and kissed me softly on the forehead.

"I'm so very proud of you, boy," the Old Man said.

I collapsed, weeping, into his arms.

CHAPTER 74

HE HELD ME as I cried.

Eventually, when I could speak again, I pushed away, wiping the tears from my face. "You were a Spirit?" I said, sniffling. "The whole time?"

"From the very beginning," the Old Man said.

"But why? Why didn't you tell me?"

"Think of the gaff, boy. Think of how it worked. Who was it on?"

His question made me remember all those nights he'd sat with me, telling me Fox and Bear stories, teaching me his tricks. How much I'd missed it. "The gaff was on me—well, part of it was. It was also on Shuna, too. And Artha."

"And?"

I thought about it. "The Eye," I said. "The Eye most of all. We had to trick it into sneaking Artha into the Heart."

"Yes. And if I'd told you I was Bran the Crow..."

I drew a breath. "The Eye would have known!"

The Old Man nodded. "The first thing the Eye did when it brought you to its cavern was search your memories. If I'd told you who I was, the Devourer would have seen it. It would have realized I'd been preparing you to stop it. So it never would have attached itself to you. It would have rejected you from the start and broken your mind, like it did to poor old Seamus, the thief before you."

I saw the truth in that. But it prompted a different question, one I'd asked many times these past few months. "Why me?" I said. "All those years ago, why did you choose me to fight the Eye?"

"I didn't. *You* chose you."

"What?"

"You're not the only child I taught," he said.

That didn't make any sense. "You couldn't possibly have trained anyone else. You were only ever away from me for a few days at a time."

"Ah," the Old Man said. "So. I told you we Spirits all have different knowledge, yes? Different abilities? Well, one of mine—"

"—is being in more than one place at the same time," the Old Man said.

Or rather, a *second* Old Man said. There were suddenly two of him standing in front of me.

"More than that," a third Old Man said, approaching me from the side.

I stared, stunned, until the copies winked out, and it was just the one Old Man as before.

"Quite a trick, isn't it?" he said. "I've always been rather pleased I worked it out—though it does come with a few unpleasant side effects. Regardless, as to your question, I didn't train just you. I trained many children, both before I met you and after. Twenty-three of them, in fact."

The number stunned me. I tried to imagine twenty-three Old

Men walking the globe. No one's valuables anywhere would be safe. "Why?" I said. "Why so many?"

"What's the most important trait in a gaffer?" he asked. "The one that, more than anything, will determine if you'll be good at it or not?"

"You have to have no conscience," I said. We'd fought about that many times. *What a tedious thing a conscience is*, the Old Man had always argued. *It only gets in the way of the job.*

He nodded. "For this gaff to work, I needed someone extremely good at cheating people—and Spirits and Devourers, too. But I also needed the opposite. Someone *with* a conscience."

"Why?"

"Think back to when you lost your eye. After Mr. Solomon's fire elemental hurt you. What did you want to do?"

"Quit," I said.

"Then why didn't you?"

Because Shuna had shown me the future. If I'd just walked away . . . "My friends would have died."

"Now you see," the Old Man said. "The solution was also the problem. Someone without a conscience *would* have walked away. After Lachlan had been stabbed, too. Almost every gaffer in the world would have left him there to die. They never would have stuck with the job—with their friends. They never would have reached the end.

"What I needed, then," he said, "was someone with a very rare combination. Skills and conscience both. I didn't know exactly which one of you that would be, so I raised several of you, all over Ayreth.

"Some of the children weren't talented enough; they could never have pulled off the gaffs. Others turned out to be very skilled, even more than you, but they lacked the empathy needed to see the job through. I found them all the best homes I could and continued with the children who remained. There were five of you at the end. Five final candidates. So I tested you all."

I realized what he was talking about immediately. "The cure for the weeping sickness," I said. "When we gaffed that poor woman and her dying daughter."

"Yes."

"But . . . I failed that test."

"No, boy," he said gently. "You were the only one who *passed* it. The others were troubled by what we'd done. Three of them even confronted me. But of the five, you were the only one who refused to continue if we didn't change. That's when I knew you were the one. I didn't choose you. You did."

He really had set up the gaff perfectly. Placed all the right pieces, played all the right moves. Once again I stood in awe, even as I remembered how much it had upset me at the time. Yet there was still one thing I didn't understand. One wound that remained, one ache in my heart.

"Then why did you abandon me?" I said. "Why did you leave me like that? I was so alone. I get that you couldn't tell me you were Bran, but to just throw me away . . . Why?"

The Old Man shook his head. "That, boy, more than anything else, is the one thing I wished I didn't have to do. But it was the only way to make the gaff work. You see, I couldn't be around when it came time to do the Solomon job. Can you understand why?"

I thought about it. And it hit me. "Because if you were there when I snaffled the Eye," I said, "it would have seen you. It would have seen your shine. It would have known right away you weren't human!"

"Right. The Eye couldn't tell I was a Spirit from your memories, because they were *your* memories. It only saw what you saw, and you can't see magic. But once it attached itself to you, it would have recognized my glow right away.

"So I had to leave you," he said. "But how I left mattered. If I'd faked my death, for example, you would have been grieving. You never would have taken the Solomon job. If I'd just vanished without a trace, you'd have searched for me. You wouldn't have been around to take the Solomon job. And if I simply removed myself, say, by getting arrested and thrown into prison..."

"I would have searched for a way to break you out," I said, understanding. And again, I wouldn't have taken the Solomon job.

"Abandoning you was the only way," the Old Man said. "It left you desperate enough—but more important, *angry* enough—to go after the Eye. Which you knew, deep down, was a bad idea. Need, greed, and speed, as I taught you. You saw it. A calmer you would have walked away from the start."

And so at last, I understood it all. The knowledge healed that final wound, made the hurt fade. But what really made it disappear was that I finally realized the Old Man had never truly left.

"So you *were* the one who gave Mr. Solomon my name after all," I said.

He smiled, looking rather pleased with himself. "All your names, actually. Except for Foxtail's. That was Shuna's doing. And speaking of the others ..."

The shock of seeing the Old Man again had made me forget that my friends were still out there somewhere. My heart began to thump again. Were they even all right?

It was as if the Old Man read my mind—just like always. "They're fine," he assured me. "See?"

He motioned for me to look around the valley. I saw the four of them sprinting toward me from the four different plateaus where the Hollow Man had sent them. Though Gareth was the slowest of any of us, he must have had the easiest route down, because he'd be the first to arrive.

The Old Man smirked. "Watch this."

Gareth ran up the hill, puffing. When he saw us, he froze, skidding to a stop.

"Hello, Gareth," the Old Man said.

Gareth stared, barely able to breathe. "You!" he said.

"You *know* him?" I said.

"That's the librarian," Gareth said, stunned. "The one who disappeared."

I was just as stunned. "You're joking."

The Old Man winked. "You think that's fun? Watch this one."

Meriel arrived next, knives already out. When she saw me and Gareth were all right, she looked relieved, though puzzled—and wary—that someone else was with us. When she finally took a good look at the Old Man's face, her jaw dropped.

"*Brannigan?*" she said, flabbergasted. "What are you doing here?"

I stared again. "Brannigan . . . the cart driver? Who helped Meriel escape from Torgal?"

"Rather dull, driving carts for a living," he said. He nodded to Meriel. "But the end was worth it, don't you think?"

"*That's* why you were in that hood!" I said. "And why your visage was scratched out in Shadow. You did that so I wouldn't recognize you."

He laughed. "You should have seen your face. I thought your heart might stop."

Suddenly more pieces fell into place. "Bran . . ." I said. "And Brannigan. And you used to get letters at Grey's—"

"To Mr. Brantworth, Architect," the Old Man quoted. "Kept sticking my name in everyone's faces, yet no one ever saw it."

Gareth and Meriel were beyond confused. This would take some explaining, but I waited until the others joined us. Lachlan arrived next, relieved, like Meriel, that we were okay, though deeply disappointed he'd missed all the action. He frowned when he saw the Old Man.

"Hey-ho . . . where'd I know you from?" Lachlan said. Then he snapped his fingers. "You're the geezer on the omnibus! The one what named Galawan!"

If Lachlan wondered what some geezer from the Carlow omnibus was doing out here, he didn't ask. Instead, delighted, he showed him the little sparrow. When Galawan saw the Old Man, the bird flapped over to land on his finger, tweeting happily.

"Yes," the Old Man said to Galawan. "I imagine they are much nicer than Mr. Solomon was." He gave me another wink. "I rather like birds."

Foxtail joined us last. She looked confused by the Old Man's being there, and it was clear she didn't know him. "We haven't met," he said. "If you'd like to do the introductions?"

"This is the Old Man," I said to them all. "I mean . . . Bran the Crow." Their jaws dropped again. "I guess I should start calling you that, shouldn't I?"

The Old Man looked wistful. "Why don't you keep calling me 'Old Man'? I've grown rather fond of it over the years."

Everyone explained to each other how they'd known the Old Man from before. Watching them talk made him realize he'd forgotten something. He made a face. "I really should let Shuna in. She's getting somewhat frantic."

There was no visible enchantment, and he didn't wave his hands or anything. Shuna just suddenly appeared among us. The others went dead quiet, stunned into silence by the sight of the Fox.

"Is everyone all right?" she said, worried. "I couldn't—" She cocked her head at the sight of the Old Man. "Who's your friend, Cal?"

"This is—"

I was about to say "Bran," but the Old Man cut me off. "Really, Shuna," he said, scolding. "Even in this form, you don't recognize me?"

She frowned. She'd recognized something, certainly, as soon

as he'd started to speak. Then it struck her who this actually was.

"*Father?*" she said.

I don't know who was more shocked, me or her. "Bran the Crow—the Old Man—is your *father?*" I said.

"Well, someone has to be," the Old Man said, a little defensive.

"What are you doing?" Shuna said crossly.

"Same as you. Helping."

"I mean what are you doing in that form? The Pact forbids it!"

"Oh, that." He brushed his fingernails on his sleeve. "I didn't swear the Pact."

That took her aback. "Of course you did. You were there, I saw you."

"That wasn't me. I switched an actual crow into my place just before the binding occurred. Which means that somewhere on Ayreth, there's an immortal—and very confused—bird."

Shuna sputtered, outraged. "You . . ."

The Old Man wouldn't hear it. "Don't give me your lip. It's not like you've never bent the rules." He wagged a finger at Shuna. "And if you and your sisters had paid more attention when I tried to teach you the magic I knew, you'd have noticed it wasn't me straightaway. But noooo. 'Father, we just want to play.' Only Kira ever bothered to listen. And good thing, too, or we'd all be dead."

His mention of Kira made me realize something. "If you're Shuna's father . . . then you're Artha's father, too."

"Rather explains all the arguments, doesn't it?" he said wryly.

Shuna suddenly looked stricken. "She isn't . . . ?"

He shook his head, smiling, and stepped aside. When Shuna spotted the gulu shell behind him, she obviously recognized what it was, because she nearly cried with relief.

She ran over to it. For a moment, she just stood there, as if unable to believe it had all worked out. Then she closed her eyes and rested her head against the shell.

"I've missed you," she said, so quietly I could barely hear her. "I've missed you so much."

The Old Man turned away, teary-eyed. Even though I knew now who he really was, it was jarring to see him anything but sardonic.

He turned his nose up. "I have allergies," he said. This time, I couldn't smother the laugh.

The others didn't even know where to begin. They kept staring between the Old Man and Shuna. I really boggled their minds when I pointed out the gulu and explained it was Artha.

And that wasn't all. In the valley, I spotted a deer and leopard waiting. Fiona and Cailín had arrived.

"I should tell the others," the Old Man said, and he walked away to speak with them.

Shuna looked so happy to have Artha back. "Can you communicate with her in that form?" I asked.

"No," Shuna said. "But there'll be plenty of time for that now. Thanks to you."

"We owe you thanks, too. For helping us all these years. For sacrificing what you did. I'm sorry about the way I lost my temper before."

Shuna wagged her tail. "I was worried you'd still be angry with me."

I shook my head. "I finally understand why you did it. All of it.

And also, to be honest . . . it *was* a really good gaff."

"It was, wasn't it?" The Fox looked rather pleased with herself. "But it's you who played it out. All of you," she said to everyone. "We owe you everything."

Lachlan's eyes brightened at that. Uh-oh. "In that case, Your, uh . . . Foxness," he said, "can I ask for something?"

Meriel whapped him on the arm, horrified. "Lachlan!"

"What is it?" Shuna said, amused.

"Well, I didn't get to see you in the vault," Lachlan said, "'cause I was snoozing at the time, which was not my fault, right? Anyway, I was thinking . . . I ain't never touched a Spirit before, have I?"

Shuna walked up to him, ears out in a foxish smile.

He could hardly believe it. "Really?" He kneeled. Carefully, hesitantly, he reached out to touch her. When nothing alarming happened, he sank his fingers into her fur.

Gareth and Meriel stood back, eyes wide. Still amused, Shuna looked at them and said, "Go ahead. When you have fur as soft as mine, there's no point in wasting it."

They kneeled beside her, too, stroking her fur in wonder. Only Foxtail stayed back, waiting.

The others stepped away, sensing something was happening between the two. Shuna walked up to her. Foxtail crossed her arms on her chest and bowed her head in reverence.

"You've done so well," Shuna said, proud. "Now it's time to return."

"Hold yer socks. What's going on?" Lachlan said. "What are you gonna do with Foxtail?"

"She was never meant to stay like this. Only until the job was done."

"Wait. Are you taking her away? No!"

"It's all right, child. You'll see."

"No! Stop!"

Meriel had to hold on to Lachlan to keep him from running over there.

"Are you ready?" Shuna said.

Foxtail nodded.

The four of us stood together, Foxtail apart. And we watched as the magic that bound her came undone. One by one, the rivets that fixed the mirrored mask to her skull spun loose. They fell into the grass. When the last rivet dropped, the mask fell, too.

And as that mirror came free from her head, Foxtail changed. Just like I'd seen the crow turn into a man, the girl transformed. She grew smaller, body shifting, until a young, dusky-colored fox stood where the girl had been.

And she *squealed*.

Foxtail squealed in delight as the voice she'd lost when she became one of us was finally returned to her. It was a sound of pure joy, pure rightness, to be who she really was again.

Everyone stood stunned. Even more than when they'd seen the Old Man. "Shuna's sneezing snout," Lachlan said. "Foxtail . . . is a *fox*?"

Foxtail chattered at him, almost like a laugh—*heh-heh-heh-heh-heh*—and sprang through the grass, happy in her own legs again. She was a little bit gangly, clearly still juvenile, but as I watched her, I recognized her. And I finally understood that one time in Shadow I couldn't explain.

She was the fox. The fox who'd lost her family in the woods, whom I'd carried away to safety. All this time, I'd wondered if the magic in Foxtail's mask prevented her from dreaming, and that's why I'd never seen her in Shadow. Turned out I'd seen her before anyone else.

Lachlan chased after her, whooping with delight as I turned to Shuna. "I *knew* you were lying," I said.

"About what?" Shuna said.

"You told me Foxtail wasn't like you."

"Actually, what I said was that Foxtail wasn't a supernatural, magical creature."

"She's not?" Confused, I said, "What is she, then?"

Shuna gave me a funny look. "What does she look like?"

"You mean . . . Foxtail really is a fox? A *fox* fox?"

"Of course."

"That doesn't make any sense."

"Why not?"

"She's too smart to be a fox."

Shuna glared at me. "Every time. Every time I see you, I think, *He can't possibly get any ruder.* And yet you make it happen."

"You know what I mean. She understands our language. She behaves like a human. She knows things a fox couldn't possibly know."

"Well, yes," Shuna said. "You can't just make a fox human without a little adjustment. It would be a disaster. So when I changed her body, I changed her mind, too. Then I imprinted what she'd need to know to fit in."

"But . . . why?" I said. "Why make a fox a human? Why go to all that trouble instead of just telling us what we needed to know?"

"I'd think that would be obvious by now."

Obvious? Why would it be . . . *Oh.*

"The *Pact*," I said. "You aren't allowed to interact that way with humans. Except—"

"Foxtail isn't human," Shuna finished. "I gave her a human body, and human intellect. But being human's more than that. It's why I had to cover her with that mask. If the Eye had seen her lifeglow, it would have known what I'd done. Her soul's color wouldn't match."

Now it all finally made sense. "Foxtail was what let you follow us so closely," I said. "How you always knew what we were doing. *She* told you."

"That's right."

"And if you really needed to speak to me, you could set it up through Foxtail. She was your inside man!"

"And as someone we know loves to tell us," Shuna said, "nothing makes a job easier than an inside man."

I barely knew what to say. "You really are an incredible gaffer."

She half laughed, half sighed. "Well, I am my father's daughter."

Foxtail sprang away from Lachlan as he tried to catch her, leaving him rolling down the hill in the grass. She ran up to Gareth and Meriel, who both watched her in wonder as she chattered her foxish laugh.

Then she came toward me. She approached me hesitantly, like she was afraid of what I'd say. I'd known she was different. But not *that* different.

I reached out and touched her. Her fur was warm. "You might be," I said, "the most amazing thing I've seen today."

She squealed, happy. Then she ran off toward Lachlan to teach him to pounce.

"You'll take care of her, won't you?" Shuna said quietly.

"Me? Of all of us, I'd think Foxtail could take the best care of herself."

"Oh, she could certainly survive," Shuna said, "but she doesn't have much in common with other foxes anymore. I told you that to change her, I had to change her mind. When I changed her back . . . well, I didn't return her mind to the way it was. If I made her wholly a fox again, she'd lose all her memories. She wouldn't remember you. Any of you. And you mean so much to her. I just couldn't do that."

"Oh. Well, of course she can stay with us." I watched her pounce in the grass. "I doubt Lachlan would let her go even if she wanted to."

∩∪

We watched them play for a while. Well, Gareth and I did. Meriel soon started chasing after Foxtail, too.

At the same time, Gareth kept glancing down to where the Old Man was talking with his other two daughters. Gareth still looked stunned—but also pleased—to discover that his vanished librarian really was a Spirit after all. I could tell he had something else he wanted to ask about, but he was too awed by the presence of the Fox to speak up.

Apparently Shuna could tell, too, because she said in an encouraging voice, "What is it, Gareth?"

"Er..." He nodded toward the Dragon's Teeth, which were still lying in the grass. "W-what should we do with these?"

She shrugged. "Keep them, if you like."

I stared at her. "Keep them?" I said. "A part of the most dangerous creature ever to exist, and your answer is, 'keep them'?"

"They're just mindless artifacts," Shuna said. "They have their powers, but they never held any true consciousness. You probably shouldn't stab anyone else with them, though."

I could have used that advice a while ago. Gareth collected the swords, wrapping them carefully and placing them back in Foxtail's pack. And after some time, the Old Man finally returned from talking with the Deer and the Leopard.

"So," he said. "All's well that ends well, wouldn't you say?"

I caught the meaning in his voice. My chest tightened, and my heart sank. "You're leaving again, aren't you?"

"I have to," he said sadly. "It's been a long time since my family's been together. We need to talk. And I've been thinking about other things, too, over the last thousand years. Our problem about leaving a trail when we travel through Shadow. I have some ideas. And I owe it to my girls to help them think through it.

"It's more than that, though," he said. "Now that the Devourer is dead, the primeval magic will become still. It won't crack the world anymore. But it needs time to grow calm. We Spirits can help that by remaining in Shadow. At least until the magic settles.

"It's not forever," he insisted. "I *will* return. I won't ever abandon you again. And though you didn't realize it at the time, I think you know now, I never really did."

Something occurred to me then. "You know, after you left, I still talked to you," I said. "In my mind. At first, it was just to curse you. But as time went on, I actually started . . . talking. And the thing is, there were a few times I felt like you were there. Really there in my head, I mean. This might sound crazy, but . . . was that you? Did you do something to me before you left?"

"Why, boy," he said, indignant. "Am I the kind of fellow who would convince a young child to walk through Shadow into his soul core, then leave a piece of himself behind, hidden where no one could find it, not even the Eye? And then erase that boy's memory, so he'd have no recollection that it ever happened? Just so I might look out for him from time to time? Do you really think I'm that kind of man?"

"Of course not," I said, trying not to smile. "I apologize."

"As well you should." He clasped Gareth's hand in farewell. Then he leaned in and whispered in Gareth's ear for a minute.

Whatever he said, it made the boy's eyes go wide with wonder and joy. As Gareth stood there, happier than I'd ever seen him, the Old Man patted him affectionately on the shoulder, then picked up Artha, cradling her shell in one arm like she weighed nothing. "Time to go."

Shuna shook out her fur. "I'll come see you sometimes, too. I can't exactly leave my favorite gaffer behind, can I? Who knows what kind of trouble you'll get into otherwise?"

"I'll look for you," I said.

She smiled. "Be well, Cal."

She went to say farewell to the others. As the Old Man headed to say goodbye to Meriel, he snapped his fingers. "I almost forgot. I got you a present."

"You did?" I said, wary.

"Don't worry, you'll like it. I *know* you'll like it."

"What is it?"

"I left it over there." He pointed to the north. "Well, a few miles over there, anyway. About a half day's walk, actually."

"Why would you leave it so far away?"

"I didn't know how all this would turn out. If the Devourer re-formed, I didn't want your gift to get ruined."

"If the Devourer had re-formed," I said, "a busted present would have been the least of our worries."

"I don't know, boy," he said. "It's a *very* nice present."

CHAPTER 75

WE WALKED A half day to the north, like the Old Man told us, before we found it. Lachlan spent most of the time romping beside Foxtail, and the rest pestering me with questions. "What do you think it is, eh? Oh—d'you think it's a *pony*? I ain't never ridden a horse before."

"For the millionth time, Lachlan," I said, "I have no idea. And I wouldn't get your hopes up. You don't know the Old Man's sense of humor. I wouldn't put it past him to make us walk all the way out here to find nothing but a half-eaten banana. It's probably nothing spectacular."

I was wrong.

I first caught a glimpse of it as we climbed over a hill. For a moment, I thought my eyes—both eyes again—were playing tricks on me. But as we crested the top of the slope, there was no doubt of what I saw.

It was an airship.

The ship was tethered to the ground, ready to board. And I'd seen one like it before. In fact, it looked awfully similar—

No. It was the *same* airship. The *exact* same airship as the one in my soul core.

Stunned, I barely remembered walking down that hill. A man

waited on the deck, looking bored. When he spotted us coming, he called out to a carriage waiting nearby. A man in a top hat and waistcoat exited the carriage to join us, holding a clipboard.

"Good afternoon, sirs, miss," he said. "And, um . . ." He looked puzzled to see we were accompanied by a fox. "Apologies. My name is Dudley Bannon. I'm a solicitor with the firm of Bannon and Crane. Are you"—he checked the clipboard—"Callan of Perith?"

Lachlan jerked a thumb at me. "That's him, mate."

"Mr. Callan. I am here to deliver one airship, the *Crow's Heart*, constructed to the precise specifications of a Mr. Brantworth, Architect, to be transferred over to your possession." He handed me the clipboard. "Sign here, please. And here . . . and here."

I barely remembered signing, too. "*My* possession?" I said.

"Indeed, sir. The ship now to belongs to you. Mr. Brantworth has also established a fund which will pay for a Weaver's rebinding of the engine, or other repairs as necessary, in perpetuity. In addition, an instructor"—he motioned to the man on the deck of the airship—"has been provided a temporary berth, for the purpose of teaching you how to crew it. You may engage his services for as long as required. Do you have any questions?"

"What?" I said.

"Read the contract, Mr. Callan, it's all in there. If you need anything else, please don't hesitate to contact me at my firm's office in Carlow." He handed me an embossed card. "Good day to you, sirs, miss." He doffed his hat and trundled off in his carriage.

Gareth looked dumbfounded. I knew just how he felt.

"Wait," Meriel said, incredulous. "This airship is *yours* now?"

The *Crow's Heart*, the man had called it. "No," I said. "It's ours."

"Shuna's snout," Lachlan said, kneeling in the grass, his arm around Foxtail. "Can we go somewhere, then?"

"Sure," I said, and I couldn't stop smiling. "We can go anywhere you like."

ACKNOWLEDGMENTS

It's been my privilege to have so many talented folks helping put these books together. I'd like to say thank you to the following:

To Jenny Bak, Lynne Missen, and Suri Rosen, all of whom offered insights that made this story immeasurably better.

To Dan Lazar, a champion as always.

To Tamar Brazis, Gaby Corzo, Krista Ahlberg, Sola Akinlana, Tony Sahara, Theresa Evangelista, Lucia Baez, Brianna Lockhart, Lauren Festa, Tessa Meischeid, Kate Doyle, Sam Devotta, Sylvia Chan, and Trina Kehoe at Viking, Penguin Random House, and Penguin Random House Canada.

To Cecilia de la Campa, Torie Doherty-Munro, Alessandra Birch, and Sofia Bolido at Writers House.

To Edel Bhreathnach, and to the monks at Glenstal Abbey for their linguistic assistance.

And finally, to you, dear reader. Thank you for helping Cal, Meriel, Lachlan, Foxtail, and Gareth pull all those gaffs. I hope you've loved spending your time in this world as much as I've loved sharing it with you.